The
Iterations
of
Caroline

Also by Roy Blomstrom

Silences: A Novel of the 1918 Finnish Civil War

The
Iterations
of
Caroline

Roy Blomstrom

CIP data available from the publisher on request

Issued in print and electronic formats

ISBN: 978-1-7750526-4-7

The Iterations of Caroline is a work of fiction.

Cover: H. Leighton Dickson

Shuniah House Books

Shuniah, Ontario, Canada

www.shuniahhousebooks.com

To the students in my science fiction classes
who learned to look at our commonplace world
with transcendent eyes.

To all the Bernies
who instinctively asked the right questions
and weighed the "right" answers.

And especially to all those
who wondered about
the reality of a multiverse,
built of times and places,
and ached to see it all.

CONTENTS

1 # DARLENE

We all agree, more or less, that the break in continuity—the first one, the one that most of us remember—occurred in July, near the beginning of my summer holiday. Minor breaks may have happened before then. The problem—well, *one* problem, anyway—is that none of us have had *exactly* the same experience.

For me, that first day went like this. My wife, who was still Darlene then, sat in the living room in a recliner, nursing a twisted ankle and watching an afternoon soap opera. Meanwhile, I was finding nothing of interest in the morning's newspaper.

Darlene looked over at me. "David, go upstairs and fetch my hairbrush, will you? I want to do something with this mess." She motioned at her hair, which, to my eyes, looked perfectly fine. She was sending me upstairs for other reasons—she was bored, and I was reading the newspaper and not showing much interest in her. We both knew that.

A few minutes earlier, she'd dismissed my suggestion that she re-wrap and ice her ankle. An hour before that, she'd insisted that she didn't need an over-the-counter pain reliever. So I knew she could make the walk herself. And still I said, "Sure. On the dresser?"

"Should be. Thanks, dear."

I put the paper down, climbed the fourteen steps to the second floor, turned right at the landing, took a few paces to the bedroom door, and turned left to enter. The dresser, just inside the door, held the brush. I turned left again.

Easy enough to recall, right? It should be, but my memories aren't consistent.

When I try to reconstruct any past event, especially this one, I can't be sure if I'm remembering what happened or what I *believe* happened. Sometimes I remember two or three different versions, and they all seem equally real, equally plausible. It helps if I try to remember an event as a series of steps, a sequence of turns, or a set of linked actions. The wonky memories usually fail the chronology test.

So. While I'm *fairly* certain of some things about that day, I'm unsure of others. I know it was in July because I had finally cleared mental space from the previous year's teaching but hadn't yet begun prepping for the start of school in September. In August, I'd re-read the novels I'd teach, but I was nowhere near ready to start that yet.

Here's another thing I know. That day, when I turned left into the room, I knew in a fraction of a second that someone else was in the room with me, and a collision was imminent. My next step would send me right into him, and him into me. Simultaneously, we both tried to stop, both raised an arm in self-defense—he his left arm, I my right. But it was too late. Momentum carried us into each other.

And yet—the "unavoidable" collision never happened.

Instead, I toppled forward, arm outstretched, straight into the side of the dresser, which shook. I rebounded to the floor with a crash.

No one else was in the room. But someone had been there—an intruder.

Darlene called from below. "David? Are you all right?"

"Yes, I'm fine." I picked myself up, finding I'd given my ribs a solid whack. Worse, I'd swept the top of the dresser clear of its little boxes and bottles, lipsticks and chains and earrings and bracelets. Painfully, I got down on the carpet to pick up things and replace them. The hairbrush had fled under the bed.

The intruder, if any, had left no sign. So what had I seen? Holding the brush, I sat on the edge of the mattress, my chest pounding.

"David?" Darlene's voice held a touch of theatrical anxiety.

"It's okay," I called. "I knocked some stuff over. I'm cleaning it up."

Mother to child: "Don't forget the brush."

"I won't. Be down in a minute."

My hands still shook. Horses galloped in my chest. What the hell had just happened?

I ticked off my symptoms.

My face tingled, but I hadn't lost sensation in my hands or feet, so no stroke. No difficulty speaking. No dizziness or inability to focus.

Hallucination? Seizure, maybe? One that lasts only a fraction of a second?

I reviewed the experience in sequence. What had I seen? Forget the "other man in the room" for a moment. What had I *actually seen*?

I'd turned *toward* the dresser, but I hadn't *seen* the dresser. I had seen—

what? Something else.

I stood up, eyes open, trying to remember. The room itself seemed to be interfering with my memory of the event. *Remove the distractions*, I told myself, and closed my eyes.

I'd seen a man. Yes, and behind him, the double doors of the bedroom closet. But the closet doors should have been behind *me*. And where were the bedroom windows?

"David?"

I opened my eyes. "Coming." I went downstairs.

Darlene had changed the channel, and she had my newspaper.

"Did it get boring?" I tried to sound normal.

"Did what get boring?"

"Your soap."

"My soap?"

"The soap opera you were watching."

"Talk show, you mean. Goddamned if I'm going to get myself hooked on soaps just because I tripped coming indoors. Damn this shit-stick ankle, anyway."

"Sorry. I guess I wasn't paying attention." I was puzzled. Darlene almost never used profanity. She worked hard to keep her bitterness sweet, and the perpetual tension between us unacknowledged.

"Not the first time." Before she went back to reading, she threw one last dart. "Did you remember the bloody hairbrush at least?"

"Here, I'll put it on the end table beside you." I edged past her and set down the brush, right beside the ashtray with the lipstick-stained butt still in it.

"Thanks."

Ashtray? Where had that come from? "I'm going to go to the bathroom," I said.

"Not something I need to know, darling. You're a big boy now."

And a liar, I thought. I went back upstairs. I peeked into the bedroom before I entered, but no one peeked back at me.

Why did I feel that the bedroom windows had been larger? Had the bedroom seemed brighter? No, it wasn't just that.

I walked over to the spot where the intruder had surprised me.

In that fraction of a second before I did or didn't collide with him, I'd seen not only the closet doors that should have been behind me, but also the door to the ensuite washroom and a second set of bedroom windows.

It was as if someone had divided the bedroom with a mirror — one that ran wall to wall and floor to ceiling, and an inch from my nose.

Though my upraised arm had blocked my view of the other man's face, I recognized him.

The face was mine.

Somehow, I'd bumped into *myself*. Falling, I'd swept the dresser clean of Darlene's crap and cosmetics, while the mirror winked out of existence.

Like Alice, my brain whispered. *Like Alice, eh?*

#

A lot has changed since then. Especially me.

One night a few weeks later, I found myself standing in thirty feet of warm, clear, fragrant water on the soft and sandy bottom of the ocean just off Santa Flora, California. The place isn't on your maps, by the way. But you've guessed as much, haven't you?

It was near midnight, and the long rolling waves, leftovers from a Pacific storm, passed overhead on their way to the shore. The moon, undulating above the water's surface, split into two or three silver ribbons and joined again to become something more rounded. Schools of angelfish swam by in sheets that flashed, flew, and disappeared when I stretched my arms toward them. Occasionally a cruising sand shark approached, smiled its malevolent upside-down smile, and banked away into the darkness.

Tired, I curled up on the ocean floor to sleep, as mermen do, and dreamed.

I dreamed that I was a young man again, a teacher with a wife who loved me, a dog, a minivan, a house on the shore of Lake Superior half an hour's drive from Thunder Bay.

No, that's not quite right. Those things were *in* the dream, but they weren't mine anymore. If I wanted them to be part of my past life, I could choose them. If I didn't, I could relinquish ownership of them to someone else that I — both lender and borrower — could also be. A different iteration of myself, as I've come to think of it.

The dream fragmented, a dream with a storyline only partly mine. For instance, I've never had a dog.

When first light awakened me, I swam slowly to shore, my gills open to the rich salt water. From time to time I stopped and let myself drift slowly down so that I could enjoy the ocean's flora unfurling their colours in the morning sun. As the water shallowed, I waded shoreward to the sandy beach. Then I walked three blocks to the corner BurgoMeister and had breakfast. No one there said anything about my wet clothing—some of them, too, had slept through the night in ocean dress. For them, and for me, it was a normal start, except for our dreams, to a not-unusual day.

#

Back upstairs in the ensuite bathroom that first afternoon, the afternoon of the mirror, I tried to sort out my thoughts. Something had happened. It had happened to me. Something like it might happen again, or it might not.

Were there consequences, though? That seemed a more productive line of thinking. The horses in my chest, which had quickened their pace as I returned to examine the bedroom, slowed again to a sedate trot, reined in by reason.

Nothing of *real* significance seemed different. I was the same person I'd been. I wasn't suddenly on some other planet or locked away between the covers of *Alice in Wonderland*. I sat in my own home. Downstairs, Darlene had turned down the volume of the TV—tuned now to one of those reality shows, not a soap opera. She was undoubtedly reading my paper, brushing her hair. And, perhaps, smoking.

Interesting. Why did I *still* think she'd been watching a soap opera? Because I'd been sneaking peeks at it, that's why. I knew as much about the storyline as Darlene did. In fact, she loved that show so much that she'd twisted her ankle for it. A week ago, she'd rushed inside from a trip to town and stumbled over some garbage bags—I'd left them near the door, so I could take them to the landfill in the van when she got home.

For two days, she'd sat with her elevated ankle wrapped and iced, napping and popping painkillers. Meanwhile, I'd kept up with her show—I'd even learned the characters' names. Then she'd declared her ankle "mostly well," except when it suited her to be waited on, but I'd maintained my interest in her soap.

No. She *hadn't* been watching a talk show. The soap opera was "her" show.

So why had she lied? Did it have something to do with her lingering resentment about those garbage bags—the ones she'd tripped over, the ones that stood in for me?

And what about this smoking thing? She'd quit years ago, when I'd also given up drinking. Forgoing beer was no hardship for me, but Darlene had struggled mightily to get past her desire for a smoke. She'd kept half a pack in the kitchen junk drawer as a sort of memory, the way I had stowed a couple of coasters from my former favourite pub under my cufflinks. Had she sought out that pack for some reason? And when— while I'd been upstairs getting her hairbrush? And smoked the whole thing while I was upstairs not-meeting myself in the mirror?

I finished up in the bathroom but didn't feel like going downstairs yet. In the bedroom, I sat in the armchair that lets me look out over Amethyst Bay—beach and islands in the foreground, the tawny cliffs of the Sibley Peninsula behind. I wanted to look at something stable, unchangeable. I needed a few more minutes before Darlene realized I wasn't around.

About fourteen kilometers along and across the bay, just to the left of the break in the cliffs that marked the village of Pass Lake on the peninsula, I could see a little white dot—a house on the road leading into the village. Past that house, the road curved to run between the old railway bed and the small lake that gives the village its name. Now, I saw another dot beside the original—a dot I didn't remember. Another house? It was too far away to tell. I frowned at the dot, which bothered me the way the whole talk show/soap opera thing did. And that ashtray.

Downstairs, I called, "Darl, you need me for anything? I'm going for a drive."

"Live it up. Hey, what's with that *Darl* shit all of a sudden? You know I don't like it."

I didn't. I'd always called her Darl—our joke, a short form of Darling, not Darlene.

I picked up my keys from the ledge where they always were. Outside, the woodpile was stacked just as I had left it, and the lupines grew wild in shades of purple, pink, and white in the same spots beside the driveway. They looked like the exact same flowers, but who pays attention closely enough to know?

I took the Corolla, not the minivan. No sense wasting gas. At the end of the driveway I turned right, heading toward the highway. I made a left turn up the McKenzie Beach Road, crossed the railway tracks, and turned right at the top of the hill.

Wait a sec. *Railway tracks*? When the Kinghorn portion of the Canadian

National Railway line had been decommissioned, the rails had been torn up. But they were back. What the hell?

Right and left, north and south. What if I *hadn't* just fallen into the dresser? What if I had fallen into ... let's call it a left-hand version of the world. Would I be able to tell?

I stopped my spinning mind. *Crazy thoughts. Just drive.*

On the highway, I headed east toward Pass Lake. At the turnoff, I drove down the long hill and passed under the old railway trestle, and after that, the nine-hole golf course. All exactly as it should have been on a fine summer day.

The road wound upward toward the village. At the top of the hill lay a picnic area, where a historical plaque explained that nine thousand years ago the location was the site of an Aqua-Plano Indian settlement. Just beyond, I pulled over in front of the house I could see from my bedroom window. Beside it, there should have been nothing but trees. Instead, I could see the cement foundation of another building—which I'd also seen from the bedroom, across the bay.

But what did that prove? I wouldn't have seen anything until the foundation had been poured—maybe a couple of days ago. Even then, I wouldn't have seen anything unusual at first, from nine miles away. I swiveled to look across the road where the CNR line, mocking me, still sported rails.

I didn't know what it meant. I turned around and headed home.

Just past the roadside park, I saw the speed limit sign: 50 mph, not 80 kph. And that wasn't all—somewhere on the way to Pass Lake, I'd started *thinking* in the old imperial units—feet and miles, not meters and kilometers.

Unless someone had changed the signs—and, I noticed, the speedometer and the odometer of my car—I wasn't where I thought I was.

Worse yet, maybe I wasn't *who* I thought I was, either.

2 # TERRY FOX

In high school staff rooms, arguments often have no *weltansicht*—no shared world view, no common ground. English, history, and science teachers all look at the world differently, and their perceptions colour their arguments.

Is *Brave New World* a good novel?

Yes, says the English teacher. Look how well Huxley has used language and symbolism to make the case for guarding against the dehumanization of people by science and technology and the Machiavellian morality of big business.

No, says the history teacher. Huxley couldn't see past the British upper-middle-class social institutions. He just melded the pop science, politics, and paranoia of the 1930s into a novel that explores the silly idea that every politician's dream is to create a political system based on make-work projects for clones.

It's worse than that, says the science teacher. Huxley was an amateur biologist with no understanding of quantum mechanics and physics, and he was completely out of touch with the true nature of reality—quantum reality. Even if he'd understood it, he couldn't have written fiction about it because at the quantum level, analogies don't work.

Game, set, and match to the science guy this time. "How about those Maple Leafs?" says the English teacher. "Detroit'll crush them," answers the history teacher.

#

You're not in Kansas anymore, my brain told me—but maybe it, too, was malfunctioning. How does a drunk know when he's drunk? I used to know—until I'd stopped drinking. I needed more evidence before I could conclude that something was very, *very* wrong.

But first, I needed to go home and tell Darlene, who might not be Darlene, that I was going to town and would be late for supper.

On the way home, I started thinking about the weather. If a person suddenly found himself in a different world, wouldn't the weather also be *suddenly* different? Unfortunately, I had no idea what the weather had been like just before I fell into the dresser. I hadn't paid attention to it — like the lupines in the driveway and the wood stacked in the woodpile. When I pulled into the driveway, nothing about my home seemed the slightest bit different.

What if those speed limit signs were some kid's idea of a practical joke? But that wouldn't explain the car's speedometer. Leaving the car in the driveway, I walked into the house, singing out, "Just me, home!"

Darlene didn't reply. She never did.

In the family room, she again watched a talk show. I started to pick up the newspaper sections and flyers scattered around the floor. Darlene watched, annoyed as usual by what she considers one of my more irritating compulsions. I shuffled the sections together and set the paper on the coffee table.

"I'm going to town — maybe the bookstore," I said.

"Stop by the mailboxes and pick up the mail."

"Want me to bring some supper back?"

"Don't bother. I'll make a TV dinner for myself."

"Maybe I'll drop in on Charlie. See what he's been up to." I'd known Charlie since elementary school.

"Carlos, you mean?" Darl turned her attention back to the TV without waiting for an answer.

I left, with no intention of visiting Charlie, or Carlos, either.

I very much regret that now. Since I left "home," Charlie hasn't existed in any world I've visited. Not as Carlos, either.

#

I checked the car — which was metric again. Then I headed for Thunder Bay, a distance of about thirty *kilometers*.

At the highway I turned left. But maybe, I thought in my increasingly paranoid state, it *wasn't* left; it was something else. It still *felt* left. Then again, which way is left if you've become the mirror image of yourself, maybe more than once? I didn't know that I *had*, but I wasn't sure that I *hadn't*.

What I did learn, about thirty seconds and a half-kilometer of driving later, was that the road signs had changed again. The speed limit was 55 miles per hour and I was twenty miles from the city. Internally, I shrugged. I'd always preferred feet and inches, even if they were officially gone by my seventh birthday.

Other than signage, nothing seemed different. The birches and aspens along the highway were still in full leaf, the rock cuts still their dappled combination of dark grey and rusty orange. I passed the garbage dump and the Canadian Pacific Railway overpass at the proper times. Near the Terry Fox Lookout, I decided to stop. From the lookout, I'd be able to see most of the city. Would its major features be the way I remembered them?

The monument sits atop a bluff just off the highway, with a large parking lot and an information centre. It's always been one of my favourite places, in part because I can appreciate the views without having to look down. For most people, the main attraction is the monument—a bronze statue of Terry Fox in full stride, eyes fixed on the horizon, face resolute as he prepares to swing his prosthetic right leg ahead. Evening, when the light of the setting sun illuminates his face, makes for a great picture.

Years ago, a vandal cut off one of the statue's hands. Everyone in the city was upset. The sculptor fashioned and attached another hand. At least that's what happened in the world I'd left.

This statue still missed its left hand. Moreover, the base of the monument looked marked, as if people had chipped off and pocketed bits of the amethyst decorating it. I was no longer in my world. I was somewhere else. And I didn't like this place.

The view, mercifully, was the same. From the edge of the escarpment, I looked at the spreading harbour of Thunder Bay, blues and silvers, and noted no radical changes. The Sleeping Giant across the bay, Pie Island, and even a faint line of Isle Royale lay in their proper spots. Some extra smoke came from the paper mill, maybe, but nothing significant. I got back in the car, heading for another vantage point.

Hillcrest Park, atop the High Street hill, can't really decide what it is. On one end, a manicured sunken garden is planted with colourful annual flowers, a popular backdrop for bridal photos. On the large, well-manicured grass nearby, kids throw footballs and Frisbees in the summer. Ancient cannons of no particular historical significance are set in a low stone wall, pointing toward Lake Superior as if guarding the city against invasion by hostile lake freighter. A humble and tiny World War II armoured personnel carrier with accompanying historical plaque stands safely inside a protective iron fence, ready to help if needed, if someone would please let it out.

I parked to the right of the carrier. What was I looking for? Even the question didn't make sense. A *good* question has the answer tucked inside it. But I was looking for anomalies, with no guarantee that anything I noticed would be at all helpful. After all, a memory of a place isn't a photograph. If Lewis Carroll's looking glass (or, failing that, a conveniently large rabbit hole) appeared before my eyes, I might be able to pass through it into my old world. But "Where is that rabbit hole?" isn't even a *sane* question, let alone a *good* one.

It seemed likely that I'd be stuck here forever. That thought triggered others, mundane ones. For example, I was getting hungry. Back into the car, then, and off to Sleepy Pete's, one of the few restaurants in the city that serves relative quiet along with really good food. I needed both.

#

There are two ways of looking at the world — as a place of order or as a place of chaos.

The chaos school (that's not the one filled with people who say there are just *two* ways of whatever) likes to argue that little events can have enormous unanticipated consequences. You know the analogy — the gently fluttering wings of an Amazonian butterfly set in motion a sequence of events that causes a hurricane that devastates Florida.

The order school likes to point out that even apparent chaos holds an element of predictability. You might not be able to determine in advance where an individual smoke particle from a cigarette will land, but you know it will rise in a column of warmed air before dissipating. That's what smoke tends to do.

On every Earth I've ever been, except one (and I've visited quite a few), the sky looks basically the same: one moon, one sun, the usual constellations of stars. What happens on the various Earths doesn't seem to bother the cosmos at all. Or maybe I'm just not allowed to spend time on the really *weird* Earths — the ones that might kill me.

Similarly, epic events in history aren't particularly significant in the grand scheme of things. On one world I visited, Hitler won the Second World War, but that world's Thunder Bay looks pretty much like mine, where he lost the war. It's as if over time, the world pulls itself back together again. Even that world where humans can breathe underwater has fast food restaurants on every corner.

And in Hillcrest Park, on every world I've seen, you can still find some melted glassy rock. It's debris scattered by an asteroid that smashed into the Sudbury area, a thousand kilometers from Thunder Bay, two and a quarter billion years ago. *And so it goes*, as Vonnegut said. I have no idea what it all means. But it's how things are.

#

Sleepy Pete's had undergone a name change. It was Sneaky Pete's, now. Inside, it still looked the same, right down to the stack of complimentary newspapers beside the door. I picked up one and waited to be seated.

"Just me, non-smoking," I said to the young woman who appeared with the menu. I didn't know what smoking laws were in restaurants here so played it safe.

She frowned. "It's *all* non-smoking. C'mon, you know that."

What bothered me more than her borderline rudeness was that she thought she knew me. I didn't recognize her. Maybe in this world I'd replaced the fellow I bumped into—me, though I found it hard to think of him as me. It would be awkward to end up eating supper across the table from myself.

She led me to a booth by the window. "Your waitress will be with you shortly." I noted that she didn't say *server*. "Care for anything to drink?"

"Coffee."

She dropped the menu and left without a word. Before I picked it up, I bet myself that changes to the menu would be minor. I was right: only the restaurant's name was different. I lingered over coffee and a meal. Eventually, I used my credit card (it worked!) to pay, then I left without tipping. It's how we meek exact revenge on the curt.

Even long July days end, eventually. The sun was low in the sky as I left the restaurant. I decided to drive out Highway 102, use Mapleward Road to get to Oliver Road and then head due west to Kakabeka Falls. I had no real plan. I just wasn't ready to go back to Darlene.

Along Mapleward Road a ground fog rose, and after a while I might have been anywhere. I recognized the fire station as I went by, but it was hard to see any houses. And then, as I rounded a curve, oncoming headlights.

Someone in my lane!

I didn't have time to turn the wheel before we collided head-on.

But there was no collision.

Of its own accord, my right foot planted itself on the brake pedal, and the car screeched to a stop. In the rear-view mirror, I saw no taillights, no other vehicle, nothing but empty road. No car in the ditch. And no fog.

To hell with Kakabeka Falls. I wanted to go home. At Oliver Road I turned left toward town. At Highway 11-17 I turned left again. I was home before ten.

The porch light wasn't on. I couldn't find the right key to unlock the door.

Frantic, I knocked on the door.

"Where the *hell* you been?" rasped the woman who opened it. It wasn't Darlene—not recognizably *my* Darlene, anyway.

Where the hell had I been? Good question. And where the hell was I now?

3 # DARLENE III

Early in my travels, I thought everything that happened *to* me happened *because of* me. God, the universe, or some indefinable something kept track of me and, every once in a while, set a gateway before me, one through which I could enter another dimension, a different universe, a place selected especially *for* me.

I was one of the chosen, I thought. But I wasn't. I was mistaken about that.

#

The woman who answered the door was not Darlene, though she could have been. If sailor-swearing Darlene had magically fixed her ankle, added thirty pounds, and never left off smoking, that is.

"So where the hell were you?"

I answered without thinking. "I stayed in town, had supper with Charlie."

"Bullshit! Why didn't you phone me?"

"Sorry." It seemed pointless to say that I'd told her before I'd gone—I hadn't told *her*, after all.

"You're not sorry. You're drunk again, asshole, not sorry. And that means you've been with that little piece you keep on the side. The only time you can't keep a story straight, drunk or sober, is when you've been with her. Charlie, my ass! You don't have a friend named Charlie."

"I'm not drunk." But as I said it, I recognized that the smell of alcohol in the air was, in fact, coming from me. Or my clothes, at least. On this side of the rabbit hole, I (the one who lived here) certainly had been drinking. But I (the one who'd just arrived) was pretty sure I was more aromatic than drunk.

"Look, I need to use the bathroom, okay?" I pitched my voice to match this woman's husband—resigned. World-weary. Wheedly.

"Go piss yourself."

I gave her a mock salute. Upstairs in the bathroom, I collected my thoughts. That near-collision. What had come toward me—or rather, who—was this woman's husband. Somehow, I'd jumped ship again.

I looked closely at myself in the bathroom mirror. A touch too much beard, and itchy, too. I'd shaved this morning; the husband of the woman downstairs hadn't. I touched the mirror's surface. Glass—just glass. What did I expect?

As I came downstairs, I called, "Hey Darlene, I'm going to see if the Crystal Beach store is open. I'll be back soon."

I was getting very good at the quick lie. I had no intention of returning to this place, this woman, ever.

Her voice drifted from the family room. "Jesus, keep our names straight, okay? I'm Darryl, remember? Darlene must be your bitch's name, right?"

No answer required. I slipped out the door, got in the car, and headed for the highway again. If I drove back to this world's entry point, maybe I'd exit. Not a great plan, but better than staying with this Darlene. Er, Darryl.

At the highway, the fog had returned. I turned on the radio and pushed the first button, set to CBC. Nothing but static. Manually, I tuned the radio from one end of the dial to the other. Four stations, but none was a CBC affiliate. No wonder my other self drank—a lot, apparently. Married to Darryl, and no CBC. I turned off the radio.

Why were the differences so pronounced here? I tried to think.

The first time, I'd entered, or perhaps exited, in my home. The farther I went from home, the weirder things had become. The second transfer point (were they gates?) had been on Mapleward Road, on the other side of the city.

So what? So at home, things were more or less the same on both sides. The gate, to give it a name, was farther from home, and I was also further from me. At least, from the person I'd been that morning. Every version of Darlene had gotten worse, too—more estranged and alienated from me.

And I was second-guessing everything.

At Highway 102 I turned right. North Country Plaza looked normal. On the other side of the road, however, a gas station had replaced the small restaurant I'd known in my world.

Before Darlene and I grew apart, and went from loving each other to just living with each other, I joked that she and I kept all the restaurants in Thunder Bay going. If we didn't eat at a newly opened place, it was bound to fail. *Trendsetters* we were, I'd tell her. She'd laugh. As time passed, she didn't laugh as much, and I stopped trying to think of witty things to say for her amusement. That's how love dies, I guess. Not in a hail of bullets, but in a rain of silences.

I never made it back to Darlene—that first Darlene, the Darlene of our courtship, the Darlene of the "we" that we had been. Somewhere, a butterfly had flapped its wings.

It took about ten more minutes to get to Mapleward Road. I turned left, heading to the S-curve, just past Government Road, where I hoped to find the gate. There was fog once again, the kind that swirls in patches.

I slowed as I neared the curve. In the ground fog, I took the curve at just a few miles an hour. The car's lights made the fog feel more dense.

No headlights came toward me. No gateway. Nothing. So no point in stopping, either. At Oliver Road I turned around and headed back up Mapleward, again slowing at the curve. Maybe the direction of travel made a difference.

And then headlights! A car approached. But it was in the other lane, nothing to worry about.

Then the lights drifted over to my side of the road. Gateway be damned! I had no intention of going to another world by smashing through another car.

I stamped on the brakes. The oncoming vehicle also squealed to a stop. I took a deep breath and then got out. A second or two later, someone got out of the other vehicle.

But the timing should have been perfect. I and I, the other one of me, should have opened our doors at the same time, like dancers in a quantum ballet.

Instead, I heard a woman's voice and saw a slight silhouette. "Please, you've got to help me. I'm lost. Terribly, terribly lost. I'm sorry about making you stop but I'm—" She sounded near weeping.

"You gave me a hell of a scare." I kept my voice calm and composed. "No harm done, though." I walked toward her car. "You're on Mapleward Road. If you keep driving in the direction you were going, and stay in your own lane, you'll end up on Oliver Road."

"I know that!" Her voice broke. "That's not the problem." Her voice climbed in pitch. "The problem is that some things are in the right places, but all the rest is different!" She began to cry.

I felt the way you feel when a dream feels real. As I thought of what to say, I wondered how it would sound when I said it.

"Lady, listen. First, let's get our cars off the road, where it's safe." She wasn't listening. I spoke slowly, patiently. "Just pull your car off the side of the road, okay? You can't leave it parked here in the middle."

She wiped her face with her hands and took a deep breath. "You're right." She started back to her car and then she turned back to me. "I—I don't know where I am. Can I follow you somewhere? Can we get a cup of coffee or something, and maybe you can show me—oh Jesus, you must think I'm crazy."

"No, not at all. How about you pull around behind me, and we'll go to the doughnut place that's on the way to the mall?"

"I don't—I'll just follow you, okay? I'm not really sure where that doughnut place is. Or the mall."

"Sure."

In the car, I waited for her to do a U-turn and pull in behind me. Then I headed for the Better Cup Café.

There were *two* of us. And she thought *I* might know where the hell we were. Small chance of that. But at least there were two of us now.

4 # CAROLINE

The Better Cup Café, almost empty of customers that late, was brightly lit. The stainless steel counter, white coffee mugs, and chromed utensils caught the light from the ceiling's recessed halogen lamps and threw it about like sparks from a welder's torch.

Under the lights, the mysterious woman shed at least a little of her mystery. She was in her early forties, a few years younger than I was. She dressed modestly—a light jacket against the cooling summer evening air, a casual top, dark skirt, flat sandals. She looked like a normal, ordinary woman, with beautiful green eyes and red hair.

"I'm David." Still wary, I chose to keep my last name to myself.

"Caroline."

In the actinic light, Caroline seemed as ill at ease as I was. She measured out two even spoons of sugar and stirred her coffee with more attention than required. Then, abruptly, she stopped and looked at me.

"You must think I'm crazy." She dropped her eyes, perhaps afraid I'd agree with her assessment.

"No. I don't. Tell me what happened tonight."

"It wasn't just tonight." She looked up again, appraising me. "Listen, I can't—I can't just start talking about it to you without knowing anything about you."

I saw no point in easing into it. "You want to know if I'll believe you when you tell me something unbelievable. Like, maybe, you went through a hole in the universe and came out on the other side."

"Yes!" There was no hint of relief in her voice.

I gathered my words with care. "Bear with me. It's not easy to say this. What's happened to you once, I've gone through twice. Just today. Maybe three times, I don't know. All in the past few hours."

Though it was warm in the coffee shop, she put her hands around her mug.

"Cold?"

"Scared." Another pause. "Where are we?"

"Thunder Bay, The Better Cup Café." I said it lightly, with a reassuring smile. "We're on Earth, a different Earth. Maybe. It's like the one we left, but ...." I left the sentence hanging, giving her a moment to run away from the crazy man.

Instead, she stared into her coffee mug. "This has happened to you *twice*?"

"As far as I know." I immediately wished the words unsaid.

"What do you mean, *as far as you know*?"

I began at the beginning and tried to keep it to bullet points, but still I talked for almost twenty minutes.

I tried to wrap it up. "That first time, in the bedroom—it was dramatic, noticeable. The second time, too, in the fog. But maybe sometimes they happen so subtly that we just shrug them off. Maybe you wake up one morning and the dollar's down a dime, or your partner reveals a secret love of country music, but nothing else seems odd. Or maybe you wake up in this other place and discover that terrorists who learned to fly planes by playing a computer game, while hiding in a Florida retirement community, crashed *real* airliners into the World Trade Center."

Caroline looked as if she wanted to say something but couldn't.

I forced myself to shut up. The silence stretched between us for a few minutes.

Eventually, she asked her question. "Can we get back? Is there a way to, I don't know, undo this?"

"I don't know. Before we met on Mapleward Road I was hoping I could go home by sort of backing out through the entry points. If I could find the gates, the holes—whatever you want to call them—if I looked for them, the other versions of me would be looking too, and we could just replace each other and all go home."

"But?" She raised one eyebrow.

"But the gate I'd gone through earlier wasn't there anymore. I thought your car was *my* car coming from the opposite side."

"You didn't run into me, though."

"Lucky you. I was too afraid of being wrong to risk it." It was my turn to stare into the mug, watching the lights of the ceiling mirrored on the black surface of my coffee. At last, I asked, "Why were you on the road, tonight?"

"Long story."

"I told you mine. You tell me yours."

"My husband. For a year, he's thought I've been cheating on him. I wasn't." Her voice had become flat, deliberately unemotional, while she nervously checked my face to read my reactions. "Two nights ago, I thought he was going to kill me. He was drunk. He came in the bedroom with a shotgun. He made me get dressed, ordered me out of the house into the car. I thought he was going to take me someplace else. There, he'd—" Her voice broke.

She sipped coffee to regain her composure. After a breath, she went on.

"I headed toward the passenger side but he kept the gun pointed at me and waved me over to the driver's side. Then he yelled at me to go the hell away. So I did, though I didn't know where. I thought of my friend Sharon, who has a condo—maybe she'd let me stay with her. I drove over there. She wanted to involve the police. But I—"

She clasped the mug, staring as one of her thumbs worried the other. "Sharon hadn't had supper so I went to pick up pizza. I got completely lost. It was like someone had renamed streets and moved buildings around. Finally I got oriented, found the pizza, and got back to Sharon's."

"This was last night?"

"Yes. I spent last night there, with Sharon."

"And who's your husband?"

"His name's Rey. Reynaldo Reynolds. My last name's Reynolds."

"David Williamson. Reynolds sounds English-Canadian. But Reynaldo—is that Spanish?"

She shook her head. "Portuguese. His grandparents emigrated almost ninety years ago. He doesn't speak a word of Portuguese, but his mother wanted to name him after her father. Then again, my grandparents were Quebec Irish, the Moynihans, and I can't speak either French or Gaelic. Sorry, I'm babbling."

"Did you know he owned a gun?" I steered the conversation to more urgent dangers.

"No. I have no idea where it came from."

"Was he abusive before?" I sat quietly after the question, allowing her to think and tell me what she was comfortable saying.

"No. Not really. Well, sort of. I mean, he didn't hit me. He'd just get, I don't know, angry. He'd shout. A lot. But I can't imagine why he'd buy a gun, especially a shotgun. He was no hunter. What would he use it for?"

I didn't want to suggest the obvious. "Okay, so that was last night.

When did you—you know, pop into this place?"

"I don't know. Nothing dramatic happened to me, not the way it did to you."

"Not tonight, at least. But maybe earlier. Maybe yesterday, your husband—"

"Rey, but—"

I could see her mind working at it. I helped her a little. "Yes, but likely not *your* Rey. That's my guess, anyway. The Rey here, who threatened you, owns a shotgun. The two of you may have a different history here."

Caroline picked up a spoon and stared at it. "When you went through the first time, you said another you must have gone through, too, but the other way."

"Yes."

"How many of *me* are there? Just me? Or me, myself, and I?" For the first time, she smiled—a guarded smile, but a real one.

"Maybe just you. Whatever was going to happen to you happened to her instead. And she's somewhere else."

"Lucky her. No shotgun in her face, slightly improved husband. And I'm stuck in a world where I'm married to Al Capone."

It was my turn to smile. "I think Capone favoured tommy guns." I paused. "So that was yesterday. What about today? How did you spend the day?"

"Sharon, my friend, works at the bank. The one near Laurier High School—"

"Whoa. Where? There's no Laurier in Thunder Bay."

"On Parkway off Edward."

"In my Thunder Bay, that's Sir Winston Churchill. Or it was. It's torn down now."

Caroline blinked. "After Sharon left for school I watched TV, made myself a sandwich, tried to call Rey, but he didn't answer. I didn't leave a message. Looked over yesterday's newspaper."

"Notice anything odd in the paper?"

"No, but I wasn't really looking, either. Around two I decided I couldn't just sit around anymore. I thought, since Rey'd be at work, I'd go home, get some clean clothes, and get back to Sharon's. After that, I had no idea."

"And you got lost trying to drive home?"

"No. That part was okay. My suitcase is still in the trunk. I left Rey a note saying I wasn't coming home for a while and I'd call. Then I thought of my cousin."

"Let me guess. The farther you got from home, the weirder things got."

"Yes! I couldn't find her. By the end I was using major landmarks, like the grain elevators and Boulevard Lake, but I still couldn't find the right street. I hadn't missed it—I drove up and down every street, but her street wasn't anywhere."

"So what did you do?"

"Something stupid." She sighed. "I went back home, to our apartment. I let myself in quietly. Rey was fast asleep in the bedroom, with the shotgun propped up in a corner. It shocked me. I thought, 'If he wakes up, he'll kill me, I gotta get out.' So I drove off. No plan, just to leave."

Caroline breathed more rapidly, trying to stave off tears. "I don't know *what* I was planning to do. I turned up Mapleward Road because it was there, and the name was familiar. Then the fog rolled in, and it was dark, and I didn't know how to get back to town. And then I saw your headlights." She took a deep breath and exhaled quietly, gathering herself again. "I pulled into your lane. I needed someone to help me. I didn't know what else to do."

She stopped talking, and I didn't know what to say.

After a moment of uncomfortable silence, she said, "Tell me more about what happened to you. It's your turn to be the storyteller. You gave me the outline, but I don't know the details."

I unfolded my story slowly, carefully, like a map I was afraid of tearing. All the while, Caroline scrutinized me. When I finished there was a long silence.

At last, she asked, "Now what?"

"Beats me," I said. "I'm no Captain Kirk." I tried a smile, but got none in return. I looked out the window. The sun was coming up. The coffee mugs had been refilled a number of times.

Caroline's next question surprised me. "What about Darlene? Your wife, not one of the other Darlenes. Won't she be worried sick?"

"Maybe, but another me is likely there, too. I can't do anything about it." I set aside thoughts of Darlene, of might-have-beens, of other versions of our marriage. I'd never be able to explain to Darlene what happened, especially when I didn't know myself. Caroline, sitting across from me with narrowed eyes, might hold answers, or we might figure them out together.

I let my awkwardness show in my voice. "Please don't take this the wrong way. I don't mean anything by it—but I think, until we figure out a few things, you and I should stick together for a while. Problem is, I'm awfully damn tired. I can't think. Would you mind if we got some sleep? Checked into a hotel or motel? Or something?"

She looked closely at me. "Okay. But just sleep, nothing else."

"Agreed. Just sleep. Where can we leave your car? We only need one, and if we're together, there's less risk we'll be separated. Can you find your friend's place again?"

Caroline nodded. We drove in tandem to Sharon's place, put a note under the windshield wiper, and left. Caroline never saw the car again.

5 # MOTEL AND DUMPSTER

The motels along Cumberland Street cater both to short-term tourists on tight budgets and to regulars—travelling salesmen, workers who value their pocketbooks, people on disability pensions, and couples who arrive suddenly at any time of day. Caroline and I checked in at the Lakeland Lodge at eight a.m. without luggage and without any problem. Caroline got the bed. I remember taking off my shoes.

Caroline woke me six hours later. "You snore."

"I know. Sometimes the echo wakes me." My mouth tasted of stale coffee.

"I couldn't sleep. There's still a couple of doughnuts in the bag if you want one. And coffee—not real coffee, but maybe good enough."

I sat up slowly and swung my feet to the floor. Before fumbling through the bag, I rubbed my eyes clear of sleep.

Though Caroline claimed not to have slept, she seemed rested. The eddies of frenzy, so apparent in last night's fog, no longer swirled about her. I bit into an apple fritter, motel coffee at the ready.

Apparently she'd also been thinking. "You said we needed to talk. So here's a thought. If I came from a mirror image of your world, the steering wheel of my car should be on the opposite side. But it isn't."

I hadn't thought about that. "You're right. It should be, but it isn't."

I tried but couldn't think of anything to say beyond that. Was her observation important in some way—or not? My brain wasn't yet in gear, but I didn't want to look foolish, so I nodded as if I were gathering insight.

Finally, hoping sensible words would come out, I started to think aloud. "Okay. How about this. Your home world and my home world aren't the same place, going by what you've said. But maybe your home world is my world number two. Or maybe it's a different world entirely. We have to figure out which of those possibilities is true."

"Why?"

Good question. "Well. If your home world is my second world, I propose that we head for your apartment."

"Because?"

"If there's a way back to your world and I go through the gate with you, I'll be just one step from my home."

Caroline frowned. "Wouldn't this have to be your *third* world? I'm thinking about how the steering wheels on our cars are on the same side."

Clever. "What if, in your world people drive on the left, thinking it's the right?"

Caroline's left eyebrow shot up at the screwball logic.

"Okay, probably not. But I don't have any other ideas. How about you?"

"My apartment it is, then."

#

For many years, long before this all began, I wondered if I had a brother. The idea started when I was about eighteen. I attended church then, and I'd been invited to make a Youth Night presentation of some sort. At the end of my speech, a woman I'd never seen before approached, showed me a picture, and asked if I recognized the person in it. I looked and saw my double—a year or two older, perhaps, but so like me that I thought she was showing me my own picture as a setup for some sort of practical joke.

But no, she was from one of the small towns west of Thunder Bay— Atikokan, Fort Frances, Kenora—I can't remember which. She was visiting some friends in town, members of the congregation, and had come to Youth Night with them. I remember very little else about the incident, just the picture.

When I got home from church, I told my mother.

"That's strange, isn't it?" was all she said.

I'm certain that my memory of the Youth Night presentation is correct. But there's a related memory I'm not so sure of. A few weeks later, I came home from school to find my mother crying in the living room.

Between sobs, she said, "Did you know you have a brother?" She then told me she'd given up her first child for adoption.

This memory has a lot more texture—but it's not solid. The details never quite come into focus. I don't know if it's real or not. I don't even know if it's mine.

Sure, I've been mistaken for someone else from time to time—who hasn't? But occasionally, someone who knew me well would ask why I hadn't said hello the other night, when they'd seen me at a place I hadn't been. Students would tell me they'd seen me on a bus or in a store or in my car. At the grocery store or in a shopping mall, someone would call me by another name (usually John) as if I were a familiar friend.

It's one thing to accept that you have a double, a doppelganger—most of us bear a striking resemblance to a few of Earth's other eight billion people. But it's not as easy to come to terms with the idea that your double may be related to you.

And then, of course, there's that other possibility. The one I've learned to live with.

#

On the way to Caroline's apartment, I had an idea. "What does the Terry Fox monument look like?"

She didn't have to ask why I wanted to know. "It's on that bluff just off the highway. It's a bronze sculpture of Terry Fox and it sits on a long pedestal that has provincial flags carved into it. The sculpture is of Terry running and he's facing west."

"Was one of the statue's hands ever cut off?"

"No! What kind of a question is that?"

"At home, one year someone cut off his left hand. The sculptor had to replace it. In my second world, the hand is still missing."

"So do you think we should go by the monument?"

"Maybe after your apartment. I can't think of any more efficient way to learn about this world than by starting with what's most familiar—in this case, your life here. There must be some reason we've ended up in this together."

Caroline considered. "I guess that makes sense." Her voice dropped in warning. "Rey may be there, you know."

"I know. We'll just play everything by ear."

After a few more blocks, Caroline asked, "Do you think we're on the right side of the street? I mean, the correct side? Yesterday, before you and I met, I sometimes felt a bit backward, as if I were driving in Britain."

"Maybe your brain's adjusted to your changed circumstances."

She accepted the statement without comment, though she could have argued that perhaps *my* brain had adjusted.

When we arrived outside her apartment building on Arthur Street, it was obvious that no amount of planning would have helped us at all. Two police cars sat on the street in front of the building, and another cruiser was parked in the alley, an ambulance behind it. I turned onto Selkirk Street and parked close to the corner. We crossed Arthur and mingled with the crowd gathered around the ambulance.

Caroline approached a bystander. "Stan, what happened?"

A man turned around. "Hey, Caroline. They found some guy's body in the dumpster this morning. There's blood all over the side entrance door. Somebody really messed him up."

I rose on tiptoe to see over the people in front. The attendants put a man's body on the gurney. I caught no more than a quick glimpse before they covered it, but it was enough to recognize the face on the dead man.

I spoke barely above a whisper. "Caroline, we should be going."

"But—" She looked at my face and bit back what she was going to say.

I took her hand and we walked away from the crime scene. It took all my willpower to keep from running, but I didn't want to attract attention.

In the car, she asked, "What's going on?"

I shook my head, focusing on driving. We went several blocks on Selkirk before I turned a corner and pulled over. I knew she was scared—and so was I.

"I'm dead. That was me on the stretcher."

"You? It can't have been. You're right here."

"But I saw. It was me. Which explains why I didn't turn up at the S-bend last night, doesn't it? I was busy being dead in a dumpster."

Caroline spoke slowly. "Stan—that fellow I was talking to—he lives upstairs. He made it sound as if that guy—you—had been murdered."

"I think he's right."

"What?"

"I think I was murdered."

"But why?"

"I think I was coming to see you. I think that in this world you and I are, you know. Friends. Or, you know. Something."

"Ah. And Rey is the murderer?"

"Best guess."

"But you and I—"

"Yeah. That last Darlene, Darryl, here or somewhere like here. She accused me of having someone on the side. I thought she was just argumentative—she seems pretty tough in this world—but maybe the version of me she knew does. Did." Darryl's voice, rough and biting, rang briefly in my ear, and I let it pass. "Maybe she was right."

"Me."

"Uh huh."

"How would we have met?"

"No idea."

Caroline fiddled with a loose thread on her sleeve. "So now what? This place makes me very—something. I don't have a word for it."

"Me neither. What if we go see your friend, Sharon? She can give you an idea of what your other self, the other Caroline, is up to. That Caroline might be still in this world, but maybe not. And we need to know where Rey fits. All this stuff seems so unlikely, but maybe there's some kind of pattern to it, and we don't see it yet. Maybe."

"What happens if we run into me? Isn't there some sort of rule about two of a person not being able to be in the same place at the same time? Like one of us has to blow up or something?"

"You're a science fiction fan?"

"No. I can't stand it, in fact. But I saw *Back to the Future*. Isn't there a rule like that?"

"I don't know. This isn't science fiction. It's something else." I started the car. "To Sharon's, unless you've got a better idea."

"Not better, but I do have an idea. How about we go someplace safe, out of sight, and I'll call Stan. He may know things we can't learn from Sharon."

"That's a hell of a good idea."

Caroline reached into her purse. "I've got my cell, someplace." She rummaged. "No, I guess I don't."

"Maybe they don't have them here. Or who knows, maybe yours was confiscated by the Universe Police at the border crossing. There's a pay phone in the Thunderbird Mall, though—in my world, at least. It's not too far, but far enough. We can't hang around too close, since I'm dead."

Caroline smiled and then, suddenly, winked at me. I think she meant to be playful and conspiratorial, but there was something else in it, too. Flirtation.

In spite of myself, I blushed. I hoped she didn't notice. When at last I dared take my eyes from the road to look at her, I found her already looking at me, amused.

"What?" I tried to sound dignified.

"I've never had a conversation with a corpse before."

"It's nice to know that you have some standards."

"Some."

I thought about Rey and wondered if he was mean enough to kill me twice. I hoped we wouldn't have a reason to find out.

#

The Thunderbird Mall was more or less as I remembered it, with phones down the hall from the main entrance, close to the hair salon.

Caroline used her own quarter to place the call.

"Stan, it's Caroline. You got a minute?" She shooed me away. *Car*, she mouthed. I left her to her conversation.

6 # STAN

Funny how your own particular circumstances determine what you become interested in. For instance, in my case, quantum physics.

Some quantum physicists (especially those PhDs who are adept at math and magic) believe that our sense of time is just an illusion. Neither the past nor the future exists—they're more like directions than events. Their apparent reality is a consequence of the universe spinning off an infinite number of versions of itself. Look down one path and you peer at all of the "evidence" for the existence of the past, everything from dinosaur bones to your Aunt Mildred's old love letters to Uncle Charley. Look in the opposite direction, and you peer into a future that was propelled into being by the events of the past, with a lot of randomness built in.

But what you see is no more real and in motion than the picture created by a movie's thousands of individual images. Once in a while, in this movie you think is your life, the projectionist splices in scenes from another film starring someone who looks remarkably like you, though not quite as handsome. And you discover that weird things have begun to happen. Your stock market picks soar or sour. Suddenly, your children are doing well in school—or they run off to join the circus.

Personally, I like the theory. I just don't believe it. But then, I'm good at neither math nor quantum physics.

#

Caroline came back to the car almost half an hour later. Most of that time, I'd been trying to note all the little things that made this world different from my own, while remaining inconspicuous. It says something for my powers of observation that she walked right up to the car and tapped on the window before I noticed.

"Short call," I said as she got in. "Did you find out what you needed to know?"

"I did, and after I talked to him I got something for you at the bookstore. I think you'll find it interesting." She raised a small plastic bag.

I stopped her. "Wait—I'll look later. First, tell me about Stan."

"Okay. Stan here is much like the Stan I know. He's a little more gruff, a little more inclined to gossip. But he and I have the same relationship here as at home."

"Which is?"

"He's like a protective older brother, one who's spent too much time living on the wrong side of the tracks. He's Ukrainian, you know? Originally Stanislav, now just Stan. He's always trying to make sure that nobody takes advantage of me or gives me a hard time."

"So, do you need his protection?"

Caroline smiled. "Not really, but I'd never tell him that."

I smiled back. "Go on. What was up at the apartment building this morning?"

"Well, in a nutshell, you were right. You and I were 'an item,' as my grandmother would have said. And everybody seems to have known, except for Rey. When he found out, he went more than a little nuts. Stan says that Rey didn't work this morning—he just hung around the building, and when you showed up, he killed you."

"Gun?"

"Baseball bat."

"Ouch." I winced.

"It's exactly what I'd expect."

"You approve?" I said with mock seriousness.

"No. Just—that level of violence is part of his character. If I cheated on him, of course he'd kill my lover and then he'd kill me. Which, by the way, I think he did."

"What?"

"Stan said a smaller figure in a body bag was brought out shortly after we left, and it was rumored to be a woman, but he couldn't see, of course. He was relieved to hear from me."

"A woman." Dread settled on me, smothering any further attempts at humour.

"Yes. Me. I think Rey killed both of us. He's been arrested." She paused. "Stan's going to have a strange day when he finds out that the mysterious dead woman is me."

"I'll say." I could think of nothing less inane to say.

"I think we should leave my car in Sharon's driveway, don't you? Seeing that I'm dead and all."

I nodded. Impassivity, along with humour, were my tools for covering the horror I felt. To me, her death and mine were real events. I knew that death hadn't come to *us*—to her and me. Nevertheless, people who were also us, or other versions of us, were now dead. Caroline, for all her light banter, seemed to feel that, too.

I didn't want to think anymore. "You bought something?"

"Two." She reached into the bag. "It occurred to me that we might need these." A map of the city and a small world atlas.

I smiled a bit ruefully. "You're a smart woman, Caroline."

"You think we could use them?"

I debated telling her what I really thought, decided not to, and focused instead on the maps. We'd certainly need them. In this world I was dead and, in all likelihood, so was she. We had to leave the city. Too many people knew us. Also, I wondered when we might expect to find a gate out of this place. If a requirement for a gate was that at least one of our counterparts had to come through to replace us—well, we weren't likely to run across a gate near here anymore. Two good reasons for maps.

"They're a great idea. Let's find someplace where we can take our time looking at them. Do you know anyone in Nipigon?"

"Nipigon?"

"Uh huh. I don't know a soul there, and if you don't, either, it might be a safe place to spend a little time."

"Sounds good. I'm hungry, by the way."

"I think I can spring for a meal."

I headed for the expressway. A short way up the highway we passed a speed limit sign—90 kph. We were back to life with the metric system. I had no idea how or when.

In this world, miles or kilometres, the two of us were on the run.

7 # GEOGRAPHY LESSON

Nipigon is the first larger town on the Trans-Canada Highway east between Thunder Bay and Sault Ste Marie. The Nipigon River Bridge on the east side of town effectively divides Canada in two. You can't cross the country by car or truck without crossing that bridge. The town itself is on Lake Superior, but since the highway skirts Nipigon's north side, most tourists never see much of the place.

On our way, we'd checked the Terry Fox monument outside Thunder Bay. The statue of the runner had both his hands. Although I was relieved to see it, I wondered what, if anything, it meant. As we drove toward Nipigon, I pondered. Had I shifted worlds again, away from the world where his hand was missing? Maybe I hadn't seen it correctly before. Maybe the "me" that had seen it lay on a stretcher. I dropped that thought.

Caroline and I chose a booth at the River Restaurant, not far off the highway. She sat beside me in the booth so we could look at the atlas together—but we waited to open it until we'd demolished the fish dinner special and the server had refilled our coffee.

"Well, here goes." I started to open the atlas.

"Wait." Caroline put her hand on mine. "Not yet. Let's think a minute. What do you expect to find?"

"Pattern." The first word that came into my head.

She sighed. "Look, if we're going to be spending time together—and it sure looks like it—you have to stop being a macho monosyllabic protector and start being my fellow traveller. I have a perfectly good brain, you know. Try bouncing an idea or two across it." She shifted in the booth and sipped coffee. "Okay, try again. What sort of pattern?"

I tossed out what I had. "Here's a hypothesis: the farther away from the gate, the stranger the world will look. So, the map of someplace like India, just as an example, will be more distorted than, say, Mexico."

"And if that's true, what will it mean for us?"

"It'll mean—hmm. I'm not sure what it'll mean."

She nodded. "That's better. Honesty is best. Now, let's see what kind of amateur scientist you are."

I found a political map of North and South America and frowned.

"Well?" Caroline said. She had shifted closer to me.

"It all looks okay to me, but—"

"You were never much good at geography, right?"

"'Fraid so."

"Quiz time." She quickly turned over the atlas. Then she took another sip of coffee. "What's the capital of Brazil?"

"Rio de Janeiro, isn't it?"

"Brasilia."

"Are you sure?"

"Positive."

"So. We have a problem. I could be wrong about Rio for a couple of reasons. Maybe I'm not good at geography. Brasilia really could be the capital. Now that I think about it, I remember reading that the Brazilian government built the city to be the capital. But, it's also possible that Rio could be the capital in my world and Brasilia in yours."

Caroline considered. "So even if I notice something seriously out of whack, it might seem perfectly fine to you. Not very useful, is it?" She sighed. "I may have wasted some of our precious cash on a bad idea."

"You paid with cash?"

"Not a good idea?"

I shook my head. "Cash should be our currency of last resort. Let's keep using the credit card as long as it keeps working."

She nodded, glum. "Sorry."

I sipped coffee to buy time. "Actually, the atlas could be quite useful." Her face brightened and I felt better. "We met at a place that was the same for both of us. So, maybe ...." I wondered how to finish the sentence.

"Maybe what? Stop speaking in ellipses."

"Circles, you mean."

"No, I mean ellipses, Mr. English Teacher. You know, an ellipsis, more than one. When you leave out part of a sentence because you expect the other person to fill in what's missing so the sentence makes sense grammatically?" She smiled smugly.

"I thought you said ellipses like in math."

"As if." She almost laughed.

"When did I tell you I was an English teacher, anyway?"

"When we were at The Better Cup."

I didn't remember that. Interesting.

"Now, finish that thought. The 'maybe-it-wasn't-such-a-bad-idea after all' thought."

"Suppose there are a bunch of gates. If they have to be where things are the same for both of us, we might be able to find them on a map."

"Because we'd agree that for both of us, the map looks okay at that point." Caroline thought for a moment. "So most, maybe all, would be in Thunder Bay. We need a city map. They sell them by the checkout."

"It's a good start. But Thunder Bay might not pan out. We left the city a couple of hours ago for a pretty good reason. So unless we see something remarkable on that map, I don't think we should go back any time soon. Our 'twins' won't be there. Therefore, no gate."

"Are you sure?"

"Of course not. Let's look at the city map." I slid out of the booth and came back from the checkout with the city map.

Caroline had pushed the atlas across the table. She unfolded and positioned the map so we both had equal access. For five or six minutes we examined it in silence.

"Well?" I said at last. "What do you see?"

"I'm not sure. Most of the streets are right, I guess—they have the right names and they're in the right places. Of course, we can't see if the right buildings are on them. But I *can* tell that the streets around my cousin's place are completely haywire."

"Which explains why you got so lost."

"I guess. There are other things, though. Like here." She pointed at the road that ran along the base of Mt. McKay. "That should be Nor'Wester Road, not Ojibwe Road."

"I think it's named Chippewa, like the park."

"The park is Nor'Wester Park, if you mean the one on the lake. At least that's what *we* call it."

I considered for a moment. "They've got a bunch of Thunder Bay maps beside the register. Would you mind buying another one for us?"

"Another one?"

"I have an idea."

"Which you aren't going to tell me until I get back, I suppose."

"The explanation needs the map. And some of those coloured pens."

"Right, of course. What's a teacher without his coloured pens? Will you need a pocket protector to go with that?" I got up so she could get past me, then sat again.

In a minute she was back from the register with the map and pens. "I used cash," she said, unrepentant. She sat down immediately, blocking me in.

"Okay, here's the idea. You take your map to that empty booth over there and mark on it every single thing that doesn't match your memory of the city. No matter how small. Use Xs. I'll do the same with mine. Then we'll put the information together."

"Oh, I get it." She took the green pen to a different booth.

Twenty minutes and a slice of apple pie later, we were ready to amalgamate the data.

I said, "Let's use my map. I'll mark what you found in red pen."

It took just a few minutes to add her green to my blue. "Aha," I said.

"I don't see any pattern—no, don't tell me."

I forced myself to stay silent for a full minute before suggesting, "Squint."

"An hourglass! Shade in the parts with a lot of X's, and that leaves a white hourglass in the middle, where neither of us saw any changes."

"Yes. Maybe not quite an hourglass. Just two circles intersecting."

"Of course." She blinked rapidly, and I could almost see the thought forming in her mind. "The centre of one circle is at the bend on Mapleward Road. And the other is the apartment on Arthur Street."

"Yep, two gates. Except, of course, you and I died in the apartment building. So one of the gates wasn't used."

"But the other one was, and there's no other option on the map. Just the two."

"In Thunder Bay," I pointed out. "But Thunder Bay is not the world."

Caroline let the statement go without comment. "You know what I don't get? I keep thinking about what's happening like this—one world, or universe, or whatever, is bumping into another, like two big bubbles touching. But wouldn't that mean that they'd touch at only one point?"

"That makes sense. But it might not work that way."

"Why not?"

"Well, for one thing, universe-sized bubbles are awfully big. So maybe what you picture as round would look, for all intents and purposes, flat, so there's more area where they touch. And if the universe isn't perfectly round, sides can touch in several places." I felt myself warming up. "And then there's this. If the universes have more than three dimensions—some physicists think so—then trying to imagine them as bubbles just doesn't work. They'd look like something else."

"Stop." Caroline said. "You're giving me a headache." I stopped. She sighed. "Now what?"

"How about sleep? I don't want to start on the atlas. The waitress looks nervous about us hanging around so long."

"There's a motel near the bridge. I don't think anyone will have cancelled my credit cards yet."

"The motel it is, then."

"Same rules."

"Same rules," I agreed.

#

Memory is the least reliable of all witnesses. Sometimes the events we remember so clearly never happened, as our friends are wont to remind us. And sometimes, as I have so unwillingly learned, the events we remember really did happen, but we're no longer part of the world in which they occurred. Often, the chains of cause and effect have breaks in them that we're completely unaware of. We just feel foolish that memory has tricked us again. Or we wonder if maybe, this time, it's Alzheimer's.

Many of my "ancient" memories involved religion. That's really all I can tell you about that, because a lot of those memories—the ones that were part of the world that gave birth to me—were replaced by others. An ancient philosopher, Sextus Empiricus, thought that one way we can tell dreams from reality is by virtue of reality's continuity—today's story always picks up where yesterday's left off. But dreams are all broken up. The nighttime storyline has no glue. A lot of my memories are like dreams now. They have built-in discontinuity. I have a sister in only one, however. In all the others I'm an only child—except for that doppelganger, over whom my mother cried. That story appears in some.

But mostly, I can use continuity to distinguish dream memories from this tale of a man and woman, this specific man and this specific woman, who once wandered through universes like children exploring a house of mirrors.

Here's a "memory" I now have of a religion I was raised in, somewhere. Its adherents believe that all religions that purport to be "revealed" in some way—the ones that claim God spoke to someone or did something that someone else saw—are false. So much for all the major religions and a good proportion of the minor ones, right? These people, of whom my parents were two, believe instead that we are not equipped to know how *everything* came to be. We are, after all, pretty stupid.

So, those parents said, there's no reason to build temples or churches or to invent rituals or to proscribe behaviour. Instead, be sensible. Try to get along with people; keep the world from becoming a wasteland; let the giraffes have some space, too; learn about things so that you don't get hurt or end up hurting someone else inadvertently; and don't be afraid to be happy. If you want to believe some other stuff besides that, for instance that God's name is Allah or that He or She enjoys hymns, or that fish, not meat, should be eaten on Fridays, that's fine, too. Just be sure that science and common sense don't put insurmountable obstacles in the way of your Friday meals. If that happens, put on your cloak of humility and find something a little less silly to believe.

And faith? Well, those parents believed that if you don't make yourself the centre of everything, things will work out all right. Belief in the impossible is neither a requirement for salvation nor a reason for turning off your brain when you think about the meaning of life. Belief in the unknowable is your own affair.

I think if Isaac Asimov had invented a religion, instead of the Three Laws of Robotics, that's what he would have put together. The only flaw— or perhaps just its biggest—is that no two people seem to agree on what constitutes common sense.

#

Sometime around six a.m. I woke from a vivid dream in which Caroline and I were on TV and the owner of the motel was calling the police. I couldn't get back to sleep. I knew our faces likely hadn't been on TV—bodies in body bags are much more visually dramatic. Also, they wouldn't have found our photos in time for the evening news.

However, the local paper was delivered early in the morning to the communities outside Thunder Bay. And those morning papers would be in the news rack beside the front desk, right now.

I pulled on my pants and woke Caroline.

She rebelled. "I thought we were going to stay in Nipigon for a while."

"We paid for the motel with a dead woman's credit card."

"But the credit card people won't figure that out for a while. At least not till time to pay the bill." She yawned.

"But the motel clerk might read the newspaper. And what if he sees pictures of us?"

"Oh." She sprang into action. We were in the car—showered, teeth brushed—inside of twenty minutes.

"Now where? Thunder Bay?"

I'd been thinking. "*Through* Thunder Bay. On to Winnipeg, maybe. Going south to and through the U.S. border is out of the question—too many uniforms. We should head in a different direction than authorities expect. We can decide exactly where after we've had a chance to study that atlas of yours. And we should aim for a place some distance beyond Thunder Bay. When there's just one highway, the police can easily set up a roadblock and—well, two corpses driving in a car might look suspicious."

"We have to get out of here."

"We are." I replied as we pulled out onto the highway.

"No, I mean we have to get out of this world, for someplace else."

"Well, first let's just get away."

A few minutes down the highway, Caroline asked, "Do you think we might get lost? What if the highway leads someplace other than Winnipeg?"

"I don't think it does. I've been to Winnipeg often. So far, if a place is familiar to me it doesn't change much."

"You haven't said that before. Is this something you just made up?"

"Yeah," I admitted. "Or maybe I remembered it? If it's true, we won't find any big changes until we're farther away. But you can take a peek in your atlas from time to time."

"I think I'll do that." She pulled out the little atlas and turned pages for a while. "Looks okay."

"Told you."

"Doesn't hurt to check."

I found I couldn't argue with that.

#

Over time, we learned a few things. For one, the more similar our new universe was to our old one, the longer we could stay in it. We fit better, or something. When we were swallowed by a place that wasn't a particularly close match, our new home spat us out like a seed from a slice of watermelon, plunking us back in the blink of an eye.

Or, as I learned much later, the hard way, after Santa Flora, it put us through a lot of pain trying to remake us to fit. We ended up with a set of gills, a terrible pain in the neck, and a bunch of very peculiar memories—some of which weren't our own but felt just as real anyway.

All of which—the universe's "fit," the fickleness of memory, the shape of universes, you name it—put a real crimp in trying to present an accurate record of what happened. Still, this theory seemed to work.

#

Just after noon, we turned off the highway and headed into Kenora. The Manitoba border was about an hour away.

"Where are we going?" Caroline asked.

"How about the mall in Kenora? We can get something to eat."

"Bathroom first."

The mall was much as I remembered. I parked between two pickups in a crowded section of the parking lot.

Caroline got out first. "Race you."

"That's your bladder talking."

"Damn right." She hurried toward the entrance. I followed a few paces behind.

Inside, Caroline glanced at the information display, oriented herself, and headed at top speed for the washrooms.

I waited in the hall until she returned. "There's a restaurant by the entrance."

"I saw it." She raised a quizzical eyebrow. "Did you think I'd miss it?"

"Your mind seemed to be elsewhere."

"This is a mall," Caroline countered. "I've been in one before."

The restaurant was an omelette-and-beef-dip place with poor lighting but nice smells. We sat by a window that looked out over the parking lot. I ordered the beef dip and Caroline chose an egg salad sandwich.

When the waitress left, I said, "You forgot the atlas in the car."

"Oh, hell. I'll go. Where did we park?" At my look, she added, "I was a little distracted."

I pointed out the window. "See the red pickup? Other side."

Caroline looked. "Rey!"

"Rey? I thought he was in jail." I looked, too.

"Well, he's out. He's over there, getting out of the car, just past the pickup and one row over!" The pitch of her voice climbed.

"What the hell!?" Stunned, I watched a dark-haired, broad-shouldered man about my age—*Rey, this is Rey*—walk swiftly toward the entrance. "We have to get out of here." I threw a couple of twenties on the table—a perfect time to use cash. "Out the door, turn right, go a few stores, and duck inside one. I'll be just behind you."

We entered a shoe store before her husband got into the mall.

I grabbed Caroline's arm. "Let's wait a second to give him time to go into a store, then try to make the exit at the other end. Walk quickly, but not so fast as to attract attention."

"But Rey—"

I cut her off. "He doesn't know we're here. He thinks we're dead, remember? He's just running, out on bail or something."

We headed for the exit. Outside, I looked back—no sign of pursuit. "I think we made it, but we've got to get to the car."

"Rey's going to see us!"

"Maybe. But malls are built so that your attention is always on the shops inside. Few windows."

"Maybe he knows our car. He's closer to it than we are."

"I don't think so—if he did, he'd have parked right beside it." I had no idea if that was true, but it sounded good and it kept Caroline moving.

We got to the car with no sign of Rey. When we were buckled in, Caroline said, "Let's get out of here."

"Not yet. If Rey comes out and sees a car leaving the lot, he may look at it closely. I think it's a better idea to let him return to his own car and leave ahead of us."

"But if he knows your car—"

"We'll be up a creek," I acknowledged. "But lots of cars look like mine. Scrunch down. I'll watch, and if he heads this way, we'll get out of here."

She slid down in the seat. "I don't like this one little bit. I can't see anything. Tell me what's going on."

"Will do."

A moment later, Rey appeared at the mall entrance. He chose a route to his car that took him well away from us. I had a good view of him and kept Caroline apprised. As Rey neared his car, Caroline sat up slightly.

I had to check. "Is it really him?"

"Absolutely. Are we going to follow him?"

"I want to see which way he turns when he leaves the parking lot."

Rey's car pulled out slowly. At the exit, he turned left.

"Well?"

"I think he's heading back to Thunder Bay. If he'd meant to go to Winnipeg, he'd have turned the other way."

"He could be setting us up."

"Yes, but I don't think so. He came here to be *seen*. He wants the police to think he's fleeing west, but he'll head toward home."

"But Thunder Bay? That doesn't make sense."

"Or maybe Ignace or Dryden. He'll hole up, and in a week or two, when the cops have taken down their roadblocks, he'll be free to go wherever the hell he wants."

Caroline was quiet for a moment. "Okay. Now what?"

"Let's give him a few minutes, then head to Winnipeg."

Soon we were on the highway, heading west. Caroline hadn't spoken since the mall, so I broke the silence. "Penny for your thoughts."

"What?"

"Penny for your thoughts."

"What does that mean?"

"You know—tell me what you're thinking."

"Is that an expression or something?"

"You've never heard it?"

"Never."

"Where have you been all your life?"

Both of us knew the answer. We were in a world that was like, but not the same as, either my world or hers. In *this* environment the two of us were, in some fundamental way, alien to each other.

After a moment she said, "I've been thinking about the man at the mall. I don't think he was Rey."

"I know, not your Rey—"

"No, not that. Stan said the police had picked Rey up, remember?"

"He might be out on bail. Or he could have escaped."

"Not yet. And escape is pretty unlikely, right? A suspect in a double murder? They'd have to be Keystone Cops to let him escape. And there's more. I think the man at the mall was left-handed. Rey is right-handed."

"Your Rey."

"Yes, my Rey."

"What makes you think this other guy was left-handed?"

"The car door—he used his left hand to open it. People always open doors with their dominant hand, right?"

"Damned if I know. But if Rey isn't your Rey and he isn't the double murderer, then who is he?"

"Damned if *I* know. Maybe he's *your* Rey." She smiled.

"Hah. You make a lot more sense when you're not saying anything."

Just under an hour later, we crossed into Manitoba.

8 # STEINBACH

Every province has a town like Steinbach. Some have several. Steinbach is to Manitoba what Listowel is to Ontario — a car town, a place that escaped being "just another farm town" by embracing cars in a big way. Car dealerships have sprung up all along Highway 12 North, each one offering the "best" deals in town. From the moment you pull into town, you feel eyes peering through every dealership window to place a value on your car. If you talk to someone, you're a red '97 Chevy, or a tire kicker. And maybe, if it's your third visit and this time you brought your wife along, you're a customer.

I'd left Manitoba 1 West to stop at Steinbach because I was still hungry. Also, I needed to collect my wits before Winnipeg. I pulled over in front of a small restaurant on Main Street. The sign above the entrance looked like a hubcap on a brick tire, and the restaurant promised good home-style food. I turned off the ignition.

"There's something I don't understand," Caroline said. She'd been silent for most of the trip, surprised by the billiard-table flatness of the Manitoba prairie and the great blue dome of the cloudless sky.

I guessed. "Rey being left-handed."

"Mind-reader. You're pretty good."

"Not really. Played the odds — it had to be about something that happened in Kenora. I've been wondering something, too."

"Why Rey is left-handed?"

"No, why you aren't."

"What? I've never been left-handed."

"I've been trying to figure out the rules that govern these gates. What should happen is this: every time we go through one, left and right are reversed."

"So if you go through one as a right-hander, you come out as a leftie?"

"Right. I mean, correct. The catch is, you'd still feel like you were right-handed. Since everything has flipped its direction, including whatever it is in your brain that keeps track of things like left and right, nothing should seem different."

"Okay, I guess that makes sense."

"But it doesn't, not really. If you pass through once, your handedness gets switched. Pass through again and it goes back to normal. Go through an odd number of times, you'd change from being a righty to being a lefty. But if you went through an even number of times, you'd still be a righty." I stopped at Caroline's "hold on" look.

After a second or two she said, "Got it. Go on."

"Well, the problem is that you consider yourself to be right-handed."

"And I only went through once." Caroline was a quick study. "So I should be a lefty, and you went through twice, so you should be a righty."

"Right. Both senses."

"And you should be able to tell that what I call right, you call left. But in this world right is the same for both of us."

"Nicely reasoned, Holmes. So what's your conclusion?"

Caroline considered. "One of us, or maybe both of us, miscounted."

"Possible. Or?"

"Or sometimes we pass through without knowing it. All we can say for sure is that both you and I have either gone through an odd number of times or an even number of times. We're both odd or we're both even."

"That's what I think, too. Of course, I'm sure that I'm less odd than you."

"That's troubling."

"You don't like having a higher eccentricity quotient?" I could not elicit a smile from her.

"No. That we can 'move' without even being aware of it. That we don't have to pass through something. Whatever it is just gobbles us up." Caroline stopped suddenly.

"What?" But I knew. "Rey?"

"Yes. If he's left-handed now, he's not the person I left behind at the apartment. He's someone else, another Rey. Or maybe he's still the same Rey with another trip under his belt. At any rate, he knew we were going to Kenora. He's hunting us, David."

"Yes. But there's nothing we can do about that. Let's go eat."

The restaurant lived up to its promise.

#

On one of my many excursions into new worlds, I went back home—not the home I started from, but one of its analogues, the house on Lake Superior in which one of my other selves still lived. For no reason in particular (a psychologist would say, "Yeah, right"), I broke into the house when the occupants were away and searched the bedroom for a keepsake from my early years of teaching. I used to write poetry, and I kept the poems I liked best in my chest of drawers (the middle drawer, under t-shirts). I wanted to know if this self wrote the same poems as I had, or different ones—or none at all. Had he written poetry and kept his poems? Perhaps he'd done something else, like woodworking.

It turned out that this self and I were similar, but not the same. Here's one of his poems.

The Knight of the Yellow Rose

Slowly
the keeper of the yellow rose
began to fade.

At first,
when he found he could no longer hear clearly
and when the taste of food grew slight,
he thought he'd caught a cold
or was simply growing old.

But one morning,
standing on his balcony,
the sun so red above the farthest shore,
he turned and saw his shadow –
lighter than the shadow of the cross
upon the wall –
and in his hand a rose
more manifest than flesh.

And one day,
working in the garden by the house,
he felt the earth begin to seep
into his hands and feet and side,

And lying down
he placed the yellow rose beside him on the ground
and dreamed
of Arthur and Excalibur, the Lady of the Lake,
the Table and the Garden and the Apple and the Snake,
the Rose forever yellow, the Child forever wise,
and one man's life a dream of love
through someone else's eyes.

As I read it, I-as-he remembered writing the poem and feeling that it said exactly what I wanted it to say. Now, it spoke of something quite different, something I could never have imagined so many years ago. It wasn't perfect, but it was better than the poem I'd written, and I was envious. I put it back in the drawer and left the house. A few hours later I was somewhere else. And, as well, a little bit more *someone* else.

#

After we finished our sandwiches and coffee, I risked asking a question I'd toyed with for some time. "Caroline, who were you before you were Caroline Reynolds?"

"Before Rey, you mean? I was Caroline Nelson, bookkeeper extraordinaire. My parents had a mom and pop store in Red Rock, just off the highway on the way to Nipigon. I kept the books for them, did the ordering, that sort of stuff."

"Nelson's. I know it. I spent part of a summer in Red Rock, at the end of high school."

"Summer job?"

"Yes. I couldn't find anything in Thunder Bay and then, through a friend, I landed a job at the mill in Red Rock. At the end of the summer I couldn't decide if I wanted to stay on or head to university as planned."

"But you left."

"Believe it or not, I flipped a coin to decide."

Caroline smiled, then grew thoughtful. "If you'd stayed, we'd have met."

I knew what she was thinking. "When I was eighteen, you were about ten. You'd still have married Rey."

"Maybe." She gave me a foxy smile. "But Rey's pretty close to your age. You might have given him some competition. Finished?"

"What?"

"Are you finished? Your food. Shouldn't we go?"

"We'd better." There's another job we have to do."

"Oh?"

"Yeah. We need a license plate or two."

#

I was proud of myself for considering the car's plates. Some motels and hotels, especially those in downtown areas, require you to give your plate number—at the very least, the province or state the car's registered in. That way, they're not in the business of providing free parking. If a car parked in the lot doesn't match a paying guest, they can have it towed.

New plates would fix two car-related problems for us. After "my" death, police might have alerted folks within relatively easy driving distance to look for my car. New plates would thwart conscientious hotel staff. And if Rey, whether right-handed, left-handed, or ambi-sinister, had trailed us to Kenora, he might himself go looking for us in Winnipeg. Cruising hotel parking lots for the red Corolla would be a crude method of searching for us, but it might work in the end. And Manitoba plates would throw him off. Maybe.

Rey, of course, had far more sophisticated tracking methods. But we didn't know that yet.

And so in our ignorance, we spent part of the afternoon hunting red Corollas in Steinbach. It was actually a pretty fun project to do together—harder than it might seem, given the staunch conservative streak running through the province there. But at last we found one and "borrowed" its plates. We left ours as a sort of payment.

A couple of hours later, we checked into a downtown hotel in Winnipeg.

9 # LOST

If you have only one day in Winnipeg, spend the morning at the Forks and the afternoon in Assiniboine Park. We'd found an affordable hotel on Main Street, with parking in the back, inside pool, complimentary breakfast, and a clean room with two comfortable queen-size beds. Best of all, it was within easy walking distance of the Forks.

We woke early, went down to the breakfast room and had waffles, toasted bagels, fruit, and first-rate coffee. No other guests were around.

"Have you ever thought about what you'll do if you can't make it home?" Caroline asked.

"We'll find a way to get back."

"What you mean is, you'll find a way to get back to *your* world, and I'll find a way to get back to *mine*. Right?"

"I suppose so."

"What if neither of us can?"

"I still have to try." She didn't ask, but I knew she wanted to know. "Darlene and I have a history. I—I have to try to keep it going."

Caroline set down her bagel. "I don't want to go back."

"What about your mother and father? Rey will be in jail. You won't have to worry about him."

"My parents are both dead. Lung cancer got dad ten years ago; heart attack last year got mom. So family equals cousin for me. No immediate family on Rey's side anymore, either. Not that I got along with them when there was." She took another bite of bagel, sipped at her coffee. "I start fresh, wherever I end up."

"That's good, isn't it?"

"Sure." She took a bite of melon. "It depends on what the place is like, though. And the people. I want it to feel like home. You know, I've never given a second's thought to what I couldn't live without or what makes me happy. I've always focused on moving *away* from things that make me sad or afraid, not *toward* anything." She cut a pineapple chunk in two with the edge of her fork. "How about you?"

"I'm a compromiser, I think. I'd have made a good accountant. *This* side of the ledger must balance out *that* side of the ledger. If I have to do *this* thing, at least later I'll get to do *that* thing. My life doesn't really have highs and lows. It's all in between."

"Is that good?"

"Is it better to be passionless than to love or to hate?"

"No." Caroline looked at me. "No, it's not." She returned her attention to her fruit bowl.

After breakfast we walked down Main to York Avenue, went under the railway overpass, and turned right.

Most of what had always made the Forks interesting to me also existed in this version of Winnipeg. No Manitoba Theatre for Young People, but the skate park and the naked eye observatory in the Oodena Celebration Circle were still there. I told Caroline how you could use the observatory's tusk-like sighting sculptures, set in a circle, to find stars and constellations. The Johnson Terminal building still had a restaurant, a pub and, in the basement, an antique store.

I deliberately steered us away from the Forks Market until it got close to noon. Finally, I said, "Enough of the antiques, already. We need to get supplies."

"Supplies?"

"For where we're going to spend the afternoon." I started up the stairs.

"And where is that?"

"We're going on a picnic."

"Picnic? We're running for our lives to a picnic?"

"In Assiniboine Park. There's a zoo, conservatory, cricket pitches, picnic tables. It's a nice place to spend part of the day."

"Are you out of your mind?"

"No. I really do want a picnic. We can sit outside in the sun, eat some sandwiches, talk."

"We don't have sandwiches."

"Which is why we're going to the Market."

I knew Caroline would be enthralled. The Market at the Forks is made up of two floors of the irresistible sights and sounds and smells of food. Fresh fruits and vegetables add colour to tables and displays. Hamburgers crackle on grills, and espresso machines roar. The aroma of bread, straight from the oven, hangs in the air. People crowd into boutiques that sell items from all around the world.

In short order we had bread, the makings of fine sandwiches, and bottled drinks. We headed back to the hotel and our car, each of us carrying a bag.

Caroline said, exasperation edging into her voice, "You know, David, I still don't know why we're having this picnic."

"I'd like to have a close look at what's there in the park."

"David, stop it. Any time you don't know what you're doing, you try to pretend you have a plan and go all cryptic. Just cut the crap and tell me straight out what's going on in that scrambled egg container that passes for your head." She stood still.

I could see she was pissed. "Okay, here's what I think. A zoo, especially one with a lot of stuff in it, is a perfect place to get an overview of this world. A zoo is a world in miniature. You see plants and animals from all over."

I'd given her something to think about. We started walking again.

"You'll be able to tell how similar this world is to ours?"

"To mine. Yours could be different from either of those."

"To yours, then. And all this is to check your theory, the one where the farther we are from a 'gate' or 'entry point,' the odder the world will look."

"Yeah. Also, the more we know about this world, the better the chance that we'll survive in it, especially if your husband comes for us with a baseball bat."

"Ex-husband. Or shotgun."

"Whatever."

"I want the corned beef with the Havarti cheese." She was prepared to call a truce.

"Done." So was I.

#

I have no idea how I find my way from point A to point B when I'm driving. I doubt that I keep the whole route in my head, only parts of it— a turn here, a sign, a rock cut, a long straight stretch that ends in a sharp left. But something there, in my memory, gets me where I want to go. I can find my way, unerringly, almost seven hundred kilometres, from Thunder Bay to Assiniboine Park in Winnipeg, even to the very parking spot I used twenty years ago when I first visited the place.

I wonder sometimes how much of the route would have to be different before I became lost—everything along the way, or just a few of my favourite guideposts? That particular stop sign, that traffic light? What would it take for me to notice?

And in a related matter: How much of me would have to change before I'd notice I'm not me anymore?

#

It was close to noon when I parked the car. Subs and sodas in hand, we found a picnic table on the edge of the cricket pitch. The July sun was intense—bright but not dazzling. The day stretched around us into one of those soft, lazy afternoons that make summer so pleasant. At a table a dozen yards away, a family of four chowed down on their lunch. The father and mother smiled at each other, the children good-naturedly shoved each other around.

Caroline watched the family for a while, then turned to me. "This is what it's all supposed to be about."

"Yes. Sometimes we ask too much of life, don't you think?"

"I always wanted kids." She seemed wistful. "Rey couldn't stand them."

"Why am I not surprised?"

"What about you and Darlene? You didn't have kids, either, right?"

"True. Not my choice. Nor Darlene's. We would have if we could have. We had a dog." Except that *I* hadn't. Or had I? I vaguely remembered a dog, but fuzzily, as if the memory weren't exactly mine.

"Doesn't count." Caroline looked me over, thoughtfully. "Do you love your wife?"

"I love the person I married."

"That's not what I asked."

"Darlene got tired of me, I think. We became friends."

"You got off easy. Rey went silent and then he went mean."

I risked a question I'd been considering for what seemed like years. "You and Rey—why did you marry him?"

"Oh, who can say? He was charming. Good-looking. Great hair, and he was proud of it. Plus he had this Marlon Brando thing—you know, rebellious, a little disrespectful of everyone and everything. He owned a motorcycle. And he smoked." She raised her eyebrows at me. "I was smitten."

I smiled. "Your parents must have disapproved mightily."

"Pretty much. Of course, that sealed the deal. God, we're so stupid when we're young." She glanced at the kids at the neighbouring table. "It was all show for Rey. Everything was a performance. He thought of himself as a character in a play, and I was part of the audience. Except when I played the role of the valued object, something to fight over. The role he chose for *himself* most of the time was the con man. He was always happiest when he could boast about how he'd fooled someone who trusted him." She stopped and shook her head. "Can we talk about something else?"

I waited a moment. "You like this place?"

She brightened. "Very much. If the whole city were like this, I wouldn't mind living here."

"Lots of mosquitoes in the spring, lots of cold in the winter."

"But it looks like a place that people want to take care of. They have spaces to relax and play. It's not all about business and bullshit and having pile carpet in a corner office with a window."

"You're right. There's a museum and a planetarium. Even a ballet, for anyone who wants to look at guys stuffed into tights. And a racetrack and a hockey arena and a football stadium for those who prefer their guys stuffed into tights with padding."

"Door number one for me," Caroline said.

"That's funny. No, not you. This place—the park, I mean—it's exactly the way I remember it."

"So?"

"So I thought it would be a lot different, the way that Thunder Bay is so different. You know, the further we get from a gate, the more differences we should find? Kenora wasn't its old self."

"Oh?"

"No big fish."

She looked at me, eyebrows drawn together. "Again? No big fish? Is this something I'm actually supposed to know?"

"There's a giant fish, a fiberglass statue. In my world, it stands at the bridge that leads from Kenora into Keewatin. Remember the part of the road that goes along the shore of Lake of the Woods?"

"I remember the bridge. I don't remember a fish. Would I have noticed it?"

"Hard to miss. It's about twenty feet tall—a muskie. Come to think of it, there wasn't a bypass around the town, either. We had no choice but to come all the way in."

"But Winnipeg?"

"I can't think of a single substantive way that's different from the place I know."

"Maybe that's because it has a zoo."

I stared at Caroline. "The next time you complain about me being cryptic, I'll remember this. Your turn to explain."

"Well, this place has things in it from all over the world. Animals and plants and—"

"Cricket players."

She ignored me. "All those things, except maybe the cricket players, were brought here. That means this place, and therefore maybe most of Winnipeg, is sort of representative. Maybe?"

I put my hand on her arm. "Wait a sec." I thought for a moment. "Are you saying that because we're in a place that's made of things we're familiar with, all brought together here—that's somehow caused the whole city to remain more like the Winnipeg I know? Or the one from your world?"

"I'm not sure. Is that what I'm saying?" Suddenly she burst into laughter.

"What's so funny?"

"I just had this thought." She took a deep breath. "This must be what you feel like all the time. You're always looking at things, figuring, working out why something is like it is."

I smiled and raised my sandwich in a toast to her. "To Winnipeg."

"Portage and Main," she replied. We both took bites.

A long silence ensued. I found myself gazing at nothing more interesting than my sandwich, listening intently to the sounds of the park, as if just by listening to the normal music of everyday life I could hold the world together for a while.

When I looked up, Caroline stared over my left shoulder. "Oh God."

I turned to see a man striding purposefully toward us, a man I recognized.

"David, what do we do?"

"Just sit. Nothing's going to happen out here in public."

Rey slowed to a saunter as he neared us.

"Cute couple." The bite of his voice perfectly matched his sly half-grin. "Caroline, come with me. Right now."

"No." Her voice trembled.

In reply, Rey patted the right pocket of his jacket, then slowly pulled a pistol partway out. After checking to be sure we'd both seen it, he slowly put it back.

"Yes. And now. Or it's first him, then them." He tilted his head toward the family at the nearby table. "Then you. You get to be last."

Caroline remained seated.

Rey regarded her carefully. "No escape, Caroline. Look behind me. See? Just at the edge of the trees?"

She looked over my shoulder. "There's another one."

I couldn't make sense of it. "Another Rey?"

Rey let his smile deepen into malevolence. "Two heads are better than one. I brought a friend. We share some of the same ideas. Oh, and there's a third, but he's waiting by your car. Let's go, Caroline ... *sweetie.*"

She rose. "I don't have a choice, David."

Rey turned to me. "As for you, Davey my boy, you sit for a while and enjoy the rest of your lunch. It's no big deal to me to shoot up this place, but I'd prefer not to. When our mutual friend departs, you're free to go. But I advise against trying to rescue Caroline. You tried that once. Terrible results."

"At the apartment?"

"No, no. Different situation. Though I *am* the one who killed you there. Sorry, the other you, I mean." He smiled again. "The pronouns don't quite work, do they? No, I mean your rescue attempt at the mall in Kenora. See you." He began to walk away, then stopped. "Come along, dear."

Caroline reached across the picnic table for my hand. While she held it, she looked into my eyes with an intensity I'd never seen before. Then she just let go.

I watched her back as she and Rey walked. They got into a beaten-up Ford Taurus and left the parking lot. For several minutes I sat at the table, my eyes on the other Rey who stood unconcernedly a few hundred feet away. At last he waved goodbye and disappeared into the trees. Rey had apparently circled about to pick him up. I ran for my car.

I tried it at the mall, did I? I thought. *Wrong. This I didn't. But this I is going to try it—right now, as a matter of fact.*

10 # NOT AGAIN!

I wished for a plan, but I had only the beginning. I needed to get Caroline out of Rey's clutches, and I suspected Rey would take her back to Thunder Bay. *Why* was immaterial at this point—I'd follow wherever they went. *Sometimes*, I told myself, *the beginning of a plan is enough. The rest will come.*

I ran to my car. But when I turned the key, nothing happened. I popped the hood and looked for obvious problems—which is what I saw. The battery was missing. I gently closed the hood. I'd left the car unlocked for my own convenience. *What a fool I am.* And like a fool, I looked around the parking lot to see if the battery happened to be sitting on the ground somewhere. It wasn't.

One of teaching's perks is that, sometime or another, one of your students will teach you how to steal a car. If you're lucky, it won't take the form of your car going missing from the teachers' parking lot. What I'd learned is that unless you happen to have a drill and the right kind of screwdriver, stealing a car is difficult and, in contrast to the movies, time-consuming. I had none of that—no drill, screwdriver or time—so I improvised. I looked for cars more or less like mine, broke a window, popped the hood, and stole its battery.

A few people passing through the parking lot saw me remove the battery. Some watched as I popped the hood on my own car and installed the stolen battery. No one seemed to think anything of it. In no time at all I had transportation.

While I worked, I weighed my options. Rey, I reasoned, wouldn't want to attract attention, especially from cops. He'd probably keep to the speed limit. I felt no such compunction. I was going to rescue Caroline, end up with a speeding ticket, or go to jail—in someone else's universe, awkward as that would be.

What would Rey do? If he'd entered Winnipeg on Highway 1, as we had, he'd likely take the same route out. Through the city, traffic and stoplights might slow him down. Instead of heading east, I headed west out of the park and got on the Perimeter Highway, which encircles the city. A longer route, but I'd avoid traffic and lights.

Fifteen minutes to the Perimeter Highway, and twenty-five more to the Highway 1 interchange. Once there, I had no idea whether I was ahead or behind Rey. Nor did I know with certainty where he was going — another matter entirely. On Highway 1, I sped up to make up time. After twenty minutes without catching up, I figured I was in front. I slowed down to the speed limit.

Assuming I was ahead of Rey's car, now what? I knew what his car looked like, and Rey would easily recognize mine — which I wanted to avoid. I monitored the rear-view mirror to see if he were catching up to me. My worry grew. I also needed a washroom.

Of course! Caroline would start complaining soon, too, thanks to our soft drinks. If our luck held, she'd be in full whine by the time the four of them — the three Reys and Caroline — hit Kenora. With even more luck, she'd urge a stop at the mall for some much-needed relief. Rey, cruel though he was, wouldn't let her pee in his car.

Just past Falcon Lake, I said goodbye to Manitoba and passed the Ontario information centre. Not long after, I entered Keewatin, a town that, along with Jaffray Melick and adjacent neighbourhoods, amalgamated with Kenora proper in 2000. Then I went over the bridge and past the fiberglass fish.

The fish was back!

I'd moved again — I wasn't in the same world that Caroline and I had been in on the way to Winnipeg. But what about Caroline? Was she still there, or was she here, in this one? There was no way to know. All I could do was head for the mall and hope I'd know what to do once I got there.

Along the way, another puzzle cropped up. On the way to Winnipeg there'd been no Kenora bypass. On this trip I'd just passed a sign for it.

I tried to pinpoint what that meant. Sometime between leaving Winnipeg and arriving here — no, not necessarily. I could have changed worlds at *any* time after we'd left Kenora on the trip *to* Winnipeg. Which meant the Assiniboine Park picnic could have been in this world and, therefore, Caroline's abduction could have been, too.

Hell, it didn't matter. I was wherever I was, and she was where she was, and I hoped it was the same world. I had to get her back.

Just off Main Street I turned down to the mall, parked a few spaces from the rear door and ran in. *Now what?* I walked through all the way to the double doors of the front entrance, finding inspiration nowhere. At the front doors, I stood in a corner to watch for Rey's car.

If Caroline came to the mall, she'd head for the washroom. But Rey probably wouldn't follow her in—he wouldn't worry about her escaping, because mall bathrooms don't tend to have windows. Would he worry about her telling someone she'd been kidnapped? I didn't know and couldn't guess. So I had to be in the bathroom when she came in, and, right under Rey's nose, get her out and to our car. Correction—under Reys' noses. Reys 2 and 3 would likely still be with him. But they'd probably stay in the car, because he'd want to avoid the attention a set of triplets would create.

In less than a minute, the battered Taurus pulled in. Rey got out first, then Caroline. And yes, Reys 2 and 3 stayed in the car. From the way Rey kept his hand in his coat pocket I knew that he'd threatened Caroline with his gun.

I went into the women's bathroom, which was empty. So far so good, but I still had no plan or weapon. I couldn't see anything to use, not even a toilet plunger. Not that I knew what I'd do with it. I stood just inside the closed door and listened for Caroline and Rey.

At last, I heard Rey's voice through the door—quiet, but with undisguised menace. "Do your business and get out. Two minutes, sweetie. If you're not out, I come in. Don't forget this, and don't cause problems because you'll get someone killed. Understand?"

"Yes." Caroline sounded calm, compliant. The door opened, trapping me for a moment against the wall's porcelain tiles. Caroline let the door close on its own after her.

"Hey," I whispered. "Caroline."

She turned around and raised a finger to her lips. At my nod, she pantomimed striking Rey over the head, then raised her hands to ask, *Is that the plan?*

I shook my head and showed her my own empty hands. *No weapon.*

She looked quickly around the bathroom and pointed at the soap dispenser.

Bash him on the head with it? I pantomimed.

She shook her head. She signalled *Wait* with her raised index finger. In a stall, she flushed one of the toilets.

We had maybe thirty seconds until Rey would come in.

At the sink, Caroline made dipping motions with her hands, then pretended to wipe her eyes. I frowned in confusion. She pointed to the soap dispenser.

She wanted me to rub soap in Rey's eyes. *Blind him,* I mouthed.

She nodded, relief showing in her own eyes.

Silently, we formed the plan. Caroline would leave the bathroom in a hurry, walking quickly so Rey would follow her. I'd slip out, get behind Rey and lather him up. After that ... well, one thing at a time.

At one of the dispensers, I filled both hands. The dispenser label said *Antibacterial*. I hoped that meant *burns like hell when applied to the eyes*. I got into position behind the door so Rey wouldn't see me. I nodded and she opened the door.

"Right on time," said Rey as she stepped smartly past him.

I waited a beat and came out. Caroline was a half-step ahead of Rey, whose right hand still guarded his coat pocket. In three long strides, I caught up. I wrapped both my hands around Rey's face from behind and hung on, scratching at his eyes with my slippery fingers.

The soap did its job.

"Shit!" His hands went to his face. He bent over, and my feet momentarily left the floor. Like a rodeo bronco, he spun to throw me off. Frantically I grabbed his neck with my left arm and reached into his pocket with the right. Somehow, I grabbed the gun and flung it through the open doorway of the nearest store—men's clothing. Had I been the slightest bit more rational I might have kept it, but you know how it is. In that moment, I wasn't doing a lot of clear thinking.

Thankfully, Caroline managed the *coup de grâce*. She leaped into the fray and pushed Rey and rider through another shop doorway. As I toppled from his back, he crashed into a display of men's shoes.

"Goddamn bitch!" he yelled, completely ignoring me in his credits.

I regained my footing and Caroline pulled me down the hallway toward the rear entrance.

"Fuck!" Rey announced it to all and sundry. "Fuck. Fuck."

We were almost out the door when Rey changed his improvised rap to "Bitch. Shit. Fuck! My eyes! They goddamn blinded me! Fuck!"

Then we were out. The car was where I'd left it. "Come on." I drove slowly out of the parking lot, down a side street, and into the rear parking lot of a small restaurant.

I put it in park and turned off the ignition. "So, how are you?"

"Much better now, thank you. Now what?"

"Now we sit here for a minute, until I stop shaking. And then I go into that restaurant and use their bathroom."

"Me, too. Thanks to you, I never got to go."

11 # REYS 2 AND 3

"So shouldn't we get out of here?" Caroline wanted to know when she returned.

"We will, once you tell me all about the trip from Winnipeg."

"Okay." She thought for a second. "Rey hustled me to the car, told me to sit in the back, and after a couple of minutes the other Rey joined us and then the third."

"Rey2 and Rey3."

"Rey2 sat in the back beside me. He and Rey aren't equals the way you'd expect. Rey2 always deferred to Rey—the real Rey, Rey1. Rey1 did most of the talking on the way to Kenora."

"About what?"

"Nothing, really. Cars, sports. You'd think he was out with the boys. He didn't ask me anything about you or me or Winnipeg. He seemed to have zero curiosity."

"Odd."

"Maybe he just wanted me to think he already knew everything."

"Rey2 just sat in the back and said nothing?"

"Pretty much. Sometimes Rey1 would say something and end with, 'Isn't that right, little buddy?' and Rey2 would grunt or nod. Once in a while he'd say 'Right,' or 'Yup,' but most of the time he was quiet." She added as an afterthought, "Rey3 seemed sick, though."

"Sick?"

"Dopey. Especially near Falcon Lake—you know, where the golf course is. In fact, that's the only time I heard him volunteer anything. Something like, 'It's going to happen again. My head hurts.' Rey1 said, 'One more time. You'll feel better soon.' A minute or so later Rey3 said, 'I'm a little better, but it's not gone.' He fell asleep in the front seat."

"That must have been where the gate to this place was," I said.

Caroline reflected for a moment. "So we're not in Kansas anymore ... again?"

"You got it, Dorothy. Didn't you notice the fiberglass fish?"

"Nope. Missed it again. I'll have to take the tour sometime."

I heard humour in her voice but saw none in her eyes. I reached over and took her hand. She neither resisted nor rewarded me. We were negotiating, it seemed. I let go slowly.

I tried to inject some hope into our situation. "I've been thinking. I taught a guy a few years ago—interesting guy, probably not neurotypical, relevant interests. I think we should go see him."

"You're showing off. What do you mean, not neurotypical?"

"You know, like Asperger's, the condition. You've never heard of it?"

"No. What are you talking about?"

She was puzzled, and so was I. Was this a difference in our "home" worlds or a difference in our interests, or just chance?

I tried again. "Have you noticed on TV, all the shows with geeky, socially inept characters? In *House* or *Bones* or all those *NCIS* shows? For the past, oh, decade?"

"Never heard of them."

"Huh. Okay, when you were in high school did you ever know someone who was sort of in his own world? Maybe interested in just one thing and unable to see that no one else was interested in it?"

"Are we talking about sex, here?"

"Ha. But no, something else. Anything—airport runways, stamp collecting, animated films. Very intensely, and in very specific ways. If you expressed the least bit of interest, he'd be your friend for life—you'd never shake him off. Ring any bells?"

"Sherry. We called her Creepy Girl. She was into shoes."

"Shoes? Excuse me while I indulge in a stereotype, but aren't all high school girls interested in shoes?"

Caroline raised an eyebrow. "No excuses, and not what I mean. Sherry had over two hundred pairs. Not just new ones she'd bought. She'd ask for your old ones—sometimes even the ones you were wearing. She could tell you all about them. What they were made of, where they came from, who designed them. All she really noticed about you was your shoes."

"Okay, I see your point. She was probably neuro-atypical, maybe with Asperger's. Some in Silicon Valley call it 'geek syndrome.' There, it's an advantage. You devote your whole life to the work. In the real world, well. It can be—"

"Intense," Caroline finished. "So you taught a guy."

"Bernie Elgar. He was fixated on time travel. In high school he read all the science fiction he could find, got all the top marks in math —"

"But never had a girlfriend. Okay, so what happened to him? More to the point, what's time travel got to do with our situation?"

"Second point first. I don't know if time travel is at all related, but I hope it has some connection. Maybe in the math. Maybe something else Bernie knows about. He can at least tell us more about this parallel universe crap we're in."

"Don't call this place *crap*."

I ignored her. "As for Bernie, himself, he works as an electronics tech for a TV repair shop. At least the Bernie I know did. He makes enough money to keep himself in reading materials and, best of all, he's not living at home with mom and dad."

"Girlfriend?"

"One thing at a time. He's still pretty geeky."

"So we're going back to Thunder Bay?"

"Yep, the sooner the better. With luck we'll be there and gone before Rey and his little buddies arrive."

"It's getting late, and that's a long trip."

"That's why we're going to fly. Kenora has an airport. Fingers crossed there's another flight out."

"Jet?"

"Turboprop. We'll rent a car when we get to Thunder Bay."

"Paid for how?"

"Mr. Credit Card," I said. "It worked in the last universe we were in, didn't it?"

#

Someone once said that in the course of a lifetime, we'll get to know about 10,000 people well enough to say hello, even if we can't attach a name to the face. Only a few will become our friends, and fewer yet will attract us enough to become potential spouses. The remainder, some 9,900 or so, get a quick once-over before we focus our attention elsewhere.

In this crazy life, I've met at least four Bernie Elgars, all geeks of various degrees of intensity. One could pass for normal, if not for his immense wealth. He's solid and likable, a person you'd enjoy as a son-in-law. One Bernie gave me the best advice I've ever received, but being in the same room with him for more than half an hour was ... difficult, I'd have to say. Another Bernie was pleasant enough—you'd risk eye contact, only to find him a little too intense for you to feel completely comfortable. And one was a geeky student completely without friends.

But all of the Bernies had strong cores, without a mean bone. They were fundamentally decent people, eager to help, eager to be useful. The person at the heart of all Bernie Elgars is a good man.

That's as close as I get to understanding a person's soul.

I've met a few Carolines. All have been similar, but none exactly alike. And that's everything I know about the mathematics of romance.

12 # BERNIE

We were lucky. A flight to Thunder Bay left less than an hour after we got to the airport. My credit card went through. A car would be available upon arrival.

I felt guilty for having stolen the battery in Winnipeg, and I wanted to return it somehow. I thought about leaving a note on our car windshield explaining that its battery had been "borrowed" in Winnipeg in the zoo parking lot.

Caroline pointed out that perhaps no one in this world had stolen the battery. It was also possible that the person who acted on the note would steal our present car.

On the plus side, I got to tell Caroline that she was now the one handing out headaches.

The moral of the story seemed to be that there are some crimes you just can't pay for.

In Thunder Bay we registered as Mr. and Mrs. Berkelmann at a Cumberland Street motel that was clean enough to pass muster, where we could park the rental out of sight of the street. Once more Caroline insisted on the "two beds" rule. I spent part of the night fantasizing that at some point she would leave her bed and crawl into mine, but her head never left her pillow. And then it was dawn.

I opened my eyes. Caroline was already showered and dressed. There went another fantasy.

"How the hell did you manage to get showered without me knowing?"

"You sleep like a baby through the snarfling blasts of your own snoring," she countered. "What makes you think a little running water can wake you?"

"Hmph." It was all the wit I could muster. I'm not a morning person. "What time is it? I should call Bernie."

"Just after seven. And yes, you should. You know the number?"

"Phone book."

"Here." She reached into the top drawer of the night table that divided her realm from mine. I held out my hand. She continued to hold onto the phone book. "Wait. What are you going to say to him? Think it out."

Good idea. I tried a thought. It sputtered a bit, then caught. "How's this? Ever since I retired I've been trying to write a book, sort of a science fiction thing about parallel universes, and I want the science to be plausible—"

"Good enough," Caroline interrupted. "Clever even. Make the call. But don't sound like an idiot." She gave me the phone book.

"This is Bernie I'm calling, Caroline. He won't care what I sound like. He's going to get to talk about time travel with someone who will listen to him."

"You said parallel universes."

"It's all time travel to him. Every conversation we've ever had started as one thing and ended as time travel."

"Call."

"Dress first."

"Call first, then dress, breakfast later. He might be going to work early."

"All right." There was no point in arguing. I looked up his number and dialled. The phone rang twice before he picked up. "Bernie, it's David Williamson. Listen, I've got a problem you might be able to help me with." And the ball was in play.

#

Bernie lived in exactly the kind of place you'd think he would—a basement apartment on a side street on the edge of the city's run-down south core. Caroline and I rang the bell at the side door of what had been a nice two-story house seventy years ago. Now the paint peeled from the clapboard siding, the shingles had curled and cracked, and the chimney sported three different colours of brick.

We heard feet on the basement steps. "Mr. Williamson!" Bernie opened the door. "Nice to see you. Come in, come in!"

"Thanks, Bernie. Nice to see *you* again. Not working today?"

"Brought it home last night." Bernie paid no attention to Caroline when we entered. He didn't say anything to her, or ask me about her, as he led us down the steep stairs. Had there been an obvious connection between Caroline and time travel, he might have been more socially attentive. But there wasn't yet, so he wasn't. His conversation was directed solely at me. "The boss lets me fix stuff here, but I have to wait a couple of days before I bring it back to the shop."

"Oh?"

"He thinks if the customers knew how fast I can do this stuff, they wouldn't pay the prices he charges, so he makes me keep it out of view for a while. I don't mind. I got other things to do."

Caroline smiled at him. "Another of life's little mysteries solved." For the first time Bernie seemed to notice that she was present in human form.

"Bernie, this is Caroline."

"Pleased to meet you, Mrs. Williamson."

"Reynolds."

"Okay." Bernie's voice stayed matter-of-fact, even as he turned to me. "You're writing now?" He wanted to get to the important stuff. That we were still standing in the middle of his living room bothered him not at all.

"Trying." I sat down on a dilapidated sofa. The cushions had lost so much of their firmness that I fell backward and had to grab an armrest for support. Caroline settled herself comfortably beside me with no loss of dignity.

"You want a soda?" Bernie tried his best to play host. "I got chips, too."

"No thanks," I said.

"Sure," Caroline said.

"It's warm, though. You still want it?"

"I don't mind." She smiled again. I could see Bernie becoming more engaged. He went into the kitchenette, returning with two cans—one for himself and one for her—in one hand, and a kitchen chair in the other. He didn't offer glasses, and when I thought about it, that was probably best. Bernie's apartment would have made Pigpen despair. And I strongly suspected that Caroline would have left the Coke untasted.

"Okay, Mr. Williamson." Bernie settled himself into the chair. "What do you want to know?"

#

When I was in elementary school I had a friend who had emigrated from England to Canada with his parents and younger sister. He spoke with a pronounced British accent. Over the years, as you might expect, the accent faded until it disappeared. An unintended side effect, however, was to generate in me an interest in the processes involved in language change. So now, whatever world I'm in, I listen to how people, especially young people, speak the Queen's English.

On my home world, English is rapidly becoming more highly inflected, a little like the Swedish I learned as a child. The monotonous drone of some music notwithstanding, English sounds have become more musical. The letter *d* at the end of a word is sometimes pronounced *t* now, so *cupboard* sounds like *cubburt*. S sounds are changing into *sh*. You're as likely to hear *firsht* as *first*, *shtood* as *stood*, *shcool* as *school*, and so on. *Picture* used to be mispronounced mainly as *pitcher*; now it's *pickshure*.

Some of my memories are not holding up well to the changes that I myself have undergone. I'm not always sure whether I'm remembering what happened to me, or to some other version of me. But my memory of language seems to be staying solid. So, when all else fails, that's what I use to tell me how far from home I really am. And, believe me, I've come a long way. In my home world, Bernie would have said *pop*, not *soda*. At least I think he would.

#

In the car on the way to Bernie's, Caroline and I had gone over the plot of the fictitious novel I was "writing." I outlined the story as we sat in the living room.

"Most of it sounds like it might work," Bernie offered when I'd finished. "But I don't think the beginning makes sense."

"Oh?"

"That mirror effect. It's hokey. It's like those watery portals that the military sends soldiers through into another universe, you know, on TV or in bad movies."

"You don't think it could be that way?"

"Sure, it could, but it's stupid-looking. I'd stay with the instant change between places—the gates. It'd happen like that more often, anyway."

"But not *always*?"

"No. Early on, most likely. After that, not so much. But it doesn't matter how likely it is; it's the visuals that count. That's why *The Time Machine* is so hard to film. And your head is just like a movie screen, right?"

"I guess so. But Bernie, the problem I told you about—how do I get the two main characters back home?"

"You want it all to be logical, right?" At my nod, he looked sober. "I don't think you can. See, it doesn't matter what those two do. The multiverse is in control, and it operates by its own rules. That's why time travel is possible, theoretically, but you can't build some kind of machine to use it."

"But this isn't time travel. It's—"

"Yeah, I know. Different universes. Same thing."

"Same thing?"

"You think time has direction. You know, like a river, flowing, never coming back on itself, like that. But it's just as valid to think of time as a place, an infinitesimally small and unmoving spot in the river, but not the river itself. From that spot, an observer would see everything move and interpret that apparent motion as the passage of time, but really, at that spot no time passes. That place is timeless. And so is every location in the whole scene—it's all made of spots, after all. That's why if you want to write equations to describe how all the forces in the universe are related, you can drop the idea of time. If you keep time in, some things don't work."

I glanced at Caroline. Her eyes had glazed over. Mine would be next.

"It's all a matter of resolution." Bernie, oblivious to our incomprehension, waved his arms about. "All this is really quite different than it looks. It's not solid. It's probably not even made of atoms and electrons and stuff. The deep structure is more like harmonics, vibrations in whatever the universe is really made of."

"Universe? Before, you called it a 'multiverse.'" I'd noticed that difference, among everything else I hadn't really understood.

"Sorry. I've gotten into the bad habit of using some terms interchangeably. Multiverse is much more accurate. You've been reading up, haven't you?"

"Not yet. I'll have to, eh."

Bernie smiled. "It's really interesting, you know. Makes you think."

"Could you give me a summary?"

"Sure. The multiverse is ... it's everything that is. All the universes—

an infinite number, almost—that there are. Some of them really old, some are young. It's got way more than three dimensions, which is why you can get places where the universes touch, places where things are similar. See, you think your characters are going from one universe to another, but what's really happening is that the universes are already where they are. Think of the characters as places instead of people. What they do doesn't matter." Bernie looked at me hopefully, willing me to understand.

"I don't get it."

"There's nothing they can do to go home."

He had Caroline's full attention now. "Nothing?" Caroline said.

It startled Bernie. He had lost his awareness of her. "Don't think so." He couldn't see how his words affected her. What mattered to him was the puzzle.

For a long moment, nobody spoke—Caroline because she was too upset at the thought of not going "home," Bernie because he was lost in the wonder of it all. As for me, I didn't know what to say.

Caroline broke the silence. "Rey2."

I understood. "Bernie, what if there's a second villain—a carbon copy of the first, from another universe."

"See how hard it is to keep from saying that? He's from another part of the multiverse. He wouldn't be exact, though, not in real life."

I didn't ask why. "Can he—"

"Exist along with his twin? Sure, no problem. But not for long. If he's not a good match to the universe, he'll pop out. Like in graft-versus-host disease." He gave a little laugh, then looked at me to see if I had got what to him was a very good joke.

I smiled for him. "He gets headaches and he seems to be able to detect the portals somehow." That was Rey3, not Rey2, but the rules, whatever they were, would apply to both.

"Yeah, it might be like that. I never thought about the mechanics of it. He could just go 'Poof' and disappear. Or 'Bang!' I don't know. Headaches, though. That's really interesting. Some bacteria seem to be able to feel quantum effects, or at least they behave as if they do. Huh, headaches."

Caroline, sitting forward, asked, "Would the two of them go ... out together?"

"I don't think so. There's no reason they would. They're not glued to each other, or entangled, just because they happen to be in the same universe. I think. I mean, I don't know."

Caroline came at it again. "Okay. So, the one that doesn't fit, would he go back to where he came from? Or forward to some other universe?"

I realized that Caroline wasn't asking about the Reys. She was asking about *us*.

"Hmmm," Bernie said. "I have to think about that. Is it important to the plot?"

I looked at Caroline. "*I* think it is." She nodded.

And off Bernie went again, though we'd heard all we could, and more than we understood.

An hour later Caroline and I were still disengaging ourselves from Bernie. We stood at the top of the stairs. Caroline had her hand on the doorknob.

"Mr. Williamson," Bernie began.

"Just David, Bernie."

"I can't call you that. Is that okay?"

"Sure." I knew some habits were hard to break.

"I want to tell you something."

Dear God, I thought, *please let it be something short.* Caroline and I were both overwhelmed. "Shoot."

"You won't remember this. When I was in your English class, one day the kids started laughing at me because I said some stuff about time travel, and you told them to stop because you were interested in it and because I knew more about it than you ever would. And then after class you took me aside and talked to me about why the kids were laughing." He stopped for a moment. "If you hadn't done that, I would never have tried to have a life. It might not look like I have a life, but I do. I've got a job and I take care of myself. I even have some friends who like me. I have to work at it all the time, but it's worth it. I just wanted you to know that."

Caroline had taken her hand off the doorknob. I could feel her looking at me.

"Thank you, Bernie. But—"

"Mr. Williamson, you're not writing a novel, are you?" His eyes, which so often saw nothing when he looked at people, saw through me with no difficulty at all.

"No, I'm not." I let the words hang.

"It's real, isn't it?"

"Yes."

"I wish it were happening to me."

I cast about for what I wanted to say. "Bernie, you understand that I'm not the David Williamson you know. I'm not the one who taught you."

"Yes."

"I think you should call him, sometime. Tell him what you told me. He'd want to know."

"Yeah, I will."

"We have to go."

"Mr. Williamson? Take care of each other, okay? That's what it's all about."

We were still outside Bernie's, getting in the car, when Caroline said, "You told your Bernie the same thing, didn't you?"

"Yes."

13 # TIME TO GO

I don't know when, exactly, the world started to look pixelated, but it was long after I'd written "The Knight of the Yellow Rose," yet long before Caroline and I had our conversation with Bernie. It was, I suppose, before I—me, that is; my version of David—first experienced any shifts. I think. It was a sort of quantum physics equivalent of the "dark night of the soul," but I don't remember the precise moment. I think that's partly because for each of the Davids that I am, the moment was different. My composite memory isn't up to working out a consensus. It happened, yes, but it's all fuzzy now.

Regardless, the moment of pixelation became a dividing line in my life. Before, the world was solid and predictable. Afterward, it had all the solidity of a ghost and all the predictability of a game of Plinko.

Here's what I mean by "pixelation." Literally, the world stopped being analogue. I'd look at the coffee cup resting on the kitchen table and wonder if someday, when I reached for the cup, my hand would pass through it. The relative reality of everything seemed to be a question of resolution, like a digital photograph. The more pixels per square inch, the more real the photograph seemed to be—but that reality was an illusion.

Emotionally, pixelation was something else. All the common sense went out of the world. Nothing and no one—not even Darlene, though we were years into our marriage—seemed real anymore. It wasn't a black depression, but it was certainly a grey one, and it showed no sign of ending.

The odd thing was, the pixelation didn't extend to the other senses. Things that I could touch or smell or hear or taste retained their solidity, their reality, their analogue nature. Even the music on my CDs, when I had some, stayed real. My brain, apparently, wasn't much bothered by inconsistency. But all my trust in things visual leaked away.

Caroline ultimately brought me back and made the world solid once more.

#

"We're going where?" Caroline asked as we left Bernie's.

"Lunch."

"Lunch? That's what you're thinking about? Bernie just told us that we can't ever get back home, and you're hungry?" She laughed. "We had breakfast less than two hours ago."

"I know, but I can't think of what else we should do. A bowl of soup won't hurt."

"Chicken soup, I suppose."

"Yup."

"What if the cops are looking for us? There's the credit card stuff, the battery theft, our own double murder—you know, little things like that."

I latched onto the thing I'd been thinking about. "I don't think we're dead here. Bernie would have mentioned it."

"Maybe he didn't know."

"He's a news junkie. He'd have known. Every couple of years there's some news on TV about time travel. That's enough to keep him watching." I turned onto Arthur Street and headed for restaurant alley. A bowl of soup really would be good.

There was no reason that soup should make me think of Bernie, but it did. I realized there was something I should have asked him. "Shit!"

"Don't—"

"I know, I know. We have to go back. I just thought of something."

"What?"

"I should have told Bernie about the memory problems. I forgot."

"Ha ha. What about memory?"

I turned around in the parking lot of a fast food outlet. "I don't want to talk about it yet. I might lose my train of thought."

In no more than ten minutes, we were back at Bernie's. But as we pulled into the driveway, something felt off. I got out and ran to the open side door. Bernie had locked it—a sturdy, aluminum storm door—when we left. Now it stood open, and the thin aluminum frame was bent.

"Stay in the car!" I yelled to Caroline, who got out anyway. She was going to do what she was going to do. I started down the steep stairs.

"Bernie!" I called. "You okay?" I could hear the TV set, louder than it should have been.

Bernie lay face down on the floor of his living room. He'd put back the kitchen chair, but the pop cans still sat on the coffee table. I heard Caroline on the stairs.

"David? What's happened?"

I knelt, carefully amid all the blood on the cheap rug, and turned Bernie over. He'd been struck with something hard enough to crush his skull. "Rey's killed him."

"Rey?" Caroline was in shock. "Rey was here?"

"Dammit, dammit, dammit!" I said. Only anger could keep me functional. "He knew we'd come see Bernie. How does he even know about Bernie? That son of a bitch let us talk to him for as long as we wanted, then when we left, he broke in and killed him in cold blood. What the hell is going on?"

Caroline pointed. "There's something in his hand. The right one."

I looked. Balled up in his fist Bernie held a crumpled piece of paper. I opened his hand and took it from him. I uncrumpled the paper.

Later was all it said.

I showed it to Caroline. "Rey must have put it in his hand after he killed him."

"It's his handwriting," she said. "What does it mean?"

"The psychotic bastard is playing with us. He knew we'd be back and he knew why."

"I don't think so. He didn't ... couldn't know we'd be the ones to find the body. Could he?"

I shrugged.

"We have to leave."

She was right, of course. We could do nothing for Bernie now. We ran back up the stairs to the car. I backed out as quickly as I dared. I didn't want to attract attention.

"Do you think Rey called the cops?" Caroline asked.

"You can bet on it."

"Plan?"

"I got nothing. You?"

"Maybe, but it's not fully born. Can we go someplace I can call Stan? I want to see if we're alive here. It may have some bearing on what we do."

"Makes sense. It's as good a start as any."

"Will Rey know?"

"You mean, will he know what we're doing? I have no idea. If he does, there's nothing we can do about it. He didn't know I was lurking in the washroom at the mall. Maybe he knows some stuff, but not everything."

"Okay. Well, in my world, the pizza place on Memorial Avenue has a phone. Let's start there." As I changed direction, she added, "And now I want to know what you were going to ask Bernie."

"I was going to ask him—wait, give me a sec." I collected my thoughts. "See if this makes sense to you. Bernie said that we have to think of people as places, places that are touching, not as people travelling from one location to another. And he said the multiverse has more than three dimensions. But what he doesn't—didn't—know is that you and I have these jumbled memories, and in your case annoying quirks as well, that seem connected to our other selves."

"And?" No humour.

My thought was falling apart. I felt stupid for making the "quirks" comment. "I wanted to know if our jumbled memories changed what he thinks. Thought. Maybe we can go home somehow."

Caroline arrived at her own conclusion. "Well, as useful as it might have been to ask, Bernie's dead. But Stan's alive. Let's make that call."

I nodded. "I have another thought."

"As good as the last one?"

"If we, the other David and Caroline here, are alive—"

She cut in. "We should warn them about Rey."

"Right."

As we drove, I kept checking the rear view mirror for Rey, but he was nowhere in sight.

"Caroline?"

"Yeah?" Her voice was tired but she was not annoyed.

"Bernie's death—does it bother you?"

"Yes. A lot."

I looked over to see tears running down her cheeks. She was making no effort to wipe them away, keeping her face emotionless even as the tears flowed.

I found it hard to continue. "I can't stop thinking about the fact that everyone and everything is multiple. It feels like being in a war. One death has meaning, a thousand deaths is an exercise in statistics." Even as I said it, I felt cold, distant. It's always been how I react to horror that can't be borne.

Her voice was subdued, quiet to the point that I could hardly hear it. "Yes." Then she recovered her control. "But goddammit, Bernie was a nice guy. Rey has to be stopped from doing whatever he's doing, no matter where he's doing it, or to whom. And you and I are going to take care of each other. Those are the rules. There's no voting. One person is as many as all."

She was right, of course. Even about the physics.

#

The pizza joint on Memorial Avenue also served coffee. I was still nursing my mug when Caroline came back to the table. Only a few other people were there. The lunch crowd wouldn't arrive for an hour yet.

She didn't even sit down. "We have to leave."

"You talked to Stan?"

"Tell you in the car. We have to go right now."

I left money on the table and followed her out the door.

"Give me the keys. I'm driving this time."

I didn't bother to argue. She pulled out onto Memorial Avenue across two lanes, ignoring the traffic streaming along the busy street, and turned left.

"Jesus Christ!" I added my voice to the chorus of horns and tires that accompanied her manoeuvre.

Her words were short. "They'll stop." She changed into the right lane and picked up speed.

"Where are we going?"

"My place. Our place. The apartment on Arthur Street. Stan says Rey called him just before I did. Wanted to know where I was. Stan didn't know for sure, but he told him he thought you and I were grocery shopping."

"So we're not dead, and you don't live with Rey."

"Right."

"And you and I ...."

"Apparently."

"And Rey is going where?"

"Rey will hang around the apartment until you and I—the other set—come back with the groceries."

"And then?"

"Your guess is as good as mine."

"Where would you go grocery shopping if you were, you know, the you that lived here?"

Caroline thought. "Rey always insisted I shop close to home. He'd give me exactly the amount that he thought I'd need. When I got home he'd check the receipt against the change."

"Control freak."

"So if I were free, I wouldn't do any of that. One place I'd stop for food would be the deli on Edward Street. Deli food was taboo to Rey—way too expensive, too snooty or something. 'Food is just fuel,' he always said. The deli."

"If that's the place I know, we can park in front and wait for 'us' to arrive. After that, I don't know what to do."

Caroline bit her lip. "What if Rey knows what we're thinking? He knew about Bernie. Maybe this is the 'later' he taunted us with. Maybe he wants to get all of us at the same time."

"Maybe he does. We have no way of knowing. It's still a good plan."

We pulled into the deli parking lot a few minutes later. Caroline turned off the ignition. Simultaneously, a knock came on my window. Caroline put her hand back on the key—she couldn't see past me and was taking no chances.

I looked. "Jesus! Caroline, unlock the doors!" As she did, I rolled down the window. "Get in the back, both of you!" They piled in.

"Took you long enough to get here," said Caroline2. She immediately closed her eyes.

David2 said, "We'll chat later. Right now we have to get the hell away from here. You two trade places—David has to drive."

As I started the car, David2 said, "Caroline, close your eyes."

"What?"

Caroline2 said, "It's important." That seemed to be enough. Beside me, Caroline closed her eyes.

At Edward Street, I turned north. "Where are we going?" I asked.

"Your choice, but someplace we can talk, eventually." David2 poked me in the back. "Don't tell us where, not a word. Just go. Rey sometimes can see what Caroline, my Caroline, sees and hears."

"Got it." I added, "We came to warn you—"

"Not us," said David2. "The ones you came to warn are dead. Rey— one of the Reys—got them as they left the apartment. Bernie's our best bet. If anyone can make sense of this, he can. He's probably in danger, too."

"Not anymore," I said. "He's dead."

"Damn," David2 said. "Drive!"

14 # CRISSCROSS

I opted for an old motel on Cumberland Street. When we got there, David2 and I steered the Carolines, their eyes still closed, across the parking lot. Before we let them open their eyes, we drew the blinds and put away all the motel pamphlets and stationery.

"Pretty generic," I said.

"Okay, you can open your eyes," David2 told the Carolines. "Do you know where you are?"

Each Caroline shook her head. One of them added, "Not a clue."

The room was large, with two queen-sized beds and a couch. The two Carolines took the couch. David2 and I headed for the closest bed simultaneously, each of us intending to prop a pillow against the headboard. But then, realizing how that might look, we both raced for the one chair in the room instead. David2 won. I sat down on the edge of the bed and wondered how identical twins manage.

"Caroline." I picked one of the Carolines at random—I couldn't tell them apart.

"You want that one." She pointed.

"Sorry." I decided to confess. "I can't tell you two apart."

"Men!" both Carolines said simultaneously.

"Same rules," said my Caroline.

"Ditto. The men get the bed closest to the bathroom."

"Well, that's that, then," said David2. "Let's talk. But remember, nothing of value to Rey."

Caroline2 asked the question on my mind. "Do you think this will work?"

David2 answered, "I have no idea. But it's how we think he works at the moment, right? So we go with it."

"Okay, then. Background first?" I suggested. "How did you two get, you know, here?" I swept my arm to take in the whole world.

"Car." David2 answered idiotically.

"No, I mean—"

"He knows what you mean," Caroline2 said. "He's just yanking your chain. My guess is that you two flew in from Kenora. We drove. What I don't understand is—"

"How we could occupy this universe together," David2 finished for her. "We'd have to have split in two or something when we entered."

"Somewhere around Falcon Lake, right?" I said.

"More likely between Dryden and Kenora," David2 answered. "This side of Kenora. We were going to Winnipeg, but Rey intercepted us in Dryden when we stopped to pick up some pop. He had a gun and he forced Caroline into his car."

"Did he have another Rey or two? You know, doubles?"

"No, no doubles. Why?"

"Tell you in a minute. Let's hear the rest of your story."

"He took my keys so I couldn't follow him, and then he and Caroline drove off, heading for Winnipeg. Am I forgetting anything important?"

His Caroline shook her head.

"And, let me guess, you got Caroline back in Kenora. But how?"

"Caroline's got to tell you this part," David2 said.

Caroline2 leaned forward on the couch. "In the car, Rey said we had to get to Winnipeg as fast as possible because David and I would be there, and he didn't know where we'd go after the park. Which made no sense at all to me."

"It does to me." I said. "Do you know roughly what time this was?"

"Maybe three o'clock, three-thirty at the outside."

"Caroline and I were there then. One other thing—did he ever say anything about a 'little buddy,' a friend, someone else?"

Caroline2 thought. "Yes, now you mention it. It was really nutty, something like, 'This is going to be tricky because my little buddy's popped.' Something like that. I thought—well, never mind what I thought. He'd say stuff like that when I was married to him. He thought it was funny."

"Okay." I turned to David2. "So Rey and Caroline are off to Winnipeg, but you don't know where they were going. What did you do?"

"Well, that's not exactly right. I kind of thought they were heading for Winnipeg."

"I don't understand."

For a long time, David2 said nothing at all. He sized me up, weighing whether to tell me something important against the possibility that I wouldn't respond well. I could read his intent with no trouble at all. Clearly, I didn't possess the poker face I thought I did. Good to know, if my future ever included poker.

"What's your wife's name?" he said at last.

"Darryl. No, Darlene."

David2 looked at me. "Picture her."

"What?"

"Try to picture her. What does she look like? Picture her doing something with you—maybe on a holiday. What does she look like?"

"She ...." I couldn't keep my mind on the task. Every time I tried, the images scrambled. Sometimes she looked one way, sometimes another. Some of the things I "remembered" I knew I'd never done. Other things seemed to have been deleted—or cropped, maybe. For example, I could remember being with Darlene at Yellowstone, stopped by the side of the road, but I couldn't remember why or what happened next.

David2 stared intently at me. Caroline, my Caroline, looked agitated, worried.

"I can't seem to ...." I couldn't express it.

"Hold on to the storyline?" David2 suggested.

"Yes. That. Things are mixed up."

Again, David2 went silent. Then he said, "This is the fourth day since all this began, isn't it?"

I thought about it. "Yes. Well, the fourth new day. The fifth if you count the afternoon before."

"Have you worried about Darlene?"

Worried? No. In fact, I hadn't thought about her at all. Nothing at all like the concern I felt when she'd stumbled on the garbage bags and twisted her ankle—I worried she'd twisted her back or really hurt herself. But as I thought about it, the worry from that time seemed distant, almost as if someone else had felt it.

I said, "I just assumed she'd be okay."

"Seriously, did you think about her? Did you worry?"

"Sure." Who was I kidding? I was talking to another version of me about something he must have experienced, too. Reluctantly, I admitted the truth. "No. I haven't thought about her at all."

"That's right. Odd, isn't it?"

I wouldn't have said it that way—what I felt was guilt. But he was right: I'd left a few days ago. I should have been worrying about Darlene, wondering if everything was okay. Why hadn't I?

"Now comes the hard part," he said. "What is she doing right now?"

"How should I know?" I tried. "Holy shit!" Darlene was on the phone to the police about Caroline and me. They'd just found Caroline murdered outside the apartment that Caroline and I shared. The police wanted Darlene to come down to the station.

"Rey," my Caroline said. "He's parked across the street from that deli, waiting." She'd put herself through the same exercise, with similar results. "I think he'll wait a few more minutes. But I'm not sure."

I recognized on David2 the ironic smile I'd used on my students. "So, now you know how I kind of knew that Rey and Caroline were heading for Winnipeg."

I couldn't think of anything to say.

David2 said, "So Rey—the one that comes after Caroline and me—is excellent at 'seeing' what we're likely to do, at least over the short term. He's better at it than we are, and we're better at it than you two are."

"Is he reading our minds?" I interrupted.

"Not exactly. It's something else." He looked at my Caroline. "When you saw Rey sitting in his car just now, where were you?"

"Here, with all of you. Wasn't I? Did I leave without knowing it?"

"Sorry, that's not what I meant. You saw something, sort of like a movie. I'm asking where the camera was in the movie, if you were the camera. Understand?"

She nodded. "I was...I was in the deli, looking out the window."

"Exactly. Every time I 'see' what's going on, I'm looking at it from a place that's reasonable for me to be. For instance, I'm never looking down at the action from far above. I'm someplace that's both possible and probable—just as it's not out of the realm of possibility that you went into the deli and saw Rey parked across the street."

I didn't like this. "Is there a way to block him, so he doesn't see us?"

"I don't think so. He can't control what he sees any more than you can. It's not mental telepathy. It's more like seeing a probability, the likelihood of a particular outcome happening. It's as if several possible futures were stacked up like a deck of cards, and you could look a short way into the deck, maybe the top card or two."

"This is nuts!" my Caroline said. Caroline2 nodded. "I don't understand how we can look at what someone else is going to do. We have *some* control over our *own* lives, but over someone else's? That's crazy."

"David," I said, "I think there's a flaw in your idea. It's not a deck made up of futures—it's alternative versions of the present, not the future. I 'saw' Darlene being told about Caroline's murder, but there was no indication that I was dead. I was there, at home—sorry, at Darlene's."

Caroline gave me a look I couldn't decipher, exactly, but she didn't look happy.

I went on, "So when Rey told your Caroline about hurrying to Winnipeg because we'd be there, he based that on a vision of us *planning* to go there. He hadn't 'seen' us there in the future."

"Hmm. That works. And I'd bet that even if he *had* made it all the way to Winnipeg, you wouldn't have been there. Not in *his* world."

"I just want all this to be over," Caroline2's voice edged toward despair. "I want to be in a world where things don't change, where you wake up where you went to sleep the night before." She began to cry. "And I don't want some Rey to be trying to kill me." She couldn't continue.

My Caroline, dry-eyed, rubbed Caroline2's shoulders. My Caroline didn't seem as emotional as her counterpart. It was as if they were sisters rather than twins.

David2 knelt in front of his Caroline and took her hand. "We'll get out of this." And that wasn't something I'd have done. But Caroline2 took deep breaths, calming herself.

I hated to interrupt their moment, but I needed more information. "If we do the unexpected, maybe we can keep ahead of the game."

Caroline2 shrugged. "Maybe." She was trying to participate. She wiped her face and exchanged a smile with my Caroline.

I said, "There's still something I don't understand."

David2 turned around. "What?"

"How can the four of us end up in the same place? It seems unlikely. With an infinite number of places to go, why all four of us, and why here? Before one of the Reys killed two of us, there were at least six of us and God knows how many Reys. What's with the cluster—why here, why now? "

David answered, "If you're wondering if we're being manipulated in some way, I don't think so. It doesn't feel like that to me."

"Me neither," Caroline2 was back in control of herself. "It's more like—"

"We're doing it to ourselves," David2 finished.

"What's Rey's part in it?"

"Don't know," David2 said. "I just don't know." For a while the four of us were silent. David2 spoke first. "But we can't just sit here and think about things that don't have answers. I want to hear your story—we can learn from it, I can feel it."

I started at the beginning. Somewhere in the middle, I had a sudden thought. I turned to Caroline2, "You were married to Rey and so was she." I pointed at my Caroline. "Which Rey is hunting us?"

David2 answered. "It might not be just one Rey, but they all have a leader, a boss. He thinks Caroline is *his* Caroline, and he wants to kill her and everyone who, he thinks, is on her side. He's completely focussed on getting rid of her. He's psychotic and talented, and I hope to God there's just one."

15 # RANDOM CHANCE

When I finished my story, David2 asked, "You think Rey knew you went to see Bernie?"

"Looks that way."

"I'm not so sure."

My Caroline piped up. "It doesn't seem right, to me, either. I think it was *you two* Rey thought went to Bernie's. He wasn't going after David and me—he was going after *you*. And Bernie, of course. And that means..."

"That he was *another Rey*," I said, anticipating. "Multiple Reys are after us—the one who belongs in this world, plus some we've brought with us. Shit!"

Caroline put her head in her hands. "One of them, God only knows which, is sitting across from the deli. At least he was a half-hour ago. But we have no idea where the others are. They might be on their way here."

"We have to leave," David2 said.

"I agree," I said. "Even though we just got here. And you two shouldn't tell us where you might be heading. One of the Reys might be tuned in to us right now."

"Makes sense," David2 agreed. "And I like your idea about being as unpredictable in our movements as possible."

"Will we see you again?" Caroline2 asked.

My Caroline touched her arm. "I don't think so. We don't know how long it's going to be before we're zapped into some other place. It may be soon, or it may be never. But we can't try to stay together. It's too dangerous—not just for us, but for the people we know."

"Like Bernie," David2 said. He turned to me. "Brother David, I'll try to throw off our Rey by randomizing our movements. I'll use a coin or something to choose where we go. I suggest you do something similar."

Of course I understood. I'd been about to suggest the same thing. "You two should get out of here, right now. We'll leave in a few minutes, after you've disappeared. It would be best if we didn't know even which way you were going. The more any of us knows, the more likely it is we'll be caught."

"Let's go," David2 said.

The Carolines hugged. "Be careful," they said simultaneously. Caroline2 followed David2 out the door. We closed it behind them.

"Now what?" Caroline asked.

"Now we wait."

"Not for long."

"No."

"You're going to use a coin, too, to make decisions for us?"

"Yeah."

"Don't talk out loud, okay?"

I smiled. "I won't." We sat in silence for almost ten minutes. Once, I walked over to the window and peered out by the edge of the curtain. No sign of Rey.

Caroline broke the silence. "Flip a coin."

"What?"

"Now. Flip a coin. Do some kind of heads or tails thing." At my look she added, "Just do it."

I got a quarter from my wallet. "You call it. But who's making a decision?"

"I am. Why should you make them all?"

I flipped the coin.

"Heads," she called as the coin was in midair. It landed tails.

"You lose."

"Ninny, it doesn't work that way." She came over to the bed and kissed me lightly on the lips.

"Well, I won, anyway. Can I flip again?" I asked. "Raise the ante?"

"Nope. Well, maybe later."

#

The human genome has twenty-three pairs of chromosomes, thirty thousand or more genes, and a billion or so three-letter words made from the four protein letters of the genetic alphabet. It's full of meaningful text, along with stretches of what the scientists call junk because they don't know what it's for, and little chunks of mutation-induced mistakes. It's the physical me, and it comes with a good deal of my personality and attitudes built in.

Whatever travels between the universes, I don't think it's my DNA. Getting all those bits and pieces into proper alignment just couldn't be done. It's the other part of me, whatever that is, that moves between worlds. Maybe it's a set of instructions for assembling me. Or maybe, as Bernie said, I'm more a place than a person, a lane marked Merge, and there's no movement at all except for the cars passing through.

#

Caroline had kissed me, but I couldn't even savour it. Rey picked that moment to kick the door in.

"It's later!" His voice was manic.

Before I could react, he'd cold-cocked me with a baseball bat.

When I woke, I lay on the floor beside the bed. The door was still open, and Caroline was gone. This time I had no idea where she was, or if she was still alive.

I quickly learned that I was in no shape to spring to her rescue. As soon as I moved, a wave of nausea felled me, and I threw up uncontrollably four or five times. I could not seem to get past kneeling on the floor. Rising to my feet was impossible. There was something wrong with my ribs, too. Every breath I took caused pain. Evidently Rey hadn't stopped beating me once I hit the floor. There was blood all over my shirt and more blood in the vomit.

Using the side of the bed for support, I tried again to stand. Bent double, lurching, staggering, I made it to the door and closed it. Then I set out for the bathroom.

Impossible though it seemed, I looked even worse than I felt. A lump the size of an egg protruded above my left ear. My nose skewed to the right and was crusted with blood. I touched the point at which it seemed to want to head off in a new direction. Broken. With both hands I grabbed the end of my nose and tried to straighten it. The pain was like a fire that someone was trying to put out with pepper. I fought against an urge to sneeze that was almost invincible. It passed most reluctantly, leaving me leaning against the counter, sweating and shaking uncontrollably.

Caroline. Where was Caroline? I couldn't charge out of the motel to find her. I just wanted to sleep. No, I couldn't sleep—if I'd had a concussion, that sleep could be my death. I needed to stay awake. I'd just lie down on the bed and close my eyes to keep the nausea at bay. I lay down and tried to position myself so that my ribs wouldn't punish me too severely for breathing.

When I woke up, the room was dark except for a narrow band of light shining between the curtains. I turned on the light above the bed and looked at my watch—almost 4 a.m. I'd slept and I'd awakened, so I must not be dead. I turned off the light and closed my eyes again. Traffic noises woke me just after seven. It took me a full ten minutes to turn onto my side and get my feet onto the floor. I tried to sit up. Bad mistake. I threw up again, not quite managing to clear my pants. At last, I stood and shuffled to the bathroom.

I meant to step into the bathtub fully clothed and take a shower. What the hell, my clothes couldn't get worse.

I did have the sense to try to get my wallet out of my pants pocket so it wouldn't get wet. I needn't have bothered. It wasn't there. Robbed as well as beaten.

One thing at a time, I thought, and turned on the water. As soon as it hit me, I passed out. Sometime later, I woke curled up in a fetal position on the bottom of the tub, pounded by water. I didn't seem to have sustained any further damage. Slowly, so slowly, I worked myself into a sitting position and let the water, now cold, beat down. I stayed there until the cold water motivated me enough to get out of the tub.

It wasn't easy, but I made it. I even turned off the water. I shuffled to the couch without a plan beyond sitting on it and feeling sorry for myself while worrying about Caroline.

A knock on the door, however, caused me to detour. If it's Rey, I thought, he's welcome to finish the job. I opened the door, and there, once more, stood David2 and the other Caroline. Darkness welcomed me with open arms.

16 # REPRIEVE

I woke to find myself lying on the couch. Someone, probably Caroline2, had placed a wet washcloth over my eyes.

"Found your wallet," David2 said.

"How did you ...." I began. It was hard for me to find and frame my thoughts. I couldn't continue. I'd gone as far as I had words for.

"Just after we left, we spotted Rey coming to the motel, so we doubled back," David2 said. "We didn't think you and your Caroline would have left yet."

In lieu of a nod, I managed an imperceptible movement of my head. I hoped it was close enough.

"He had a clone-buddy in the front seat with him."

"Caroline. What about Caroline?" It was becoming easier to think.

"They have her. We know where, and they probably won't leave before morning, so we've got time."

"Wait, what time is it?"

"Just after three in the afternoon. I know. We have to save her, and we will. But you need to hear the rest of the story first."

"Sorry. Story. Sorry story." I seemed, to myself but to no one else, incredibly clever. I wanted to laugh at my little joke and have everyone else enjoy it too.

David2 continued despite me. "When we got back here, Rey had finished with you and was coming out with Caroline. He tossed your wallet into the hedge—he wasn't the slightest bit interested in it. He just wanted it to look like you were mugged. The other Reys stayed in the car."

"Like in Kenora." My words came somewhat more easily. I was waking up more fully.

"Caroline looked white as a sheet." He paused for a heartbeat. "She must have tried to stop him. She was a little beaten up, and his face looked like someone had taken a rake to it."

"She's okay, though?"

"Oh yeah. She was still scrapping with him as he dragged her to the car. He made the other Rey sit in back with her."

Caroline2 took the washcloth off my forehead and went into the bathroom to wet it with cold water.

"You said you know where she is."

"The Rey in the car asked where they were going, and the Rey struggling with Caroline said they'd take Caroline back to the farm. But they didn't leave right away."

Caroline2 had returned with the wet washcloth for my forehead. "They were probably waiting to see if we came back. Of course we watched them wait for us."

"And I was trying to take a shower, which didn't work out well." I winced. "This farm—where is it?"

Caroline2 answered. "It's not too far out of town, on the way to Murillo. Rey's parents owned it, and when they died it became his, but he never did anything with it. It's pretty run down. There's a tumbled-down barn, and a small house. The old cedar silo is still in pretty good shape. They're probably staying in the house—it's a long way from the road, and it has a basement and a root cellar."

"I can't just stay here," I said. "I have to go."

"*I* have to go," David2 said. "*You're* in no condition to go anywhere."

It was hard to disagree. "But what will you do?"

David2 smiled. "I'll do what you'd do, and just as well, too." He looked me in the eyes. "Right, brother?"

"Right."

"While David's gone," Caroline2 said, "I'll look after you, but not here—we'll move you someplace safer."

"Where?"

David2 said, "Can't say, just in case we're wrong about how Rey picks up information about us."

"Transportation?" I asked. "We need a car."

"We have one, the one we drove here. I'll call a cab to take me to where it's parked."

The motel phone rang. Caroline2 reached for it.

"No!" David2 yelled. "That could be Rey. Let it ring. He might be checking to see if my bro, here, is dead."

The phone rang a dozen times or so before falling silent.

"You'd better call the cab from the phone at the front desk. If he calls this room and the line is busy ...."

"I miss my cell phone," Caroline2 said.

David2 said, "I'm going. Caroline can answer any questions as well as I can. See you in a while."

"Be careful," Caroline2 and I said simultaneously.

For some minutes after he had gone, Caroline2 tended to me. "You're a mess," she said at last. "Why the hell didn't you get undressed before you tried to shower?"

"No point. I'd puked on my pants. And anyway, I couldn't move much." I shrugged. It hurt.

"Your clothes will probably dry *on* you as well as they would if they were *off*."

"You and my Caroline are quite different, apropos of nothing."

"A bit. I wouldn't have gotten so physical with Rey. I might have shot him in his sleep, but I'd never confront him directly. My 'sister' has more fire in her belly than I do. Different background, I guess. Rey and I were married just a few months. At a guess, your Caroline married earlier and stayed with him longer, am I right?"

"Yes, I think so. Here's a guess. Your David and I are quite a bit alike."

"Yes, but you *think* more, and he *acts* more."

"I'm not sure I like that."

"He was never married to Darlene. She was his high school sweetheart, but that's all. After high school he met a young woman by the name of Camilla Fontaine."

"My college crush. French father, Italian mother."

"When he first told me her name, I thought he was making it up. They lived together for a few years, but nothing came of that, either. Then he and I met and the rest is history."

"And you and Rey?"

"He was my live-in boyfriend for a while before we got married. Mean bastard, but charming. It took me just a few months to see what a dead end he was. I told him to hit the road—instead, he hit me. One thing led to another. There were court injunctions against him, which turned him into a bona fide stalker. He terrified me for years after the breakup. I thought it'd be all over when David and I got married, but Rey didn't change at all. He got even more nasty, more sneaky."

"Do you know a guy called Stan?"

"From the apartment block? Yeah. Nice guy. Before David showed up in my life, Stan used to look after me, like a brother. He took a beating from Rey once for that. Why do you ask?"

"My Caroline knows him, too. Another question—are you and David from the same world? I mean, is your David the same one that you've always known? I'm sorry, I'm not being very clear about this."

"I know what you mean. Yes, he is."

"Any idea how many times you've, how do I say this, made the trip to another universe?"

Caroline2 laughed. "It's hard to tell. Twice, anyway. Sometimes I think it's been more. I'm not one hundred percent sure. What about you and your Caroline?"

She and David might be from the same world, but still, I wondered whether her David was the only David she'd ever known. I decided not to ask and answered her question instead. "She and I met on Mapleward Road one night. She'd just gone through a gateway into a new world. I'd gone through a couple of times, at least. As you know, it's hard to be sure."

"So you and she are from different worlds."

"Yes. No cliché."

"And since then?"

I knew what she meant. "Travelling buddies. Separate beds." I blushed.

"You'll need to work on that, won't you?" She laughed. "You look as if you're feeling a little better. "

She was right. I was coherent again, if not pain-free.

"We'll get her back for you."

"I hope so."

David2 returned about twenty minutes later. "You look better."

"I'll feel a lot better once I know that Caroline is safe."

"Me, too. First we get you moved out of here. Then we'll plan. We'll have to make up a lot of this as we go, but we might as well plan what we can."

It took both of them to get me into the car and out again at our new "no questions asked" motel, a place as sleazy and decrepit as the last. The drive was agony.

David2 opened the motel room door. "You won't be much help at the farm."

"I can at least act as a sentry. I thought of something—the three of us need to be able to stay in contact with each other. What if we pick up some FRS radios from an electronics store? To hell with the cost. We can pick a common channel and trade info. You can prop me up against a tree, or set me on a hill."

"Or leave you right here," David2 said. "You're in no shape for this."

Caroline intervened on my behalf. "He's right, David. He can help. The radios are a good idea. Rey's not likely to twig to what we're doing."

"We'll need weapons, too."

"This is Canada," David2 offered. "You can't just pick up a gun at a convenience store."

"Canadian Tire sells machetes."

"Machetes it is, then. Unless we find something better."

"Torches and pitchforks would be nice." Caroline smiled. With David2's help, she lowered me onto the bed. I was asleep almost instantly.

17 # THE FARM

Shakespeare and Milton understood evil. What motivates Iago in *Othello* to do what he does? Is it, as he says, that his ambition has been thwarted? Or is it, as Shakespeare implies, that Iago's behaviour is fundamentally inexplicable, that Iago's proffered explanation of it is rooted in nothing more than a desire to laugh at the gullibility of others?

And why, in *Paradise Lost*, does Satan lead the angels to rebel against God? Is Heaven so unsatisfactory? Or is Satan just the sort who throws rocks through stained glass windows because he gets a kick out of it?

Mark Twain, too, understood evil. In *Huckleberry Finn*, the villainous King and Duke are buffoons of the first order, but their larceny is successful nonetheless. Their victims are innocents who mistake buffoonery for art, and law for justice. They also believe that all evil advertises itself as evil by *looking* evil.

Iago and the rest helped me stop asking "Why?" Why was Rey the way he was?

Rey Reynolds never felt a need to explain. He wasn't afraid of death, though he'd be annoyed when death brought an end to his pleasure. Killing wasn't even a game to him. It was just something he did—it was in his nature to do it. And the longer he spent "travelling," the better he got at it.

#

According to Caroline2, the farmhouse sat at the end of a winding driveway that led uphill from Oliver Road. The adjoining fields, though overgrown with hay and small scrub poplar, didn't provide any real cover for someone trying to approach without being seen. The only hope of remaining undetected, at least for a while, was to approach after dark. Which, at this time of year, meant after the summer twilight ended near 11 p.m.

While I slept, David2 and his Caroline shopped for clothes for me. By six o'clock, they were back with shirts, trousers, underwear and a pair of shoes. Finding things to fit me was, of course, not difficult.

I woke up when they returned—not because of noise, but because of the aroma of fried chicken. They'd brought supper.

We ate, talked about "home," and waited for the summer sun to set. Just past eleven o'clock, David2 parked half a mile from our target and shut off the engine. The low cloud cover made it darker than normal.

I'd been consigned to the rear seat. For most of the trip I'd held onto the back of the front passenger seat to keep my ribs from rubbing against each other.

David2 turned around to point at me. "You aren't in any condition to try to get your Caroline out. Stay in the car, and we'll be in touch with these." He passed me one of the FRS radios. "Use channel ten."

"Ten."

"If things start to go wrong, I'll call. Can you drive if you have to?"

"If things go badly, I'll be able to drive."

David2 gave me that look that meant "You're lying through your teeth and I know it, but I'm going to rely on you anyway."

I returned the look, punctuating the message with my middle finger. He smiled, shaking his head in a manner both worldly and dismissive. I hadn't yet mastered that gesture.

"Pissing contest over?" Caroline2 looked at her David. He nodded. "And you?" She gave me the same look.

"I suppose so."

"Good. We have work to do."

She and her David got out and started up the driveway. In a few moments, they'd been swallowed by darkness. There was nothing for me to do but sit and wait. The night closed in. I couldn't even read the time on my watch. I saw nothing through the car windshield, heard nothing beyond the confines of the back seat.

Then someone tapped lightly on the window beside me. My heart leaped into my throat.

"David?" I peered through the window.

A flashlight shone into my face. "Get out." Rey's voice was quiet and full of menace, without a trace of bluster or posturing.

"David and Caroline?" I asked. I couldn't frame the full question. I was certain that He'd killed them.

"Two down, you to go. Get out."

"You killed them?"

Rey sent his voice a mocking octave higher. "You killed them?" He switched to his normal tone. "They were coming to kill me. I killed them first, is all. Now get out!"

I hadn't the slightest doubt that Rey was telling the truth. It was too much. I didn't know what to do. Frantically, I rolled away from the window, as if sitting in the middle of the seat would somehow keep me safe from Rey and the reality of death.

The light from the flashlight shifted away. Rey flipped the light to hold it by the bulb end and swung the flashlight at the window. The window glass exploded into my face, shattering into a thousand small pieces.

"Out!" Rey reached in, hit the unlock button, and yanked open the door. He grabbed me by my shirt collar and pulled me out. Then, as if it was something he did all the time, he felled me with a blow to the side of the head.

I couldn't see. I certainly couldn't get up. I prayed to lose consciousness but was denied even that. My right hand went to my ear and came back wet and warm with blood. The light returned, inches from my eyes.

"Messy, messy. And about to get messier."

I said the only word that made sense to me. "Caroline."

"Is that a question? Can't put together all the words?"

The light shifted again and reflexively I brought both hands up to ward off the blow I knew was coming.

But Rey merely stood up. From his full height, he pointed the flashlight at me. For a few seconds, he said nothing.

Then, "Bitch is smart. She got away. This afternoon."

It didn't make sense to me. "Got away?"

"Caroline? Yup. Oh, I won't have too much trouble finding her again, but for now she's gone AWOL."

"I don't understand."

"Of course you don't. I'm not explaining anything, either. She's gone and you're not. She's alive and so are you—temporarily, both of you. Got about two minutes, if you're wondering. Then it's bye-bye time. Time to shuffle off your mortal coil."

"The others..."

"Are dead. Yes, including that other Caroline. I wouldn't grieve too much for her. She wasn't the real thing."

"How ...." I couldn't figure out how to ask.

"Did I know you were here? Or how did I kill them?"

"Here." I tasted blood, now running into my mouth. I wiped it away.

"Let's have your wallet."

It made no sense. "My ...."

"Wallet, wallet, wallet."

Pain and fear and a terrible weariness meant I did what I was told. I retrieved it from my right front pants pocket and handed it to him.

Reynolds put the flashlight under his armpit so he could flip through the wallet's contents with both hands. He pulled out a leather flap in the bill compartment. "This right here is the 'secret pocket' that nobody knows about." He laughed. "And lookee here—somebody put something in it. What can it be? Well, well. It's a bug—an electronic one, not a creepy crawly. A transmitter, like you can buy at any fashionable spy store. Good thing your little buddy saw me throw your wallet away, huh? I'd never have known what you were up to if the little fishy hadn't gone after the bait."

"Bait," I managed. My mind and my voice were equally dull.

"We're monosyllabic today, aren't we?"

"Caroline is bugged, too."

"Well done. Yes, she is." Reynolds paused dramatically. "And would you like to know where she is?"

"Yes."

"Me, too. Let's just have a look." He handed the wallet back to me. From his breast pocket, he took out a phone. "I just love this thing. So small! So convenient! Caroline's bug sends me her GPS data and I see an X. X marks the spot. X, in this case, being your Caroline. She used to be mine, you know."

I didn't respond. He bent down to give me a look at the screen. "See? There she is. Not very far away, either."

It took a moment for me to orient myself. Caroline was perhaps a mile from the farm, several hundred yards off the main road. Was she coming this way?

Suddenly the X disappeared. Rey had been staring with all the intensity of an overzealous schoolteacher. "What the hell?"

I said with mock innocence, "Did I break it? So sorry. Or, you know, maybe she found your bug."

"No!" Rey shouted. "No way she could figure that out."

I shrugged, which hurt. "X doesn't seem to mark the spot anymore."

The flashlight caught me a glancing blow across the left cheek and instantly went out. I couldn't see anything except the glow of his tracking device. But neither could he. I couldn't walk or run, but I could roll and crawl, and I did.

In his rage, Rey didn't know what to do. He started after me and then stopped, instead heading back to the car to turn on its headlights. I rolled off the road and into the scrub, and then I crawled parallel to the road but toward the car. I needed to get behind it so that its headlights wouldn't betray me. I heard the slam of a car door and then footsteps on gravel as he searched the road margins. Twice he stopped to listen for me, and I lay very still.

"Fuck this!" he shouted. "Fuck you, and fuck the bitch!"

The car door opened again. I could hear Rey ranting as he searched for keys, his elation when he found the spare key in the glove box. He spun the car in a wild turn and headed down the farm road. He was going after Caroline.

I lay in the underbrush and listened to the blood coursing in my ears. My heart hammered away.

Rey didn't get it. The tracker wasn't broken. Caroline hadn't found the bug, either. She was gone—just not here anymore. Rey might find the woman who had taken Caroline's place, if one had, but he wouldn't find *her*.

And if she was gone from *him*—I didn't like this thought at all—she was gone from me, too. And I might never find her again.

I didn't have time to be happy for her, or sad for me. Rey, once he realized he wouldn't find her, would come back to finish me off. Nothing would save me this time. I lay still, thinking of Caroline, and gauging my ability to move. My focus was interrupted by a gentle but insistent beeping coming from the road just to my left. My radio must have fallen out of the car when Rey yanked me out. I turned it on.

"There's no one here," a voice said.

"David?" Was it David?

"Yeah. We're in the farmhouse. It's empty. No sign of either Rey or your Caroline."

I started to laugh, though it hurt like hell. Damn, Rey could lie.

18 # SEPARATION

Like the word *love, separation* has many meanings. The worst separation is to be separated from yourself. Vampire movies and stories about insanity scare us in part because we understand that victims are leaving behind their identity, everything they are. They're transformed, but not into another kind of person—into another kind of *thing*. To me, it's that loss of self that makes Alzheimer's terrifying. It's why some people have trouble with retirement, something that should be pleasurable. It brings to mind depressing questions, like "Who am I now? What am I?" "What will I become?"

When we lose a loved one, we lose a part of ourselves too. When they were alive, we'd notice things, and commit them to memory so we could tell our loved one about them. When someone is gone, we still notice those things, but we stop filing them away. The audience is gone, the one we used to share those moments with is beyond listening. And because we don't share those moments with anyone, perhaps ever again, we change, too. After time passes, it's hard to remember who we were, long ago—that we experienced a particular moment and wanted to tell someone special about it. Eventually, we stop even noticing things that we once studied so intently.

"I am what I am," Popeye said. Life grows better or becomes worse or just changes in ways we can't anticipate. We leave the old self behind and become someone else. And always, we are what we are—not who or what we've been, and not who or what we will become.

#

Of the next six days I have no memory at all. David2 and Caroline2 hauled me to the farmhouse and, with some difficulty, cleaned me up. They then used David2's cell phone to call a cab which duly picked up three drunks—twins, one of whom was dreadfully intoxicated, and the woman who claimed to be their sister. God bless the Davids of our worlds for keeping their credit cards paid up, and God bless all taxi drivers who ask no questions and tell no tales.

On the seventh day I came to, fully. I woke out of a dream in which, as a game show contestant, I picked door number three. Caroline was not behind it. But the first person I saw when I opened my eyes was Caroline—no, that was Caroline2. David2 watched TV, much too loud, and a buzzer sounded when a contestant picked the second door. The wrong one.

Caroline2 looked at me, head tilted. "Well, you look like you might stay with us for a while this time."

"Stay?" I had no idea what she was talking about.

"He's coming out of it," she said to David2 without taking her eyes off me. "Do you know what day it is?"

I realized she meant me. "Not for sure. Tuesday?"

"Missed by that much." She held up her right hand, index finger and thumb half an inch apart. "What month?"

"July?"

"Got that one. Good. Want to try to sit up?"

I was, apparently, lying on a couch. We were in another nameless motel room, blinds drawn. David2's game show told me it was morning, sometime around ten or eleven. "Okay."

"I'm going to put my arm behind your back to help. David, get a couple of pillows off the bed to put behind him. And turn that thing down."

"Ten-four." The volume diminished. I felt Caroline2's arm behind me. As she lifted I tried to sit.

"Holy Christ!" The pain in my ribs was unbelievable.

David2 got the pillows in place. "Broken ribs, maybe. You had the shit kicked out of you. But they'll heal. Caroline taped you up pretty good."

I relaxed into the pillows, still hurting.

"Drink." Caroline2 brought a glass of water to my lips. "Small sips. It's the one thing you've been able to do, other than cough a little blood, scream a bit, and pass out."

"I remember the radio," I said. "Head hurts."

"Concussion," David2 offered. "You've been in and out for six days. We couldn't risk taking you to Emergency, and we haven't been able to get any food in you, just water. You must be hungry as hell."

I was. But suddenly I couldn't see my guardian angels anymore. They were blotted out by bright light, followed almost immediately by darkness.

"Passing out," I tried to say.

When I came to again, my mouth felt as if I had been eating fibreglass insulation. "Where's—" A coughing fit put an end to my question.

Caroline2 knelt beside me. "Welcome back, after a brief two-hour nap. Where's your Caroline, is that what you mean?"

I nodded, trying to forestall more hacking. Caroline2 put a glass of water to my lips and I drank thirstily.

"We don't know." David2 put down his newspaper. "Don't know where Reynolds is, either. I don't think they're together, though. I think she's—"

I interrupted. "Gone. Down the rabbit hole."

"'Fraid so."

"And left me behind."

Caroline2 gave my hand a maternal squeeze. "You'll find her. She's ... special, especially to you."

"I remember something," I said. "Reynolds, he said she was 'the real thing.'"

"The real thing?" David2 echoed.

"Yeah, something like that. He was way more interested where she was than in me. Oh, he was going to kill me, all right, but—for fun, I think."

"Odd."

I had a sudden urge. "I gotta pee." I tried to get up, but my ribs insisted that I needed help. "David?"

"Sure. Caroline, I'll help him lean forward, then you get under his left arm. Slowly up and slowly to the door."

It was easier than I'd anticipated. My ribs preferred that I stand. At the door to the bathroom I said, "I'm okay from here. When I was unconscious how did you do this?"

"David built, uh, a contraption. It was quite clever." Caroline2 sounded proud.

"Sorry," I said. "This can't wait." They let go and I used doorframe and counter to get to the toilet. I pushed the door shut behind me, unzipped and started to relieve myself. I was pissing blood. "Bastard must have kicked me in the kidneys."

"What?" David2's voice came through the door.

"I said—" A wave of dizziness hit me. I just managed to get my right hand out to keep me from smashing into the wall as I toppled forward. Steadying myself, I let the nausea pass and finished my business. Then I looked into the bowl. No sign of blood. *Diluted*, I thought. I flushed, zipped, and slowly washed my hands. I opened the door.

My friends were gone.

A newspaper—not the one David2 had been reading—lay folded neatly on the bed. Someone had changed the colour of the couch.

It seemed that the universe had gobbled me up and spat me elsewhere.

I looked in the mirror: same face, same clothes. But my ribs felt better—not healed, exactly. More as if I hadn't been hurt so badly to begin with.

Where was I, though? Was this the universe where Caroline had gone? Or was I completely on my own?

19 # WANDERER

Once upon a time, one of many lifetimes ago, Darlene and I drove along one of Thunder Bay's minor thoroughfares. A cyclist appeared, suddenly, in front of me. He'd been coming down a steep road that intersected ours, and at the bottom of the hill he found he couldn't stop and would therefore die. I saw him first in my peripheral vision, coming from the right. Even before I turned my head, I hit the brakes. The car slowed just enough for him to pass safely in front of me.

The amount of detail I retain of this incident astounds me, even today. I remember his hands on the bike's brake levers. His wheels were fully locked. He'd looked toward the windshield, but glare kept him from seeing me. The muscles in his face stood out. His body was rigid. His eyes held absolutely nothing—not terror, not relief, just a look of certainty. He knew he was going to die and couldn't stop it. He was locked into a chain of events that would carry him, chained, to his death. But the brakes did their job, and we didn't hit him.

As soon as he cleared the car, I took my foot off the brake. I looked in the side mirror. He'd started pedaling again.

Beside me, Darlene shook uncontrollably. When I'd braked, she'd been thrown forward and her seatbelt had locked. She'd been reading, and she clutched the book.

Her voice held wonder and dread. "He almost hit us. He'd have been killed. We'd have run right over him."

"Yes."

"Are you okay?"

"I'm fine. It was close, though."

That was the truth. But if someone had told me what would happen and wanted me to predict what I'd feel afterward, "fine" wouldn't have been anywhere in the answer.

How often do we behave the way we think we will?

Sometimes, I wish I didn't react as I do in crises. I hate that moment of disengagement—the moment when I don't know if I'll come back whole, able to feel again. The moment when I don't care.

#

When I found my friends gone, it took a moment, but I finally realized that I was the one who'd left. I sat on the couch to regroup. It felt the same as the old one.

Next, I closed my eyes. Why? Perhaps I thought that since I'd "recently arrived," I'd be more closely connected to the version of me I'd been in this world. If I closed my eyes, I might be able to remember his experiences and know what he knew. Or maybe I was just goofy with leftover pain and the loss of Caroline, and closed my eyes to get away from it all. It's hard to know.

Still. Just a week earlier, David2 had first suggested I concentrate on people I knew. That in trying to picture them, I might see a little of what might be happening to them. I started with the exercise he'd used — remembering my wife's name. Here, in this place and maybe the one next to it, she was Darryl, not Darlene. But Darryl—I tried to picture her. She was completely unreachable. I couldn't see her at all.

Reynolds, then. Where was he?

Nothing.

I didn't know how to do it. I'd done it before, but I couldn't do it now. Maybe going from a world where you're half dead and pissing blood to a world where you're just beaten up and goofy is too big a jump. Maybe when a universe swallows you whole, you end up with so many layers of onion between where you've been and where you are that you can't see through them.

Or maybe it's not like that at all.

So, I knew my wife's name here was Darryl. But that could be in my head as a scrap of memory from the David who'd married her. No ESP required. Or maybe my brain was engaging in some self-deception, just for fun.

Caroline. Reynolds had said that Caroline was "the real thing." And suddenly I knew that Caroline was alive. I couldn't see her, but she was alive. Somewhere—here? Could she see me?

She seemed to be far away. And that seemed to be all I could know. My "peeping through universes" battery was discharged for now.

I kept my eyes closed for another couple of minutes, hoping for something more, but nothing else happened. So I opened them. Immediately, I checked to see if the couch was the right colour—I wanted to be sure I hadn't travelled somewhere else while my eyes were closed. I hadn't.

Now what? Caroline was gone. It wasn't likely that I'd find her by doing the logical thing, especially because I didn't know what that was.

But a trip to see Bernie, if he was alive here, would be a good choice.

In general, staying alive seemed to be a good idea. I felt the way Jonah probably felt after being swallowed by the whale. For him, at some point, all the big questions must have become little: *I wonder if there's anything to eat. What can I use to make a bed?*

My ribs still hurt. Whatever I decided to do, I'd do it slowly. But when this universe swallowed me, it had also made the doughnuts and coffee disappear. I made a plan—after a short nap, I'd get something to eat.

I woke about an hour and a half later, stretched gently and very, very carefully, and looked around the room. No surprises. Then I went to the door and opened it.

Surprise! Definitely not Kansas, Toto.

20 # OZ

If you were a fall-down drunk in Thunder Bay, even with a really bad case of I-don't-know-how-I-got-here, you'd still be fine. Assuming you were outdoors, perhaps arising from a snowbank, you'd need only a second or two to get oriented. Thunder Bay's landmarks—the lake, the low mountain range—are visible just about anywhere in the city. If the landscape around you is flat, you're in the part of town that was Fort William. If it's hilly, you're on the Port Arthur side. There's really no way to get lost.

So when I opened the motel door, I knew exactly where I was—in a motel on Cumberland Street, about a mile north of the Port Arthur marina. That's what the big landmarks told me. But Cumberland Street was two lanes instead of four, and the city ended just north of the motel. No houses, no gas stations or tiny businesses past Grenville Avenue.

No car parked outside my room, either. To get coffee, I'd have to walk.

I closed the door behind me. Walking out to Cumberland Street, with my various and sundry injuries, was harder than I would have liked, but easier than I expected. Cumberland runs north-south, and I turned south, toward downtown. Where a doughnut shop should have been, I found a small park with flowers and benches. They looked inviting in the light of a July afternoon. Even after so short a walk, my ribs told me they wouldn't mind if I sat for a minute. I told them I wanted a cup of coffee, and we'd wait to sit until then.

Where Cumberland should have joined Water Street, it didn't. This Thunder Bay had never made Water Street the main traffic route on this side of downtown. No overpass crossed the railway tracks to give access to Marina Park. There was no Marina Park, either. Instead, an old grain elevator sat awaiting demolition. I kept walking.

The Prince Arthur Hotel was where it should have been, but Red River Road—the street heading west, away from the water—was still called Arthur Street, according to its sign. In this world, Port Arthur and Fort William had never amalgamated and never had to rid themselves of redundant street names. I was in Port Arthur, not Thunder Bay.

The cars that passed were modern, but I saw far fewer from Europe, Japan, and South Korea. So I hadn't gone into the past—if that were even possible. Instead, I was in a more old-fashioned version of the world I'd known. Apparently Port Arthur hadn't replaced its streetcars with buses—streetcar tracks ran down both lanes of Cumberland Street and up Arthur, too.

I crossed Arthur Street at the lights, then Cumberland, looking for a particular restaurant on Arthur. Finally, I found it, a little café that had been my regular teenage hangout. It showed its age, but its name, Athenian, was still on the big glass windows. People sat inside, eating.

My ribs, which had been demanding to know when we'd sit down, didn't appreciate my gentle pull on the door handle. I sat down at a booth.

"By yourself?" The waitress seemed world-weary and not afraid to show it.

"Yes." I looked around.

"Counter."

"Counter?"

"If you're by yourself, you sit at the counter."

Oh for God's sake, said my ribs. I moved to the counter. My ribs didn't appreciate my less-stable seat on the round and somewhat wobbly stool.

In a moment the waitress was behind the counter, pad in hand.

"Money?" she said.

"Money?" I parroted.

"Do you have money? Cash? No credit cards, no cheques, no scrip."

Scrip? "I—" Did I have money? I fished for my wallet. There wasn't much in it, and I wasn't even sure my money would work here. "How much for coffee?"

She looked as if I'd asked for an explanation of relativity. "Dime."

The world of lattes and cappuccinos was far, far away. I took out a dime.

"I don't want it now. When I give you the check."

I'd made some progress, I felt. I'd confirmed that I had a dime, and she'd looked at it, albeit not closely. Even if the dime was somehow not okay, I was sure she'd just kick me out of the restaurant, not call the police on a counterfeiter.

"Coffee?"

"Yes. Cream and sugar. That's not extra, is it?"

"Don't get funny on me. It's been a long day already. I may be a little long in the tooth, but I still got some bite." She smiled. The gruffness evaporated.

"Sorry." I smiled back. "I'm not from here, so I'm not used to ...." I let it trail off.

"I *thought* you were new. You haven't been in here before?"

"Maybe as a kid. I used to live here, went to school here."

"Mmm," she said. "You look familiar. I wouldn't have known you as a kid, though. I've only been here a while myself. Enjoy your coffee."

When I finished, I paid my check without incident at the cash register. Outside, I walked up Arthur Street once more. I passed Eaton's—still a department store, I noted, not a telemarketing center or a big box store. I crossed Court Street, aiming for the library at the top of the hill. Over coffee, I'd developed at least a hint of a plan.

As I climbed the hill to the library, I looked across Algoma Street and stopped in my tracks. The spot where Central School once stood was empty, not turned into Magnus Theatre. Waverley Park remained, but up the hill, where my old high school should have been, stood a row of very old houses. In this world I couldn't have gone to Port Arthur Collegiate Institute. That wasn't good. I wondered if I'd even been born in this world. Although from what the waitress had said, it was possible that I lived in the city somewhere.

In the library, I wanted to do three things: look at some maps, check the phone book to see if I was listed, and call Bernie. If he existed here at all, and assuming Rey hadn't killed him.

The maps were easy to find. I took a world atlas and a current Port Arthur/Fort William street map to one of the reading tables.

Start with what you know, I told myself. I thumbed to a map of North America. It looked okay. Wait. The part of Alaska that runs down beside British Columbia was part of Canada here, as was Isle Royale in Lake Superior. I didn't know enough geography to spot smaller differences.

I checked Europe. Finland was part of Russia. There was no Northern Ireland. Germany was still divided.

What about places still farther away? I turned to the South Pacific. Australia was called Cook's Land, of all things. Tasmania was the Tasmanian Protectorate. New Zealand seemed unchanged. I couldn't remember much about what it ought to have looked like, but it felt "familiar."

I put the atlas away and unfolded the map of Lakehead and Area. At the scale of the map, the differences between what I knew about "my" Lakehead and this one were striking. Here, Port Arthur and Fort William had never grown together. Parts of the cities were "right" but many more were "wrong." One encouraging note: the area around Bernie's house in Fort William was much as I remembered. The immediate area around the motel on Cumberland Street was recognizable, but beyond the streets I'd walked, the city got unfamiliar fast. After ten or fifteen minutes with the street map, I went to the phone by the main entrance to call Bernie.

Local calls were five cents. I looked up my own name in the phone book. Not listed. I looked up Bernie's name and number, fed the pay phone its nickel (twelve-sided, not round) and dialed.

The phone rang six times.

"Hello?" Bernie's voice.

"Bernie, it's David Williamson."

"Who?"

"David Williamson." He didn't know me. "I taught you English a few years ago."

"Williamson? Mr. Williamson?"

"Yes." There was a long pause.

"I want you to answer a question, Mr. Williamson. Will you answer it?"

"I'll try." What the hell was going on?

"What lives in the fluorescent lights?"

I smiled. "Bugaboos." One of the lessons I used when I taught *A Canticle for Leibowitz* focused on the fact that we know very little about how the world works, especially when electronics is involved. We accept, as an article of faith, that electrons are somehow involved in what happens inside a fluorescent light, but most of us don't really know more than that. So I told the students that what really happens is that intelligent bugaboos live inside the tubes. They keep a close eye on the light switch, and when it's flicked to the "on" position, they run rapidly back and forth inside the tubes. Their body heat creates the light we see. When the switch is "off," they stop running and rest for a while. No sense in getting burned out.

"We have to talk," Bernie said. "Where are you? I'll pick you up."

"I'm calling from the Waverley Library. You have a car?"

"Yes. Why?"

"I don't know. I just didn't think you'd have a car. I'll be waiting inside the main door."

"Twenty minutes." Bernie hung up without saying goodbye. That much, at least, was typical Bernie.

Exactly twenty minutes later, a newer model black sedan stopped in front of the library. I went down the steps and got in.

"It's good to see you," Bernie said.

"You, too, Bernie."

We drove for a few minutes in silence. Finally, I couldn't stand it any longer. "Bernie, why did you ask me about the lights?"

"Because you're dead."

I laughed. "Now that's funny. The last time I saw you, *you* were the dead one."

He looked over at me. "This is gonna be good, isn't it?"

"Yup."

21 # THE WIZ

The first thing I noticed when we got to Bernie's place was that the house had undergone a makeover, with fresh vinyl siding on the walls, and new, modern windows—sliders and plate glass. Second, the old house on the driveway side of Bernie's was gone. In its place was a double driveway and a fenced-in yard, with some small trees and a flowerbed.

"Your landlord's been busy."

"Oh, I bought the place from him a few years ago, just a couple of years after I rented that basement apartment. That's where I still like to work."

As he shut off the car, he looked over at me to gauge my reaction. It was a most uncharacteristically Bernie thing to do. My Bernie would have looked for a reaction only if he were talking about time travel. And he wouldn't have smiled at all.

"You bought the place?"

There must have been a little too much incredulity in my voice—something which, again, my Bernie wouldn't have picked up on—because he laughed.

"I know, I know. I'm the last person you'd think could afford it. But I made a little money a few years ago. Now I have a winter place in Florida and an apartment in Geneva. But as I said, I like to work here. Come on in. I'll put some coffee on."

At the side door of the house, Bernie tapped the keypad of what seemed to be an elaborate lock/intercom system. As we headed downstairs, he said, "Don't be alarmed if you hear someone moving around upstairs. That's just Fred. He's one of my bodyguards. I have two. Johnny was in the car that followed us here."

"I didn't notice."

"Good. You weren't supposed to. I don't really like having them, but I've got a contract with a company that insists I have bodyguards. They're nice guys, mind you, but they're in my space."

The basement looked as if an interior decorator had worked with Mission Control to design a geek's paradise. Two desks, each with a monitor and keyboard and little else, sat so that a person could rocket from one to another on a single office chair. One corner of the basement held a small kitchen nook with a counter and sink, a small refrigerator, a coffee pot and a microwave. Opposite was a living area—couch, coffee table, entertainment unit. A large and very well-vented black steel cabinet occupied another corner. Bernie saw me looking at it.

"Computer." He went over to the kitchen. "Fred! I'm making coffee. Want some?"

A voice wafted downstairs. "Sure."

"Ask Johnny, will you? It'll be ready in a couple of minutes. I'll bring it up, and you can take it out."

"Sure thing, Mr. Elgar."

I finally found my voice. "This is ... wow. You must have made more than just a little money, Bernie. How?"

"Long story." Bernie hunted in the cupboard for coffee and filters. "You remember I was interested in time travel when I was in your English class?" He turned to look at me as if he needed to know the effect his words were having.

"Sure."

"One day you took me aside after class was over and sort of told me how the world worked, how things were."

"I ... that wasn't me, Bernie."

"I know." Both sadness and concern coloured his voice. "It was the other Mr. Williamson, the one who was killed. We'll get to that. Cream and sugar?" He looked in the small refrigerator.

"Just sugar."

"Good. No cream." He took a small sugar bowl from one of the cupboards and fished in a drawer for spoons. He put one in the sugar bowl. "None of us uses cream, so I don't buy it very often. Thought I might have had some, though. Why haven't you asked me how you were killed?" He acted if his last question were an extension of the failed hunt for cream.

I'd been hanging around watching him make coffee. Now he motioned me to the couch. I sat.

"Because I think I know. A guy called Rey Reynolds killed me, right?"

"Ahh, that's interesting. But no. Who's Rey Reynolds?"

I had questions of my own. "Who killed me?" I was stumped.

"Wife." Bernie didn't hesitate. "She thought you were having an affair and smothered you in your sleep after she'd doctored your coffee with something—sleeping pills? Rat poison? I'm not quite sure. At any rate, you weren't. Having an affair."

"You know this how?"

Bernie shrugged. "I had Johnny look into it. He's good at that. Her trial comes up in a week. The lawyer will plead her not guilty by reason of insanity, but I don't think the judge will buy that. He's ignored lots of those pleas before. She'll be found guilty, executed, end of story."

"Executed? Jesus. Canada doesn't execute murderers."

"This Canada does. It does a lot of other things I don't like, too."

"Bernie, I'm ...." I didn't know how to finish that sentence.

"Not from here? Yes, I know. I recognized your voice when you called. That was a strange call. But I was sure it was you. I've found that sometimes it's best not to try to come to grips with what's happening, especially if it's two-heads odd. If you hadn't known about the bugaboos, though, I wouldn't have come to get you, even with Johnny tailing me, ready to shoo away bad guys. I wasn't a hundred percent sure—seventy, maybe. The bugaboos clinched it." He glanced toward the kitchen. "Coffee's ready. I'll serve."

While he headed up the stairs with mugs for Fred and Johnny, I sipped my own and thought.

When Bernie returned, I said, "My wife. What's her name?"

"Starts with a D. Funny name. Darryl, I think." He looked at me for an explanation. When I didn't volunteer one, he sat down on the couch beside me, mug in hand, and put his feet up on the coffee table. "Fair question, and a good one. Now, tell me your story. I assure you I'll believe it all, even your wife's name."

For the second time, to as many Bernies, I started at the beginning.

#

"Well?" I said when I'd finished.

"Well, I believe you. It's way too cockamamie a story to be false. Let's have a look at those ribs of yours. Pull up your shirt."

"I don't think I can."

"Too shy?"

"No, my ribs are telling me they refuse to let me raise my arms."

Bernie laughed. "Stand up." He slowly and carefully pulled up my shirt and took a look. "Fred, come down here a minute, will you?"

Fred looked like everyone's idea of a bodyguard, complete with shoulder holster and no-nonsense face.

"Mr. Elgar?"

"Have a look at this. What do you think?"

Fred inspected me as if I were a slab of beef. "Down here, these might be broken. Most likely not, but it wouldn't hurt to tape him. I'll get the kit." He headed up the stairs.

"Fred's had some experience with repairing people who've been in a fight. If he says you need to be taped, it's a good idea."

In less than five minutes, Fred had me taped up. I felt much better. The idea that my ribs rubbed against each other was becoming just a memory. I could even risk slightly deeper breaths. Fred left with the kit.

"He's good," I said.

"You have no idea." He paused. "You want to know how I made my money, don't you?"

"Yes, but I also want you to tell me what you think I should do next. I haven't any idea."

"The story about the money first. It'll establish my credentials. More coffee? It'll keep you awake through the story." Bernie poured us each a full mug before he began.

"You know I was interested in time travel when I was in high school. I assume the Bernie that you taught was, too. I had other interests — namely, math and physics. So I went to the University of Waterloo on scholarship and promptly flunked out. I was too involved in some things and not enough in others. After that year I came back, got a job fixing everything from appliances to computers, and rented this basement.

"One night I was working on a client's computer and I started thinking about what you'd have to do to make a quantum computer work. I played around with some of the assumptions, got interested, and began to read everything I could get my hands on. There wasn't much on the Internet, but I looked at all of it. Soon I was deep into superstrings, the multiverses and their theoretical levels and properties, and so on, and your eyes are glazing over, so have some coffee. I promise not to start talking in calculus."

Obediently, I took a sip. He was wrong about my eyes glazing over.

He was a very good storyteller. The subject matter, after all, was life or death to me.

"I was fiddling with a toaster when I saw a way to make the ergodicity in quantum fluctuations work to make parallel computing possible in the Level III model of the multiverse."

He looked over at me then. "I know what I promised, but sometimes there just isn't simple language for what I do. Here's what happens, though. Imagine that you have access to 10 to the 10 to the 10 to the 7 universes, and in each one a computer works on a slightly different part of a very large calculation. In the blink of an eye you collect each computer's part, put them all in order, and presto! The solution appears. It's neat. And I'd figured it out.

"I'd stayed in contact with some Waterloo profs. I wrote up my work and sent it off to one, who passed it on to some other folks. My career as an appliance repairman was over."

"The military hired you, right?"

"No, a Japanese electronics firm. Turns out my work has all kinds of interesting applications for entertainment. Next year, it'll launch the first holographic TV set. The broadband bottleneck problem is no more. In fact, a lot of formerly insurmountable problems are currently being surmounted. The only limitation now is the number of people who can work on any given thing. The technical problems are gone."

"But the military?" I persisted.

"Can't do a damn thing about it. I posted my work on the internet the same day I sent it to my prof. It's all open source, for any and all to play with. Or work with."

"What about the Japanese company?"

"They hired me as a consultant. Well, actually they didn't. They bought the right to use my name by hiring me. They give me a humongous salary and the freedom to do anything I like. Oh, and they contribute a couple of bodyguards for public display, and background security like you've never imagined." He smiled.

"You're not really just a consultant, are you?"

"No. I'm a little more than that, but it's a nice word."

"Bernie, my world—the one I started from—it's a lot different. It has more people, it's richer, everyone has lots more gadgets and better houses and better roads. But this?" I swept an arm to indicate everything in his basement. "We don't have anything like this."

"Maybe *this* is what brings my world into better, uh, 'alignment' with yours. It's one of the ways in which my world will ultimately repair itself. We got hit really bad—*really* bad—when the Spanish flu exploded in 1917. It wiped out three-quarters of the population. That's a lot of people. So when my world's population comes back and this world becomes more like yours, someone on your world will discover how to improve the rudimentary quantum computers you undoubtedly now have."

"Maybe." I didn't want to think about the possibility that I'd never see my world again, so I changed the subject. "The computer in the corner there, is that a quantum computer?"

"No, it's an old IBM from the days of programming with punch cards. I bought it on E-Bay. Sentimental, maybe. The quantum computers are very small, very simple."

"Jesus." Reynolds had killed God only knew how many Bernies. Thank God this one had got away. "Bernie, this Reynolds, he's a dangerous man. You need to be careful."

"I know. I will be. Let's see what we can find out about him, and then I'll get to Part II of Everything You Wanted to Know About the Multiverse." He called up the stairs. "Fred, could you bring down another chair for Mr. Williamson?"

"Yessir," wafted down the stairs.

"Former military guy," Bernie whispered.

Bernie sat in the computer chair, and I moved the kitchen chair Fred had brought so I could see both screens.

But Bernie reached for a phone instead of a keyboard. He picked up the receiver. "Peeper, get Search for me, will you?" After a moment, he said, "Hi, Alice. Got a guy here who's going to tell you all he knows about a couple of people. Fellow named Rey Reynolds is primary; secondary is Reynolds's wife, Caroline. Multiple spellings, expansions, variants. Filters are security and unusuals. I suggest Caroline be the start point. Upload my way, number one. Thanks, Alice." He handed me the phone. "She'll walk you through."

For the next hour, Alice asked me every question imaginable about myself, Caroline, Rey Reynolds, even Darryl. I wondered if she was real, or if Bernie had developed artificial intelligence, too. Frequently she came back to a question she'd asked earlier. Did I remember the name of the high school Caroline had attended in Red Rock? Was it Nip-Rock High, or some other name? Had she mentioned a teacher, an administrator? Did

Caroline say Red Rock or did she say Nipigon? Had she ever been to school in Port Arthur or Fort William? How did Caroline meet Rey?

On it went. Eventually, Alice said, "I think that's it. Been nice talking to you, Mr. Williamson. You can put Mr. Elgar on again." I handed Bernie the phone.

"Hi, Alice. How long until the data's in and correlated?" There was a short pause. "Okay. Thanks again." He returned the phone to his desk and then turned to me. "Five minutes, and we'll know how much a problem Mr. Reynolds is likely to be."

"Five minutes?" I let my astonishment show. "That's all? She asked me a million questions."

"I'm sure she did." Bernie grinned. "But she's going to use a qc—that's a quantum computer, not a Queen's Counsel—to find and crunch the information she needs. It will take about a nanosecond. In that nanosecond, the qc will look for every instance the name Reynolds has occurred in all recorded media for the last hundred years, and filter out the useless stuff. Every newspaper and magazine in electronic format, email, all accessible databases. The rest of the time, so five minutes minus that nanosecond, she'll be on the phone, informing the required parties of what we're doing, making sure the right people are told to do the right things. Like that. When she's cleared the bureaucratic hurdles, she'll transfer a summary to this computer, number one, on a secure connection. For the qc there's no such thing as time. In fact, if time really did exist, the qc wouldn't be able to work."

"And you figured out how to make a qc work."

"Yup."

"Jesus. Wait a minute. Time doesn't exist for the quantum computer?"

"Doesn't exist for us, either. Not really."

"What the hell?"

"We really live in the multiverse. It's much like the one the other Bernie told you about. He got a few things wrong, but he was basically correct. Imagine you're standing at a street corner, there's no traffic, and you can't decide if you want to cross with the light or against it. In the multiverse, the instant that the situation arises, the universe containing you splits. In one universe, you cross with the light. In the other, you cross against it. Both of you are unaware of the splitting, and both of you have the same memories up to the time the universe divided."

"But that's not how it is for me. I know when things change."

"So I understand. I don't know why it's like that for you. I just brought up the multiverse so that I could explain why we don't need a concept like time. Speaking of which, the data's up. Let's look, and then we'll get back to your particular situation."

I leaned closer to the monitor so that I could see what he saw. It wasn't much help.

He flipped rapidly through screenful after screenful of columns and figures. "I'm going to print this so I can study it at my leisure." On the other desk, a printer came to life. "I can tell you what I think it shows, but I reserve the right to change my mind after I do a real study."

"Shoot."

"On this world, my world, neither a Caroline nor a Rey Reynolds has ever existed. Nothing, not driver's license records or birth certificates or news items, seems to hint at them being part of this place. On the other hand, you have a complete history. In a word, don't worry. Ray Reynolds won't show up here."

"I showed up here. And after I was dead."

"That you did—I think because you could. Mr. Reynolds, for all kinds of reasons, can't. I think."

"This multiverse. The way I seem to 'travel' in it is changing. When I started, it seemed that I had to exchange places with someone. Now, I don't know what's going on. There's no logic to it anymore."

"Well, I'm sure some logic is at work, but it's not possible for us to see it, possibly because of the nature of multi-dimensionality."

I gave Bernie the raised eyebrow.

"Some problems in math and science can be solved only if more than three dimensions are allowed in the equations that describe reality. When mathematicians allow for ten dimensions, just about everything observable starts to make some sense, including gravity, dark matter, the apparent acceleration of the expansion of our universe, even the way the Big Bang happened. But we're not built to 'see' or to think in more than three dimensions, so we have no way of directly experiencing this ten-dimensional reality except through math. We're like the Platonists who thought that the true reality was the realm of ideal forms, which we ordinary folk saw only as shadow figures on a cave wall." Bernie paused. "I guess I picked up something from your English class after all. That's from *The Republic*, isn't it?"

I nodded, though I honestly didn't know. How much more of myself would I have to lose before I was no longer me? I drank some coffee—lukewarm, now, but still drinkable.

"Here's an analogy. One day you're in your kitchen and you notice a small round circle on the floor. The next day, the circle is slightly larger. You leave it alone—too lazy to clean up the spot, maybe, or too curious. Each day the circle grows a little more. One day, instead of growing, it shrinks. The next day it shrinks some more, and the shrinking continues until the circle is completely gone. What have you seen? Perhaps a colony of bacteria growing and then dying on your vinyl flooring. But if you allow for an extra dimension, it's not too difficult to imagine that a sphere has passed through your floor, and something about the vinyl flooring made it 'visible' as a spot on its way through."

"Okay. But if you think I'm drawing some kind of conclusion from this, you're wrong."

"Bottom line," Bernie said, his voice kind, "you've been experiencing some very strange things. For some reason, you travel among some individual universes of the multiverse. All that's real. I don't doubt you for a second. I know how the quantum computer works, though I don't know how *this* works.

"But I can tell you three things. First, in the multiverse everything that can happen, everything that is possible, happens somewhere. It's not *probable* that pigs can fly, but somewhere in the multiverse, pigs have big wings and fly. If it's possible, it's out there, and you may end up visiting one of those places, so be ready for anything.

"Second, Rey Reynolds isn't here and neither is Caroline, but I think there's a strong probability you'll see both of them again. For example, I'd bet that if you went back to that last universe, David2 and Caroline2 would both be dead in the motel room with Rey wiping the blood off his baseball bat. It's possible you were 'popped out' so you wouldn't be killed, and you were popped into *this* place because it's safe. Rules of physics may govern such things, but I don't know what they are. I can, however, promise you I'll be thinking about them. At this point, though, my guess is that you won't stay here too long. After all, you're technically dead.

"Which brings me to the last point. Most of the universes in the multiverse are inherently unstable. There's a number that scientists refer to as Q and, yes, I remember that Q was the mischievous 'god' in some of the *Star Trek* episodes. The number is the ratio of two fundamental energies, and in order for a universe to exist in a stable form, Q has to have a value of about 1/100,000. Well, there's a tiny, tiny difference between what the number is and what it ought to be. It's a difference the qc has allowed us to measure. At some point, this universe is going to 'wink out' and everything will be gone."

"Soon?"

"Perhaps. But when I say 'soon' I'm using the word the way geologists use it when they try to predict earthquakes—when the next 'big one' will hit. Your presence here is a pretty good indicator, I think, but I don't know if we'll disappear tomorrow or a million years from now."

"Is it my fault?"

"Not at all. You have no more influence on the future than litmus paper does on whether a solution is an acid or a base. You're just an indicator, one of many, and not necessarily a big one. No offense."

"None taken. When it happens, then what?"

"It'll be instantaneous. In the deck of cards that is time, there will be no next card."

"Oh."

"More coffee?"

"I don't think so." Upstairs I could hear Fred moving around.

"Look, how about this. Your ribs could use some time to heal. You're welcome to stay here as long as you like. If and when you feel like leaving, I'll set you up with a new identity so you don't have to hide because you're dead. I'll even make sure you have access to a bank account and all that."

"Oh, you don't have to—"

Bernie cut me off. "I know that. But, hell, what am I going to do with a gazillion bucks in a world where coffee costs ten cents? Besides, you can drop by from time to time, or email me. Tell me what you notice about this world compared to yours."

"But." I was still trying to take it in.

"Bottom-bottom line: what's going to happen is out of our control. Another thing, in case it's escaped you: the multiverse isn't all that's ten-dimensional. We are, too. We're conscious of three dimensions, unaware of the other seven. Trying to understand a ten-dimensional situation using three-dimensional logic—well, that's asking a bit much. In the multiverse it's not true that what you see is what you get."

Bernie stopped talking. For a minute the room was quiet.

"Darlene—sorry, Darryl. My, my wife. Is there anything you can do for her?"

"Ah, no death penalty?"

"Yes, please."

"I'll take care of it."

"Thank you." I found myself thinking of Caroline. "You got any more of that godawful coffee? Mine's cold."

22 # INSTABILITY

For my money, the most plausible of the pedagogical tales of travellers is E. M. Forester's *A Passage to India*. Forester asks, *What can a person learn in a truly foreign environment?*

His answer: Only what one is capable of learning—and even then, only if the foreign environment isn't so alien as to be indecipherable. Beware, says Forester. It's always possible that what you *think* you know will be erased by what you *learn*, and *that* will be replaced by the feeling that you have misconstrued it *all*.

#

I stayed with Bernie for almost two weeks—into August—before I felt strong enough to leave. He set me up in a small bedroom upstairs, next to Fred's, with Bernie's own a few steps down the short hallway. Where Johnny stayed, I have no idea. All the time I spent at Bernie's, Johnny never showed his face indoors.

The house itself had received more than just a cosmetic makeover. As Bernie pointed out, the windows and walls were bulletproof. Downstairs, behind what seemed to be the basement wall, was a safe room with a heavy steel door, its own power supply and ventilation system, and a communications capability even NASA would have envied.

The black car parked in the driveway could survive a land mine, machine gun fire, and loss of its tires, and still keep rolling along. If it became submerged, its passengers wouldn't even begin to get wet for an hour, and they wouldn't run out of air. Its exact location was always known to those who needed to know.

Bernie always called me Mr. Williamson. He couldn't bring himself to say David any more than Fred could call him anything but Mr. Elgar.

When Bernie and I talked, it was almost never about parallel universes, and it was *never* about time travel. He tried to ask me about things he thought I was interested in. Sometimes we talked literature, sometimes gardening, sometimes sports—a topic that worked only if we stayed well north of anything specific about teams or players. Once, Bernie asked me if I thought hockey could be improved by making the ice surface perfectly circular. I said I didn't know.

"Here's what would happen," he began, and we were off for an hour of silliness. He was fun to talk with.

When Bernie was at work downstairs in what he called his "happy place," I read the magazines and newspapers Fred brought into the house. Far from making this world seem more like home, my reading served to increase the sense of distance.

Nothing provided one second of relief from my longing to see Caroline again.

One day, down in the basement, I watched Bernie doing a crossword puzzle. What would have taken me half an hour, he finished in three or four minutes. He wrote in the answers as quickly as he could read the clues.

I said, "You're very good at that."

"If you do a bunch of them you discover the 'filler' words, things like *pi* and *erg*. I do them first, and the rest is easy."

"Do you play with words the way that you play with numbers and physics?"

"Some. I like rearrangements for some reason."

"*Elgar* and *regal*, you mean?"

"And *large*."

"*Alger*. As in Horatio Alger."

"*Glare*."

"Okay. I give up."

"Want a beer? A *lager*, perhaps?" He grinned.

"No thanks, I don't drink."

"Are you sure?"

"I used to be sure. But I might start, even if I don't."

#

A few days before I left Bernie, late one evening, he and I sat outside in the yard. The air was cooling off as evening gathered, and more than a few stars were visible despite the city lights.

During a pause in the conversation, I said, "The sky's different here."
"Oh?"

I pointed south and a little west. "There. I should see two stars, Yed Prior and Yed Posterior, but only one seems to be there. They're not very bright, but I should see them both anyway, right?"

"You made up those names, didn't you?"

"No. I liked astronomy as a kid—not the way you like time travel, but enough. Yed Posterior is only a little over a hundred light years from Earth, which is pretty close, and it's a yellow giant. Giants are usually red, but this one doesn't have any carbon or cyanogen in it, which makes it older than our solar system, even older than the supernovas that blew things around in the galaxy. Old enough that it may be close to fusing helium instead of hydrogen."

"Hmm. And how far away is it?"

"Hundred and, I don't know, five, ten light years."

"You're sure it's the Posterior one that's gone missing, not the other one?"

"Pretty sure. They're close together, though. It's funny, you know—as far as I can remember, this is the first world where something has been different in the sky."

"I don't know stars. Do you mind if we go in? I want to check on this."

"Sure." I was glad I hadn't said *winking out* when I told him about the star nearing the end of its life span—but he'd thought of it on his own. He went downstairs; I went to my room. Sometime in the night I heard him come up to his room.

The next morning, despite having stayed up so late, Bernie was up before me, as was Fred.

I entered the kitchen. "Well?"

"Kick in the ass. There's no record of your star."

"What does that mean?"

"I really don't know. A big change like that—a massive component of the galaxy—wouldn't that make this world impossible? You can't just remove a star and expect everything else to stay in place. Orbits would change, for one thing." He fell silent. "There might be other deletions or additions, too. And there's no way to check." He shrugged. "*Que sera, sera,* I guess."

Bernie and I went over all the documents he'd provided for my new identity. The bank card and credit card were both supported by a considerable sum of money in a brand-new bank account. From it, I bought myself a used Corolla, still in pretty good shape, and arranged to pick it up that afternoon.

Bernie had thought of everything. I was Richard Glendenning, now— still an English teacher, but from Fort Frances, not Port Arthur. I had a new social insurance number, driver's license, health card, hospital card, birth certificate, and an assortment of membership cards, photos, and coupons. All were cosmetically "aged" and packed into my old wallet. Bernie had sworn I was in no danger of running into Rey Reynolds in this world, but the new identity made me feel much better anyway. I'd be hard to trace. Bernie had even made arrangements for a corroborating voice at the end of a phone line if I ever needed a personal reference. I also had a phone number to call if I was ever in trouble, and a secure email address where Bernie asked me to send whatever observations I thought might interest him.

"My other stuff—the things that used to be in my wallet—what happens if I actually make it back to my old world?" We stood in Bernie's driveway. Johnny, a few feet away on the sidewalk, pretended to smoke a cigarette.

Bernie said, "I guess you'll report your wallet stolen. But you and I both know that's not what you really have in mind, is it? It's Caroline."

I smiled. "Yes. If I had to choose between finding her and being returned to my world, I'd choose her. No contest." We were both silent for a moment. "The stuff in my wallet. It won't, uh, destabilize your universe or something if I disappear and it's left behind, will it?"

Bernie smiled, but it was a rueful smile at best. "I don't think that's quite as serious as our galaxy losing a star. If it actually has. Now, let's go get that car of yours from the dealership. Let me know how the credit card works out. It's new. I think it'll work anywhere, and I'll keep your account here topped up."

"Anywhere? You mean other worlds, too?"

Bernie nodded. "Of course. Sadly, if it *does* work in other worlds, you won't be able to tell me about it. I won't be there. But if there is a Bernie where you finally end up, show him the card. Maybe it'll be something he'll enjoy working with."

"Bernie, I owe you an awful lot. And there isn't any way that I can repay you."

"It's not a debt. It's ...." He never finished the sentence. We both understood.

Fred came out of the house with the keys to Bernie's black car. "I'll drive you to your car. That okay, Mr. Elgar? I've told Johnny to keep his eyes open."

"That's fine, Fred." Bernie and I shook hands. I hated to leave, but it was time.

23 # FREE

Of the memories that I know are mine, two school-related ones stay with me.

The first is from Grade One. (I didn't go to kindergarten.) I finished my work ahead of the rest of the class and raised my hand to ask the teacher what I should do.

She said, "Do whatever you like."

I knew I wasn't supposed to leave my desk and wander around, so I looked for something to work with, play with, examine, or read. I had a pencil, a workbook (but it was for work, not doodling), an eraser—and basically nothing else.

So I sat in my seat and rocked. First I rocked back and forth, then I rocked left and right. At that point the teacher noticed and asked, "What are you doing?"

"Rocking." I was puzzled—couldn't she see? And she'd told me I could do whatever I wanted. This was it.

"Fine," she answered. Unfortunately, the rest of the class had noticed, too, and giggles spread. So I stopped rocking.

For the first time, but certainly not the last, I felt the hot blush of embarrassment set fire to my cheeks.

The second memory from school is of my first real kiss. It was summer. I had just finished grade nine; she had finished grade eight. For three weeks that summer I was the older man in her life. As soon as we started that first kiss, the one no one ever forgets, I realized I had a problem. If we weren't going to bump noses, one of us would have to tilt our head and swerve. I assumed it was my job, so I tilted and swerved — and collided with her. She, too, had arrived at the same conclusion. However, I was a left-handed kisser, and she, like most people, was a righty. Our noses met—and, because her front teeth protruded somewhat, there was also some slight clicking of enamel.

She sighed. "That way." She gripped my ears like the handlebars of a bicycle and performed a passable imitation of a chiropractic adjustment.

After we came up for air, she asked, "Better?"

It certainly was. I played a right-hander from then on, until she dumped me.

It takes a long, long time before we figure out even a few of the rules of the world we live in, and how to gain some measure of freedom from them. Sometimes, as Wordsworth said, "The world is too much with us."

#

Both Bernie and I knew what I'd do next. In this world, I knew I wouldn't find Caroline, but I wouldn't run into Rey Reynolds, either. So I'd explore this world until, I hoped, I was suddenly elsewhere and, I even more fervently hoped, closer to Caroline.

Bernie and I also knew that he'd delve into astronomy, hoping that when I went elsewhere, he didn't wink out as a consequence.

I'd never been to the Yukon, so that seemed as good a destination as any. I spent the night in a nondescript motel in Kenora. The next morning, I talked myself into going to the mall for breakfast, where I sat thinking about Caroline and feeling sorry for myself. Bernie's credit card, however, worked fine.

I was in Winnipeg by noon, in spite of my dawdling. I drove around the city for a while. It looked older than the Winnipeg I'd known, and older than the version I'd visited with Caroline. There was no Canadian Mint sheathed in copper-coloured glass, no Perimeter Highway. Instead of 650,000 people, the population was probably less than 250,000. It was still the center of the grain industry, and the corner of Portage and Main still bustled, but it lacked the Museum of Man and Nature, the Planetarium, the Symphony Hall, the Royal Winnipeg Ballet, the elevated walkways, and the underground mall.

I returned to the feeling I had the morning I found myself in Port Arthur, in a world of ten-cent coffee and quantum computing. This world had been interrupted and then fast-tracked. Since I had nothing better to do than to satisfy my curiosity, I looked for a library and found one, the Cornish Library, on West Gate near the Assiniboine River. I wanted to find out what the Spanish flu epidemic had been like.

From the outside, the library was imposing—according to the cornerstone, an old Carnegie Foundation Library built in 1914. I started up the concrete stairs and was almost knocked flat by a teenager who burst through the doors and, on his way ownstairs, pushed me roughly to one side.

"Hey!" I yelled. "An 'excuse me' would be nice."

He replied with a raised middle finger and charged across the parking lot.

I turned away and went into the library. The air smelled of a century of study and quiet reading at oak tables, directed by cards in a real card catalogue. It also had a plaque about Nellie McClung, the suffragist and politician who, in both my world and hers, had required the government to declare that women were, indeed, *persons*. She'd given lectures in the library basement.

I started with the twenty-year-old set of Encyclopaedia Britannica. Five minutes after I found a spot at one of the tables, I had the answers to a bunch of questions. In my world, the Spanish flu pandemic in the fall of 1918 had caused the deaths of thirty million people. In this world, it had killed closer to two billion—and while "my" flu had seemed to target the young and healthy, this flu had attacked everyone equally.

Of course the world had gone on—just without the possibility of birth for either Caroline or Rey Reynolds. I found other differences. The Great Depression had lasted an extra two years, so World War II had begun a little late. The Korean War arrived on time, and Kennedy became President of the United States and still got assassinated. But nobody had gone to the moon. I closed the book and stared into space, miserable. I wasn't interested in this alien, foreign place now. I wanted to go home.

No. I wanted to be with Caroline.

I had the same feeling I'd get, sometimes, on a vacation trip. However interesting my surroundings might be, I didn't belong.

Since then, I've had that feeling a lot. When you've sampled some of the 10-to-the-really-big-number universes that made Bernie's computer work, you feel more than a little disengaged. You're in one more shoe store in one more cookie cutter mall. So the Spanish flu killed almost two billion people here? Interesting. The loafers with the neoprene soles? Not as nice as some of the 10-to-the-whatever pairs I've considered buying in other universes, but nicer than most. Perhaps another day.

That day, the world was pixelating on me again, and this world wasn't even mine. I wondered if Bernie was happy. He seemed to be. I wondered, too, how I'd feel if Caroline were here with me. Truthfully, not nearly as disengaged.

I returned the book to its shelf and left. In the parking lot I looked around for my car. It was gone.

My first thought, with a flicker of excitement: Had I jumped?

But no—nothing seemed different.

"Mr. Glendenning?" I looked up to see a nondescript, nonthreatening man in khaki shorts and mismatched shirt.

"Yes?"

"Oh, good. I was supposed to find you inside the library, but now I don't have to. A gentleman asked me to give you this." He handed me a note, neatly folded, then walked back to the bus stop from which he'd evidently come.

I opened the note. *Your car was jacked. I'll get it and return it to the motel on Portage. Johnny.* He obviously didn't want to show himself, or make life easy for me, by dropping it off at the library.

So I went back inside and called a cab. It arrived half an hour later, and twenty minutes after that I was at the motel. So was my car. I paid the cabbie, walked to the car and got in. The driver's door was unlocked; the key was in the ignition. It had been in my back pocket when I went into the library.

The note on the dash read, *The kid took your key. He apologizes. Johnny. PS Bernie says hello and says to tell you that once you leave Winnipeg you're on your own.*

24 # YUKON

From Winnipeg to Portage La Prairie, only the soil was rich. The Great Epidemic had so effectively culled the world of its population that although Canadian grain still dominated the region's economy, the worldwide market had never materialized. The resulting farms seemed a hodge-podge. Large tracts of wheat still grew beside the road, but some farms had backyards full of pigs and chickens and large vegetable gardens and broken-down tractors. This farm had modern farm equipment; that one worked with a team of horses. The homogeneity I'd expected wasn't there. These prairies wore rags in public and promised no riches. After all, the night sky was missing a star or two.

Portage La Prairie, about fifty miles west of Winnipeg, turned out to be a town of perhaps five thousand people, not like the place I remembered from a much-less-savaged land. It had the same City Hall, designed by Thomas Fuller, who'd helped design Canada's Parliament Buildings. But in the spot where I remembered a modern elementary school instead stood a pretentious-looking old building called Landsdowne College, built at least a century earlier. One of its main-floor tenants was a clothing and shoe repair shop called Rich's Stitches. The usual assortment of modern convenience stores and gas stations were dwarfed by a huge clapboard structure called the Hotel Leland, untouched by a paintbrush for decades.

I stopped to buy a map at the convenience store across from the hotel. This was no world in which to rely on memory for direction. In my world, the Yellowhead Highway branched off Highway 1 shortly after leaving town. But the city's bypass hadn't been built in this world, so checking seemed the safest bet.

At the back of the store, among the greeting cards and magazines, I found a small stack of maps, all of them combining the United States and Canada. Sure enough, the top of the map showed the narrow strip where almost all of Canada's population lived. The most northern Canadian city it showed was Edmonton. On the reverse, I found the part that continued from Edmonton into Alaska. That would have to do.

I handed the young woman behind the counter the map and a dollar bill.

"Tourist? Noticed the plate—Ontario."

"Been visiting friends in Winnipeg." A lie, but small. "Going up to Saskatoon before I go home."

She passed across my change. "Taking #1, then? Road's better. Safer. Been some jackings on 16. Even if you take #1, you might think about not driving at night. Maybe stop in Brandon."

"Thanks, I'll do that." I walked out to the car. I hadn't had the foresight to equip myself properly or plan a little more thoroughly before I left Bernie's. Instead, I'd left my life in the hands of road signs and friendly counter clerks.

I got in, rolled down the window for a little air, and opened the map. I could make Brandon easily before dark. There, I could decide if I wanted to head north and pick up 16 at Minnedosa or continue along Highway 1 to Regina, Saskatchewan, and from there take 11 to Saskatoon and parts farther west. I'd play it by ear—take my time. I didn't have anything important to do, after all.

And so I poked along. The wheat-lands of Manitoba, on the flat, black earth of what had been the bottom of an ancient lake, turned into the prairie grasslands and cattle country of Saskatchewan, acquired some rolling hills, then became the oil fields of Alberta.

I stopped frequently to rest, have a bite to eat, and talk to the locals in restaurants and fast food places along the way. I slept in mom and pop motels and gassed up the car at Texaco stations with their sheriff's badge logos.

In Grande Prairie, Alberta, I met a man who liked to put a few spoonfuls of ice cream in his tea. Closer to the Yukon border I drove past a brush wolf hunting along the roadside ditch.

Things I wanted to tell Caroline about.

Five days, give or take, after leaving Winnipeg, I pulled into Whitehorse in the Yukon. I stayed at a nice motel connected to an RV campground and played golf at a beautiful nine-hole golf course just outside town. I also avoided the opportunity to bungee-jump from a hot-air balloon—it might have beautiful views, but I'd never be able to open my eyes to enjoy them. I ate most meals at a downtown restaurant with tablecloths. In general, I played tourist for a week.

And always, underneath it all, I missed Caroline.

I wondered whether all my days would be like this now, drugging myself with minor amusements so I didn't think too deeply or feel too much.

Exactly a week after I arrived in Whitehorse, I decided it was time. I bought a small tent, some groceries and camping equipment—a plastic cooler and water jug, a small propane stove, a camper's mess kit, a small battery-powered alarm clock. I considered spending time in Kluane National Park, maybe hiring a guide to take me up onto the glaciers.

But maybe I wouldn't. Either way, I needed to move on.

That evening, I went to bed early.

I was in Toronto walking along the beach down by the water filtration plant, west along the boardwalk in a cold morning mist in late March, where pet owners could let their dogs off leash. Dirty ice capped the rocky breakwater a few hundred feet from shore, and small rolling waves lapped at the sand. Occasionally, a jogger ran past—always the same person. I'd hear his feet behind me, and I'd think, "I should turn around so I can see his face," but always, before I could turn around, he'd pass me, and I'd see only his back.

Numbered fitness stations lined the boardwalk, with equipment and a sign showing how to use it—chin-up bars and swinging rings and ladders. I noticed that the numbers decreased in the direction that I walked.

The jogger went by again. "Look for the signs," he said. He turned his head and yelled back, "Read the signs!"

I noticed, for the first time, small warning signs posted on metal poles between the boardwalk and the water. I walked toward the nearest sign, getting some of the fine beach sand in my shoes. The sign showed an icon of a medical syringe with a red circle around it and a slash through it. The message underneath: "Do not pick up needles or syringes. Contact the lifeguard." I returned to the boardwalk and walked west once more.

"That isn't what I meant," the jogger said on his next pass. "Read the signs!"

Coming toward me, I saw a young woman carrying a leash. Her dog ran back and forth in the sand between the water and the boardwalk. When I looked closely, I saw it wasn't a dog at all. It was a brush wolf, hunting along the water's edge.

The young woman came alongside me. She looked a little like Caroline. "They follow a trail we can't see. He isn't mine, I'm just taking him for a walk. He thinks we're hunting, though." Her laughter sounded nervous.

Then I was on Queen Street, a block or two from the beach, on the sidewalk, looking across the street at a store selling coffee beans. On the overhang of the roof, a young woman sat smoking a cigarette, purse in hand, legs crossed demurely. She watched the traffic, especially the passing streetcars. She looked up and saw me staring at her across the street.

She laughed. "I think he got on the streetcar. He's just a brush wolf, after all. I told him he ought to exercise more."

"Where—?" I began.

"Is Caroline?" she finished. "Damned if I know, I just walk them."

I woke up. The alarm clock read 5:30, but it was obviously day already, thanks to the August sunlight. I peeked through the curtain. My car was still parked where I'd left it. So far so good. I told my paranoia to reconsider trying to convince me that the dream had been a harbinger of a shift to another world. My paranoia deferred comment.

After dressing and shaving, I went out and checked the trunk. The gear I'd bought for the Kluane trip was still there, but my desire to go had abated.

Bernie had asked me to notice the differences and similarities between this world and mine. It seemed like a job to do—so why not do it seriously? I could pick up a laptop in Whitehorse—at the Chilcoot Centre, a shopping mall.

Then what? Well, to tell Bernie about differences, I'd have to visit places I'd been to "back home," in my world. It wouldn't be a hardship—I'd visited Banff and been to Vancouver. So, south—then I could even cross the border into the States and head toward California. After that, who knows?

I felt better. My new work wasn't "real" work, just make-work, but it would be useful to Bernie. And it might keep me from thinking about Caroline all the time.

25 # SOUTH

Only a few memories of my grandfather are really mine. This one is. I'm very young, and my grandfather, my mother, and I are sitting at the kitchen table eating supper at the end of a warm summer day. Through the kitchen window I can see storm clouds approaching from the west.

"It's going to rain," I say.

My grandfather looks up from his plate, as does my mother. I'm so young that they've never before heard me draw conclusions about the weather. My mother smiles.

My grandfather answers, "Yes, but the really big storms come over the lake. From the east."

"From over there," my mother adds, pointing away from the window. "Where the sun comes up."

"Why?" I ask.

"That's just how it works," my grandfather says. Apparently the *why* of forecasting systems wasn't especially important to him.

Today his words could seem brusque, as if he'd grown tired of me and my questions. But when I was a child, we didn't have weather satellites or made-for-TV animations of weather fronts. It was a time of faith in simpler explanations.

My grandfather never got to see any photographs of the earth from space; and he never needed to abandon his theory of weather for something less magical.

#

After leaving Whitehorse, I retraced my original route. By late afternoon, I was back at Watson Lake. I stopped beside the famed forest of signs, more than ten thousand of them, hand-lettered by visitors. Erected on posts, each sign pointed the way to a traveller's home, most providing the distance as well. I walked for some time in the sign forest.

Of course, I didn't put up a sign of my own. Where would it point, and in what units could I express the distance?

One week and a thousand miles later, I was in Vancouver.

#

The north-to-south trip through British Columbia was a revelation. Here, as the *Britannica* revealed, the 1918 Spanish flu had killed three out of every four people. In the space of one year, the world's population fell from a couple of billion to five hundred million, the same population as in Shakespeare's time. In the trenches of World War I, the death toll from the flu topped ninety percent. The war to end all wars ended, not because of the military intervention of the United States, but because the Spanish flu destroyed the armies.

One consequence was that the Alaska Highway wasn't built in the early 1940s, as in my world, but in the late 1970s, and even then, it wasn't finished. Part of the route I followed from Whitehorse to Vancouver, through Fort Nelson to Fort St. John and Williams Lake, was basically a dirt-and-stones trail. At Hope, the asphalt reappeared. The Corolla's undercarriage stopped sounding like I'd run over a punk rock drummer from a steel drum band, and settled back into playing classical timpani.

On the plus side, from those bad roads, I saw a landscape full of crispness and defined edges, features my world had lost to air pollution. Here, the air was clean, still fresh and pure. Remove most of the human race and if you're one of those still standing, you can breathe the air without chewing it first. That's just how things work.

26 # VANCOUVER

I'd kept Bernie up-to-date on my travels until I hit all the dirt roads. So once I was in Vancouver, I sent him a catch-up email with some data I thought he'd find interesting.

Hi, Bernie:

Vancouver has come as a surprise. For one thing, the housing is affordable. In my world, a modest three-bedroom bungalow costs as much as a dozen nice cars. It's less than a third that amount here. The other surprise? Most of Old Chinatown still exists. The high-rise buildings, parks, museums, and redevelopment that came in the 1970s in my world never happened here. Some of the old houses, from the early 1900s, still stand, though they're mostly unoccupied. The old neighbourhoods are a shambles, however. I feel like I've travelled back in time several decades.

In contrast, some parts of downtown are delightful. It's possible to drive and sightsee simultaneously. In my world, you'd be dead behind the wheel in a few minutes. Talk about aggressive drivers! Incidentally, have you ever heard the term "road rage?"

Last night I drove to the campus of Simon Fraser University up on Burnaby Mountain. I wasn't sure it would exist. Several years ago, Darlene and I spent time in Vancouver, and I felt certain that my memories would still be fairly accurate. As I told you during one of our talks, I'm not the man I was. The view from the top of Burnaby Mountain is still spectacular, but the Vancouver we visited was much larger. Here, the bordering towns aren't run together like warm urban ice cream. They're still towns, separated by substantial tracts of undeveloped land.

One interesting fact: my hotel has a welcome package—you know, full of information on how to escape from the motel in case of fire, how to find the pool if you can't. It also has a short history of Vancouver, which didn't mention the 1886 conflagration that destroyed most of the city. I guess that it didn't happen—though perhaps after a hundred years or so, it doesn't matter. Most of a city like Vancouver is apt to be newer than that.

By the way, have you found out anything yet about our missing star? Will I be whisked off soon to some other world?

Another thought: I know that neither Caroline nor Rey will appear here, but is it possible that Rey could send someone in his place? What do you think?

David

Ten minutes later I received Bernie's reply.

Last question first. It's possible. Watch your back. And to save you the trouble of asking: no, I don't know how it could happen. But remember, in the multiverse, if something isn't forbidden, it's possible—however improbable it may be.

The star, by the way, seems to have existed until a few million years ago. In its place is now a black hole, lots of high-energy radiation, the usual. Fortunately, the mass of the hole is approximately equal to the mass of the star—good news for the equations that describe the stability of the universe. It appears that my world isn't likely to blink away any time soon. Tentatively, the schedule calls for the sun to blink first. It'll swallow the earth four or five billion years from now, long before anything else big happens.

As for your personal situation, that's more complex. You might want to talk to a man I know at Simon Fraser. His name is Kunal Raj Singh. He has two doctorates, one in astrophysics and the other in philosophy. I'll let him know you may drop in. If you decide to see him, bring him some tea—real tea from India. Also, don't try to contact him in any way. There's a reason for this. Just go see him. And don't forget that to everyone, you're Richard Glendenning, not David Williamson.

Don't worry about deleting this email from your laptop. It'll do that all by itself, just like the others.

Bernie

PS. Sorry for all the don'ts.

I had to laugh. Long ago and far, far away, I'd taught another Bernie to avoid unnecessary repetition of any expression in a research paper. This Bernie's apology was for that Bernie, delivered by someone I'd never taught to someone who'd never taught him. Bernie would have thought all that out as he added his postscript. As for the tea from India, my guess was that it would identify me as the "genuine" Richard Glendenning to

Dr. Singh.

At the university's information kiosk the next morning, I found Parking Lot B and the TASC2 building. Dr. Singh opened his door at my knock. He sported a neatly trimmed salt-and-pepper beard and moustache. With his dark blue turban, he wore attire from a movie—white shirt, conservative blue tie, black sports coat, and trousers.

After I introduced myself, he said, "I understand you have brought me some tea, Mr. Glendenning."

I held it out. "Yes."

"From China?"

"India."

"Very kind of you." He placed the package on top of a pile of papers, then turned to me. "Do you walk?"

"Walk?"

"Yes. Do you enjoy walking?"

"Yes." I expected that this was the right answer.

It was. "Let's go for a walk, then. I'll show you the campus."

Outside the building we cut across the campus, then crossed the ring-road to a walking path. We strolled through a bit of forest and then, suddenly, the forest gave way to an open area with a beautiful view across Burrard Inlet.

"This is Burrard Mountain Park," Dr. Singh explained. "They tell me they're planning to build a restaurant near here."

"Nice location."

"Come look at the sculptures." We headed toward the Ainu sculptures that made up the Playground of the Gods. He pointed at the totem poles. "They look indigenous to North America but they're actually Japanese." Then, "Bernie tells me you have a question."

I stopped walking. "Several, actually. What has he told you about me and my, uh, situation?"

"Everything he knows. It's most interesting. Had anyone but Bernie told me such a story, I wouldn't have believed him. As you're undoubtedly aware, though, Bernie is incapable of lying. What would you like to know?"

"I want—I want to know what's happening to me."

"That's not an easy task." He pointed at the sculptures. "What do you see there?"

"Totem poles." Atop each of the dozens of poles sat a figure—a bear, an owl, a whale. "Carved by the artist and his son, right?"

"Yes. But the bear, for instance, isn't a real bear. It's a representation of a bear, an image, a likeness. And what is this likeness made of?"

I felt as if I were in a class. "Wood."

He nodded. "If we could look at this wood closely, so closely that we could see the carbon atoms of which it is made, what would we see?"

"Isn't there mostly just empty space between the atoms? How could we see—?"

Dr. Singh's raised hand stopped me. "The wood wouldn't look like wood anymore, would it?" He gave me an impish smile. Bernie must have told him about the lesson on repetition. "In fact, just as the carving of a bear is not a real bear, the wood we see is a representation to our eyes of something that's quite different at a deeper level." He paused. "It's a *metaphor* for wood. And the atoms are themselves metaphors. They're made of subatomic particles so difficult for us to imagine that we gave them names like *strange* and *charm* and *bottom*. More metaphors. Below them, at a level of reality that is completely unlike our own, there may be superstrings and God—or, perhaps something else entirely. So what, then, are you, Mr. Glendenning?"

I considered my answer carefully. "A metaphor of me."

"Well done. I believe it was Vonnegut who said that science is magic that works. I'm an astrophysicist, as you know, and Bernie is an authority on quantum computing. I tell you frankly that ninety-nine percent of the time I have no idea what he's talking about. And when I ask him to consider a problem in astrophysics or, worse yet, in philosophy, his eyes glaze over. Each of us takes the other's knowledge on faith. When we talk, we use metaphors that we hope help the other person understand what we really mean."

I looked at the sculptures again—solid to my eyes. But I knew what he meant.

Dr. Singh went on, "Bernie believes that the next big thing in computing will be a unified system that lets scientists of all sorts work together. 'Academic networking,' he calls it. It sounds like the computer world's equivalent of scientists going to a bar for drinks after work, to share their half-baked ideas and fully cooked metaphors. He thinks that letting down our hair in an informal environment, where ideas and personalities can mingle more easily, will help science advance much more quickly. He thinks the highly structured system of conferences and papers and university-based research projects is too constraining. He may be on to something really useful. It may work. But I think it's more likely to be just another way in which we geeks entertain ourselves."

I bit my tongue. "In TV's early days, it was thought of as an educational tool. Of course, its potential for entertainment took over."

"Pandora's box." He glanced at his watch. "I need to get back for class." We started back toward the university. After a few minutes, he stopped. "Mr. Glendenning, I don't know—I can't know—why you travel between worlds. The astrophysicist in me can't explain it; the philosopher is at a loss for words. But this is what I believe. What happens to you is meaningful. It is not random happenstance. Despite my earlier suggestions, I feel strongly that this metaphor of you also contains real substance. I think you'll learn at some point how to control, a little, what happens to you."

"It sure doesn't feel that way."

Singh chuckled. "Do you believe in atoms, Mr. Glendenning?"

"Yes." I didn't know where this was leading.

"Even without having seen one, felt one?"

"Yes."

"And what of quarks? Do you believe that atoms are built of them?"

"I suppose so."

"And the immense space between the nucleus and the electron. Do you believe in such an emptiness?"

"Yes."

"What about strings and superstrings?"

"I'm not sure."

"Me neither, but they seem to be good enough metaphors for now." He paused. "Mr. Glendenning, we've been walking a while. We've travelled some distance, have we not?"

I looked around. "Yes."

"Don't you find it odd, that when you rise from your chair and walk across a room, all these atoms, these quarks, and who knows what else— maybe even fuzzy little violins—get up and walk across the room as well? The astrophysicist in me can't explain how this is possible. I can't even determine where I begin and end. The philosopher can't help. In the end, we're like clouds, Mr. Glendenning. We look solid, but up close we're insubstantial. We're made of magic—magic that works."

As we neared his building, Dr. Singh asked, "Are you planning to stay in Vancouver?"

"Perhaps." I hadn't really thought about it either way.

"Go south, instead. Go where you've never been. Look around with eyes that see only the *reality* of this world. Open yourself to it."

"Open myself."

"I'm from India, Mr. Glendenning. What do you expect me to say?"

I laughed. "Dr. Singh, what's the significance of the tea? Was it some kind of test?"

"Oh, no. I just don't get away from campus often, and I'd run out of tea."

We walked the rest of the way in silence. Outside his building, I thanked him for taking the time to talk to me. Then I headed south.

27 # BORDERLINE

The first thing I noticed at the Canada-USA border was a big nothing where the Peace Arch should be. The man who'd built it in 1921, Sam Hill, had been a casualty of the Spanish flu in this world. With his death, the expression, "What the Sam Hill!" died too, even though it had nothing to do with him or anyone else named Sam Hill.

It's amazing what you can find out if you have a laptop, access to a search engine, and some curiosity.

It's also amazing how easy it is to get into the United States on one of Bernie's passports. Because there was no lineup, I was in Blaine, on the other side of the border, in less than ten minutes.

I-5 took me south past Custer and Ferndale, then into Bellingham, where I pulled off the interstate and drove around until I saw a sign for the Scandinavian Motel. The word *Restaurant* hung slightly askew below the motel's name. The main door was flanked by two enormous wooden Scandinavian loggers, created by an artist who had abandoned hammer, chisel, and riffler rasp in favour of a chainsaw.

Inside the office, the clerk greeted me. "Canadian, eh?"

"Ja." We didn't parry further.

Lunch/supper was a Big Sven, Scandifries and *kaffe*. The *kaffe* explained why I was the only patron there at three in the afternoon. No double-doubling could turn it into real coffee. I spent the rest of the day in my room watching TV and prowling this world with laptop and various search engines. I doubted that Dr. Singh would have approved of the way I chose to "open myself" to the experiences of this world, but I needed the break.

Early next morning, I headed south once more. I knew where I wanted to go. The interstate took me past Mount Vernon and Arlington to Marysville, in search of family. I'd once had some in Lake Stevens.

The little Lake Stevens that lends its name to the town is shaped like Africa. Downtown is on the north side of the lake (think Somalia), but every square inch of the shoreline is taken up by housing—small cottages, enormous three-story dwellings, old buildings on decaying timber foundations, new structures on level concrete pads. In the downtown section, some streets are actually parallel, but for the rest, the curving lakeshore, hills, and watercourses determine the road direction and shape. It takes a long time for a newcomer to figure out which routes take you where.

People who live in Lake Stevens usually work elsewhere—Everett, even Seattle. The town has morphed from a recreation area to a bedroom community, with boats and water-skiers. The little farms once outside town are now mostly inside it, and people raise children, not livestock. Still, a short distance from the lake, you'll see plenty of places with small barns, some horses or goats, even lamas and alpacas.

The smaller communities a few miles away are full of big box stores, landscaping enterprises, and giant sporting goods establishments. And if you like to gamble, you can find half a dozen casinos within a half-hour drive.

On my home world, my father's brother lived in Lake Stevens. I'd visited five or six times—a time or two when both my uncle and aunt were alive, once when only my aunt was left, and a few times later to see their daughter, Samantha, and Samantha's husband, Gary. After my aunt died, they'd built a new house behind my aunt's old home.

In this world, I didn't want to visit them—not as this version of myself, whom they didn't know. I certainly didn't want to walk in looking like the doppelganger of someone who might be sitting at their kitchen table. I wanted to drive by my aunt's house to see if it was still there.

Truthfully, I just wanted something to be the same as in my birth world.

I got onto Lakeshore Drive—every place with a lake has a road with that name—and turned up Purple Pennant Road, then angled to the right at Nyden Farms Road and slowed down. The house wasn't there. The neighbours' places on either side were there, but the land between them sat vacant, except for the stand of mature pines. I stopped, engine running.

I tried to remember the house: concrete block foundation, Insulbrick siding, single-pane windows, green trim. It was hard, like trying to make out the tune of music coming from so far away that you hear only the bass notes. I could remember my aunt's general appearance, but not her face.

Often, when I lose a word I find it by "hunting" for the first sound in the word or for its first few letters. It's as if my mind stores words alphabetically, just as it stores them in pairs of opposites and by rhymes. If I find the "ghost" of the word, the word entire soon pops into place.

I tried hunting for my aunt's face by finding its pieces. I knew she had blue eyes, and a round face.

But it was no use. In this world, I had no aunt. It felt, to me, that she'd never been born. My uncle had never found her, or loved her, because she'd never existed. He hadn't cleared away most of the pines to build that first house for her on this lot. They hadn't raised a family here.

In the car, I began to weep at the loss of what had never been. When I was emptied of tears, I sat for a while in a dull stupor before I left.

From the vacant lot on North Nyden Farms Road, I drove into downtown Lake Stevens, found a window seat at a restaurant, and ordered a sandwich and coffee. While I waited, I looked out the window.

Caroline came out of a clothing store across the street.

I couldn't move. I could hardly breathe. Caroline. She glanced at the restaurant and headed toward it—toward me. She came in and sat at the small table just ahead of mine, her back to me. The server went to her table almost immediately.

"Coffee," Caroline said. "And a slice of that lemon meringue pie you save for your *special* customers." She smiled at the waitress.

"Sure thing, Robyn," the waitress said.

Robyn? I looked at Caroline's cheek, her hair, the way she sat. She looked exactly like Caroline, even though her accent was Washington State, not Canadian. Bernie had searched records in both countries, and he hadn't found her. I didn't know what to do.

The server brought my sandwich and coffee.

"Refills are free. Just catch my eye. I'll give you the check now, no rush, pay me when you're ready." She went to Caroline's table. "You doing anything special tonight?"

"No. Why?"

"I was thinking of heading over to Tulalip and donating some of my tips to the casino."

"Sounds like a plan," Caroline said. "Pick me up?"

"Sure. Maybe seven or so?"

"Done deal, no heels."

"No heels on the floor, no heels at the door," the server said. "Just you and me and comfortable shoes."

They laughed and the server went to refill coffee cups.

I had to know who this Caroline was. I walked over to her table. She looked even more like Caroline from the front. "Excuse me," I said. "I saw you come in. I heard the server call you Robyn, but you look a lot like a woman I know named Caroline. You don't have a sister by that name, by any chance?"

"No." There was some suspicion in her voice. "Nice name, though. I'd have picked it if I'd had the choice. When people hear Robyn they think I'm saying the bird. In grade school I used my middle name, Sandra, but I got over that before I went to high school." She looked at me closely. "I don't think we'd have gone to high school at the same time."

"No, I'm a little older. My name's Rick, and if we'd met at high school, it would have been in Canada."

"I thought you sounded different. I was in Canada once. Victoria."

"Nice place."

"Yes."

I couldn't make myself continue the conversation. "Look, I'm sorry to bother you. The resemblance—it's really remarkable. Nice to meet you." I went back to my table as the server brought Robyn her coffee and pie.

I finished off my own sandwich, gulped down coffee, and left.

Caroline—Robyn—was not the Caroline that I knew. She wasn't one of the other Carolines, either. She didn't seem to have a Rey in her life, and certainly no David. I was a complete stranger to her and could be nothing else. In this world, someone had drawn a line that couldn't be crossed, a border for which I carried no passport. Here, on this side of the line, our lives didn't touch—had never touched.

And yet. How odd. As the movie says, of all the restaurants in all the worlds, she'd walked into this one.

Robyn and the server were going to the casino in Tulalip tonight. Absurdly, I decided to check it out. Perhaps one of the Reys would be there. *She might be in danger*, I told myself. It was a completely foolish thought. She was in no danger whatsoever. I just wanted to ... I don't know what.

#

The drive to Tulalip took less than fifteen minutes. In the casino, a set of totem poles stood in the center of the lobby. According to the explanations, at the top of the Story Pole, an eagle folded its wings around a creature with the head of a wolf and the body of a man. The creature symbolized all living things, human and wild, and the process of their transformation. It told the story of a time when humans and animals spoke the same language and shared the same culture.

A memory hung just beyond my ability to call it forth. *What the hell had drawn me to the casino? It had been a mistake to come.* A conviction grew that something dangerous was going to happen—not to Robyn, but to me.

I was just about to leave when I remembered the dream—the jogger in Toronto at the beach, who'd said, "Look for the signs." And the woman on the roof, who looked like Caroline, had said something about the brush wolf and the streetcar. Here I stood in a place I had no reason to be, looking at a pole topped with the animal of my fevered dream.

Dr. Singh would have loved this moment. He'd tell me to open myself. As if it all meant something.

"Drink?"

I hadn't seen the hostess approach. "Thanks, but no."

"Magnificent, isn't it? I see it every day, and every day I find something different in it." She stared up at it.

"What do you see today?"

"Today?" She thought for a moment. "Today my feet are hurting because of the heels they make me wear, and one of my kids has a fever and I'm worried about that, and all the lights and the sounds in the casino make this whole place seem unreal. I'm tired and I've got hours to go yet. Today, the totem is something solid, made of wood by someone who had something to say. It's the most important thing in this whole place."

"Wasn't there a sculptor who said he never made anything out of stone? He just chipped away to let what was inside it get out?"

"Michelangelo. He'd have liked this. Let me know if you change your mind." She left.

I looked up at the totem again. *Metaphor,* Dr. Singh had said. Was the wolf turning into a man, or the man into a wolf? Would the transformation end up with a complete wolf *and* a complete man? Or was the transformation complete already, the creature in its final form, neither this nor that?

In my dream, when I asked the woman on the roof where Caroline was, she'd said, "Damned if I know. I just walk them." *Them.*

28 # BRUSH WOLF

I decided not to stay overnight in Lake Stevens. I knew myself well enough to know that if I did, I'd try to get to know the Robyn-Caroline from the restaurant. Which, I also knew, would not be a good idea. The woman was, for me, a simulacrum of the real one, and neither of us would be good for the other. So that evening, I left town.

Maybe it was the wooden canoe outside the entrance of the casino. Maybe it was the sense that, at the ocean, change is the norm. Maybe simply because I'd never been to Ocean Shores. In any case, I wanted the water, the big expanse of the Pacific. I headed south, through Seattle and Tacoma, which hadn't stitched themselves together in this world. Then on to Olympia, Aberdeen, and Hoquiam, each smaller than the place before.

Ocean Shores—especially by the standards of this universe—was a surprisingly robust tourist community sitting on a long strip of sand. I expected something less commercial, more stripped down. I drove south along Point Brown Avenue past bars, antique shops, galleries, restaurants, hot dog stands and homes; then I angled onto Discovery Drive which, I discovered, became Marine View Drive and took me north before it meandered into Ocean Shores Boulevard. At last, I found a respectable-looking, newer franchise motel.

"Any rooms left?" I asked the clerk.

He tapped a few keys on his computer and nodded without looking at me. "Ground floor or second?"

"Do you have non-smoking?"

"Yes."

"Non-smoking, please, on the second floor."

"Sorry, the only non-smoking room is on the ground floor. That okay?" He was forced to look up because I had decided to simply nod until he did.

"That's fine," I said, to reward him. When he finished the paperwork, I asked, "How do I get to the beach from here?"

"Go north, and when you get to West Chance a La Mer turn left. You can drive on the beach and park pretty much wherever you want. Continental breakfast," he continued as if it somehow pertained to the beach, "is from six to nine in the Pirate's Hall." He pointed to a small open area behind me, its wall-mounted screen tuned to a golf channel.

"You play golf?"

"No, but a lot of our patrons do. Hope you enjoy your stay with us at Knightside."

I'd been dismissed.

West Chance a La Mer was right where he'd said it would be. I drove onto the beach, where several hundred vehicles of all kinds sat in half a dozen crooked lines. It reminded me of pictures of Dominion Day celebrations in Port Arthur in the 1930s, when crowds of people who had no money to spend gathered at Boulevard Lake to meet friends and have picnics.

North and south of where I'd left the asphalt for sand, the lines amalgamated, thinned, broke into sporadic clusters of cars and trucks, and then became widely spaced individual vehicles. I drove until I had a long stretch of beach to myself, then I got out. From my stash of camping equipment, I fetched a folding lawn chair and sat watching the waves break on the beach.

In spite of my desire for the neverending vista of the Pacific Ocean, I've never been fully comfortable on an ocean beach. No matter how sunny and warm things are, no matter how far I can see, I always think about an approaching tsunami. When I drive toward a beach I note where the high ground is, in case I have to head for the hills. Most of the time I can control my fear, but when I find myself paying undue attention to the beach balls and surfboards, I know it's time to leave. I don't like being the kind of person who'd wrestle a beach ball away from some kid when a wave comes in and I need a life preserver.

I kept my tsunami-watching paranoia more or less under control, and then the woman and her dog came by. I saw the dog first—I couldn't help it. It had legs like a small pony and weighed at least a hundred and fifty pounds. Its steel-grey body was easily as tall as I was—then again, I was sitting in the lawn chair. Its massive chest and grizzled, rough-hewn head gave it an aura of power. It bounded along the water's edge like a greyhound, then stopped suddenly where a wave retreated to sniff at something left behind, then doubled back to its owner, who jogged determinedly along the beach.

Most dogs are single-minded when they find something to play with. Not this dog. When it saw me, it charged.

"Clarence! Stop!" the woman yelled.

The dog stopped and sat on its haunches a few feet away, looking down at me. I tried to look as unthreatening as possible. I couldn't remember if that meant looking a homicidal dog in the eyes or playing corpse-in-a-chair. I chose to look at the owner as she approached.

"Sorry about that. I hope Clarence didn't frighten you." She was trim and fit, younger than Caroline, one of those early-thirties women who make all their sentences end with a gravelly drop in tone.

"No." However, I noticed that my hands had gone, of their own accord, to guard the family jewels. As casually as I could, I moved my arms onto the armrests.

"Okay." She spoke to Clarence. The dog got off its haunches and padded slowly toward me, nose first.

"Jesus, he's big."

"Irish Wolfhound. Diana."

"You called him Clarence."

"He's Clarence. I'm Diana."

"Yes, of course. Sorry. I'm—" For a second I couldn't remember if I was supposed to say Richard or David. "Richard Glendenning."

"Pleased to meet you, Richard. It's okay to pat him. He doesn't bite. He's just a puppy and he likes to be petted."

If this dog wanted to be petted, I decided, I'd pet it. Clarence's fur felt coarse.

"Wolfhounds were used to hunt wolves, weren't they?" That used up all the knowledge I had about wolfhounds.

"In packs. His owner told me once that they were used in warfare, too, against the Romans or something. He isn't mine, by the way—I'm walking him for a friend. Clarence thinks we're hunting, though. It's weird—like following a trail humans can't see."

She laughed a little nervously, then asked the dog, "You're hunting now, aren't you?" He looked at her curiously, not quite sure what he was supposed to do.

She turned back to me. "Wolfhounds were pretty well extinct by 1800 or so, but those left were bred with Great Danes, Mastiffs and Deerhounds, tailor-made to look like the original Wolfhounds but without the aggressiveness. Clarence here is really good with children. Aren't you,

Clarence?"

The dog looked at her, glanced at the water, then returned to staring at her face.

I said, "I think he wants to go back to hunting."

"Okay, Clarence." The dog bounded off. "He loves running with other dogs when there are some around—plus pretending to be a brush wolf hunting ferocious shellfish."

I laughed.

"Been nice talking to you. See you on the return trip." She started off after the dog.

For a while I watched her running along after Clarence. Then I closed my eyes for a moment. That was a mistake.

I woke because the sun, which had been gently lowering itself into the blue-green water of the Pacific, had suddenly disappeared. Cold air, along with the crash of waves, shocked me awake. The sun hadn't set, but it had gone behind low, dark clouds. The wind, stronger now, blew in gusts off the ocean. I shivered. It was time to go.

I folded the lawn chair and put it in the trunk, then got in behind the wheel.

As I reached for the armrest to pull the door closed, something hit the door with the force of a brawler's kick and slammed it shut.

I saw a snarling face at the window, paws scrabbling at the door. This wasn't Clarence, a pretender to the title of Wolfhound. This dog was the real thing, the beast that made the Roman centurions flee. Its thick leather collar had inward-facing metal spikes.

I looked beyond the teeth to see Diana, the dog-walker, running toward the car—carrying a leash made of chain. She clipped the leash to his collar and yanked him away. She mouthed "Sorry" as the dog snarled and barked. As I watched, she pushed down on his hindquarters to force him into a sitting position. After a second or two, she shouted "Home!" They headed along the beach, the dog trotting beside her obediently.

I drove slowly across the beach to West Chance a La Mer and the Knightside Motel on Ocean Shores Boulevard. As I passed Diana and the dog she waved.

I raised a hand in reply, a little too late for her to see it. My mind was on Bernie's credit card. I hoped it still worked in this new world.

29 # POP

Human beings are born with the gift of adaptation. Those of us who live in the year 2000-and-something know that what we become, or what we try to become, will be nothing like our "destiny" would have been in the year 1600-something, when just staying alive was a hard-scrabble fight.

We have the freedom to grow, to learn. Our brains recognize the world's dangers and rewards. They let us remember things, and they allow us to make other people's experiences our own. With some effort, we can learn to anticipate—we can read about the past and extrapolate a future from the patterns we see.

The point is, what we are is a very *fluid* thing. But I found that nothing prepared me for jumping from world to world. When you jump from universe to universe, you leave home as one person and arrive elsewhere as mostly the person you were when you left, but with bits of someone else attached.

It takes a long time to learn to cope with that person's unique talents, and use what that person knows.

#

As I drove along the beach, I felt more *fear* than simple *worry* about the credit card. Somehow I knew I'd awakened in one of the "harsh worlds" where the milk of human kindness was in short supply. Mostly, I was afraid that it was a world that included a Rey but not a Caroline. That would be hell.

The desk clerk addressed me as "Mr. Williamson," and my credit card worry returned in full force. Apparently, I was Richard Glendenning no longer. I decided not to check the name on the card in front of the clerk. Instead, I nodded and smiled and went to my room. The key card in my pocket didn't work. I went back to the lobby.

"Could you re-key this for my room?" I asked. "It doesn't seem to work anymore."

"Sure. Happens all the time." He took the key card and, within a minute, handed it back. "I forgot to tell you, a man came in and asked about you. I told him you were at the beach. Did you run into him?"

"No." I kept my voice casual. "Fairly big fellow, dark hair, forty or so? Canadian accent?"

"Sounds like him."

How long ago had I been on the beach? Ten minutes? I didn't have much time. I tried the key card again, and it worked. I repacked my belongings and stowed my case in the back, behind the passenger seat.

I came back into the lobby, trying not to hurry. "Something's come up," I told the desk clerk. "I won't be staying."

"No problem, sir. I'll charge you for the time spent, how's that?"

"Fine."

It took forever for him to complete the checkout process. When the time came to pay, I found I could pay in cash. I hoped that the bills weren't different from normal.

"Credit card's in my luggage." I handed over the money.

"Yes sir." He counted the cash and filled out the receipt.

I headed for the car. My heart pounded and my face was flushed, but I kept my walk under control. I headed for West Chance a La Mer. I needed to get out of town and onto Highway 12. What would Rey expect me to do?

To escape from him, the logical thing would be to take different roads at random. However, even in my new multiverse without the extra-virulent Spanish flu, this part of Washington State wasn't highly populated. Roads, especially ones that led somewhere useful, were few and far between. If I could get to Aberdeen, a town of about 17,000 people, I could hide out for a while.

But Aberdeen was a choke point. Only a few roads led in and out, and most crossed bridges. If I went fifty miles farther, to Olympia, I'd have a wider choice of escape routes. And that's exactly the choice Rey would expect. So I went with Aberdeen.

An hour later I sat inside the car, inside a rental storage shed, in Aberdeen. Absurdly, I felt fairly secure. Rey could drive every street in the town and check every motel parking lot, but he'd never find my car. I had no idea how he'd known to look for me in Ocean Shores, and that bothered the hell out of me. But if it was mental telepathy, I now wore the biggest metal hat of all time, and I was equipped with a submarine sandwich, a couple of bottles of water, and the camping gear in the trunk.

It was dark inside Unit 4, but I wouldn't turn on lights. Someone might notice that the shed door wasn't locked. From a few dozen feet away, it looked shut. But if Rey found me, he could flip up the door and walk in. So, in the dark, I tipped back the Corolla's seat and napped.

When I woke up, my wristwatch told me my nap had lasted nine hours. The shed was uncomfortably hot. I felt like a dog trapped in a car with the windows rolled up on a sunny day. Light leaked into the shed — from underneath the door, from spaces between the walls, ceiling, and floors, and through a random spray of odd holes in the door and rear wall. Bullet holes? It was time to go.

I got out of the car and rolled up the shed door. I wasn't prepared for the brightness outside—or for the woman who stood, arms crossed over her chest, in front of me. I shaded my eyes.

"It's about time you showed up," she said.

"Caroline!" It was all I could think to say.

"How did I get here?" she prompted. "Where have I been? Is that what you want to know?"

"How did you find me?"

"That's for another time, which we don't have much of now. As to how I got here, well, I drove. Right now, the important thing is to get away from here. We have to go south, but the Reys will be looking for us."

"Rey was here yesterday, looking for me at the motel after I fell asleep."

"On the beach. I was very impressed with the way you handled the snarling dog, by the way."

"You saw that?"

"I've been following you."

"Following me." I was turning into an echo.

"It's a long story. But not now. Get in the car and unlock the passenger door."

"Right." We got in the car and I drove slowly out of the shed. When I had cleared the door, Caroline had me stop.

"Pull ahead a bit so my car can get past—I'll leave it in the shed." She got out and a minute later pulled up in a nondescript green import. We rushed it in.

I got back in my car. Caroline was already in the passenger seat.

Caroline was here! Yesterday, I'd been almost certain that I'd never see her again, but here she was. I didn't want to consider that this Caroline might not be the one I knew, but I couldn't help it.

Instead of asking about it, I said, "How did Rey find me?"

"It's a long story. But first, think of him as *a* Rey, not *the* Rey." We headed off, and she gave me directions. "Go right at Simpson Avenue. That'll put us on 101. Keep following the signs. We'll cross a bridge and then head south." She was silent and seemed to gather her thoughts.

"*A* Rey," I prompted.

"Yes. He's not as ... fully formed, I guess, as the one who killed our doubles. Rey, the real Rey, is extraordinarily powerful. He can sense where you are if you appear in a world where the laws of probability allow you to be." She laughed a little. "You know, I hate cleaning, but I'd much rather be cleaning the house than talking about this stuff."

I was supposed to laugh, too, so I did.

She seemed to relax. "Anyway, if he senses you, he makes the Rey that's in your world come after you. If it's possible to send more than one Rey, he does. I don't know how he does that. He can, so he does."

"Caroline." I had to ask but didn't know how.

"Am I *the* Caroline, *your* Caroline? Is that what you want to know?"

I could only nod. Luckily, I was driving, so I didn't have to look her in the eyes.

After a time, she said, "I don't know." It was her turn to feel uncomfortable. "Are you *my* David?"

I waited a moment to see what felt like the truth, but I didn't know. "Close enough? Let's go with that."

"Deal. I'm sure we'll know at some point. A bridge is coming. Stay on 101."

"Where are we going?"

"Portland."

"Oregon?"

"We'll stick close to the coast. That's the safest route. The Rey who's after you will assume that we'll be on I-5. When he can't catch up to us, he'll think we're *behind* him and try to intercept us at the Castle Rock. When we don't show up, he'll head for Portland. He knows we're going there."

"He knows?" *But I don't?*

She nodded but didn't explain. "Try to relax. It's a lovely trip. The scenery, especially on Highway 4, is spectacular."

"You've made this trip before?"

"No, I just know. One of me was here as a young girl long ago."

I understood.

30 # MEANWHILE

We said little until we were far from Aberdeen, south-bound on Highway 101. I focused on the traffic; Caroline seemed preoccupied with her own thoughts.

At last, I broke the silence. "Back at the farmhouse, with Rey, what happened?"

"That's a long time ago. Weeks. More than a month. It was awful. After he broke into the motel and kidnapped me, he forced me into the trunk of the car. Out at the family farm, he put me in the cold cellar."

"Cold cellar?"

"Farm girl talk. At the side of the house there was a second cellar with a door to the outside. Back in the 1920s, when the farmhouse was built, people stored potatoes and such in cold cellars."

"Oh, a root cellar. The doors opened from the top, right?"

"Yes. So back to the farm—he locked me in the cold cellar. It was dark, musty, and full of spider webs and the smell of mildew and rot."

"Nice."

"I knew he wanted me to scream, so I didn't. If our doubles were on the way, I worried screaming might make them—especially David—do something hasty. So I kept quiet."

"Rey told me he killed them," I said.

"He didn't. He lies, remember?"

"I know. They're the ones who took care of me for a week."

"Okay, so you're in the motel...."

"Battered, concussed, confused, and confounded. Nose broken. Awake long enough to do some emergency repairs on myself and lie down on the bed."

"So while I was in the cold cellar, you took a snooze."

"Involuntarily." I fast-forwarded in my head, preferring not to remember the injuries. "David and his Caroline showed up. We hatched the plan to free you. It even had a high-tech component, radios."

"Fancy." She sounded more amused than impressed.

"Yes. Caroline had overheard Rey say he was going to take you to the farm, so that's where we went that evening. I stayed in the car, because I couldn't move, and David and Caroline headed for the farmhouse."

"And Rey?"

"He showed up at the car." I described briefly how he'd beaten me up with a flashlight. From the corner of my eye, I could see Caroline wince. "Anyway, sometime during the beating he told me you'd got away and he'd killed the other David and Caroline."

"That's kind of funny." She seemed thoughtful. "Sorry, not the beating. But the rest, about me getting away, he accidentally told you the truth. It's not that hard to escape from a cold cellar. After I knew he was gone, I pushed up on the old doors, and they came off at the hinges. Then I ran like hell."

I laughed. "Speaking of high-tech, he showed me this gizmo, a tracking device. He'd planted bugs on us. Mine was in my wallet. I have no idea where yours was. He could see you on this screen. You were a fair distance from the farmhouse, then suddenly you weren't. Anywhere."

"Let's come back to that. What happened to you?"

"He got really pissed off when you disappeared. He whacked me so hard the flashlight broke. It was suddenly dark as hell, so I rolled away from him. Then he sort of lost interest in me. Hey." I was puzzled. "Does even Rey, *the* Rey, the *main* Rey have a boss?"

"What? Why?"

"Well, maybe he was *ordered* to keep you alive. He's sadistic, and he's evil, but he's nobody's fool."

"Huh." After a moment, Caroline added, "I don't think so."

"It's not just Rey that wants you; it's somebody else, too."

"Nope."

"How do you know that?"

Silence. I tried again. "Maybe *boss* isn't the right word. Maybe *Alpha Rey* is closer. Someone more powerful than *your* Rey, more dangerous, more, I don't know, an *über*sociopath." This last thought seemed to affect Caroline. She turned her head away to stare out the window.

We drove for a few minutes in silence.

At last, I said, "Tell me what happened when you winked out."

"I don't want there to be an *über*sociopath. The idea alone frightens me." She sighed. "When I was in the cold cellar—"

"Root cellar." I flashed her a smile.

"*Cold* cellar, wishing like hell Rey would just go away, he of course hung around for the longest time. I could see a little daylight through the cracks in the door. The light faded as it became dusk and then night. Most of the time Rey just stood smoking or sat on a wooden kitchen chair he got from the house. He didn't want to talk to me, and I sure as hell didn't want to talk to him. Like we were strangers—but we weren't. Or shouldn't have been—we'd been married."

"Maybe he had the car bugged, the one the other David got—the one we drove to the farm."

"Doesn't seem likely."

"Sorry. Continue," I said.

"All of a sudden, Rey said, 'Gotta go,' and left. Like he'd looked at his watch, or heard something, or I don't know what. Anyway, he knew you'd shown up."

"Remember when the other David and Caroline were with us at the motel on Cumberland, and you could picture Rey outside a deli? And I could sort of see what my wife—except she was Darryl, not Darlene—was doing? Was it like that, do you think? Did he know we had arrived because he just *saw* us somehow?"

"It's as good a guess as any. Creepy, mind you." She shivered a little.

"And he puts other Reys in play when he needs to."

"True. Also mega-creepy. Anyway. When I couldn't hear him or smell his cigarettes, that's when I broke out of the cold cellar and ran. And then, I needed someplace safe, someplace he couldn't find me. So I …."

She stopped speaking. For almost a minute she sat silent. I kept silent, too. It was almost as if we weren't driving—instead, she was back running from the cellar in that dark night, scared out of her wits, and I was there with her.

At last, she spoke slowly, feeling her way to an idea. "I think I—I made a place of safety. *I* did it. I opened a hole and squeezed myself through it. And on the other side, in that world, there was no Rey." She reached over to touch me. "And there was no you."

I noticed her hand on my arm. "You winked off the display."

"I ran away." She spoke just above a whisper. "I left you to face him—*it*, that monster—alone. I'm sorry. I'm *so* sorry."

"No, please. You have nothing to be sorry for. You didn't do that—I was with the other Caroline and David. You did exactly the right thing."

She didn't seem convinced, though she nodded. For a long time, she didn't speak.

Meanwhile, we drove through second- and third-growth forest, past hillsides that had been logged several times, starting long before the Civil War. Here and there we passed a small farm. About an hour after we'd left Aberdeen, we pulled into the town of Raymond, once a booming lumber and fishing town, now just a place struggling to survive in an economy that no longer valued its timber.

After we crossed the Willapa River, I needed directions. "Now where?"

"We're coming to Duryea Street. Go right, to Third, then left. Stop in front of the Raymond Theatre."

"Why?"

"Because it's pretty."

I pulled up in the parking lot in front of the theatre.

Caroline smiled. "They've fixed it up. When I was about ten, my parents took me to see a movie here. We were supposed to visit someone the next day." She paused. "How strange. I'm remembering something that never happened to *me*. *I've* never been here."

"One of you has."

"Yes, but what I'm remembering is as vivid and as real as if—" She stopped in mid-sentence and started to cry softly.

I didn't know if I should try to cheer her up or let her weep. It seemed prudent to say nothing.

After a minute or two, she blew her nose and turned to me. "We're quite a pair, aren't we? Most people are like trees, with roots, a single trunk, and a bunch of branches. We're more like bushes—some kind of shared root system, maybe, but the rest is a bunch of trunks with one part of the bush just a little taller than the rest."

"Why were you crying?" It felt like a risk, but I wanted to know.

"I never came here, not in my real life. My dad died when I was eight. Mom always said he wanted to take this trip, to see the Pacific Ocean and the long beaches, so far from Red Rock. But the person who came here was with both her parents. It was my tenth birthday, and my father wanted me to be able to do something I enjoyed. I loved movies and movie theatres."

"That's not a bad memory. Seems worth a good cry." I thought of my cousin and her husband who never existed, but I kept my own tears at bay. "You ready to go?"

"Sure. Turn left at the next street. It'll take us back out to 101." She paused for a moment. "You're right. It's a good memory to have."

Highway 101 bends west on the south side of Raymond and then plunges south to skirt the ocean, occasionally breaking away from the coast to venture into coniferous forest. An hour out of Raymond it closes in on the Columbia River, but before it reaches the river, the highway heads west toward the ocean and the communities of Long Beach, Seaview, and Ilwaco. We bypassed the bypass in favour of a fill-up for us and the car. I crossed Sandridge Road where 101 became 40th Street, then turned north at Pacific Way. The attendant at Sand Crane Gas directed us to the Blue Breakers Café for lunch.

After the waitress had left us to contemplate our menus, I said, "I saw you in Lake Stevens a couple of days ago."

"Me?"

"Not exactly. A woman who looked just like you, but was most definitely *not* you. She wasn't married as far as I could tell, certainly didn't think *I* was someone she knew. Her name was Robyn. She seemed very ordinary."

"How much did she look like me?"

"Lots. She was nice enough. But she'd never had someone like Rey in her life. She was carefree—the same way protected children are carefree. You know?" I glanced at the menu. French Dip, first choice. Grilled Cheese Delight if there's no beef.

"You talked to her?"

"Not really. I asked her if she knew someone named Caroline, but she didn't."

"That's not much of a pickup line."

I felt my face heat up. Caroline gave me a pixie smile and opened up her menu with a small flourish, letting me know that she had scored a point.

The waitress returned. "Are you folks ready to order?"

Caroline nodded. "French Dip."

I ordered my second choice.

31 # THE HOLOGRAPHIC PROJECTION ROOM

It's easy to imagine ourselves as part of a bigger picture, relatively speaking. For instance, imagine yourself going to the moon. It's not much of a stretch—astronauts have already been there. How about Mars? It's really just more of the same, right?

What about going to a planet that orbits a different star? It still calls up images—getting ready, boarding the vessel, entering suspended animation for the long trip. Another galaxy might require you to stretch your imagination a bit—but again, it's mostly a matter of engineering a thing, a vehicle of some sort, to take you there. Our imaginations are now primed, thanks to years of feeding on science fiction movies, to picture approaching a galaxy (spiral-shaped), rotating slowly.

It's much harder to see ourselves taking a trip in the other direction, into the land of the very small. For one thing, if you can't take your body with you, *Fantastic Voyage* notwithstanding, you leave your eyes behind.

In the land of the very small, you're built of molecules, mostly water, that are much smaller than the period that will end this sentence. Much, much smaller. The number of molecules of water in a teaspoon, for example, is two followed by twenty-three zeroes. Give or take.

Each molecule is made of atoms. The diameter of the hydrogen atom in the water is one ten-millionth the thickness of a dime. The proton at its centre is one hundred thousand times tinier than that, and the electron that is orbiting it is one thousand times smaller than the proton. Between the two is nothing—just empty space. If the proton were the size of a soccer ball, the electron would be about the size of the head of a pin. The pinhead electron would orbit the soccer ball from about twenty feet away. The proton itself is made up of weird little things called quarks, and the quarks are built of little squigglynesses. Gluons kind of hold the stuff together.

You can't go for a visit, because you're already there. That's what makes the trip so unimaginable. Going from universe to universe? Piece of cake. Every place looks more or less like home. But visiting the quantum world? Hello, woo-woo land!

#

As we sat in the Blue Breakers Café waiting for our food, I thought about Robyn, who'd come from the faux-boutique clothing store across from the restaurant in Lake Stevens. While I'd enjoyed meeting her, I hadn't been able to relax completely. It had felt somehow as if Rey would show up there and kill us both, even though Bernie had assured me that Rey didn't exist in that world.

I had no such assurance anymore—though I did have Caroline back in my life.

Caroline seemed to sense my disquiet, and she turned my thoughts in another direction. "Did you know that there's a theory that everything in the universe, or the meta-mega-multiverse or whatever, is just a holographic projection?"

"Where on earth did you hear that?"

"One of my others likes to read popular science. But that's not how I know." The mischief in her smile invited more questions.

"You are full of surprises." I refused the bait. "It absolutely would not surprise me to hear that. At least one scientist figures that the earth's magnetic field connects our brains. Surely one of them thinks we're images in someone's big movie theatre."

"Anyway." She took back the floor. "It's all related to the fact that information is stored on the surface of a black hole, not inside it. Consequently it's the surface area of the hole that is important, not the volume. And all the stuff that we see, hear, feel, taste, and smell is just math. If you assume there's a two-dimensional surface a long way away projecting things into existence, that is."

"I guess that's okay. I know I'd rather be in 3-D movie than one that's just two-dimensional."

Caroline laughed. On cue, the waitress materialized by our table with lunch. The French Dip looked really good, the grilled cheese, not so much.

"Anything else?" she asked. I looked at Caroline for my cue and then shook my head. "Just the ticket, then?"

"Yes, please."

She wrote out the bill and left it on the table.

I pointed at the bill. "What do you call this?"

"The bill. *Ticket* must be American."

"What about check, slip, and chit?"

"I always say bill. I wouldn't even try saying *chit*, especially if I'd had a glass or two." She gave me a look to let me know she knew my question wasn't casual.

It wasn't. Caroline had changed. I took for granted her warmth—the insight she brought to relationships, the emotional connectedness she felt with people. But a scientific side? That surprised me. In what other ways was she different now?

I poked at the crisp-as-a-stick fries that had come with the Grilled Cheese Delight, then took a bite of the sandwich. After I swallowed, I sipped a little coffee from a mug with a wave logo on it. Then I stopped stalling.

"I wasn't testing you." Technically, I wasn't. I really did want to know if she'd heard other words used for *bill*. "I know you're the same Caroline I first saw on Mapleward Road—you seem to have all her experiences—but you're different now. You have strong memories from your other selves. And part of you suddenly has an interest in black holes and holograms."

Caroline gestured toward her French Dip. "This is really good. You should have ordered it."

"I was going to."

"I know." At my skeptical look, she smiled. "No, not ESP. I watched your eyes as you looked at the menu."

"How'd you know I wouldn't if you did?"

She raised an eyebrow and gave me an expression that said, *If you can't prove it, don't say it.*

"But seriously. Where did you learn about that hologram? You didn't know that before we were separated at the farm—or did you?"

"I went to see Bernie. I didn't know what else to do. I busted out of the cold cellar." She raised a finger and one eyebrow to keep me from saying *root cellar*. "Then, after I ran and made that space, everything felt different, and I knew I'd gone travelling again. I knew I'd left you behind, and I'd made it happen, but I didn't know how. All I really knew was that I was safe." She reached across the table to give my hand a quick squeeze, then released it.

"So, no cars anywhere? Not the one at the end of the driveway?"

"No. No cars, no broken window, no Caroline and David, no Rey, no you. I was alone. So I went to Bernie's, hoping he wasn't dead in the world I was in."

She stopped talking. She took a bite and looked out the window while she chewed.

I tried another fry. My fork broke it in two. The pieces skittered onto the table. I put them back on the plate and decided to let them rest. "He wasn't dead," I prompted.

She turned back. "No. He was a physics prof at Lakehead University. You were the one that was dead."

"Me?" I felt affronted.

"Well, me, too. Rey had got both of us at the apartment that day. One of the Reys." She dipped her sandwich into the small bowl of light gravy and examined it, still talking. "After Bernie's initial shock at seeing me— we'd been dead several days, remember—he was quite receptive to a conversation. Hence the hologram."

"And you were relatively safe from Rey because he'd already killed you once and wouldn't be looking for you there."

"Maybe. That's probably right, but there's no real way to know."

I glanced out the window. "No, I guess there isn't."

"Can I ask you a dumb question?"

"Shoot."

"When you, uh, jump from one world into another, does it feel the same as earlier?"

Maybe she really could read my mind. But she hadn't, of course. I considered her question. "No. There's no mirror now. I don't feel like I'm going *through* anything, a wall or a film on a surface—nothing like that. I'm here, and then I'm there, just like that."

"That's what it's like for me, too. What does that mean, though?"

I'd never considered that. "I don't know."

Caroline smiled. "I believe we established that weeks ago. Neither of us knows, really. You know what I think, though? If there's someone or something—maybe a Big Boss, maybe the multiverse itself—that's doing this *to* us, it's getting better at it. If we're the ones doing it, it's getting easier for us, too."

"And your conclusion is?"

Caroline looked out the window and back to me. "You know what it's like? Growing older. Maturing. We know it's happening. The older we get, the faster it seems to happen. We know some of the things that cause us to grow up, but there's no real way to stop aging. For all practical purposes, it happens to us, and we're carried along by the consequences. In short, I don't have a conclusion. It means something or it doesn't."

"Hmm. Sometimes we lose our memories, and sometimes we acquire false ones. That's like aging, too."

"Most of us go all the way from one end of life to the other without ever knowing what it all means."

"I met a guy in Vancouver a few days ago. He says everything is a metaphor, even us."

"He should have a talk with Bernie," she said.

I laughed. "He knows Bernie, who, by the way, is a multi-billionaire in that world. Quantum computers. He's got a James Bond guy named Johnny who works for him."

"Good for Bernie. No woman in his life yet?"

"Not yet."

"Poor Bernie," she said. "What's a quantum computer?"

After we left the restaurant we followed Highway 101 south along the Pacific coast. Just past a little place called McGowan, we drove across the four-mile-long bridge that marks the start of the Oregon Coast Highway. It was absolutely straight as it crossed the mouth of the Columbia River. At Caroline's direction, I headed east on Highway 30. At Clatskanie, the highway suddenly started calling itself Quebec Route 366.

Caroline said, "It's okay, we're still in the US." Ahead of us and to the left we could see Mount Rainier, eighty miles away. Almost straight ahead and fifty miles away sat Mount St. Helens.

"Mount St. Helens looks odd," I said.

"It's still intact here. It had blown its top in my world."

"Mine too. When I visited my cousin in Lake Stevens in 1981, her husband gave me a small vial of ash from the mountain."

"I wonder what'll happen when it blows here. If it does."

Just past the cutoff to Longview, the highway bent south once more.

Caroline said, "It'll be safe to spend the night in Portland. We're not too far from there."

I'd been thinking about Mount St. Helens. "We should get a place that's inconspicuous. Maybe we should park the car far from where we're staying."

"We can decide when we get there. Rey thinks we're a lot further south on I-5."

"How do you know?"

"I just do. You can stop worrying about Mount St. Helens, too. It won't explode while we're anywhere near it."

"You know that for sure?"

"Of course not. But it's unlikely. No sense you worrying. Hey, here's something I've been thinking about. Time. We travel in space, but never time. When we jump from one world to another, we always enter at the same time we left. Why?"

"Haven't we already established that I don't have answers to questions like that?"

"Well, yes. Any guesses, though?"

I seemed to have lost my interest in speculating aloud about the unknowable. I opted for the truth with no trouble at all. "Nope, not really. My mother used to say, 'What is, is.' She meant that even if you don't understand *how* something works, you can understand *that* it works. And if you don't know the name for something, you can make up a word for it until you find out. What that means to us is, we don't travel in time because we don't."

Caroline looked at me, expecting me to continue. And apparently I hadn't lost all interest in speculating aloud after all. "Okay, there's a thing in quantum mechanics called entanglement. Physicists know how to entangle two photons. Any change you make to one is also made in the other, regardless of distance, apparently simultaneously. So maybe, in some way, you and I and Rey are entangled. We keep running into each other wherever we go. I don't know why. I think it isn't magic, but it happens. If it's because of some arcane property of the universe or multiverse or whatever, I won't understand an explanation of it, if there is one."

"That's kind of what I thought." Caroline was quiet, watching the landscape roll past. "You know, I don't buy that idea that there's no such thing as time. That time is nothing but a bunch of nows stacked like a deck of cards." She pointed out the window. "Wouldn't this be jerky, like when you see individual frames of a movie or fan a deck of cards? But it's not. It's one smooth, continuous flow."

"Maybe that smoothness is an illusion. Maybe each card in the deck is very, very similar to the ones above and below it, and we're unaware of the jerkiness. Or maybe time is made of, uh, magnetic cards that aren't totally separate, but instead are stuck together by magnetic fields of some kind." I heard what I was saying and flushed with embarrassment. "Sorry, that was silly. I apologize for my nutty side. I haven't got any idea what I'm talking about. Can you tell?"

"Yeah. You don't hide it."

I couldn't let go of the idea. "What if for us, your deck and mine and Rey's are kind of shuffled together? Sorry, bad metaphor." I wished I could make myself shut up, but the words had tumbled out of me.

"One metaphor's as good as any other. The most important thing is that for us, this is real. And if Rey kills us, he'll kill us dead."

For a long time we rode through time in silence.

"Portland's coming up in about half an hour," Caroline said finally. She was right.

32 # TSUNAMI

Oregon's Highway 30 has almost as many names as there are worlds to visit. Lower Columbia River Highway. St. Helens Road. The Banfield Expressway. Luckily, Caroline had been there before. Some iteration of her had, at least.

As we passed a set of rapids on the river to our left, Caroline pointed. "Portland's basically on the other side of the river. That's where the people live. This side is industrial."

"It's sure not the City of Roses." We drove past gigantic oil storage tanks and rail yards. "Where are we going?"

"Get off at Northwest 23rd Avenue, veer right, slow down. We're looking for Burnside." It took us a few minutes. "Next street. See the ball park? Right at the next corner. Now right again, and again here. Voila."

Suddenly we had a choice of motels.

"How'd you do that?" We pulled into the most convenient parking lot.

"You never ask your other selves for directions? Just like a man. Nice little hideout, don't you think?"

We were part way to the motel office when I said, "Wait."

"What?"

"I don't have much cash on me. Bernie gave me a credit card to use, a world ago, but it might not work here."

"Guess we'll have to find out." She started toward the motel office door.

I trailed behind like a recalcitrant child. "What if it doesn't work?"

"Then we smile sweetly, say something about how annoying this is, apologize if necessary, and get the heck out of there. That's all."

"Do *you* have any money?"

"Oh, for Pete's sake. You make me feel like we're *married*."

I scooted ahead of her, opened the door, and walked in first. Once inside, I turned to look at her. She shook her head and smiled—no anger. Such is love.

I got out my wallet and looked at the name on Bernie's credit card. Would it say Glendenning or Williamson? Williamson, it turned out.

Bernie's card worked. They key was the old-fashioned kind—metal, tagged with the room number. It had a solidity that made me feel it'd still work if we made a jump to another reality. And when we got to our room, the key opened the door. Amazing—just like in mid-winter, when a car left unplugged still starts immediately.

Our room had no smell of mould or cigarettes or insecticide, and no carpet stains or patches, no drip marks on the walls. An old flat-screen TV sat high above a chipboard-and-veneer-decaled armoire.

"Tonight, we can watch fat people who have fingers that turn skinny when they point to the side." I pointed at the large glass ashtray on the nightstand, and beside it, a tented card saying *No Smoking!* "And I guess we can smoke some smokeless cigarettes, if we have any."

"Well, I have many things to look forward to, don't I?" Caroline sat on the bed and took off her shoes. "Bed needs a bundling board, though."

"Damn."

"It's okay, we can just put a couple of the pillows between us. You can pretend it's a threesome."

"Double damn."

"You want to know why?" She was suddenly serious.

My heart stepped up its pace. "Why?"

"What if, sometime, while we're still lost—what if you die? What if Rey finds us and kills you, or we don't make the jump together and get separated forever?"

"That won't happen." Of course, I knew any of those things could happen—and, in fact, they were some of the more *likely* outcomes of our journey.

"If we—if we make love." She took a breath and looked at me. "I'll remember, always, what it was like. And if we're apart, I don't think I'd be able to go on if that's all I had. The only way to remember you. That's why I keep pretending that we're just friends." Her voice caught. She couldn't continue.

I didn't interrupt the silence she needed.

She cleared her throat at last. "Stupid, eh?"

"I wish it were." I didn't like it, but she had a point. I tried to lighten the mood. "I'm not that good, you know."

Caroline laughed. "One of my others disagrees."

"Jesus, do you trade gossip with them, too? Could we watch TV? I don't feel like taking a cold shower."

After some channel surfing, Caroline found a channel with local Portland news. A serious traffic accident, an accidental shooting, one business closing down and another opening up, two missing teenagers, the attempted robbery of a convenience store in which the robber was killed by the store owner. Neither of us really watched it. It was just the same old same old.

Out of the blue, Caroline asked, "Do you think we have to kill him?"

"Rey?" As if she meant someone else.

"Do we have to go after him instead of playing sitting duck to his hunter?"

"We'd have to arm ourselves—buy guns or something."

"That shouldn't be too hard. We're in the US."

"We'd have to fill out forms and—other stuff." I didn't like this train of thought.

"We could find out. If it's something we have to do, we could at least find out. We need a computer. Even an upscale phone. God, I miss my tablet. There has to be some way to search for information."

"Oh hey, I have a laptop in in the car. I was emailing Bernie."

"Great. But let's leave it for a bit. Could we just go for a walk or something? I'm, I don't know what."

"Antsy?"

"I need to stretch my legs, get outside. I'm feeling claustrophobic."

"You don't like the idea of killing Rey, do you?"

"No, I really don't. I hate the thought of it. But Rey is going to try to kill us, you know. That's what being married to him meant. He always set up these impossible situations that had no solution. Every second of his life he's been playing puppet master. And now he's the biggest, baddest puppet master ever."

"Come on, let's walk. The neighbourhood looks safe enough." I'd noticed apartment buildings and grocery stores and restaurants. "Most of the graffiti looks more like artwork than gang signatures. And this isn't bad, for an inner-city motel. The owners keep it up."

"Thanks, Dad," Caroline said. "Can we go out and play now?"

"Do you have a jacket or something to put on? It might get a little cold."

"Sorry, I left my suitcase back home. You know, on that other planet."

I pocketed the key. Outside, the weather was warmer than in the motel room. I decided to ignore the nervous willies that made me feel we were in danger.

"Where to?" I asked.

"Let's just go find a neighbourhood and wander through it."

"A neighbourhood."

"Yes. A place where people live, not just work. Every city has neighbourhoods. Even in the middle of most downtowns, you can find neighbourhoods."

"Lead on. Take me to a neighbourhood."

At the street, we turned toward the trees whose crowns overhung the pavement a block away. We picked streets by their potential for leading us into more greenery. After about fifteen minutes, we found ourselves on Southwest Park Place.

Caroline sounded triumphant. "This has got to lead to a park, it's right there in the name."

We came to the entrance of a beautiful park that promised walking paths and one-way winding roads.

"Any idea what the name of this place is?" I asked.

"No, none of me know." She smiled, the sort of smile that made me remember what one of her other selves had said about me.

I walked faster up the steps. At the top, we started along a path. The grass beside us was a lush Irish green that seemed never to have thirsted for either water or care. At the top of a small hill we looked around. Someone had dropped a small park map. It was weather-beaten, but I looked anyway.

"We're apparently in Washington Park, and it has something called a rose test garden."

"City of Roses," Caroline said.

It was the last thing she said before everything started to change.

Imagine yourself watching a film with time-lapse photography. In a matter of seconds a seed breaks open, from it erupts a tendril of green, its roots seek the earth, and in a few seconds you're looking at a beautiful, full-grown flower, whose petals almost immediately wilt.

Take time, itself, out of that film. For each frame, substitute a new world, a new universe. Link each frame to the next in form and feature, so the change from frame to frame is perfectly smooth. You're not traveling through the illusion of accelerated time but instead through a multitude of possibilities for a single location, each possibility morphing smoothly into the next.

"Jesus," Caroline managed. The changes swept us up and carried us away.

The trees around us transformed: darkened, grew light, turned from oak to maple, and back to oak. The ground rose and fell; there were sudden flashes of colour as buildings erupted into being and vanished. The path we were on became the sidewalk of a street that turned into dense forest that became a logged hillside. I closed my eyes, and the roiling earth pitched me down. In panic, I opened my eyes, found Caroline beside me, and grabbed her hand. The world kept changing, the pace increasing until the changes were too hard to follow.

Then, instantly, I stood upright once more, Caroline beside me, and I held on to the ragged map instead of her hand. I trembled, adrenaline fueling the tremors that shook my body.

Caroline said, "What was that? What the *hell* was that?"

"I think we went on a trip." I tried to hide the shaking in the hand that held the map. No use. I could feel hysteria building, so I clamped my mouth shut and tried to focus on my hand.

"Where are we now?" Caroline asked.

Thank goodness, she'd given me a problem—something I could work on, here and now. I looked around, trying to remember just before the movie started. I couldn't see any change. "I think we're back where we started. We got swallowed and spit back up."

"I want to go back to the motel."

"Me, too." What I didn't add was that we might have a problem finding the way.

But there wasn't. We backtracked along the route we'd taken, said hello to the desk clerk, walked down the corridor, and when I turned the old-fashioned room key, the old-fashioned door opened.

In the room, Rey sat on the bed.

33 # TWISTER

Instinctively, having been beaten so often and so well, I looked to Rey's hands. Was he holding a gun, a knife, a baseball bat? There were two of us and only one of him. My brain considered options. Could we kill him, here and now? Did we have to, yet? Eventually my brain decided we were safe enough that I could look him in the eye.

"Nice walk?" Rey asked.

I ignored him. "Caroline, is he your Rey or just another Rey?"

Rey laughed. "Even I don't quite know the answer to that one."

Caroline looked at me. "He's not the one I married."

"Oh?" Rey's voice held a challenge. "And just how do you know that? I'm not saying you're wrong, mind—just curious."

Caroline said to me, "He's arrogant enough, but he's more educated. Rey would never have said, 'I don't quite know.' He'd have just grunted something dismissive."

"Something dismissive," Rey parodied her parody of him. "You, if I may say so, speak far better than my wife ever did."

My apprehension had lessened. "Why are you here?" I hoped for a non-obvious answer.

Rey looked at me for a moment. "I don't like what I'm doing."

"Hah!" Caroline had apparently picked up at least one speech characteristic from her husband.

Rey waited a beat before he continued. "I have nothing against you, either of you. I'm not a violent person, despite what you may think. Caroline, in my world, we had a pretty good life together. Maybe not especially happy or satisfying, but functional. When this Bozo showed up, and you left me for him, I could understand. You'd already found out about Ellen."

"That—that young girl at the drycleaner's?" Caroline's curiosity trumped her disgust.

"The very same. Nice, quite 'pneumatic,' as Aldous Huxley would say. Anyway, you met this David. You're a schoolteacher, aren't you?" He swung his attention to me, in what seemed a carefully calculated gesture.

"Yes." I wondered immediately if I had given away a valuable piece of information. Did I just identify myself as the correct target? Was there even such a thing as "the correct" target? Then I caught myself: *Why do I imagine I'm somehow intrinsically important to the goings-on of the universe?*

"Schoolteachers have big egos." Had Rey read my mind? "After a while they forget they spend their lives matching wits with schoolchildren. They start thinking they're smart. Is that what you think, David?"

"No."

"Good. Glad to hear it. Personally, I spent a lot of my life bored, hence Helen, the dry-cleaning girl."

"Ellen." Caroline frowned.

"Yes, of course." Rey allowed himself a crooked little smile. "Pursuing you two has been quite the antidote, but, truth be told, I'm tired of the chase. I'm just another hound in pursuit of the fox. The real hunter, you know, is on horseback—even the most loyal dog realizes that eventually. Every *posse comitatus* has its leader, its organizer, its motivator—and it's not me. I'm just *tired*. I'd far rather shoot a little white ball into a cup on a golf course. That would be no less interesting, and far less dangerous."

"Bullshit," Caroline said.

"Perhaps," Rey conceded, taking his eyes off me momentarily. "There's something to be said for the rush of adrenaline at the moment of the kill. It's quite addictive."

"How did you find us?" Caroline refused to be drawn into a discussion with Rey.

"Let's just say I saw you as you were leaving."

"Saw, meaning you were here when we left, or saw as in you visualized us—saw us in your mind—as we left?"

"More that last bit. But until you looked at the motel sign I had no idea where you were. Luckily you looked at it. I can read a sign. Hell, I can even look up an address in a phone book. I've been in Portland for almost a month, waiting for you two to show up and getting more bored by the second. So, that's it. Game over. I'm done with the chase, and you two can go your merry way."

"Caroline," I said. "We have to go. Right now."

"Why?"

"Because he lies. They all do." Caroline and I had been standing close to the door like deer frozen in headlights. I walked past Rey to the window and pretended to look out.

Caroline sensed what was coming next. She bought me time. "Is that true, Rey? Are you a liar? Are you lying to us right now?"

Rey didn't reply for a second. Then he offered, "More or less."

I pretended to peer to the far right of the window, edging near the lamp on the night table beside the bed. "You have no intention of giving up the chase. He's coming, isn't he?"

"He?" Rey said.

"You know who I mean. The other Rey. *Her* Rey. *You* won't kill us, but *he* will." I looked left. Rey watched, relaxing a little as I moved away from the table lamp.

"No," Rey said, "He's—"

Caroline silenced him with the heavy glass ashtray she'd picked up from the night table. He fell backward onto the bed.

"Is he dead?" I asked. "Did you kill him?"

Caroline stood motionless, holding the ashtray. She was in shock, her voice toneless. "I don't know."

In the silence I heard a key entering the door lock. I grabbed the ashtray from Caroline's hand and leaped past her into the bathroom. I left the light off. Caroline didn't move—I suspected she couldn't, still in shock.

The key turned, the door opened. Rey saw Caroline standing beside the bed and his counterpart lying on it, both legs hanging over the edge, feet on the floor.

Rey didn't see *me*. My two-handed rushing smash to the side of his head dropped him like a stone.

"Oh, sweet Jesus." Adrenaline gave Caroline her voice again. "We've killed the two of them."

"Not this one." I looked at the slow rise and fall of my victim's chest. "Do you have anything—a wire hanger, even? We need to tie them up."

"Closet. It has some."

"God bless old-fashioned motels." I quickly unwound the wire. I looped it twice around the second Rey's wrists and twisted it together as tightly as I could.

"He'll just untie it."

"With his hands?" I got another hanger and tied his feet together.

Then I hauled the body into the bathroom and pushed it over into the bathtub. It was hard work.

With two more hangers (four left, I noted) I trussed up the Rey that had kept us in thrall until his partner arrived. Then Caroline and I hauled him (like his partner, still breathing) into the bathroom and dumped his body on top of the first.

"Now what?"

I had a brainstorm. "Now we tie them together." I fetched the other hangers. When we were done, the two were tied together hand to foot, neck to neck, and belt to belt.

I needed a shower, but, of course, the bathroom was occupied. I closed the bathroom door just as one of the Reys began to come to.

"They're going to start yelling." Caroline sounded almost regretful.

I wiped my brow. "I guess it's time to leave, then."

"Will they be okay?"

"Probably. I don't much care." In all likelihood, it would have been better if we'd killed them. Better for us, anyway. However, at the time, I wasn't capable of it, and I don't think Caroline was, either. Fortunately I didn't say any of that.

The desk clerk was still on duty as we passed through the lobby.

I asked, "Is there a good restaurant around here somewhere? Serves a nice supper?" He gave us directions to the Cascades Café.

In the parking lot, Caroline asked, "We aren't going there, are we?"

"No. We'll have supper, but just out of town. It won't be long before someone frees your husbands, or they do it themselves. Then we'll have cops aplenty after us."

"Maybe not." She read an imaginary headline. "Twister game goes horribly wrong for identical twins." She laughed. "They'd be embarrassed to call anyone else. I bet they'll be the only ones who come after us. If either of 'my husbands' even hangs around after they're free."

In the car, I asked, "Which way?" It was getting very dark now.

"South. We're meeting someone."

I got us heading south. "When were you going to tell me?"

"When I needed to. Bernie said I should meet them. He also said I shouldn't tell anyone, including you, until I had to."

"Which Bernie?"

"Bernie of my escape from the cold cellar. So we're back in *that* Bernie's world."

178 # Roy Blomstrom

"The one that was supposed to be safe? Two Reys in a motel bathtub suggest otherwise."

Caroline said seriously, "No place is safe forever. No place. But Bernie gave me a letter to use if we get kicked out of this universe. It'll work anywhere—it's handwritten."

34 # TINKER

I am more a tinker than a thinker. Not "tinker" in the tinsmith sense, though—I'm the fiddly kind. If I have to build something, I rarely plan ahead. Instead, when I discover I need a special tool—one I maybe should have realized I'd need—I make one out of something at hand. I don't own a store-bought cleaning brush for the barbecue grill, because I tried a wooden paint stirring stick, and it worked like a charm.

Even when I taught school, I rarely planned lessons. I tried to visualize the end of the lesson, and worked my way to it, improvising on the run. A real lesson plan would have been too restrictive—that's what I told myself, and that's what I still believe.

There's a downside, of course. Believing you'll "think of something" can be an excuse to put aside thoughts—thoughts you need to examine *right now*. Putting thoughts aside can become a very bad habit.

It was only when Caroline and I were speeding away from the motel that it occurred to me—I still didn't know where she'd been. What happened to her while I was going from Thunder Bay to Whitehorse to Vancouver to Lake Stevens, and now Portland? Portland, it occurred to me had been her idea. She'd insisted. Was that odd?

I hadn't bothered to ask. And now I had another question. *Who was this person we needed to meet?*

Overall, I felt like a dolt. I'd let myself go on a mental holiday, and it had been way too easy to do. I needed to believe in a proverb beyond just *que sera, sera.*

#

"Where to?"

"Head for the coast. Pick a route, any route, and take us south-west. But don't tell me where we are or where we're going. I'm going to sleep. Wake me when we're there."

"Where?"

"Wherever we are when you think it's time to stop."

"You're going to sleep?"

"It's a prophylactic. I don't think Rey will know where we are if I'm asleep."

"I don't understand."

She closed her eyes. "Don't forget to wake me when we arrive."

So much for finding out where she'd been during the weeks I'd been travelling.

Caroline had said we should go south-west, so I went south-east instead to get onto I-5. Later, I veered left at Salem and took Highway 22 and then Highway 20. The darkness grew. Low clouds moved in from the west to blot out the stars. The road wound and twisted through heavy forest. I had to concentrate on driving. We were almost at Bend, Oregon, when Caroline woke from her three-hour nap.

"Are we there yet?" She rubbed the sleep from her eyes like a child.

"Not yet."

"Pull over. State park."

"Where? There's no—" But there was. Just ahead a sign read Tumalo State Park.

"There. Just pull over and stop the car."

"In the park?"

"No, on the side of the highway. Just pull over. Turn off the engine and set the parking brake."

"Now what?"

She turned toward me and smiled. "Hang on. It'll be all right. We've done this before."

She was right—the deck was being shuffled again. As in Washington Park, the world began to change from what it was to other things it could have been. My stomach lurched when the car was pushed up from below and the flat highway became a downhill grade. The changes might have lasted a few seconds, maybe a few minutes. But this time was different from Washington Park. When it was over, we weren't back at our starting point—we were somewhere else.

My hands had clamped on the steering wheel. Caroline put her left hand on my right one. "It's okay," she repeated. Then, voice casual, she asked, "Did you take us south-west?"

"No."

"Good. I was counting on that. We're fine now. Rey's not here. He can't follow us here, at least not yet."

But I couldn't let go of the wheel. My body kept warning me that if I did, the world might start to change again. In my mind, I held the deadman switch, and if I let go, something, maybe everything, would stop and the world would be no more. Outside, the stars still shone in the sky. Were there fewer?

I took a few deep breaths. "Where are we?"

"Just north of Bend."

"No, I mean—did you do this?"

"We're in a safe place. And, yes, it's ... a thing I can do now. At the farmhouse I did it by accident, or unconsciously—either one, it doesn't matter. Now, if I'm not tired and I can concentrate, I can make it happen."

I considered for a moment. "So—you can control what happens to us?"

"Sort of, hit and miss. Remember after you got me back from the Winnipeg kidnapping? I told you one of the Reys had said his head hurt and that 'it's going to happen again.'"

"Yes. This is that?"

"Something like that—but I don't get headaches."

"I see."

"No you don't. You know how I know? Because I don't have any idea how I do it."

"Did you do it at Washington Park?"

"No. That happened all by itself."

Suddenly, it seemed funny. I laughed.

Caroline looked at me, caution mixed with curiosity. "Now what?"

"You sound like me. Next, you'll offer some theory about what's happening or what it might mean, and a short time later it'll turn out to have been all wrong."

She smiled. "We're a match made in heaven. But I'm hungry. Fire up the Corolla's hyperdrive and let's see if we can find a place to eat in Bend."

Fifteen minutes and fifteen miles later, we had to give up the idea of eating in Bend. It didn't exist. Where it should have been sat only a truck stop called the Snack 'n Shack. It looked like it might be part of a chain, but not one that I'd ever heard of. It had gas and diesel pumps under a high canopy, along with a convenience store. Behind the store stood a dozen-unit motel—the shack part, I assumed. Three tractor-trailer rigs were parked in the lot in front of the motel.

I pulled up at a gas pump. Caroline had seen a Restrooms sign in one of the store windows. I told her back, "I'm going to see if I can get gas."

I wanted to know if Bernie's magic credit card would work at these self-serve pumps. I looked at the card to see who I was in this world— David, it turned out—and took a breath. Following the instructions on the pump, I inserted the card, pulled it out, and all was well. In a few minutes the Corolla's tank was full, the charge accepted. I moved the car to a spot beside the store, then I went in.

Caroline sat at one of three small tables beside a window. "I've already ordered for us. We're having the Supper Special." She motioned with her head to call my attention to the lighted menu board above the cashier's counter. Sure enough, there was a Supper Special—fish and chips, house salad, beverage.

"And my beverage is ...?"

"A regular cola. I'm having the diet. And before you ask, I watched to see if the credit card worked or not."

"God bless black magic."

"Quantum tunneling. Didn't you tell me that sometime?"

"I might have."

"So after supper, then what?"

"Room for the night? I don't feel like driving any more today."

"A room it is, if they have one."

Our meals arrived in care of the cashier. "Two supper specials who gets the diet?" she said, all in one breath.

Caroline looked up at her as if the question was unnecessary.

The cashier caught the look. "Some of the drivers are a little on the heavy side," she said, by way of explanation. "They figure a diet drink, or coffee with some of that artificial sweetener stuff, will give them back their belt lines." She nodded at me. "*He's* trim enough, but I always ask. Anything else I can get youse?"

I spoke up. "We've been on the road all day. Are there any rooms left at the motel?"

"One. Two queens, though, so five bucks more. You want to look?"

"No, I want to eat. I'm sure it'll be fine."

The cashier added, "Mattress is good, and the room's clean. You wouldn't think it, but drivers are picky about stuff like that."

"We'll take it," Caroline said.

"Checkout's at eleven. Breakfast runs until then. You want, I can put the room and the meal on the same ticket. Breakfast, too."

"That'll be fine," I said. "Do you need my credit card?"

"Naw. I seen it worked at the pump so no problem. Enjoy the meal."
Back at the counter, she sat on a stool and started to read a newspaper.

"Excuse me," I called to her. "Is that a local paper?"

"What passes for one. *Eugene Sentinel-Courier*. Got stuff about Eugene,
Springfield, sometimes Redmond and Prineville. We run an ad in it on
weekends. Don't bring in many customers, though. You can have it when
I'm finished, if you want."

"Thanks." My supper was surprisingly good. When we were done, I
looked over the store's products, and added to our tab a highway map of
the western states, two bottles of water, a bag of chips, and two chocolate-
cake-and-icing confections shaped like hot dogs. Also two toothbrushes
plus a tube of toothpaste, since we had donated the previous ones to the
bath-tubbed Reys as we fled the motel.

I moved the car to a spot in front of the motel. The room key—metal,
tagged, and well worn—turned easily in the lock. The room smelled
slightly of deodorizer, but it looked clean. However, there was no TV and
no telephone—just a radio on an end table and a Gideon Bible in a drawer.

"Do you think they have wifi?" Caroline asked.

"I doubt it. If you want, I'll bring in the laptop and you can try it out."

She shook her head. "I was just wondering."

I turned on the radio—AM only. Slowly, I tuned the dial from one end
of the band to the other. Nothing. The bigger cities, if there were any in
this world, were either on the other side of the mountains or too far away
for the signals to carry.

"Maybe later there'll be some skip from the east."

She yawned. "Skip?"

"With the right kind of atmospheric ionization, radio signals can be
reflected over long distances. Late at night, AM radio hauls in stations a
thousand miles away."

"I'm not staying up late, and neither are you."

"I'm not?"

"We have some business to take care of before we leave here, so we're
getting up early."

I glanced pointedly at the bed that was beside her, and she laughed.
"Not yet. We'll talk about that in the morning, too."

I opted for a dramatic sigh and took off my shoes.

35 # BACK STORY

The next morning, we woke early and headed to the Snack 'n Shack for breakfast. There was a new cashier at the counter, which worried me. What if we'd gone travelling during the night? Every time I shifted from one world to another, I had to learn a whole new back story to explain myself. I knew very little about the person I was here, which presented challenges. My heart rate accelerated a bit.

I looked closely at the new cashier. She seemed to be a slightly heavier version of the one from the previous day. I hoped she wasn't a double.

"You must be the folks in nine," she said. "Shelley said you'd want breakfast. Add it to the tab, right?"

We picked the same table. "You look very much like the woman that was here last evening. Are you two related?"

"Sisters."

My heart rate slowed. "Ah, I see."

"Yep. She's not much for mornings, and I don't like the late shift, so it all works out. Now, what'll youse have? Eggs are fresh and we got pea meal bacon, imported from Vancouver. That's back bacon rolled in cornmeal. I don't know why they call it *pea* meal."

"It used to be rolled in dried peas," Caroline offered.

"Canadians?"

Caroline nodded. "And I'll have some."

After we'd eaten, Caroline and I walked back to the motel. As we got to the door, I asked, "So are you going to bring me up to speed on what happened to you? You told me about Bernie, the physics prof."

"Yes." Caroline's voice held hesitance and something else—sadness?

I put the key in the lock and turned it.

She sat down on the edge of the bed. "Promise me something."

"Sure." I picked up the single wooden chair and flipped around so I could sit with my elbows resting on the top of the back.

"Promise me that you'll try to remember—I'm the same person I was before Rey kidnapped me at the farmhouse. I'm the very same person. Just with some additions."

"Yes, your other selves."

"Not just that. Promise me." Caroline looked at me closely as I said the two words. Satisfied, she started her story.

"Remember Bernie's basement? That's where I ended up—but it took a while. I'd walked almost halfway to town before I got a ride from some guy, an old farmer from Murillo. When he asked me where I wanted to go, the only place that might be safe was Bernie's. I couldn't remember the address, so I told him downtown Fort William. Once we got downtown, I found it. Bernie must have thought I was crazy, but he let me in anyway. I used your name, said you were in trouble."

"Whoa, whoa. Wait, a sec. It's late at night or early in the morning, and Bernie just opened the door and let you in?"

"Ye-es." The hesitancy again.

"What aren't you telling me?"

Caroline was silent for a few moments. "Sometimes, if I ask a person to do something for me, the person just does it."

"Just does it."

She nodded. "Even when it's an odd thing. Even if the person doesn't really want to. If it's something the person might do, I can sometimes cause that choice to happen."

"I see." It was my turn to let some doubt creep into my voice.

"I sort of make them choose to do what's best for me."

"I don't understand."

She sighed. "I don't, either. It's like I'm getting stronger—more skilled."

"Let's put that idea aside for a sec. Tell me about Bernie. He let you in, and then what?"

"Then he put the coffee pot on, and we talked. Yes, about you, or at least the you that had taught him. Then I got into our story, the real one, how I met you and—"

I interrupted. "Whoa again. You told him about us meeting on Mapleward Road, and why you were driving on it in the middle of the night in the first place? And he just sat and listened? He didn't seem skeptical or call for the guys in white coats?"

I smiled to take the edge off what I'd said, but her expression let me know I hadn't been very successful.

"Yes." This pause was long as she marshalled her thoughts and put her ducks into rows. When she was ready, she looked me in the eyes. "It's another thing I didn't know I could do. Not then, anyway. I can make people listen, keep them enthralled. Is that the word I want?"

"It's as good as any." I thought about the Rey sitting on the bed in the motel room, talking until his partner arrived.

"So Bernie listened to the whole story. He asked questions about details sometimes, but mostly he just let me talk."

"He believed you?"

"Yes." It was her turn to try for a smile. "After all, he was talking to a dead person, remember."

"Touché! So you told him our story, including, I suppose, the parts about meeting him 'before.'"

"Yes. Then he told me about himself. He began by saying, 'In this world, I'm...' and off he went as if I hadn't been saying anything out of the ordinary at all."

"Well, once Bernie focuses on something, he won't let go of it. His normal isn't like most people's."

"We talked for a long time. When I couldn't keep my eyes open anymore, he suggested I go to bed—he slept on the couch. When I woke up in the morning, he was gone. He'd left me a note—make myself at home, that kind of thing. He'd drawn a little map of where the food was in the fridge."

"A map?"

"So I could find the bacon and the eggs, I guess."

"The hard things for him are the easy things for everybody else. His world is kind of reversed, I think."

"And it's not so nice. I spent most of the morning and afternoon watching TV. The American channels were full of horrible programs where people were made fun of, or challenged to do dangerous things, or encouraged to surprise the people who loved them with hurtful confessions of past affairs. The Canadian ones weren't much better. I stayed indoors in case I was wrong about Rey not being in this world I'd fled to. Which reminds me, 'fled' isn't really the right word. You know how when a wild animal is startled, it instantly leaps away from danger before it runs like hell?"

I nodded.

"It was like that. I 'jumped' into Bernie's world. I was startled into it."

"I think I understand. But you've got control over it now, right?"

"A little. You know how a baby just kind of flaps about until she figures out those fuzzy waving things she sees in front of her are her own arms? And then she learns to move them deliberately, and long after that she gets to wrap her fingers around a bottle of milk and drink? That's what it's like."

"So where are you now? Drinking yet?"

"A bit. I try. But sometimes I forget to hold on to the bottle."

"And Rey?"

"He's figure-skating. What about you?"

"I've just started noticing the fuzzy waving things."

Caroline gave me a half-smile then stared down at her hands folded in her lap. "We're both changing, but it scares me to choose. I don't mind when the world changes around me—I can adapt. But I'm afraid that someday I'll choose to stop being myself."

I was just smart enough to keep my mouth shut. Caroline didn't want my sympathy or, worse yet, my advice. She didn't need me to say anything. She wanted me to listen.

"And another thing—I don't want my relatives and my friends to change, either. If they change, they won't really be mine, anymore. Unless we change together, and what's the chance of that? You and I keep hopping from one world to another and can't always stay together. You know those vampire movies where the head vampire is about a thousand years older than a normal human? What scares me isn't the business about having to drink someone's blood to stay alive, or having to stay out of the sun. It's having to watch everything change around me—maybe one day I just won't care about anything anymore. All those endless cycles of building and destruction and reconstruction, and styles that come and go, and people always dying away from me, while everything that's supposed to be worth living for is mine, and then it isn't mine, and then it is again."

The flow of words stopped, and the flow of tears began.

I sat beside her on the bed and put my arm around her shoulder. She leaned against me, the tears falling into her lap and onto her hands, folded as a child would fold them in church for prayer.

I covered her folded hands with one of mine, as if making a roof above a cabin. "That's not how it's going to be for us. Do you love me?"

"Yes."

"And I, you. That's what makes the difference. Rey loves nothing.

That nothing is an emptiness that he can't fill. I think he knows that. I think he knows that he'll never, ever, have a moment like this one."

"But he's so strong, and so mean."

"And all dead inside."

We sat for several minutes without speaking, each of us holding the other. At last, I said, "It's going to be okay."

Caroline nodded, though I knew she thought it wouldn't be. Breaking the spell, she reached over to the night table for a tissue to wipe her face.

I stood up. "Want some coffee? We can try out their foil-wrapped, two-serving, breakfast blend gut rot."

"You make it sound delicious." Caroline was working hard to pretend to feel better.

I deliberately wasted time pretending to decode the instructions on the coffee maker, to give us both a chance to return to something closer to normal. When I thought an acceptable interval had passed, I tore open the foil package of coffee. "How long were you at Bernie's?"

"A week, I think. Then we tried experiments. At first, I tried to move from Bernie's world into a different one. Bernie suggested the technique."

"There's a technique?"

"Sort of. Bernie had a desk lamp that he liked. It was really a god-awful looking chintzy thing with a pink lampshade. He suggested that I concentrate on the lampshade and try to change its colour. So I did. I made it blue."

"You made it blue?"

"Not exactly. It isn't possible, according to Bernie, to change the colour. What I had done, instead, was to take a teeny-tiny step into a world in which Bernie's desk lamp had a blue shade. To get the blue colour, the universe I started from was replaced by a universe in which the main difference was the colour of the lampshade. As long as only the colour of that lampshade changed, all the rest—Bernie and me included—would stay more or less the same as in the world I'd left. We could even pick up the conversation where we had left off."

"Wow. But I don't really get it."

"The change was so smooth I didn't even know it had happened, except for the shade. I was supposed to nod to Bernie when the lampshade turned colour. When I did, he asked me what colour it had been. I told him it had been pink, and he believed me."

"Interesting."

"And scary as hell."

"What did it *feel* like? Physically, I mean."

"Besides scary? Like when you're playing tennis, and your hand keeps the racquet making contact with the ball. You know *you're* moving your hand into the place where the ball is going to be, but it *feels* like your hand is making the decisions all on its own."

"A reflex."

"Yes." She went to the window and opened the curtains a bit to look out. "The next day, Bernie asked me to make the lampshade pink again. He made me try to remember the exact shade."

"To move back into the world you had come from."

"Exactly. Before I tried, he had me look closely at the blue shade so I'd remember exactly what blue it was, the hue. The idea was that if I needed to come back to the blue-shade world, I'd have to know the exact colour."

"Too bad you couldn't take a paint chip back and forth."

"We considered it, but it wasn't practical—I'd have to find an exact match somewhere. So we just went with my memory of the colour."

"And did you get back?"

"I'm not a hundred percent certain. How could I be? I think so. I went to a room where a Bernie had a pink lampshade. It seemed the same shade of pink."

"But you're not sure?"

"No," she said. "Pink Bernie said something about a field width indicator. When I told him about Blue Bernie's paint chip idea, he said we should have done the experiment outside. There, the number of items that could possibly change would be much larger."

"So field width is the total number of items that change in the experiment?"

"If you say so. I don't have a clue. He said something about interconnected realities, not just parallel ones. He also said something about limited and unlimited entanglement. Does this mean anything to you?"

"Nope."

"He told me that some physicists believe we actually live in something he called the polyverse, so I asked him if any parrots lived there, and he laughed."

I laughed, too, and then grew thoughtful. "The Bernie I taught wouldn't have been able to laugh like that." I changed the subject. "What about this guy Blue Bernie thinks we need to meet? Who is he?"

"One of Blue Bernie's internet friends. A computer geek, and Bernie calls him a 'successful' one. I think he made a gazillion dollars out of building a quanta computer."

"Quantum," I corrected.

"Teacher." Caroline's voice lowered the standing of the profession by several grade levels. "This friend's family moved to the US after Canada shut down the Avro Arrow project. His dad was some kind of engineer and immediately got a job with NASA."

"Ah," I said.

We drank coffee and chatted about nothing for several minutes, while I tried to let her story sink in.

"So when we leave, we're heading where?" I asked finally.

Caroline took my hand in hers and looked me in the eye. "I can't tell you that. Bernie said if Rey can do what it looks like he can, I shouldn't say aloud anything that might give away this guy's name or location. Or anything else."

I nodded. "Good idea. It might also be a good idea for you to drive. That way you don't have to tell me where to turn or what route to take. You know where you're going. I don't."

"Bernie also said it might be a good idea if we made you a tinfoil hat."

"What?"

"I'm kidding," she said. "Mostly."

36 # ANALOGY

At university I took a course in English Romanticism. The prof started one of the lectures this way: "If you absolutely had to prove that you exist, how would you go about it?"

It was a good question, an appropriate introduction to the new ways that the Romantics regarded the world. It started the class thinking about the nature of awareness and the ways in which awareness is intimately connected to the five senses.

As the prof pointed out, if you touch someone, you can feel that person with your fingers. However, some people who have lost an arm feel a cramp in the missing hand, or experience the sensation of drumming fingers that aren't there. Just because you *think* you're touching someone doesn't mean you *are*.

Therefore, the brain, this prof argued, may be our only real connection to the world.

But sometimes the world that the brain connects to isn't real. Consider the world of a person with schizophrenia. Their brain insists, all evidence to the contrary, that the voices they hear, the things they see, the impulses they feel compelled to follow are real. The brain doesn't believe they're a consequence of faulty hormones or wiring.

After Coleridge and Wordsworth have whispered that people see the divinity in nature, where do you stop? Do you believe them? Do you see it yourself? And what do you see?

No wonder Romanticism exploded into Impressionism as painters tried to paint what they felt about what they saw. No wonder dramatists began to play with Expressionism and wrote plays they hoped would speak through the senses directly to the mind.

Science started to doubt Newton and, in consequence, rewrote notions of time and gravity. Suddenly, something called relativity meant E was equal to mc^2. And, later, atoms—at least those of the tinker-toy sort we were used to—were displaced by teeny tiny strings of God-knows-what that vibrate in a ten-dimensional existence to produce everything we once considered tangible and solid.

All the while, writers tried frantically to keep up with the latest truth. They scribbled furiously about the modern world, only to discover that it had changed overnight—in the dark, it had gone Post-Modern, and then Post-Post. How, in the grand scheme of things, could they write about the world when they didn't know anything about what *actually* makes it tick?

What do you do when you realize that there are things that you—and not just you, but *everyone*—can never, *ever* understand?

You take a deep breath and muddle on, that's what. It's a strategy that worked for the first fish that flopped itself onto the beach and struggled landward on its fins. It's what we always do when we don't know what to do. We do it because it's what we've always done.

#

Over the course of three days, Caroline took us south and then west toward a destination she dared not tell me, to meet a man whose name she couldn't say—a man who had existed in another world but might not exist in ours.

Sometime during the first day, after we left the Bend truck stop, I found it difficult to not comment on the things we passed. Instead, it seemed safer to ask Caroline about her past.

"Your parents had a store in Red Rock, your mother kept it after your father died, and you worked as the bookkeeper, then you married Rey, then what?"

"You remember all that? I'm impressed. You were paying attention."

"Teacher training." I tried to sound casual.

Caroline smiled in a much-too-knowing way. "My mother got herself a real bookkeeper, and Rey and I moved to Thunder Bay. I kept house for us. Rey was older and I thought he knew everything about everything, mostly because I knew so little, so I went along with whatever he suggested. He got a job, and for a while we had a normal life. Or I thought it was. But little by little, my old friends stopped coming to visit, stopped asking me to go out. Rey always had something I had to do that kept me from spending time with people. Rey's parents were gone, but he still had that farm, so we spent a lot of 'free' time out there. He futzed about, and I'd be out of contact with everyone."

I steamed, but gently. "That's abuse."

"It didn't feel like it. More like I was becoming a 1950s woman." She fell silent.

We passed through Beaver Marsh. At Highway 138, Caroline turned right. She was taking us to Crater Lake. I knew because I'd spent a lot of time looking at the Oregon map back in Washington State, when I was plotting an escape from Rey. If Rey tuned in to us, he'd see a sign for the national park.

As we approached the sign, Caroline slowed. "I'd like to see this place." She turned to look at the sign as we went past. "We could stay at the lodge."

"As long as you don't make me walk to the edge." At her look, I added, "Not crazy about heights, okay? And also—Rey?"

Caroline glanced at me, her eyes anything but casual. *Shut up*, they said. So I did.

She turned on the road to the crater and, after a mile, pulled over at a small parking area and turnaround—one with washrooms.

"I'll be right back." She walked purposefully, her handbag swinging in time with her steps. In a few minutes she was back.

"Feel better?" I asked as she got back into the car.

"Much." For the briefest moment we locked eyes. She signalled: the cup holder. She put on her seat belt, and in the same fluid movement dropped a crumpled piece of paper. She was as smooth as a magician hiding a coin from a child.

I reached for the paper. She shook her head minutely, so that Rey, if he were "watching," wouldn't have seen the communication between us.

"Don't *you* need to go?"

I understood. As I undid my seatbelt I palmed the crumpled paper and headed for the washroom.

It was darker in the washroom than I'd have liked, but I could still read it. I straightened out the paper. *Lodge,* she had written, *pretend sleep, leave, I sleep, you drive, backtrack, west anywhere.* Cryptic, but not overwhelmingly so.

I suddenly realized I needed the bathroom for more than just privacy. When I got back to the car, Caroline gave me a quick once-over to see if I had understood. I gave her the smallest of nods in return.

When I was belted in, she started the engine. "Let's do this."

It took forever to wind uphill to the lodge at the crater's rim. Here and there I could still see the last of last winter's snow in the shadowy spots beside the road. The first of the fresh stuff could begin to fall any day at this altitude—we were at almost eight thousand feet. We pulled in at the Visitor's Center, paid the park fee (thank you, Bernie), and then drove to the lodge.

Yes, said the clerk, they had one room left. However, the room they had was a loft, and expensive: $310.

I had faith in Bernie's credit card. Once again, the transaction went through.

The loft was spectacular. Caroline threw herself on the bed. "Young man, fetch the bags. There's a dollar in it for you if you're prompt."

"American or Canadian?"

"Whichever has the lower exchange rate."

I could see that she was genuinely tired. "Why don't you order room service while I bring up our stuff?"

"So long as later you don't complain about what I order." She reached across the bed for the phone. I left for the car.

It took me more than a few minutes to collect everything. When I got back to the room, Caroline still lay on the bed, the phone in its cradle.

I couldn't restrain my curiosity. "So what did you order?"

"You first, food second."

I put our few belongings on the floor beside the door to the bathroom. "Cough up the food portion."

"Cratered chicken quesadillas and the house salad with raspberries."

"Cratered?"

She held up the Guest Services booklet, pointing to the picture in the menu. "The orange and yellow circles are melted mozzarella and cheddar cheese. They serve the quesadillas on big round plates so it looks like a planet or a moon with craters."

"That's, uh, different. Cheesy."

She smiled at my joke. "Just so. There's something else I'd like to show you, but I'll save it for later."

"Later" turned out to be three in the morning. Caroline woke me from the dream of the brush wolf, and we packed up our gear. We were out and on the road in ten minutes.

"You drive," Caroline said. "You know where."

"Okay. But Rey—he's going to be able to follow us, isn't he?"

"Eventually. But Rey's a regular sleeper. Right now, his head's on his pillow and his eyes are shut, and he's dreaming about someone bosomy."

"That's *almost* poetic."

We crept down the long winding slope to Highway 138. With no moon, the headlights turned the road and its bordering pines into a tunnel. I had no idea if wildlife sat on the road, ready to surprise us, but I kept watch for the telltale flash of eyes reflecting our lights.

"You were going to show me something," I said. "What?"

Caroline reached into her handbag and took out a book. "This."

I glanced over and caught the glint of three gold letters on its cover — KJV. "A Bible? You *stole* the *Bible*?"

Caroline laughed. "It seemed like a good idea at the time. My parents were religious. Like, really religious. We said grace before meals, we went to church on Sundays, all that. I've actually read the Bible. The whole thing, cover to cover, at least four times. My family had this evening reading routine. So while you were hauling our stuff up to the room last night, after I was done ordering food, I opened the drawer of the night table. I skimmed a few pages."

She reached up and flipped on one of the car's map lights, then thumbed to find a place. "John 14:26," she intoned. "This is the bit where John is talking about Christ letting the disciples know He's not going to be around much longer, but God's going to send them the Comforter, the Holy Spirit, to be their substitute teacher."

"Okay." I tried to communicate both puzzlement and curiosity with a word that has neither at its root.

"So the Holy Spirit is a guy, right? The masculine pronoun, *he*, is always used. *He* is the Comforter. *He* is going to teach them. Except in this Bible, the Comforter is female."

"Could be a misprint."

"That's what I thought, too. So I looked up Luke. The first part of Luke is all about how the Virgin Mary got pregnant by the Holy Spirit. And lo, Mary isn't a virgin in this Bible, just a young woman, and Joseph impregnates her while the Holy Spirit looks on."

"This is important, why?"

"Wait." She flipped pages again. "I just want to check something."

We were low enough that all traces of snow had disappeared. The clouds had begun to break up as well, and here and there I could see stars.

"Aha. In my world, in Matthew, there's a story about a couple of guys who are possessed by demons, and Jesus chases the demons into a herd of pigs, and the pigs rush into the sea and drown themselves. In Mark and

Luke, you get the same story except it's different—there's just one guy and he's in a different place. Actually, Mark and Luke don't agree on the name of the place, but the names are pretty similar."

"So?"

"So this story, about demons and pigs, is one that people point to when they want to prove that the Bible has mistakes."

"And?"

"But it doesn't matter whether these are actual mistakes—what's important is that I know the Bible."

"You've completely lost me."

"Don't you see? I know the Bible, the one I was raised on. Give me a Bible from any of the worlds we're in, and I can tell you how similar it is to the one I grew up with. I think that means I can tell you how similar any world is to the world that was my home. I can count discrepancies. The more there are, the farther away we are. No doubt you can do the same thing for your world."

"Not with the Bible I can't."

"There's got to be something—some printed, factual information—you can use. What do you know about?"

"Hockey trivia. I know a lot about hockey."

Caroline was silent, eventually saying only, "Well, it's a start. Now you drive and I sleep."

"You get to sleep?"

"Damn right. And if Rey cares to check in on me, he's welcome to anything in my head."

37 # OBSERVER

Four days later, we arrived at the home of Dr. Anna Gustafsson in Cambria, California, at just after 2 in the morning. I'd driven until about 1 while Caroline slept, then she took the wheel.

The strategy was Caroline's. The whole way, I drove during the day while Caroline napped. At night, she took over and I rested. Neither of us knew what route the other would take. Caroline saw my job as getting us lost. Hers was to get us closer to our destination, which only she knew. If Ray tuned in on me, he could learn only that we were somewhere he didn't expect. If he tuned in on Caroline, she'd be napping—perhaps dreaming.

I later learned from Dr. Anna that we had taken what a physicist would call a semi-random quantum walk.

Anna was not a "guy" in any sense of the word—Caroline had cloaked her identity as another level of protection from Rey. In reality, Anna was a comfortable, rumpled forty-year-old physicist who taught at Berkley through the late spring. Then she returned to her childhood home in Cambria, where she wrote up research and kept in touch with her friends and colleagues. Bernie, who was none of the Bernies we knew, was one of her closest friends.

Anna's parents were canoe-junkies. Every year, when California got too warm for them, they headed for Canada and the lakes and portages of Quetico Provincial Park in Ontario. Anna then "borrowed" the house and slipped into something more Californian and comfortable, trading in shoes for flip-flops and shedding the academic accent leftover from her post-grad days at Harvard.

Anna's summer home was a short walk from the cliffs that made up most of the shoreline of Cambria. The exterior of the house was California Nondescript, complete with a hybrid car parked in the driveway. Inside, the home was plain, with relatively bare light-grey stucco walls.

Caroline rang the bell. When Anna answered, I of course assumed that we'd meet her physicist husband in short order. I'm a slow learner.

In my defense, I wasn't familiar with this Caroline. Not only had Caroline lied to both Rey and me about Anna, but Anna greeted her with, "You must be Nancy." So Caroline had lied to just about everyone—she'd been, I hoped, both smart enough and devious enough. She'd learned a lot while we were apart.

I tried not to stare at "Nancy."

Caroline smiled sweetly. "Yes, and this is my husband, Jim."

I had been rechristened again: David, Richard, Jim.

"Come in," Anna said. "You have the letter?"

Caroline gave it to her.

"And this is not from the Bernie I know, but from one you're familiar with?"

"Yes."

"Give me a moment," Anna said, opening the letter.

While she read, I said to Caroline, "Whoa, I'm missing something. How does Dr. Gustafsson know about Bernie's letter?"

"I called her from the Lodge when you went to get our luggage."

Anna finished reading. She turned the letter over and looked at it closely. Then she looked up at "Nancy" and "Jim."

"It's very strange indeed. On par with your phone call. However, you don't look dangerous, and the letter is in Bernie's handwriting, so let's assume it's genuine. Come with me, please. Sorry about the mess."

She led us through the living room, a tangled path through stacks of paper and piles of assorted items of clothing—and past an ugly but small purse-dog sleeping in a handmade basket-nest of some kind. The dog opened its eyes, decided that we weren't worth its time, and closed them again.

In the kitchen, Anna flipped on the light. A small table with four wooden chairs stood in front of a bay window. The almond-coloured kitchen stove and harvest yellow refrigerator were festooned with fridge magnets and notes dangling from magnetic clips.

"Sit down. Make yourself comfortable."

Attempting to be inconspicuous, I checked the seat of the proffered chair for sticky stuff. Finding none, I sat. Caroline sat without checking.

Caroline began, "Bernie suggested that we should talk to you about our, uh, situation."

Anna gave her an open but somewhat conspiratorial smile. "My Bernie, you know, is completely wasted at Lakehead. I assume yours is as well. He's the brightest man I've ever met. He has some odd interests, however, and attracts some odd people." She looked over the top of her glasses the way an old-fashioned schoolmarm might when getting ready to upbraid a pupil. "Still, I've never thought of him as the damsel-rescuing type. So, Nancy, tell me something about what you seem to be able to do."

"I don't think it's something *I* do. Up to now, I'm more done-by than doer."

"Let's leave that idea on the table for a moment. Start at the beginning."

Over the next two hours, Caroline laid out our story. From time to time Anna asked a question or invited Caroline to go back over a particular situation.

After Caroline finished, Anna turned her attention to me, and I went through the same interrogation.

When I finished, we sat, awaiting her verdict.

"Huh." For a moment, Anna sat in silence. Then, she said, "Believe it or not, I believe you." She looked at Caroline. "You definitely have the ability to change your circumstances." She turned to me. "You—you're not so accomplished, but have at least a *little* of Nancy's ... skill. "

She turned back to Caroline. "I think you're right about Rey's ability to know where you are, *and* his ability to examine your environment for clues to your location. So here's what I'd like you to do: go away and come back here tomorrow night, same time."

I tried to contribute. "Should we take two aspirins and call you in the morning?"

Both Caroline and Anna scowled at me, but Anna's politeness won out. "I have some thinking to do."

She led us out the way we'd come in. The dog's paws twitched in its sleep as it chased something. When I walked past, it gave a little lip-snort, a dreaming dog's bark. A brush wolf it was not.

"Tomorrow night. Same time."

In the car, Caroline said, "You need sleep. We passed a park. You can get some shuteye. I have a book to read."

At sunrise Caroline woke me, and I took the wheel again. We left Cambria and headed inland. If Rey chose to take a look, he wouldn't know we were at the coast.

#

Anna was watching through the window for us and urged us quickly into her house. Again, we gathered at her table.

"I've been thinking about information." She pointed at me. "You told me yesterday that Dr. Singh implied you're a metaphor."

I thought back. "He led me to say it—I don't know that he believed it himself."

"Doesn't matter. Here." She handed me a paperback book. "What do you have in your hand?" Socrates would have been proud of her.

"*The Invisible Man.*"

"Not the title, no matter how appropriate. It's a paperback book."

"Yes? So?" I didn't feel like playing Watson to her Holmes.

"It is also full of words. And the words are made of letters. And each letter can be built of code—computer code, for example—that expresses the information that's the letter."

She looked at me to see if I understood. Although I didn't know where she was taking us, I nodded like a dutiful child.

"In the quantum world—"

"There's a phrase I'm starting to hate," I muttered.

Anna ignored me. "In the quantum world, in the beginning, when the universe came into existence, all the information that was around in the first moment of the Big Bang could have been contained in that paperback book or—or, say, a one-gig flashdrive. Everything, *everything* that came into being as a consequence of the Big Bang had its origins in a very small packet of information. The whole universe was no more complex than that novel. Everything, Jim—including you—can be expressed mathematically as information. We just have more of it now."

She launched into an explanation of how some bacteria use quantum information to locate food sources—they do the quantum walk. Then she returned to the nature of information as bits of code and how everything, at its core, is an expression of information.

Caroline followed Anna's explanations better than I did. In fact, Caroline had been the one to tell Anna about Dr. Singh and his idea of metaphor.

"Metaphor is an excellent way to look at this," Anna said, "because all metaphor is built of information."

I shrugged. "So now I'm information."

"Yes." For a second Anna looked at me hopefully, searching for the glimmer in the eyes that means the student understands at last. Seeing no such glimmer, she shifted her attention to Caroline. "Mathematics, not English, is the language of the universe, but for the language to make sense, some conditions must be met."

I tried. "Like pumping up the number of dimensions from three or four to ten?" That contribution had used up most of what I'd learned.

"Yes." Anna acknowledged my participation, not my insight—she thanked me for showing up, but she knew Caroline was her better pupil. "We know that quantum information can't be destroyed. A bit, think of it as a zero or a one, is its smallest unit and can't be further divided. Photons can be entangled, not only in pairs, but in larger units. We entangle three photons and use one as the mechanism for something akin to teleportation. We can send information from here to there, without regard to distance or the speed of light, with no lag time. When the information arrives, it instantly changes the behaviour of the photon so that, for all intents and purposes, a photon itself was transmitted."

She paused as if waiting for applause.

None came. Caroline said, "Okay. But I don't see the point."

"There's another aspect. One odd thing about the quantum world is that without an observer of an action, no action happens. No observer — nothing. Add an observer, something."

Anna looked intently at Caroline. "So the observer isn't just an observer. In the quantum world, the observer is also the creator of the event."

Caroline and I looked at each other. We both got it at the same time.

"We're creating what's happening to us," Caroline said.

"But how ...?" I didn't know what the rest of the sentence was.

Anna smiled. "I don't know, and I don't think I *can* know. I can't make a pink lampshade turn blue, no matter how hard I try. After you left last night, I spent some time at it. But you can." She nodded at Caroline. "Can Jim—who, by the way, probably isn't named Jim, is he?"

Caroline shook her head like a little girl caught in a lie.

Anna said, "No matter. He's not as advanced as you are. And you're not as skilled as this Rey fellow. I think both of you can learn to do it, whatever it is you do, much better. Go away now. Come back tomorrow. I'll think about what exercises might make you better at all this."

She herded us to the door, sounding like a mother sending her children to school for the first time. "Be careful. This Rey is dangerous."

As I pulled out of the driveway, I commented, "Brusque, isn't she?"

"I like her."

"Me, too. Same park?"

Caroline thought about it. "Different park. She's right about Rey."

The following night, Anna waited in the dark at the side door. She had left the lights off.

"Come in, I have something to show you."

She led us through the domestic battlefield of the kitchen. The dog, asleep on the kitchen floor, woke as we went past. He gave a half-hearted bark and sub-vocalized growl.

"Fermi!" The dog put its head between its front paws and tried to look woeful.

"Fermi?" I asked. "Why Fermi?"

"I like word-play." Anna explained no further.

I finally figured it out—fur-me—and acknowledged that in punning, as in so many other subjects, Dr. Anna was my master.

In the living room, she offered us tea. "It'll keep you alert." So much for the idea of a soothing cuppa.

On the living room floor sat two books, *The Invisible Man* and *The Time Machine*. Flanking the books were two number-ten envelopes. She motioned for us to sit on the living room sofa. She returned from the kitchen with tea in two old-fashioned porcelain cups, presented on a wooden tray, with sugar and cream.

"You're not having any?" I asked.

Anna pointed to a cup perched precariously on top of the old-fashioned TV. "I couldn't wait."

We took our cups. Anna took the tray to the kitchen and settled into the swivel rocker opposite us.

"Now, then. Each envelope contains a piece of paper with a number on it. The number is five digits long. That's long enough to make it a meaningful number, but still not hard to memorize. Each of you, take an envelope and memorize the number. When you're done, put the paper back in the envelope and put the envelope back where you found it. Jim, yours is on your left. Nancy, you take the other one. Don't show each other and don't do anything to give the other person any clues, either."

As we opened our envelopes, Caroline pointedly moved closer to her end of the sofa, and I followed her example. After a moment or two, I became aware that Caroline was better at memorizing than I was. At last, I put my paper into the envelope and returned the envelope to its spot beside *The Invisible Man*.

"All done? I know both numbers. Of course I wrote them, but I also memorized them. And neither of you knows the other's number, right?"

We agreed.

Anna nodded, satisfied. "So let's try this. In a moment we'll close our eyes—me included. Nancy, you imagine that when you open your eyes, the two books on the floor will have traded places. Take as long as you like. When you think you've succeeded, open your eyes and say something."

Eyes closed, I felt completely apart from what we were doing. It felt like a séance or a table-rapping session disguised as science. I felt trapped in the worst-ever dream, a paid-advertising infomercial for bogus exercise equipment, crossed with a magic metal cure-all bracelet.

Caroline said, "I'm done. Eyes open."

Anna and I looked at the books. They had changed places.

"She could have moved them around when our eyes were closed," I pointed out.

Caroline glared at me, but Anna nodded.

"She could have, but she didn't. The books are tied together. Before you came, I linked the books with a piece of thread. It's glued to the back of each book. You can't see the thread because I hid it amid the fibres of the carpet. Nancy, pick up the books."

Caroline did, and showed me—the books were still fastened together.

Anna got up and headed for the kitchen. "I need to check something." She was back in a minute or two. "Like you, I have an envelope with a number, quite a long number. The number in the kitchen is a lot like my number, but it's not quite the same. Close, but no cigar."

I reached for my envelope.

"No!" Anna said. "Don't touch it."

I pulled my hand back and resolved yet again to do fewer stupid things.

"Nancy, take us back home—to my home, that is." She knelt on the carpet and put the books back. "Same as before."

We closed our eyes. When Caroline said, "I'm done," we could see the books back in their "correct" order.

"Now, Jim," Anna said. "Remember the number you memorized?

Look in your envelope. Is it the same? Nancy, you too."

We looked.

"Well?" Anna's voice held excitement.

"Same," Caroline said.

"Same," I echoed.

Anna went into the kitchen, returning with a triumphant smile. "Same."

I raised my cup to Caroline and took my first sip of tea.

Anna looked ready to clap her hands with excitement. "Tonight, you took all of us a little way from my world and brought us back. Gradually, you should start longer trips."

Caroline's voice held a mixture of curiosity and excitement. "Longer trips?"

Dr. Anna nodded. "Absolutely. The more iterations you do of this process—whatever it is that you do to move in the multiverse—the more you'll learn and the more skill you'll develop."

"Iterations?" I spoke before I thought. Anna looked at me, patient, waiting for me to say something elementary. So I did. "I just—it's a confusing term. I thought an iteration of something was just a different version. You know, the latest car model, or a slightly different vacuum cleaner. But you seem to mean something else. Specific."

Anna's smile was kind. "In mainstream culture, 'version' and 'iteration' aren't that different in meaning, and 'repetition' is a related concept. Strictly speaking, though, an iteration is a process—a series of steps—that's repeated in a meaningful way. The point is to learn something from each repetition. Maybe the result of the iteration is closer to a correct answer, or the iteration lets you find the least-bad solution. I could give you technical examples from computer science, but they're not terribly important. Really, all I meant was that if Nancy, here, deliberately performs the same actions she's shown us tonight, in ever-more-ambitious situations, she should gain skill. Perhaps over time, she'll become as skillful as Rey, or more."

"Ah. Okay." I hoped I sounded wiser.

Dr. Anna dismissed us. "Now, finish your tea and go. Tomorrow night, we start training for the Olympics."

As we left Dr. Anna's house and drove off to find a place to sleep, I thought again about Caroline iterating the actions, whatever they were, that moved us through the multiverse. I knew that each time we moved to a different part of the multiverse, we also changed slightly. Caroline had already changed in the time we'd been apart, but she was still recognizably the same Caroline I'd known, if more subtle and powerful. I hoped, selfishly, that Caroline's iterations wouldn't take her too far from the Caroline I'd grown to love. The Caroline that had room in her life for me.

38 # NO

The next night, we were a few minutes late. Barricades for road maintenance clogged traffic on not one, but two of Cambria's main streets.

When we pulled into Anna's driveway, the house's side door light was on, as usual. But something was wrong—the aluminum storm door bowed out and bent at its handle, and the screened bottom half of the door was torn. Our headlights glinted off glass that spilled into the driveway from the broken door. The entry door stood open, but the house beyond was dark.

"A break-in, like at Bernie's." My throat felt tight. Caroline looked at me.

I turned off the car but made no move to get out while I examined the scene closely, trying to mine all the information possible.

"Someone pulled so hard on the handle that the door bent."

"Rey?"

"Must be. Dr. Anna must have tried to hold the outside door shut against him. She'd thought we were early." I blinked to keep back tears.

Caroline tried to keep her voice calm. "Do we call the police?"

It's hard to shut off the brain's first response, its instinctive need to follow familiar, conditioned procedures for what to do when trouble appears. Of course we wanted help for Anna—she'd become a friend, intertwined into our lives.

"I don't think so, not yet. Let's find out what happened first."

On our way to the broken door, I said, "Touch as few things as possible." Again, a reflex from what we all absorb from TV cop shows—I had no idea whether our fingerprints would be on file anywhere in this world. I found a small stick on the driveway and used it to hold the screen door open.

Caroline went in ahead of me. "It's dark."

"Wait. I'll get the light." With my handkerchief, I groped for the kitchen light switch and flicked it on.

"God!" Caroline shielded her eyes from both the light and the scene.

A ragged trail of blood ran along the floor to the doorway of the living room. A few feet from the door, a bloody shoe print—the right shoe and big enough to be Rey's—followed the path of blood into the living room. It looked like something out of a comic slasher movie, one in which the killer went leaping after the victim on one leg.

But as I looked, I found nothing funny about the scene.

The kitchen table had been pushed into the wall and one of the chairs lay overturned. A drawer stood open, and forks and spoons and knives, some of them bloodied, lay scattered on the floor. A single spoon, its handle under the yellow refrigerator, seemed to be trying to hide from the mayhem. The dog's bed, which belonged in the living room, lay broken and upside down near the kitchen door. Fermi's cushion was gone.

In the living room, everything seemed to be in its proper place. Against the far wall, the sofa, where we'd sat for Anna's *The Invisible Man* experiment, looked untouched.

Then Caroline gasped, and I turned around. While I'd focused on the sofa, she'd followed the blood to the rocker, against the wall beside us.

In it sat something that had once been Anna.

On the carpet, fainter now, the prints of the right shoe. Faintest of all, the print in front of the entry door, made when the attacker had left.

It could have been no one else. Rey had stabbed Anna repeatedly. He'd started when she met him at the side door. He'd continued as he chased her through the kitchen and into the living room. She'd tried, but failed, to make it out the front door.

The body now in the swivel rocker, slouching as she would never have slouched in life, had been finished off with multiple slashes to her face, legs, and abdomen. Her arms and hands were cut to shreds.

Defensive wounds, my mind told me from far off. When she was dead— *please God, not before*—he'd gutted her.

The dog's cushion lay at Anna's feet. I knelt and turned it over with the little stick. It was bloody.

"Not just Rey," I said. "Two of them."

Caroline didn't seem to hear. She said nothing.

"One held her in the chair while the other suffocated her."

Still nothing from Caroline.

I looked up.

She stared at the wall above the chair, seeing and not seeing bloody hand prints.

A man's hands—not handprints of the woman in the chair.

He'd drawn a semi-circle of bloody hands, a red sunrise. Like a child, he'd used blood to draw alternating short and long lines from the circle.

Rays, I thought. *Reys*. He, they, had signed their work.

"O, God." Caroline pointed at a painting on the floor.

At first I thought she wanted me to look at Anna's knitting bag lying on its side beside the rocker, the contents strewn across the carpet, but after a moment I understood.

The painting, a brush wolf peering through tall grass at huge green waves crashing on a rocky shore, had fallen on the floor.

No, it had been placed on the floor. When we'd been in the room before, I'd only glanced at the painting. I hadn't seen the wolf, hidden by its artist in the grass.

Now something else hung where the painting had been, a collar draped over a large picture hook. Fermi. Like her, he'd been gutted, but not before Rey had driven Anna's knitting needles through his eyes.

Caroline managed to say "Rey" before the sobs started. Her body shook as she attempted to regain control. "Oh God. Rey—he shoved the needles in its eyes to make it look like an insect. My Rey wouldn't have done this. He likes—*liked*—to make little sculptures out of stones and pieces of wood, but funny things, small and harmless. He'd never have done this. Not before."

I took her hand. "He's changed. He changes, we change."

She pulled her hand back, shouting, "No! Not this! A human wouldn't do this!" She clenched her fists.

Suddenly, Anna's living room was pristine again.

Anna was gone, Fermi was gone, the blood, all the evidence of violence. In this room, Anna was merely absent—maybe running an errand or shopping at a twenty-four hour convenience store. On the wall, instead of the brush wolf painting or the body of poor Fermi, hung a painting of a toy poodle—Fermi—looking over a sandy beach where children played as the sun set.

Caroline took my hand again. "Come on, we're not staying here one more second." She dragged me through the kitchen (now untouched), out the side door (unbroken), to the car.

She got in the passenger side. "Drive. Take us somewhere."

"Where?"

"I don't care. Just drive."

I thought she was going into shock again. I was confused. I wanted to know if we were someplace Anna didn't exist, or if she simply had escaped murder here. I wanted to know ... I don't know what. Something.

"Anna?"

"She's alive, somewhere. But *our* Anna's dead." She began to cry. "O, God, I hate this. I hate it."

"Do you think Rey's watching?" I was suddenly afraid.

Caroline, furious, shouted, "There is no Rey here! There is no goddamn Rey! Start the car and drive, damn it!"

I did.

39 # THE TIME MACHINE

Fifteen hundred years ago, Anicius Boethius wrote in *The Consolation of Philosophy* that for God, all time is simultaneous. Small consolation, perhaps, because at the time, Boethius was in prison awaiting execution for the crime of being overly truthful. I'm sure he'd have been interested to know that all these years later, his words still ring true—except, of course, that time should be expressed in the plural, and God should be bracketed by quotation marks. And somebody would need to say a few words to him about the multiverse.

H. G. Wells, who wrote *The Time Machine*, wouldn't have been as interested. After all, he wrote about *his* world. In his world, not somebody else's, *plus ça change, plus c'est la même chose* was the universal theme. The more things change, the more they stay the same. Wells wrote social criticism, not just science fiction.

I had a new appreciation for Wells. For Caroline and me, the Anna that Rey killed was Anna. *Our* Anna. Same as we'd felt about Bernie. The fact that there were lots of Annas or Bernies to go around was no consolation.

#

Anger and tears, blended with hopelessness, make a powerful soporific. After just a half-hour of driving, I looked over to find Caroline asleep. I drove for another hour or so. When the road felt as if it were rolling under the car, I looked for a place to pull over. I turned up a dirt road leading to a gravel pit.

Caroline woke for a minute or two when I turned off the engine, but quickly went back to sleep.

I joined her soon after.

The low and persistent rumble of a dump truck woke me four hours later. Before the truck got to us, I had the car turned around and headed back to the main road.

Caroline woke. "Where are we?"

"I'm not sure." The pavement felt smooth under our tires. "I was on Highway 101, then State Route 46. We're about fifty miles from Cambria."

"Good." She fell asleep once more.

The highway wound through the hills and descended onto a flat expanse of farmland stretching out to forever. When the hills were behind us, the road straightened and took us southeast. After a while, it bent to the east and straightened out again, sending us like an arrow flying low under the blue morning sky. Soon the farmland vanished on the right but continued on the left.

A short time later, we came to Blackwells Corner, marked with a huge sign and the picture of James Dean. At last I knew where we were—the last place the movie idol stopped before the 1955 car crash that killed him.

I woke Caroline, excited. "James Dean!"

"What?" She tried to sit up but flailed a little. Her seatback was almost horizontal and she was pinned down by the seatbelt. Groggily, she freed herself and sat up.

I pulled into the parking lot. "James Dean. The movie star?"

"I have to pee. Tell me later."

We went into the building, Caroline leading the way. The room was dominated by a curving counter trimmed in aluminum, ringed in round bar seats topped by shiny red padded leatherette. Two customers sat examining menus while a server chatted them up, all smiles and attentiveness. She wore a black blouse trimmed in white, a pink apron over a baby blue skirt, and one of those hats where she could park the pencil from her order pad. It was 1955 all over again, except for the flat-screen TVs in the corners.

Everywhere else—every available surface, horizontal and vertical—was covered with James Dean memorabilia. Glasses, calendars, statuettes, mugs and picture frames, posters, post cards, paintings. Clothing, too—scarves, bandanas, caps, even knockoffs of the famous Rebel jacket. The wall on our left had an oversized doorway, perhaps ten feet wide. Above it, a sign said Little Bastard.

Caroline had stopped, mouth open.

"Little Bastard!" I said.

"What?" Caroline stared reprovingly.

I pointed to the sign. "Can't be. Little Bastard was the car Dean was driving on the day he died. He totaled it. It was cursed. Some of its parts were bought by people who had Spyders, and the cars all crashed, people died. Cursed!"

"Spiders?"

"Spyders, with a y—a Porsche nameplate. James Dean had a 550."

"Okay. Still have to pee." She headed for the Ladies.

I went through the wide doorway. The car was, indeed, Little Bastard—maybe not Dean's original, but a 550, right down to the *Little Bastard* painted on the grill. George Barris, the guy who designed the original Batmobile, had done the artwork.

A man appeared beside me, out of nowhere. "Still a beauty, isn't she?"

He wore one of the Rebel jackets the store sold, and his hair, dyed dark brown, was cut in a pompadour style. He held an unlit cigarette in the corner of his mouth. He looked about fifty or so, which made him too young to be James Dean—but he sure looked the same.

I risked it. "Mr. Dean?"

"Call me Martin. Dad had a strange sense of humour."

"You're James Dean's son?"

"'Fraid so. You can take my picture out by the sign. We've got a motorcycle we use as a prop. Cost you ten, though."

"I don't have a camera."

"We sell those, too. Twenty megapixels. It's got a Little Bastard logo. Good camera. It's Russian."

"No, thanks." I was more tempted by a photo of the car.

"No problem. Don't want to pressure you. Pardon the cigarette. I don't smoke, but—you know, the image."

"Your dad died when?"

"2001. The Good Book says three-score-and-ten. Dad was a few months short."

I changed the subject. "The car. I thought it was totaled in the crash."

"Nah. Dad almost was. Broke his leg, took a heck of a whack on the noggin. You know the story."

I didn't, actually, but I didn't want to let on to Martin. I knew only the story where James Dean died, cut down in his prime—not the one where he survived. I could still tell the truth. "He was a great actor."

"Not much of a businessman, though. Not much heart for maintaining his image, either. Everybody loves *Rebel* and *Giant*, of course. *East of Eden* not so much. *Digger* was a disaster. Shouldn't have done that one. The next two, either."

"I liked it." In my world James Dean had made only three movies, and *Digger* wasn't one of them.

Caroline had returned. I introduced her to Martin, then I left to find the washroom myself.

When I got back, Martin was still talking to her. "When Dad got out of the movie business, he bought this place. Said it was lucky. And I guess it was. For a while, anyway. Still does a pretty good business at different times in the year."

"Ready?" Caroline's eyes told me what I should answer.

I thanked Martin for talking to us. Before we left, I filled the tank. Then I pointed us east once more.

After a few miles, Caroline broke our silence. "Who was James Dean again? Some movie star?"

"You never heard of him? Never saw *East of Eden*?"

"No. I read it in high school. John Steinbeck, right? The teacher kept going on and on about how it was a Cain and Abel story. Or was it Adam and Eve?"

"No movie?"

"Nope."

I wondered what it must have been like to be raised in a world without James Dean in it. Caroline had grown up in such a world — and so had her Rey. No doubt some other rebel had taken Dean's place in their world's culture. After all, Caroline had said Rey had a "thing" about his hair.

A few miles out of Blackwells Corner, the farmland disappeared. The orchards became a thin green line receding in the rear view mirror.

In their place grew mile after mile of oil pump-jacks, bobbing their heads like dippy birds sipping from invisible glasses of water. We were in the oil fields of Kern County. The road, unobstructed, ran east until we came to Lost Hills, a tiny community with almost as many fast food joints as the oil fields had pump-jacks. And then the road ran east some more.

After we crossed I-5, I risked a question: "Can Rey see us?"

"No." Her voice was calm, but the question must have brought up a picture of Anna dead in the swivel rocker. She shifted position in the car seat.

I didn't want to ask her the next part of the question, but I had to. "You know this for sure?"

"One of my others says we're being protected."

"By ...?"

"She doesn't really know. But she's sure Rey can't see us, not here."

"So where are we going? We can't just keep heading east."

"Well we can, but you're right. We need a place to practice."

"Practice?"

"Getting home." She paused. "Keep going to Wesco. We can pick up I-43 there. It'll take us to Bakersfield. Then we can loop back a bit and go down to Ventura. We'll be there before nightfall."

"Your others are better than a GPS."

"I seem to have done a lot of travelling in this area, all right." Her voice was flat. "It's funny—they know how to get me to all kinds of places, but they don't know past a certain point what happens once I get there."

"Huh. I wonder why."

Caroline was silent for some time. "Maybe they think I'm going to die, but just don't want to say it."

There was no response for this. So I kept my mouth shut.

40 # BONAVENTURE

Ventura, California, when we got there, wasn't called Ventura, and it wasn't the headquarters of surfing culture. In our world, it was San Buenaventura, a small city on the California coast that had retained much of the admirable parts of twentieth-century American culture, even after the new century gave it up.

After we'd settled into our motel (usual rules, still), Caroline promptly went to sleep. In contrast, I fought all night against something dreadful—something malevolent and unreasonable. I dreamt dreams within dreams, nightmares within nightmares.

"How did you sleep?" Caroline asked in the morning.

"Fine." No bogey man had hidden under *her* bed, it seemed. "You?"

"Good." She paused and looked momentarily puzzled. "Um. There's continental breakfast downstairs. Get dressed and fed, and we'll get to work."

I did as I was told. I returned with dry cereal in a plastic bowl and a fork in hand because they had run out of spoons.

Caroline sat on her bed, making notes on scraps of motel writing paper.

"Sit and have a look at this."

"Hold on." I drew back the curtains. "Wow. What time is it?"

Caroline pointed at the clock on the night table. Eight-fifteen. "Time for you to sit down and help me think."

I brought the desk chair over beside Caroline's bed. The chair had been around for decades. Its cushion was flat and hard, the back a little wobbly.

"At least the furniture and the cutlery match." I settled in. "What's that?"

"Questions. I made a list. For instance, what in this room makes it different from all the other motel rooms we've been in? What is the unique thing—the one thing that won't likely be in any other room? And others."

"Because?"

"To take the place of those numbers Anna wrote out."

Caroline had planned an experiment—we'd "leave" the room and come back to it.

"So we need to be able to prove that we're back where we started. If we don't get back and die in an ambush of some kind." She sighed.

"How about a weather forecast? On TV?"

"How would that work?"

"You leave the room. I write down the weather forecast for someplace, then you do the same. We don't even tell each other what place we chose. Then, when we're back, we compare our forecasts with what's on TV. "

"If our forecasts, the ones we write down, are the same as the TV forecasts, we're back. I like it."

"It's not Bible trivia, but it should work."

"Let's use your laptop so we're not stuck with what's on TV."

I set up the laptop. After some fiddling, I logged on.

As I worked, I asked, "What will we change in the room?"

"Lampshade colour." Caroline added, "It's tradition."

"Okay. What colour?"

"That, Sherlock, is a secret. Leave the room—get us a coffee or something."

When I returned, Caroline got up from the desk chair. "My turn."

I looked up the weather in Aberdeen, Scotland, wrote it on a piece of paper, and put it into my pocket. She came back five minutes later.

"Now what?" I wanted to know.

And with that, the lampshade turned green.

It took a moment to register. "It's green!" It was one of my many demonstrations of genius.

"It complements my hair. Now, I'll see if I can get us back."

"Wait, wait, wait. What if just you goes back?"

"We came here together, right?"

"Yeah, but I'm not one-hundred percent sure that'll happen in reverse. Could we hold hands or something?"

"No." The lampshade was beige again.

It looked like the room we'd left. But we had to be sure.

Caroline pulled a piece of folded paper from her pocket. "Here's my weather forecast."

I gave her mine.

We each checked the other's information on the laptop.

Caroline frowned. "It *seems* to have worked."

"But?"

"One of my others is new. I was just thinking about Stan. You remember the guy who told us you'd been killed with a baseball bat?"

"Yes."

"Well, I can't. I know he existed, but I can't picture him anymore. I've lost some part of that. I think that memory is gone. It's with someone else—another me, I guess. Lost it in transit."

"We change." I tried to make it sound hopeful.

"But Stan was a good guy. I don't want to lose my memory of him."

"You won't, not forever. You'll hold onto the things that are really important."

I said it because I hoped it was true. Like, for example, she'd hold on to memories—her memories—of me, the real me. But on the whole, I didn't believe much of that.

#

During the days and weeks that followed, August closed in on September. Caroline became an unstoppable force. Anna had fueled her hope for returning home. Rey had fueled her rage.

Caroline's iterations became more complex. With each one, she became more confident and skilled—far beyond any need to check our purloined Gideon Bible, though we kept it for sentimental reasons.

At first, the trips were short—from room to room, a few minutes here, half an hour there. Then we went outdoors and went from place to place. At "home" we'd leave something behind so we'd know, when we returned, that we'd gone back to our starting point.

It took some learning. The first time we missed returning, I thought we'd be lost forever. But Caroline simply tried again, and we were back.

Over time, Caroline took us to places like and less like the worlds we'd come from. We spent longer and longer periods in each.

Once, we saw Rey walking toward us on a downtown street in Ventura—not San Buenaventura, not Bonaventure, not San Buena.

She quickly took us back before he saw us.

At last, Caroline decided she needed to travel by herself and then return to me.

I tried to be a good sport. "Why?"

"Because it's something I have to learn to do."

"But if you, some version of you, make it back to me, how will I know it's really you?"

"You'll know." Then she took a dollar bill out of her purse, crumpled it, and tore it in half. She handed me one of the pieces. "Take this. We'll match halves when I return. And not just the serial number on it—we'll match the crease lines, too."

I had to be satisfied with that. *She will return*, I told myself.

Instead, she never left.

She put her half of the bill back in her purse. Then she said, "Show me your half of the dollar." She retrieved her half from her purse.

I handed mine over.

We compared them. They didn't match.

She put her part back into her purse. "Oops. Try again."

This time, they were a perfect match—serial numbers, creases, even a slight stain that cut across the tear.

I had to sit down. "Jesus. I didn't think it would be like that."

"Me neither." Caroline gave me an impish look. "Was it good for you?"

Then I was one-hundred percent sure—she'd been gone, but the right Caroline was back.

After that, we travelled together sometimes, and sometimes Caroline went alone. When she was gone, I'd see if I could turn a lampshade a different colour, or make a butter dish hold a slab of margarine, to no avail.

In truth, I didn't try too hard. I was afraid I'd end up in a world from which there was no return.

Caroline's solo ventures got longer. Sometimes when she left, a "replacement" appeared instantly. We'd chat and I'd find out how she and "I" were getting along.

Sometimes, the Caroline who appeared wouldn't have a David—he'd have died or never been—and she'd be shocked.

Sometimes, Caroline didn't have a replacement version. Those were the days I hated most.

When she was away for a long time, I'd head to the San Buenaventura library and read up on quantum matters. Sometimes I'd stay in the motel, sorting the garbage from the technical gibberish I found online. I learned a lot of things, but nothing of much substance, nothing useful.

One day I went to the Santa Barbara Zoo to gawk at the monkeys. When I got back, Caroline was there, unhappy because she'd hit the limit of her capacity to travel.

"It's like a sound barrier or something. I can't seem to go any farther. Like the world can be only so weird, but not weirder."

"I'm sorry." I wished, not for the first time or even the hundredth, that I really understood what it was like for her.

She shook her head. "Never mind. What did you do today?"

"I went to the zoo. The monkeys don't like the feed you buy from those little machines. They throw it back at you." I brushed at my sleeves. "It makes me feel itchy."

She'd stopped listening and stared out the window. "Monkeys! Of course!" She looked at me. "Get it? I have to do it in steps, like swinging from tree to tree, or, you know, evolution. I've been going straight from this world to another. I need to jump from world to world to world—or island to island, like Darwin and those beagles of his."

"Finches. But look, I don't like this. It's one thing to go from here to there and straight back. It's something else to go from here to there, to there, and somehow back again."

"We'll go together." She said it as if it solved everything. And, I had to admit, we had no real ties to the world we were in—just to each other.

The next day, we tried her quantum two-step. It worked. We began to travel from world to world.

And that's how, after a lot of two-step and then three-or-more-step trips, San Buenventura became Santa Flora. And I became, for a few days, a merman with a taste for a BurgoMeister breakfast.

It was fun to breathe and sleep underwater. But the transition from human to merman hurt like hell, even though Caroline carefully took us through a long set of baby-step transitions. Still—so worth it.

At least in retrospect, it wasn't surprising that I eventually learned to move between worlds on my own, like Caroline. If I could remember the first time I did it, I'd describe it, but I can't.

One Friday late in August, Caroline decided it was time. I was returning from one of my trips to the San Buenaventura public library. She met me at the door.

"I need to talk to you."

"Sure. Did you know that the FFG hangs around the library?"

"I'm serious. I need to talk to you, and I need you to listen. So here's the deal: you can tell me about the FFG, whatever that is, but then *you* have to listen to what *I* say."

"Okay." She couldn't possibly have anything as interesting as I did. "The FFG is the Fundamental Fysiks Group. From the 1970s, from Lawrence Berkley Laboratory. You know, the physics hippies?"

Nothing ignited even a hint of recognition in her eyes. I kept trying. "Some of them meet at the library on Fridays. I talked to Sarah Reiser!"

"Oh?"

I gave up. "Your turn."

"It's time to go after Rey."

She won. This was way more interesting.

"Go after him?" I sounded as if I didn't understand what she meant. I did. I just didn't like it.

"I'm ready. So are you. I think."

"We don't know how to find him."

"I do."

I didn't want to ask.

Caroline was right, of course. We'd been hiding in San Buenaventura, and so far, so good. But always, always, he'd found us, everywhere else we'd been. It was just a matter of time before he invaded this safe space, too. He'd catch the two of us—or one—on a trip, and that would be that.

I knew that my visits to the library, even the oddity of finding some members of the FFG alive and well and living in San Buenaventura, weren't enough to give up a regular life.

Bernie's bottomless credit card could keep us in food, gas and motels. But it couldn't keep us safe. It couldn't buy us happiness.

Caroline had waited quietly for me to catch up.

"Okay. Where is he?" I finally asked.

"He'll be at the farm."

"So we're going back?"

"If you feel we shouldn't, we won't. But you know …."

She didn't need to finish her sentence. Yes, I knew. Rey would be there. He knew Caroline as well as I did—perhaps even more intimately. He knew that she'd need to confront him, eventually, to break his hold on her. And he knew she'd do it at the place he'd terrified her the most.

He'd killed Dr. Anna to set up the moment of confrontation. He'd check, from time to time, to see whether Caroline had returned.

"All right. But he's very strong." My own weakness overwhelmed me for a moment. But it passed. "Can you get us back to the world we were in?"

"Yes." She paused. "I went back this morning."

I tried to sound ready, hoping that feeling ready would follow. "Okay. So what comes next?"

"Find the car keys."

41 # ROUTE 66

It was early on a Saturday morning, no trace of fog, clear blue sky. Traffic would be heavy as people headed for the beaches, but we'd leave the city as they headed into it.

Caroline studied the California road map she'd bought. "Santa Monica."

"Um. That's in the wrong direction. Shouldn't we head north?"

"I've been thinking."

"Uh-oh." No reaction. I couldn't coax a smile from her.

She spoke steadily, with resignation. "When we get to Thunder Bay— if we get there, if Rey hasn't killed us en route—it'll be bad." She seemed to be preparing herself for the inevitable. "Could we take Route 66?"

"There is no Route 66, not anymore. Just pieces of it, here and there. Most of the original is under the interstates now."

"Can't we follow it home? It started in Santa Monica. Let's see if we can find it."

"Absolutely, we can do that."

"I can take us to places where it still exists. I can do that much, at least."

I didn't know if she meant she'd take us to *worlds* in which it still existed or just to *places* where the interstates had left it alone. Instead, I asked, "Why the interest in Route 66? Movies?"

"It started with my dad reading to me when I was a kid. I liked stuff by Raymond Chandler. You know—Marlowe, seedy old Bay City. That was really Santa Monica. But I watched a lot of movies, too, and Palisades Park and the Santa Monica Pier are in dozens of them, even some of the Rocky movies."

"Stallone?"

"When things started going bad with Rey, I started thinking about running away from it all, someplace that wasn't anything like home and didn't have Rey in it. Not like now, just the world I'd started in, but a different part of it—on Route 66 in an old Model A, rumbling through

Beverly Hills down into Santa Monica." She was quiet for a moment. "But that's all I did—I just thought. I never did anything, never tried to make it better. Now, though, Route 66 feels like unfinished business. I've always wanted to see it. And I want ...." She trailed off.

In my mind, I finished it for her: *I want to travel that road before I die.*

After a beat, she went on, voice chipper. "So, driver, take me to Santa Monica, and the start of Route 66."

"Sure. But where's that?"

Caroline laughed—an easy laugh, relaxed and spontaneous. "That depends on who you ask. There are three possibilities."

"Why is nothing ever easy?"

"Then life wouldn't be *real* life." She ticked them off on her fingers. "Three options: Santa Monica Pier, the intersection of Lincoln and Olympic Boulevards, and where Santa Monica Boulevard runs into Ocean Avenue. They're all in a little cluster down by the beach and Palisades Park."

"And you know this how?"

"I know a lot about Route 66. I studied up. When I had to—when Rey started doing serious damage, I learned to travel it in my mind.

I started the car.

#

It should have taken us a little more than an hour to get from San Buenaventura to Santa Monica, but the saints were not with us. It was more than two hours after we left the motel when we pulled into a parking lot at Palisades Park.

"Now what?" I asked.

"We get out and walk."

Caroline took me to a spot just across from where Santa Monica Boulevard butted up against Ocean Avenue. Set in a weathered concrete frame, a large brass plaque proclaimed the Will Rogers Highway, dedicated in 1952 to the "humorist, world traveler, good neighbor." The American spelling of *humourist* reminded me how far I was from home. Here, Route 66 was called Highway 66. I wondered if politics had got in the way.

Caroline said, "Hang on a sec, I'll be right back." She didn't go anywhere.

Then she laughed, her voice sounding a little strange. "No worries, I'm just a place marker." It took me a second to realize that it was a different Caroline.

The woman laughed at my sudden discomfort. "She'll be right back. My David is getting his own little surprise right now."

"Oh." This Caroline's voice was a little harsher and deeper than that of the "real" Caroline. "Do you smoke?" I couldn't think of other small talk.

"Yes. She doesn't?"

"No."

"That's a shame. What else doesn't she do?" Her smile was more than suggestive. "Never mind, I'm just having some fun. This isn't the place she's looking for, by the way." She examined the plaque for a minute. "We didn't have this Will Rogers fellow."

"Too bad. Funny guy."

"We need more of those. You think you're going to be able to get rid of Big Rey?" Apparently her small talk skills weren't much better than mine.

She caught me off guard, and I told the truth. "No."

"He's a tough son of a bitch. Try hard. Throw your body in front of the train, if you have to. You might get lucky. The train might derail."

"No plaque marking the end of the road. Let's try the pier." Caroline's voice was unscratched by smoke and she seemed completely unflustered by what she'd done.

She was back! I didn't tell her about my conversation with her "place marker."

Our route kept us in the park. The pier was magnificent—an old wooden structure. Like the road across London Bridge, it had small shops and kiosks on one side that sold almost everything you'd want to buy on a hot and cloudless day.

Caroline bought us ice-cream cones and a map that showed Route 66, the "Great Diagonal Way," winding down from Chicago and ending at the Santa Monica Pier.

"Just a sec." She sighted down the length of the pier to the point where it turned into asphalt and entered the city.

The woman beside me said, "She'll be right back." She gave a slight cough.

"You're ...."

"The other one. We met a few minutes ago. Nice to see you again. Could I have a lick of that?" She pointed at my cone. "My David didn't buy me one."

"Sure, I guess so." I passed her the ice cream. "Actually, Caroline bought."

She took a sizeable bite of the ice cream, then licked around the top edge of the cone. She passed it back.

"Is this the start of Route 66?" I asked.

"Nope." Caroline tasted her ice cream cone. "It didn't veer off toward Olympic Boulevard."

"Too bad," I said. "This would have been a nice starting point." We walked back along the pier.

Caroline noticed I couldn't make myself eat the rest of my cone. "You don't want that?"

"She licked it." I could feel my upper lip curl.

"Doesn't bother me. Give it here. It's a two-cone day, lucky me."

I checked my watch—nearly noon. "You want to get lunch before we try the last spot?"

"No. Are you hungry?" She started in on my cone.

"No." I tried to keep the *yes* out of my voice.

"Let's go back to the car, then. We can drive up to Lincoln Boulevard, turn right and make our way to Olympic."

"And then?"

"I'll take us to the other place before we get to the intersection."

"Car and all?"

"World and all." Caroline winked at me.

The drive to the corner of Lincoln and Olympic was easy and uneventful. As we approached the intersection, I spotted a dental building with a large, and largely empty, parking lot.

Our car was already parked there. Caroline said, "Oh, the other two are already here."

That explained the car. I pulled in beside it. "Won't someone see us? Two sets of identical twins who bought identical cars, with identical plates?"

"No, that's the whole point. Nobody's going to see us because we're here and not here at the same time. Something like that. Bernie explained it, something about somebody's cat. I didn't get it at the time. Funny. Now I do things I don't understand."

All four of us got out simultaneously. The other Caroline lit a cigarette and came to stand beside me so the smoke would drift my way. Her David shook his head in mock dismay. I gave him a look, and he raised an eyebrow at me as a sort of "Love, what can you do?" shrug.

"Well?" I asked my Caroline.

"Let's walk to the corner."

"We'll be seen."

"But not observed," the other Caroline said.

"I don't think we should be gone too long." I couldn't believe that what we were doing wasn't dangerous somehow.

"You worried your car will be extracted from the dentist's parking lot?" Every word from the other Caroline carried its own slight smell of nicotine. "That won't happen either."

At the corner, I said, "Well?"

The other David examined Lincoln Boulevard, the cross street. "The street's been straightened a bit, but this is it."

"Good," smoking Caroline said, "We're outta here, then." And they were.

My Caroline said, "I'm going to miss her. There was a time when I wanted to be someone just like her."

I kept thinking about the ice cream cone and tried not to shudder.

Caroline squinted at the intersection. "I see what her David meant. If you look closely, you can tell that the street used to be a trail leading out of town."

"Now what?"

"Now I know where the road started. The map I bought can take us the rest of the way."

Back in the parking lot, our car, but not its twin, was still there. No ticket was tucked under the wiper blade.

#

Once upon a time, Route 66 was America's main highway, at least in my world. It swooped down from Chicago, curved gently to the west in the middle of the country, and then headed for southern California. It wasn't, perhaps, the main *street* of America, but it certainly was the major highway for commerce and travel. Farm goods headed east and north along it, money and migrants flowed south and west.

When the Depression came, when bad weather and worse farming practices turned the centre of the country into a dust bowl, Route 66 offered hope—a path to the Promised Land, where the weather was always good and the soil never blew away, where teenagers could grow into movie stars, and grapes could be pressed into wine. On this highway, everybody saw something, found something, realized something for the very first time.

If you headed west on Route 66, you'd never want to go home again. If you went east, you knew you'd always want to come back.

Once upon a time. But Caroline and I headed east in a different time.

We went northeast on Figueroa Street and had just gone under the Pasadena Freeway when I spotted Dodger Stadium. Caroline was trying to hold the map open and drive at the same time.

I couldn't stand it any longer. "Give it here."

At last, both of her hands were on the wheel.

"Take Arroyo Seco Parkway. Figueroa will ramp onto it. Jesus, did 66 run through the Stadium?"

"Not quite. Arroyo Seco became part of Route 66 around 1940. The stadium was built in the early sixties. It was Chavez Ravine in those days. The Dodgers shared it with the Angels until the Angels got their own stadium in Anaheim in 'sixty-five."

"You know baseball?"

"I had a misspent youth. Rey was an Angels fan."

"Ironic."

"Good wives always share their husband's interests. At least they did in Red Rock."

In an hour, we were in San Bernardino. Two hours after that, we made Barstow by way of the National Trails Highway, which took us off the interstate, through Oro Grande, Helendale, and Lenwood. We'd driven through a land of sand dunes and desert brush. From time to time, the rusty tracks of a rail line beside the road had kept us company.

At Barstow, we had a bite to eat and filled the tank.

I studied the map. "What's your pleasure—I-40, or the National Trails Highway?"

"Route 66. That's the National Trail, and that's what I want."

And so it went. We passed through Daggett, Newberry Springs, and then skirted Pisgah Crater, drove into Ludlow and all the way to Needles.

In Needles, we got into a small squabble. We were having supper in a little Mexican restaurant that featured food with names I didn't recognize.

I had the map out. "Lake Havasu City! London Bridge!"

"London Bridge?"

"It's the real London Bridge. Sort of. A guy bought all the outside masonry, numbered the pieces, and built a replica at Lake Havasu. It goes out to an island."

"A replica," Caroline said. "And you want to see this?"

"The outside's original, even if the inside's made of concrete and steel. There's even a canal."

"Is it on Route 66?"

"Kind of. We have to deke down to get there. But people did that, I'm sure—in the 1930s, Lake Havasu was a tourist destination."

"Okay, then."

The drive took a little longer than I'd expected. When we got there, Caroline said, "It doesn't look like London Bridge."

"You're thinking of the Tower Bridge. You know. The one with the ... towers."

"I could fix this one," Caroline offered. "There's got to be a world where the guy rebuilt Tower Bridge instead."

Finally, after dark, we pulled into Kingman, Arizona and got a motel on Andy Devine Avenue.

"Jingles grew up here," I said.

"Jingles?"

"The sidekick of Wild Bill Hickock. A TV show in the 1950s. My dad used to talk about it all the time, so when it came out on DVD a couple of years ago, I bought the set."

Caroline had never heard of him.

42 # HELL

As soon as I woke, I knew something was wrong. The smell hadn't been there when we'd gone to bed (Caroline on the queen, me on the couch). I sat up and woke Caroline immediately.

The motel room had changed. The carpet was green and stained, not the clean deep blue of the room where we'd gone to sleep. Different pictures hung on the sad-sack walls, whose wallboard peeked out from the curling edges of the wallpaper.

We dressed quickly and drew back the window curtain. It wasn't just the motel room that had changed.

I turned to Caroline. "Did you—?"

"No." She turned away, examining the room. From the desk, she picked up the cardboard folder that described the motel. She held it up so I could see it.

The *King* part of Kingman 66 Motel and Restaurant had been underlined in thick, permanent marker. Under it was written *Lives!*

"It's a message, for me. Rey did this."

"Rey?"

"He was an Elvis fan. He'd call himself The King when he wanted to boast. He's letting us know—well, letting me know—he can find us."

She opened the folder and turned it so I could see it. "This mean anything to you?"

I looked: On the inside cover was written July 5, 1973. "No. It's just one day after the Fourth of July, that's all."

"Go ask at the desk. It's got something to do with Kingman."

The desk clerk recognized the date immediately—the Kingman explosion. I knew a little about it, but the clerk's story magnified what I knew a thousand-fold.

When I returned, I set up my laptop. "Give me a couple of minutes, I have to check out some stuff."

Meanwhile, Caroline packed up and loaded the car. When she came in, she looked shaken. "This isn't the place we came to last night. More than half, three-fourths maybe, of the town is gone. Our motel is the only one I can see on the street, and that's not Andy Devine Avenue anymore, either."

She looked over my shoulder at the screen.

I went back to the most relevant site and turned to face her. "When I was a kid, maybe ten years old, my parents always turned on our small black-and-white TV at supper so we could watch the news while we ate. I remember my world's version of what happened here in 1973."

Caroline listened and read the screen at the same time.

"A fire started when a spark from a workman's hammer ignited a propane leak in a railway tank car. It was a spectacular fire and it burned a long time, long enough for the fire department to arrive and a crowd to gather. When the explosion happened, the fireball engulfed the crowd, even though they were a long ways away."

I shifted in the chair to catch Caroline's eye. "Here, things were different. Almost the whole train exploded, car after car."

"Oh my God! And the town?"

I turned back to the screen. "Used to have twenty thousand people in it. Now there's a little over four thousand. It wasn't just the explosion—a firestorm made buildings spontaneously burst into flame. A lot of people died of suffocation because the oxygen was used up. Some died because it rained propane cars. Some of the railcars burst and launched themselves into the sky. Some shot along the ground into cars, homes, people. The town never recovered. It was a BLEVE event."

"Which is?"

I pointed at the screen. "Boiling liquid expanding vapor explosion."

"Rey brought us here, on purpose." In spite of the surprise and horror, Caroline's voice was matter-of-fact. "This is his version of an object lesson."

"Can you take us back?"

"I can try." We were back in the room we had rented. The carpet was blue, the walls were painted, the furnishings looked new again.

"You're strong."

"So is Rey. We were moved in our sleep."

We paid our bill at the front desk and walked out into the cool desert air. In the car, I asked, "You still want to stay on Route 66?"

"It's *my* route, not *his*. I'm terrified of him, but damned if I'm going to let him spoil my vacation."

#

We left Kingman without breakfast. Caroline directed me back to Arizona 66 and we were on the Route once more. The highway was paved, the cars that came toward us were new, but the desert beside us had no markers of time. We could have been driving at any point in the heyday of Route 66.

We crossed the Hualapai Valley and went through towns with names like Hackberry, Valentine, and Peach Springs. In Seligman, two hours later, we stopped to eat. Leaving Seligman, we picked up Interstate 40, which ran more or less atop the old Route 66 through Arizona all the way to Albuquerque, New Mexico.

Just before the city proper, New Mexico 66 took us off I-40 and into historic downtown Albuquerque. We had been on the road for eight hours and I called it quits. We found a hotel and after supper took a walk along Central Avenue, a.k.a. Route 66.

Caroline was admiring the façade of an old store when I asked her the question that had bothered me all day. "We didn't see Rey when he broke into the motel room. We didn't hear him. How did he do that?"

She considered for a moment. "I don't think he broke into the room."

"He broke into Anna's house."

"When we weren't there."

"So what do you think happened?"

"I think he moved us." She sounded almost sick. "He was in one place, we were in another, and he moved us to a third."

"You say you *think* that's what he did. You don't know?"

"No more than you do." She was quiet for a moment, apparently studying the items in the store window. "Another thing. Bringing us back this morning was hard."

"But you did it."

"Yes. But still, it seems to be getting harder to do what I do."

"Because you're trying more difficult things."

"More than that. It's like something's changing. You were right this morning—I am stronger, and I feel that. But also, the—the *weight* is heavier. Everything's getting, I don't know, sticky. It's harder to move. Or maybe move into—maybe that's what I mean. Remember Santa Flora, the changes you went through to be a merman?"

"It hurt, but it was fun."

"Besides that. Was it easy or hard?"

"Easy, once I knew how."

"Do you think you still know how?"

"Sure."

"Try it. Make this place like the world that had Santa Flora in it. Change into a merman. You don't have to be one for more than a second or two. Then change back to the person you are here."

"Okay." I tried. The only thing that happened was that I felt sudden, overwhelming fatigue.

"Let me help."

My hands went instinctively to my neck, even though she didn't seem to do anything. I felt gills—and then none.

"I can still make it happen, but it's not easy. Jesus, I feel like I've been running uphill for half an hour. Can we go back to the hotel?"

"Sure." We walked back in silence.

#

Albuquerque to Oklahoma City is an eight-hour trip along Interstate 40, but at least ten hours if you absolutely must see Tinkertown and Sandia Crest on the way.

"The Dalai Lama went to Tinkertown," Caroline argued. "It's got to have something of interest. And Sandia Crest will give us a really nice view."

She was right on both counts.

Caroline turned into a little girl at Tinkertown—a museum of carved figures set in glass-walled dioramas. The place is a carnival, a tourist attraction, and a memorial to the man who did all the carvings and made the sets where the figures live. To Caroline, it was the ultimate dollhouse. To me, it was like a giant Hieronymus Bosch painting in 3D.

Take the diorama in which God and the Devil tug at the figure of a cowboy—a gunslinger, probably—standing in a graveyard. A single boot atop a coffin in a newly dug grave tells you that the setting is Boot Hill. In front, Death stands in the guise of the Grim Reaper, scythe and all. At the feet of the gunslinger, a mariachi band of little skeletons dressed in black hats plays, two little red devils standing below them. Behind God, angels float in a blue sky decorated with white clouds. Behind the Devil, the sky is red, and at his feet burn the fires of Hell.

It's campy and creepy—and oddly powerful. It's hard to believe in things like quantum physics and the multiverse when you stand in front of it. Magic and religion and the supernatural seem far more sensible explanations of things, instead.

As we were about to leave Tinkertown, Caroline noticed a 1929 open-top Ford by the entrance. "It looks like a boat with wheels. How could people cross the desert in something like that?"

"They had little choice. They put their trust in modern technology and far away gas stations, hoped they could fix whatever broke, and off they went."

Half an hour later, we looked out over the desert from the top of the Sandia Crest. Science, in the form of geology, reasserted itself. As long as I looked *out* and not *down*, my vertigo didn't kick in. Besides, I was fascinated. I could see that this desert had once been the bottom of an ocean. The mountains had been pushed up as the Rio Grande Rift formed. I explained this to Caroline, who listened politely.

"What do you believe?" Caroline asked when I'd finished playing teacher.

I knew her question had nothing to do with my explanation. She was asking, *What do you believe is happening to us?*

"I don't know. But it's time to get back in the boat."

That night, after much meandering and extra hours of driving (because I-40 isn't really Route 66 and we had to stay true to the plan) we slept in Oklahoma City.

#

It's easy to get from Oklahoma City to Thunder Bay. On I-35, point the car north, and you'll be there in two days. It's harder if you go via Chicago and stick as much as possible to Route 66. It's also twice as long.

Interstate 44 almost follows old Route 66, but not quite. Sometimes we were a little north, south, east, west, and even under I-44, but rarely on it.

We were someplace—near Foyil, maybe, or Vinita or Afton, northeast of Tulsa—when Caroline said, "We need to have a plan."

For a second I thought she was thinking about making up some of the time we had lost in Tulsa, but she meant Rey.

"He'll either try to kill us or he'll try to send us somewhere, some hell-hole world we won't be able to escape. There's no mercy in him now, no sanity."

Outside the car, in the fields, the mechanical dippy birds sipped oil and nodded in agreement. I kept my mouth shut and listened.

"I don't want to kill him. I just want him to stop. But he never stops. He never does." Her voice cracked.

At last, I said, "We may have to kill him. I don't think he can be reasoned with, or threatened. I don't think we can run away from him, even."

We drove on in silence. Weeks earlier, we'd talked about killing Rey in the abstract. But we were getting close to home, and soon abstract would be real. There was little likelihood we could kill Rey, and we both knew it.

Route 66 spends about ten minutes wandering through the southeast corner of Kansas before it enters Missouri near Joplin. At Galena, Kansas, a little place that had once had over thirty thousand people and now had a tenth of that, we stopped to stretch our legs. If you've seen the *Cars* movie, you've seen Galena. In the movie, it's called Radiator Springs.

"People are trying to fix this place up," Caroline said as we walked past an old gas station with a familiar tow truck parked beside it.

"The world always tries to knit itself back together. Maybe it'll do that with Rey, too."

"I don't think so. I think you're right. If we don't kill him, he'll kill us, after he's finished whatever other torture he chooses." She stopped walking. "I think Rey believes I'm the strongest of the Carolines. That's why he wants to kill me."

I couldn't think of a response that would make her feel safer. We walked back to the car.

#

Joplin, Carthage, Avilla, Phelps, Halltown, Springfield, Lebanon — places to think, feel, imagine.

Carthage, Missouri, a city divided about slavery at the time of the Civil War, had been a battlefield several times. It was burned to the ground in September, 1864, by Confederate troops. For a while, it had been a ghost town of broken buildings and ashes. Still, its people moved back after the war and chased out the occupying wolves and owls.

It was named for the Phoenician city-state of Carthage, which had suffered far worse two millennia earlier. Cato the Elder, the Roman statesman, had shouted *Carthago delenda est,* to end his speeches, even those unrelated to Carthage. *Carthage must be destroyed!* In 146 BC at the end of the Third Punic War, it was. The city-state was leveled and its citizens sold as slaves. The destruction was so overwhelming that a respected historian created the legend that the land on which Carthage stood had been sown with salt so that nothing could ever grow there.

Carthage, Missouri, had living roots. After the war, it grew into a city of maple trees and manufacturing. Ancient Carthage came back to life, too. The Romans rebuilt it, the Muslims destroyed it in 698 AD, it was rebuilt once more, and now it's a suburb of Tunis, thus providing a lesson of sorts, and a definite tourist attraction.

Lebanon, Missouri, a little further down the road, was not named for the country of Lebanon, but for a city in Tennessee that called itself Lebanon for the cedars that grew there. Like Carthage, Missouri, it had suffered badly during the Civil War but survived. The country of Lebanon, of course, despite the biblical phrase about the "cedars of Lebanon," had become a land *without* cedars. It survived two thousand years of war, and was, and will be again, a nice place to visit.

Route 66 seemed to be a winding snake whose coils looped back on themselves the way history is wont to do. And the study of history, I was learning, is an exercise in irony, especially when you leap from world to world.

Pick any place on earth. If you could travel in time, you might select a time when that place is full of terror, sickness, death—horrors of every kind imaginable, you could build your own list. But choose another time, and all could be wonderful at that same place.

The corollary is that if you ignore time and go to the same location at a different spot of the multiverse, it would be the *place*, not the *time*, that determines whether you find paradise or hell.

Route 66 was not just history. It was geography. There was something important about that.

43 # CHICAGO

If the western terminus of Route 66 is hard to pin down, the start of America's Highway is even more so. The official starting point is the intersection of Adams Street and Michigan Avenue in Chicago—but the highway never started there. In my home world, the highway began at Jackson Boulevard and Michigan Avenue until 1933. In 1933, the start was moved to Jackson Boulevard and Lakeshore Drive, closer to Lake Michigan and, more importantly, onto land that had been reclaimed for the 1933 Chicago World's Fair. This "starting point" worked fairly well until 1955, when Jackson Boulevard became a one-way street running the wrong way. That's when the official starting point became Adams Street, which at least ran in the correct direction, though not from the original starting point.

Few if any people who took Route 66 to California started the trip at the official starting point, wherever that was. Instead, they went as directly as possible from their home to Route 66 and turned onto it.

Real life is not about *the* starting point; it's about *our* starting point.

#

After we passed through Lebanon, Missouri, Caroline lost some of her interest in driving the "real" Route 66. Chicago might be one end of Route 66, but the end of our journey was not Chicago. Both of us began to look to Chicago as the place we would be set free to begin our real journey— the trip to Thunder Bay and the small farm on Oliver Road that had belonged to Rey's family. It became more important to get to Chicago and then home quickly than to get there "the right way."

The lesson was over. We got on I-44 East, then went north on I-57.

We tried to give Chicago its due, when we at last arrived. We stopped at the official eastern terminus and walked around for half an hour before finding a place to spend the night. But the pull of "home," and our next chapter, was too strong. The next morning we were on our way.

From Chicago to Duluth, Minnesota, is a full day of driving. The countryside is a mix of small towns and bigger ones, forest, low hills, high hills, farms, rivers, and bridges. Even though it was just past mid-September, all the landscape had begun to change. The grass at the roadside had thinned, the uppermost leaves of the birches and poplars had begun to turn yellow, and the maples were just starting to show their first hints of the brilliant reds to come.

For a long time that morning, we talked very little, and when we did, it was about what we saw. We left Eau Claire, Wisconsin, and chose to bypass Minneapolis/St. Paul to cut diagonally toward Duluth.

I watched the road and scenery roll past, feeling as if we were once more Nowhere Particular.

The change in our conversation came from Caroline, out of the blue.

"What do you think happened to Darlene, to your wife?"

"Darlene?" For a moment I couldn't remember her name: was it Darlene or Doreen or ... what else had it been? Darryl? I paused just a second too long. "I don't know."

"You must have thought about her."

"Yes." I thought about her at that moment, anyway. Then I spoke the truth. "But everything that's been happening—it's kept me from thinking clearly."

"Do you think she misses you?"

It was a question I really didn't know how to answer—not because I was afraid of alienating Caroline, but because it was hard to express.

Eventually, I said, tentatively, "I'm not sure she even knows I'm gone."

Caroline cut through any evasion. "What if she *does* know you're gone? That the person she's with isn't you?"

"But I don't think she does. I think, to her, she has the same husband she's always had. Maybe he believes he has the same wife, too. Everybody changes a *little* every day. We take that for granted. But the changes add up, over time."

I knew Caroline's next question before she asked it.

"Would you go back to her if you could?"

I'd answered the question, for myself, weeks ago. "I don't think I can."

Caroline looked at me, silent. She deserved the explanation without having to ask for it.

I tried. "Suppose I found myself back with Darlene. How would I know it's really her? She wouldn't be the Darlene I'd left, because that Darlene would have changed while I was gone." I searched for the right word. "The *continuity* would be gone. If that other me had no idea he replaced me—what if he didn't know he'd come from elsewhere and didn't miss his home, either? And furthermore, what if he were able to love more deeply than I can? What if he could love her better?"

Caroline raised a doubtful eyebrow. "You love deeply." She paused. "So. Would you go back if you could?"

I didn't want to say it. "If I *could*, I ... I'd have to."

"Why?"

Because, I thought. *Because.* Because is not an answer, except when it's the only answer. "I'd feel guilty if I didn't." It was mostly true. Not completely.

"Do you love me?"

"Yes, absolutely." The words said themselves.

Caroline considered. "I don't think you can go back, either. I think ...." She stopped in midsentence to compose her thought. "I don't think there is a back. There's no back for anyone, anytime, ever—even for people who never skip into other worlds. There's no place we can ever return to because 'time, like an ever-rolling stream, bears all its sons away.' And all their homes."

"Wesley," I said.

"Close, but not close enough. It was Isaac Watts. Wesley put it in his hymnal, though. And I'm sure Watts wasn't the first to have had the thought. You can't go back, and I can't either—even if Rey weren't intent on killing me. There is no Darlene for you, David. Just me."

"Are you proposing to me?"

"Feels like it."

"I accept." I took my eyes off the road just long enough to give her my biggest smile. I grasped her hand. I felt wonderful.

I don't know why, but just after something good happens, my mind sometimes leaps to the next potential threat. So of course, I thought of Rey. At least I kept it to myself. I let the happiness remain one minute, two, five. Then, my hand back on the wheel, I said what I knew I had to say.

"We need to talk about Rey."

"I'm not married to him anymore." It was a pronouncement—as if by saying it, Caroline created it as fact. "Not here."

"That's not what I'm concerned about." I smiled slightly. She'd spoken remembering that Rey might be "present" in some way.

I knew she understood that we couldn't talk about killing Rey, because he might be "listening." Nevertheless, we needed a plan. So she trusted me to find a way for her to tell me information about him that I could use.

"Did Rey read much?"

"Some." She gave me a quick glance—*you're asking what I think you're asking, right?* "He read the newspaper, the sports section mostly. He wasn't into novels or magazines or anything like that."

"What about you? What have you read?" *Would she understand?*

"Lots of things. I loved Shakespeare in high school, though. We studied *Julius Caesar*, *Romeo and Juliet*, *The Merchant of Venice*, *Hamlet*, *Macbeth*. I even read *King Lear* and *Othello* on my own. Rey didn't have to read any of those. The only play he had to do in high school was *Twelfth Night*, and he hated it."

"Do you remember Fermi in *Romeo and Juliet*? The guy who starts the fight with Juliet's nurse, Amanda?" It was a risky question.

Caroline took a moment before she spoke. She knew that Fermi had been Anna's dog. She also knew that neither Fermi nor Amanda existed in *Romeo and Juliet*.

"Yes. I didn't really get the play at first, but I do now. I sort of identify with Amanda."

You are as smart as I knew you were, far smarter than I am, I thought. We had two names in a code we could use—Fermi for Rey and Amanda for Caroline. And now, we built on those.

It was almost fun. "So if Fermi was the main character in *Hamlet*, do you think he'd have killed Claudius at prayer?"

I was asking what Rey's *modus operandi* would have been. Hamlet had put off the assassination of his uncle in case Claudius, at prayer, asked sincerely for forgiveness for murdering Hamlet's father—a forgiveness that God might grant him. If God forgave Claudius, then he'd go to heaven, which Hamlet absolutely didn't want, so he had to postpone his murderous plans. So, I wanted to know, how dedicated was Rey to murdering us? How much would he be willing to risk?

"Fermi's more a twisted Othello type. If he were convinced that Claudius was going to be let off the hook by God, he wouldn't kill him right then. But he wouldn't wait too long, either. He'd be ... feverish, raging. He might be able to delay for a scene or two, but not for a couple of acts."

"Would he plan the death?"

"Some, but not really. He's an opportunist. He'd go to the trouble to set a trap, but then he'd wait for Claudius to fall into it, and kill him with his bare hands."

"Bare hands?"

"Yes, I think so. He'd want to *feel* Claudius dying."

"Othello killed his wife, Desdemona, first. He didn't kill the real villain, Iago."

"That's true. But until the very end of the play, Othello thought Iago was innocent. If Fermi knew Iago was to blame, he'd kill Iago first and Desdemona last. She'd be the icing on the cake."

We were getting too close to the story of Rey, Caroline, and me, so I changed plays. "What about *Julius Caesar*? How was Brutus lured into the conspiracy so easily?"

Caroline knew at once that Rey was now Brutus. "He wasn't lured; he was seduced. They gave him a picture of himself that matched his self-image, and he decided to become the man in the picture."

"He wasn't lured in?" I had trouble differentiating between the two words.

Caroline insisted. "He was seduced. The conspirators didn't tell him that Caesar was a tasty little fish that could be caught and killed easily. Brutus wouldn't have got involved in something so underhanded. They appealed to a higher calling. They told him that Rome needed him, that Caesar had to be killed because he was a monster in the making, and that Brutus was the only man for the job."

"Ahh." Well, this discussion had been useful. I still didn't know how I could kill Rey in one world, never mind all the worlds I had to kill him in. But now I had some idea of what needed to lie at the core of my plan.

Caroline dropped a bombshell. "I've been thinking about Rey."

Jesus! What are you thinking? Rey might be listening at this moment! I kept my "outside voice" as calm as I could. "Oh?"

"Yes." She sounded sad. "I don't see how we can ever get away from Rey, not really. He could just follow us, or maybe send one of his 'others' to do it. If we tried to kill him, he'd just go somewhere else, and we'd just kill the substitute. It would go on and on like that, until he killed us."

Clever, I thought. *If Rey's listening, let him hear us feeling hopeless. And, at the same time, make sure I am aware of the main obstacle.*

I sighed. "Still, we have to try. Do you think he'll be at the farm?"

"Yes. I do."

We had no real plan, but we had baited a trap of our own. If Rey were listening, he'd know that we planned to confront him at the farm. He'd wait there to kill us.

By 9:00 p.m. it was dark, and we had a few more hours to Duluth.

"We should look for a place to stay. If we start early tomorrow, we can make Thunder Bay by supper time."

Caroline shook her head. "I think we should get to Duluth tonight. I want to sleep in a place with lots of rooms, an elevator, and doors that a strong kick won't break down."

I let my hope show in my voice. "And one bed?"

Caroline had the grace to sound regretful. "Sorry, two. When we make love for the first time, I don't want Rey to watch."

I couldn't help noticing: she said *when*. *When* we make love. It made me even more determined to keep us both alive.

In Duluth, we bolted the door behind us.

44 # HIGHWAY 61

Instead of sleeping, I lay awake watching flashes from the green light on the motel room's smoke detector.

At first, I reviewed everything I'd known or thought about this "adventure" we'd been on, and how it worked. I started with my early and quickly debunked mirror and right/left-handedness obsessions, and cycled through Bernie's "we're places" theory (some helpful truth in that), Dr. Singh's "you're all metaphors" comment (as yet less helpful), to Anna's practical exercises, and the expertise Caroline had developed.

Mermen swam through my ruminations—how easy it had been, or seemed then, to live underwater in Santa Flora. And the difficulty I'd had even developing gills in Albuquerque. What had been the point, other than entertainment, of becoming mer-people?

A voice in my ear—was it Bernie's?—pointed out, "Anything not forbidden is possible. So, now you have a better idea of what's possible. You know what you can do—and what Rey can also do. In any given landscape, that is."

Yes. I reviewed moments of transfer between multiverses. I thought about landscapes—oceans, Sandia Crest, Lebanon, Rey's family farm. My thoughts turned back to Kingman, but I didn't dare dwell on the intense physical connection Caroline and I had felt. The most practical reason was that I didn't want to wake up Rey. But I'd also, at last, understood why Caroline wanted Rey gone before we became whatever-it-was-we'd-become. Although the likelihood that I'd end up dead far outweighed the likelihood that I'd escape and Caroline wouldn't, I knew I didn't want to be alive in any multiverse if my Caroline couldn't be there.

Maybe it was the rhythm of the flash, maybe it was resolve as we approached our showdown, maybe it was simple love for Caroline, but somehow, my brain worked its way around the puzzle pieces.

At last, I formed a plan—or part of one, anyway.

#

In the morning, Caroline and I sat in the "breakfast room" of the motel and talked of Shakespeare once more.

"Do you know *Twelfth Night*?" I asked.

Caroline made a so-so sign with her hand. "Not as well as the others."

"Do you remember where Malvolio is when Feste, the clown, convinces him to write a letter to Olivia?"

"Sure."

Relief swept over me. I knew Caroline spoke in code because she hadn't actually answered the question with information about Malvolio. Instead, she'd let me lead.

"If you were in his situation, would you write the letter?" I didn't know if she'd understand what I was getting at.

She thought for a moment. "I wouldn't need to. I'd do something different, but a lot harder."

In Shakespeare's play, Olivia's servant Malvolio was imprisoned for his apparent insanity—a fabricated charge. Malvolio believes that if he sends Olivia a letter explaining his actions, she'll order his freedom. I was asking Caroline whether she'd be able to escape on her own if Rey imprisoned her. Back when she was in the cold cellar, she'd transported herself to a world that didn't have Rey in it. Could she still do it?

Her answer told me that she could, but she felt it would be more difficult than before. The shuffling of the deck had become harder. Soon it might become impossible. We would be stuck forever, wherever we were. I hoped to make sure that was a place without Rey.

"You'd try to pick the lock, wouldn't you?"

"Darn right. With my teeth if I had to."

I waited a moment. "Hey, before we head for Thunder Bay, I'd like to get the oil changed in the car. It'll take an hour, maybe two, to find a place and get it done. Can I drop you off at the mall? You could amuse yourself for a bit, and I could pick you up there later."

She looked at me, and I could see she knew I wouldn't return.

"Sure. I'll need to get a nail file in case I have to pick that lock."

An hour later, we were at the Millwright Mall, which had a different name in my home world. Wasting no time on nostalgia, I parked close to a major entrance.

Caroline said, "I'll need Bernie's magic credit card to pull some money out of an ATM."

I reached into my wallet. As I was about to hand it over, she said,

"Sorry, just a sec. I need to blow my nose." She rummaged about in her purse and then asked, "Is your handkerchief clean?"

I handed it to her, and she made a show of blowing. When she gave it back, I knew there was something other than mucus in it. I put it in my pocket.

Caroline took the credit card and got out of the car. With just a quick smile at me, she went into the mall.

When she was safely inside, I drove away. Before we'd gone to the mall, I'd made preparations of my own. I had a full tank and cash. I could drive all the way to Thunder Bay from Duluth with gas to spare.

For half an hour, I drove around "looking" for an oil change place, just in case Rey was "looking" too. At last, I headed north.

I had no idea where Rey might be, or where his attention was. I hoped that Caroline's presence at the mall would draw him there. Although she didn't know the exact details of what I was up to, she knew I needed her to keep Rey distracted for a while.

When I left Duluth, I took the old highway to Two Harbours, winding along the lake. I parked in front of an old saddle-and-leather-goods store downtown, took out my handkerchief, and read the note Caroline had tucked in.

Keep safe, it said. *See you at the farm tomorrow night. I love you.*

I put the note back in the handkerchief, put the handkerchief back in my pocket, wondered why I had done that, and started the car.

I've always enjoyed the drive from Duluth to Thunder Bay, along the lake. I knew it well, and it was somehow comforting to revisit it before whatever came next. Fortunately, the world I was in, though not my home world, had some similarities.

For example, Highway 61. Just out of town, I entered the Silver Creek Tunnel. Both tunnels, built in the 1990s, were as I remembered them. The highway through both arched and ran in long sweeping curves through the diabase cliffs. They were also wide, so that the sightlines would be long enough to be safe.

And, as in my world, passing through the tunnels was also a little like travelling through a time machine. You started in a world where shopping malls and four-lane highways lay only a few miles behind you. You emerged a short time later into a world of tiny towns, slow speeds, and freighters that moved languidly along on the green-blue waters of Lake Superior.

Still, the trip home wasn't exactly quick. On an interstate, it would have been maybe three hours. Highway 61 had only two lanes, lots of hills, and lots of small towns where patrol cars handed out speeding tickets quite liberally. I didn't speed, but I pushed it. I wanted to arrive with plenty of time left to scout out the farm and prepare however I could. It took nearly four hours to reach the border, and I lost another hour just crossing it. Too bad this version of the world hadn't redrawn the line between the Central and Eastern Time zones.

Another plus for this world: at the border I was asked where I lived. When I said Thunder Bay, they just waved me through, as they would have in my world.

But I wasn't prepared for other changes. Like the smell of rotten eggs as I crossed the Kaministiquia River and entered the city. In this world, the paper mill on the north bank of the river still exuded what people in the old days called "the smell of money." For many an American, that smell had been their first (and last) gagging introduction to a city perpetually trying to sell itself as a tourist "destination."

In my world, the smell of the mill had been muted to skunk-at-a-distance. In this one, it was still skunk-in-the-backseat. I breathed through my mouth until I passed the airport a mile or so further on.

I felt tension build in my hands as I neared Oliver Road and then turned left. I deliberately drove past the farm, to look for cars in the driveway. Nothing. I turned around half a mile up the road. This time, I slowed down to check for cars that had been hidden from the other direction. Still nothing, so I turned up the driveway to the farmhouse and parked.

I'd seen little of the old farm property up to this point. The one night I'd been there, I'd been injured to start with, and then Rey had beaten me to within an inch of my life. Later, Caroline had described it, especially the root cellar, so it looked much as I expected. The trees lining the driveway seemed less dense than those the night of the beating, but I recognized the very old fodder silo that Caroline had mentioned, just over the rise of the small hill from the farmhouse. I walked over to it.

A small thought echoed in my consciousness: *Open yourself to this place.* It sounded like Dr. Singh. Another thought followed: *Every road has its history, but the history arises from its geography. What can I make happen here? What do I need to pay attention to?*

The silo must have been eighty or ninety years old. It was odd-looking, about forty feet tall, with eight sides built from six-by-six squared cedar timbers using cribbed wood construction. At the very top, a small dormer gave access to the interior. Up the outside wall ran a series of rungs—at some point, someone had replaced the original wood with steel bars. Beside the dormer, I could see the remains of a rope-and-pulley system for hauling up silage. As I neared the silo and stared up, I began to feel dizzy.

Up close, I could see that although the building was old, its builder had given it a foundation of interlaced cinder blocks, ensuring it would stay sound for a long time. A small door was set into the base of the silo. I peeked in. The floor was concrete, and, except for some pieces of fallen roofing, it was clean.

I needed to see the top of the silo. When you're afraid of heights, no ladder can ever be strong enough or stable enough. The steel rungs that led upward looked solid, but I didn't trust the old cedar timbers they were attached to. Still, I had to go up, so I started climbing. I managed by not looking up and not looking down, by staring at each bit of timber, and by testing each handhold before I trusted it with my weight.

Eventually, I reached the dormer. My right hand had a white-knuckled grip on the last rung to keep me from falling, so with my left, I unlatched the dormer doors. They opened out, and I had to duck as I swung each door open. A wave of dizziness washed over me. I couldn't make myself reach over to latch each door to the side of the building.

I peeked through the opening. The air that came out was fetid, full of the smell of mould and failed farm. I raised my eyes to the ceiling—the foundation was solid beneath me, but the roof was in bad shape. Many boards had rotted and come away from their trusses, leaving large gaps where birds and bats could enter.

I pulled my head out of the dormer's opening. I managed to close and latch the doors. Then I started down. My legs were still shaking when I touched ground.

Walking back to the farmhouse helped my legs. I sat on the back steps beside the cold cellar to recover fully. Then I got up and looked around the farmhouse exterior. There had to be something I could use to get rid of Rey. I looked at the environs of the house. Maybe it already had weapons or potential traps lying around—ordinary things, like that old dug well. I could take its cover off, and if Rey chased me, I could trick, trip, or push him into the well and put the cover back on. *And then what?*

Over the next hour or so, as early afternoon became mid-afternoon, I came up with a lot of stupid ideas using all kinds of features out there.

The old silo, for instance—I could trick Rey into entering, and then I'd close the bottom door. *And then what? Leave him inside forever?*

The farmhouse—Rey could chase me through it, but I'd prep by pouring gasoline on the floors so I could set the whole place, plus Rey, on fire. And keep him from running out how?

Every idea I came up with seemed to be predicated on the assumption that if I got Rey into a dangerous location, he'd never be able to escape.

But I had to account for *all* the worlds. And what if, on some world, the well was dry and had been filled in? What if the silo had two openings at the bottom? What if my matches wouldn't light?

Rey could simply go to that world to save himself. He'd come back a little later, very much alive and a whole lot more angry than when he left.

Then I remembered what Caroline had said: Rey needed to be seduced, not lured. Maybe, if I thought about that, some possibilities would magically present themselves. The Muses of Murder would whisper in my ears, and I'd know what to do.

Finally, they did. I had a plan.

45 # MAGIC

When I was in high school, I had a friend who wanted to be a magician—not a real one, just a damn good performer. One day, he announced he wanted to show me a trick.

He took a small brass lock out of his pants pocket and handed it to me. "What's the serial number?"

I read the number stamped into the back of the lock. "2983771."

"It's yours. When you go home today, get rid of it. You can destroy it, hide it, give it away—whatever, it doesn't matter. Make sure that whatever you do, it will be impossible for me to find it."

After school, I pitched the lock into Boulevard Lake from the dam. The water there was at least twenty feet deep, and the bottom of the lake was murky. The lock vanished. Even if he knew what I'd done, even if he'd seen me throw it in the lake, I'd made it impossible for him to retrieve the lock.

The next day at school, he handed me the lock—same serial number, 2983771. It took me ten—no, twelve—years to figure out his trick. He'd bought two identical locks, locks that didn't have serial numbers. Then, using an engraving tool—his father was a jeweller—he'd carved the same number on each one.

#

Mid-afternoon, I drove to the hardware store in town. I needed some supplies to do a magic trick. Then I headed back to the farm.

I'd found a heavy old hammer. The head was badly rusted, but the wooden handle felt solid under my hand. I placed it strategically on top of the well.

By five o'clock, my work at the farm was finished. If Rey hadn't been watching me, if Caroline had evaded him so far—if all the *ifs* had gone our way—we might survive the night. It wasn't likely, but it was possible.

At last, I sat down on the back steps of the farmhouse to wait for Rey.

I figured that Caroline would arrive less than an hour after he did.

Rey did, in fact, appear first, just as the sun was beginning to set. He parked beside my car, got out, and walked slowly to the steps with studied nonchalance.

"Waiting for someone?"

As calmly as I could, I said, "You. Here." I motioned for him to come sit by me. I felt like an actor in a shock-and-schlock movie.

"Giving up?"

"Nope. You?"

Rey laughed. "Not much chance of that, is there? Where's Caroline?"

"I don't know. She said she'd come here, though. Should arrive soon."

"I'll wait for her." He sat down beside me on the steps. "Did you know I was in Tulalip when you were there? I was watching you look at that totem pole with the werewolf on it."

My heart picked up its pace. "It wasn't a werewolf."

Rey laughed. At last he said, "Right. But it was no brush wolf, either. You have the strangest dreams, my friend. What do you think? Am I the wolf?"

"Maybe."

"Hey, you don't have a cigarette on you, do you?"

"I don't smoke."

"I shouldn't, either, but I do. Guess I'll have to use one of my own." He reached inside his green nylon jacket and took out a cigarette pack.

I glanced over. It was the same brand my father had smoked before the manufacturer scrapped it to add menthol to the tobacco and promote a safer smoking experience. Of course, the purpose of the menthol was not what it seemed. I suspected that Rey had never heard of menthol cigarettes, but he'd think the manufacturer's actions were brilliant.

With a quick flip and tap, he shook a cigarette from the pack and put it to his lips. From a side pocket, he retrieved a small box of wooden matches. He opened the box with one hand and took out a single match. Still holding the match, he closed the box and put it away. Curling his index and middle fingers around the match, he held it secure, and then he scratched the top with his thumbnail. It lit instantly.

Throughout the ritual, Rey had seemed oblivious to me, emphasis on seemed. He, too, was playing a role. And he enjoyed it.

"Sesquisulphide of phosphorous. Safety match." He laughed and turned teacher. "The old matches used to give factory workers 'phossy jaw.' They'd breathe in phosphorus fumes. Smokers got it too, from lighting up. Their jawbones would develop abscesses, the teeth would fall out, and there'd be brain damage too. These treated ones are somewhat safer. The matchbook ones are better yet. I don't like them, though."

As I listened, a cold wave passed through me. He'd turned teacher — like me. Had he been studying me? To better "read" my plans?

He let the match burn down near his fingers, then slowly lit the cigarette. He took a long drag before he spoke. "Caroline's coming."

He exhaled smoke and smiled, like the sharks in Santa Flora.

I heard a car turn onto the gravel driveway. "I want a twenty-second lead."

"That's pretty short for foreplay. How are you going to seduce me in twenty seconds?"

Seduce. He had read my intentions. I swallowed. *Calm,* I reminded myself.

Rey took another drag. "But for our purposes, twenty's too long. I'll give you ten from the opening of the car door. After I kill you, I'll kill my wife. Too bad you won't be around to see it. I apologize for eavesdropping, by the way."

I didn't wait for Caroline to open the car door. I sprang up, spun to face him, and hit him across the ear with the palm of my right hand. I'd planned it. He hadn't anticipated it, though.

"Son of a bitch!" He leaped to his feet. "Cheater! Game on!"

I ran toward the well as fast as I could.

46 # REICHENBACH FALLS

At the well I swung wide, taking the long route. Rey, close behind me, was gaining. He was far more fit than I was, and the slap I'd given him had pumped a little more adrenaline into his legs. He maneuvered, trying to cut me off.

I gave the hammer a quick glance as I passed and kept going. Rey followed my look and changed course to pick it up on his way past the well.

I'd gained some time, but he'd gained a weapon. I hoped it was the slap that had made him mad enough to grab it.

Thanks to Rey's hammer detour, I could change course again. I picked the route that took me up and over the hill, toward the silo. I wanted him to think I was running *past* the silo, not *to* it. But when I got close, I made for the ladder up to the dormer.

I started to climb just as Rey came down the hill. When he reached the base of the ladder, I was half way up. I glanced down. He stood at the base of the silo, looking up and laughing. Pointedly, he looked at the hammer in his hand, then started climbing.

I spotted Caroline, on the other side of the hill, running toward the silo. I needed to make sure Rey was well up the ladder, so he wouldn't change his mind and go after Caroline instead. I tried to look exhausted, then resumed my climb.

A few yards below me, Rey called up, "Where the hell do you think you're going? Straight to heaven, maybe? You are one fool of an asshole."

He started climbing again, but he wasn't hurrying. He knew that once I reached the dormer, I had nowhere else to go.

I unlatched and opened the dormer's doors. Then I went in.

The hardware store hadn't been as useful as I'd hoped. I'd found screws and tools aplenty, but not silo rungs. However, it had towel racks, so I'd created my own rungs from them. They weren't very strong. Screwing them into the inside walls of the silo had been awkward, hard, and frightening, but I had managed to get four "rungs" into place—two where a person would put his feet, and two that were meant to act as hand-holds. The two sets of rungs were about three feet apart.

Very carefully, I used the first set of rungs to get away from the dormer doors, and then moved to the next set.

That was it. As far as I could go. I was stuck, forty feet above the silo's concrete floor, on two rungs.

Rey poked his head through the dormer entrance. "Heeere's Rey!"

Of course, I thought. *Of course he'd loved Jack Nicholson in* The Shining.

Then Rey laughed. "You are one stupid hero."

His head disappeared—he'd turned to look back. He reappeared. "Caroline's coming – running like a bitch. I'll have to be quick. Better for you, though, eh?"

With the dexterity and strength of a gymnast, and none of my fear of heights, Rey swung himself onto the first set of rungs. We were no more than three feet apart now.

Rey, hammer in hand, smiled—cruel, sadistic.

I tried not to panic. The rung for his hands should have come off. I'd attached it with undersized screws—big enough for someone being careful, like me, to use it. But I'd hoped they weren't big enough to support the weight and movement of someone as big as Rey.

Unfortunately, it seemed that the towel rack had held. Rey looked at his hammer, as if he were examining the blade of a newly sharpened knife before making the first cut. Then he looked at me.

"I think I'll break your hands, one at a time. What do you say?"

"Caroline loved you. How is that possible?"

Rey smiled and brought his arm back to swing. Of its own accord, my left hand let go of my hand-hold. It didn't want to be hit. My right hand held on, bravely.

Half way through Rey's swing, the weight of the hammer and the speed of its head created enough momentum to pull Rey out and away from the wall.

And the rung tore loose.

Hammer in one hand, like a dumbfounded cartoon Thor, Rey fell, astonished, to the concrete floor, forty feet below.

It took just over a second—no time for him to think of a way to escape.

After I heard his body hit the floor, I took a breath. Then I made myself look down.

The light from the open door at the bottom of the silo was enough to show me all I needed to know. Rey's head had been smashed open. His death had been instantaneous. His fingers still curled around the handle of the hammer, but they no longer held it.

"David!" Caroline's voice came from the dormer entrance. She had climbed the silo. "Are you all right?"

I turned my head slowly, trying to keep the dizziness under control. "Yes." I couldn't nod. "He's dead."

"Don't move."

"Can't. I'm stuck here. Rung's down there." I pointed with my foot.

"I can see that. Don't move. I'm going for something to get you out."

"Okey-dokey." I blinked. "He's dead."

"Yes, I know. I'll be right back."

In less than ten minutes, Caroline had me safely down on the ground. With some large shelving brackets from the house and a two-by-ten plank, she created a walkway. I walked it, inch by inch—my eyes glued to the wall of the silo—until I reached the dormer.

Climbing down the ladder, I wondered what it had felt like to fall. At the silo's base, I sat down on the ground.

Caroline sat beside me. "That was a really stupid idea."

"Rey thought so, too."

"Why, then? "

"Why what? Why did I do what I did?"

Caroline nodded. "We could have shot him, you know."

"He'd have known what we were up to. He was the master of 'seeing.' If we'd lined him up for a shot, we'd have been killed by the Reys in reserve. Or something else."

I felt like an actor playing someone in shock. *Maybe I* am *in shock.*

I began to talk. "I didn't really know what would happen. I had no idea what I'd do. The silo made me think of a Sherlock Holmes story—*The Final Problem.* Have you read it?" I was babbling now.

"No. Nice title, though."

Guilt suddenly swept over me, a tidal wave. I put my head in my hands and tried to blot out the world. "I killed him." I took a breath. "I killed him."

Caroline took my hand. "Tell me about the story. *The Final Problem.*"

I tried to compose myself. "Doyle was tired of writing Sherlock Holmes stories, so he decided to kill off Sherlock. Professor Moriarty and Sherlock struggled at Reichenbach Falls, both went over the edge, and both died. But his readers clamoured for more Holmes, so Doyle brought him back in another story, *The Empty House*. *Hound of the Baskervilles*, too. Sherlock had faked his own death. I wondered what would happen if Rey fell to his death. What would he do if he plunged down the Reichenbach Falls? What would *I* try if *I* were Rey?"

"I know—you'd look for a way out. You'd try to pick the lock."

I nodded. "Even if it was hopeless. I figured Rey would, too. But falling would give him less than two seconds to think. Even then ... if he switched places with one of his 'others,' that person would have to be falling, too. It wouldn't provide a way out. If he tried to go to a world that had no silo, he'd still end up falling forty feet to the ground out of thin air. And he'd have just a second or two to work through all that."

I paused to find the right words for what came next. "But Rey is—was—really smart. I worried he'd find a way I couldn't anticipate. I knew I had to make it hard for him to think at all. He could have sent a lesser Rey to kill me, especially if he thought he might be in danger. So I tried to enrage him. I hit him. Then I gave him a weapon. I guess—I tried to *seduce* him, with the promise of violence, not sex."

"For Rey, that would be the most seductive thing of all. He was a brutal man."

We were both quiet. The sun dipped below the horizon. The autumn night gathered.

Finally, she squeezed my hand. "We have to clean up here. Then it's time to go home."

"Sounds good to me."

Caroline made no move to get up. "One thing."

"What?"

"If Rey hadn't taken a swing at you with the hammer, would you have pulled him off the ladder? Would you have played Sherlock and gone over the falls with him?"

I stalled for time. "We have work to do." I started toward the silo door. Partway there, I turned back to her. I had a plausible answer.

"If Rey hadn't tried to kill me with the hammer, he wouldn't have been the real Rey. My plan wouldn't have worked, because only the real Rey would fall for it. And none of the other Reys would sacrifice themselves, even for their top dog. They'd never throw *themselves* in front of the train to save him. They were *all* Rey, after all.

It was a rationalization, but it made sense.

And when I'd explained it to Caroline, I finally believed it. I'd killed Rey—the *real* Rey, the monster. With their leader dead, their *sine qua non* gone, the other Reys were no longer a threat. Without him, they were nothing.

EPILOGUE

Later, in The Better Cup Café, we chose our first—and maybe our last—world. We created it, together.

We'd left Caroline's makeshift scaffolding at the silo, but we'd disposed of the towel racks, including the one that Rey had held.

Sometime in a few days or weeks, when Rey's body was found, it would look like he'd had an accident.

That wasn't important. Where we were going, no one could find us. But somehow, cleaning up finished off the day.

This coffee shop wasn't exactly like the one where we'd first spent time together on the day we met, but it was this world's version of it. Same location, same atmosphere. And that, too, seemed the way it should be.

"I wrote a poem about coffee, once," I said.

"Well? Recite it, please."

"It's called 'Coffee.'"

"I like the title. Original."

I cleared my throat. "Coffee," I proclaimed.

> does not understand
> how space and time are warped by mass,
> but pulls its ochre bubbles 'round
> into a spinning galaxy
> that turning ever slower spins
> all time into a minute in
> a universe made sweeter with
> some sugar and a spoon.
>
> Coffee
> does not know you need
> its warmth for hands
> about the cup.

Coffee
dreams no metaphors
for wasted, wasting would-have-beens,
nor numbers all the countless times
I drink of you.

To signal "the end," I bowed my head to acknowledge imaginary applause.

Caroline smiled. "That's lovely. Have you written a lot of poetry?"

"No. I'm not good at it. It seems a waste of time."

"You're not quite telling the truth, are you?"

"Not quite. Maybe I'll write more. After."

She reached across the table and touched my hand. "Let's build us a world. One with poetry in it."

"Let's."

"And with none of those big, black, omnipresent sidewalk signs, the ones with those neon letters. The kind you don't like."

I smiled at her. "With bike paths that run beside rivers, and sidewalks so we can walk the length of the city without scurrying on busy streets or walking on people's lawns as cars pass."

"I'd like a downtown café or two with tables outside in the summer. And flowers hanging from lamp posts."

"I want Bernie to be alive and well. I want to give him back his credit card, even if he isn't the Bernie who gave it to me. Maybe we can trade it for some new documentation. It won't be a world with *another* Caroline and David. And although it might be nice to never have to work for a living, I want a world to *need* us. We'd have a *purpose* in it."

Caroline nodded. "And what about your wife?"

"Darlene? She wouldn't be around. We'd never have met." I was silent for a moment. "So, a question. A long time ago, back in Aberdeen, you said you'd been following me. How did you know it was me?"

She didn't answer at once. Her hands toyed with her coffee mug, not as if it were distracting her from thought, but as if she needed its solidity and warmth to let her say what was on her mind. When she spoke, her voice, so often playful, was serious.

"I didn't. I thought maybe, during that time we were apart and I was alone in Duluth, we might be separated forever. I was afraid you'd been swallowed by a universe I could never find."

She paused. Her silence seemed to last forever, but it was only a second or two. "When I found you, I spent a lot of time watching, looking for signs that you weren't the man I had come to love." Another infinitely long pause. "I didn't find any."

"I'm glad." I hoped she'd never find any.

After another silence, she said, "That was a dumb plan. The silo and towel racks."

"Yes. So Rey told me."

"You didn't really think it would work, did you?"

"I had my doubts."

"You were ready to play Sherlock Holmes and take Moriarty with you."

"Maybe. I didn't think I'd need to."

"Liar." Then she smiled. "You still wonder if I'm the woman you met that night on Mapleward Road, don't you."

"Sometimes. But it doesn't seem to matter. The you I love is in all of the yous that you are. It's your core self."

"My soul?"

"I don't know about that. I don't know what to call it. But soul is a good word."

"It's the same with me. And *core* is close enough. The core of each of us, for the other, is close enough."

#

So it went. We talked through several cups of coffee, far into the night and then the dawn, building the world we wanted to live in.

At last, Caroline looked directly at me. "It's time."

"Can you do this? Can you find this place and take us there?"

"I think so. This one time—this last time, perhaps."

"I have something to ask you."

"Are you proposing to me?"

"Yes."

"I accept."

She took my hands in hers, and I felt something ... *change*. The air was suddenly different—cleaner, fresher—and outside, the sky brightened over a world that looked *renewed*.

Caroline said, "Let's go outside. I have something to show you."

We stepped out into the crisp, late-September morning. A sidewalk ran beside the coffee shop. The rising sun was turning the birches' changing leaves into amulets of emerald and gold.

We were home.

"Bernie?" I asked.

"Alive and well. Anna, too."

"I'd like to see them."

"Okay, then. Let's go."

ACKNOWLEDGMENTS

Thank you to my readers. If you've made it this far, you won't be surprised to learn that I've been thinking about this book for a long time—specifically, its "what-ifs," the "knowability" of the universe, and everything that makes up our core selves.

In the list (which is by no means definitive) on the next page, I share some books I found while following my curiosity about traveling through the multiverse. You'll find titles on re-imagining history, quantum mechanics, what makes us human, and basic science. Much more information is, of course, available online.

I taught science fiction for years, after even more years of reading it. My favourite work remains *A Canticle for Leibowitz*, by Walter M. Miller, Jr. However, I recognize that many new writers at work in the field are going in all kinds of interesting directions. I need to catch up.

Thank you to my wife, Marion Agnew, for your skills and support. This story means a great deal to me, and you helped in its telling.

Special thanks to the Ontario Arts Council for a Creator Grant that supported the writing of *The Iterations of Caroline*.

Suggested Reading

Blackburn, Simon. *The Big Questions: Philosophy*. New York: Metro Books, 2009.

Brooks, Michael. *The Big Questions: Physics*. London: Quercus, 2010.

Clark, Stuart. *The Big Questions: The Universe*. New York: Metro Books, 2011.

Cowley, Robert, ed. *What If? Eminent Historians Imagine What Might Have Been*. New York: G. P. Putnam's Sons, 2001.

Crilly, Tony. *The Big Questions: Mathematics*. London: Quercus, 2011.

Greene, Brian. *The Elegant Universe: Superstrings, Hidden Dimensions, and The Quest for the Ultimate Theory*. New York: Vintage Books/Random House, 1999.

Greene, Brian. *The Fabric of the Cosmos: Space, Time, and the Texture of Reality*. New York: Vintage Books/Random House, 2005.

Greene, Brian. *The Hidden Reality: Parallel Universes and the Deep Laws of the Cosmos*. New York: Vintage Books/Random House, 2011.

Harari, Yuval Noah. *Sapiens: A Brief History of Humankind*. Toronto: McClelland & Stewart/Penguin Random House, 2014.

Kakalios, James. *The Amazing Story of Quantum Mechanics: A Math-Free Exploration of the Science that Made Our World*. New York: Gotham Books/Penguin, 2010.

Ridley, Matt. Genome: *The Autobiography of a Species in 23 Chapters*. New York: Harper Collins, 1999.

Roberts, Andrew. *What Might Have Been*. London: Orion Books, 2004.

ABOUT THE AUTHOR

Roy Blomstrom, born in Port Arthur (now Thunder Bay), Ontario, is the son of Finland-Swede parents who lived through the Finnish Civil War and came to Canada.

His first novel, *Silences: A Novel of the 1918 Finnish Civil War*, was shortlisted for the Whistler Independent Book Award and the Northern Lit award.

Roy has published poetry, stories, and essays. His ten-minute plays have been produced in Thunder Bay, Ontario; Helsinki, Finland; and at the Brighton Fringe Festival.

He lives and writes in Shuniah, a community north of Thunder Bay, Ontario.